The Exiled Blade

The Exiled Blade

Act Three of THE ASSASSINI

Jon Courtenay GRIMWOOD

orbit

www.orbitbooks.net

ORBIT

First published in Great Britain in 2013 by Orbit

A CIP catalogue record for this book is available from the British Library.

ISBN 978-1-84149-850-8

Typeset in Adobe Garamond by Palimpsest Book Production Limited,
Falkirk, Stirlingshire
Printed and bound by CPI Group (UK) Ltd, Croydon, CR0 4YY

Papers used by Orbit are from well-managed forests
and other responsible sources.

MIX
Paper from
responsible sources
FSC® C104740

*"He'd been proud of her from the moment they met.
Her fierce intelligence, the quiet fury with
which she met life full on . . ."*

*For Sam, who shares more with Giulietta than
simply red hair*

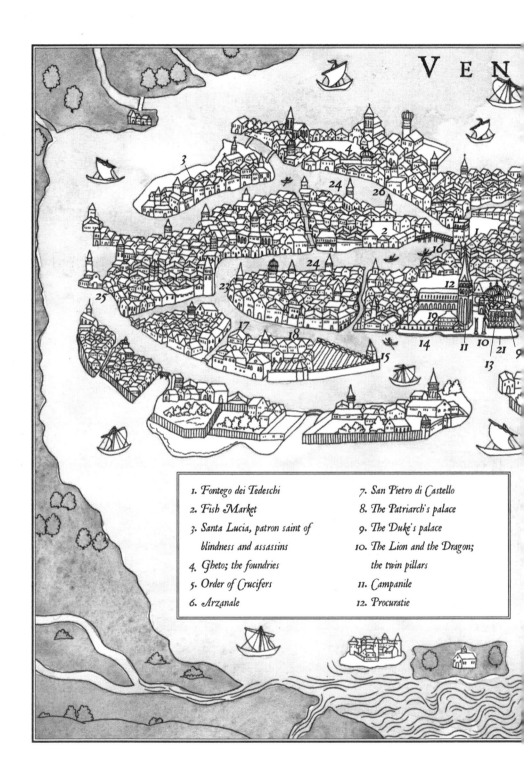

V E N

3
4
24
26
2
16
1
12
23
24
19
25
17
11
10
21
18
14
9
15
13

1. Fontego dei Tedeschi
2. Fish Market
3. Santa Lucia, patron saint of
   blindness and assassins
4. Gheto; the foundries
5. Order of Crucifers
6. Arzanale

7. San Pietro di Castello
8. The Patriarch's palace
9. The Duke's palace
10. The Lion and the Dragon;
    the twin pillars
11. Campanile
12. Procuratie

I A

22

6

8

20

The Millioni family tree

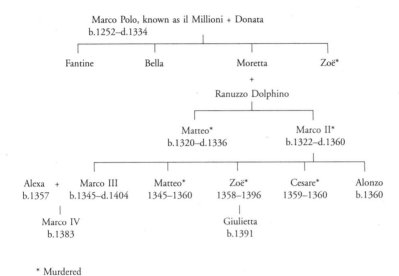

Marco Polo, known as il Millioni + Donata
b.1252–d.1334

Fantine   Bella   Moretta   Zoë*

+

Ranuzzo Dolphino

Matteo*
b.1320–d.1336

Marco II*
b.1322–d.1360

Alexa   +   Marco III   Matteo*   Zoë*   Cesare*   Alonzo
b.1357   b.1345–d.1404   1345–1360   1358–1396   1359–1360   b.1360

Marco IV
b.1383

Giulietta
b.1391

* Murdered

First Republic
1336 –1348

Second Republic
1360 –1362

Dramatis Personae

Tycho, a youth with strange hungers

The Millioni

Marco IV, known as Marco the Simpleton, duke of Venice and Prince of Serenissima

Lady Giulietta di Millioni, his young cousin, widow of Prince Leopold, mother of Leo and lover of Tycho

Duchess Alexa, the late duke's widow, mother to Marco IV. A Mongol princess in her own right. She hates . . .

Prince Alonzo, Regent of Venice, who wants the throne

Marco III, known as Marco the Just. The late lamented duke of Venice, elder brother of Alonzo, godfather of Lady Giulietta and the ghost at every feast

Members of the Venetian court

Lord Bribanzo, member of the Council of Ten, the inner council that rules Venice. One of the richest men in the city. Sides with Alonzo

Lord Roderigo, Captain of the Dogana, Alonzo's ally

Lady Maria Dolphini, heiress

Captain Weimer, new head of the palace guard

Amelia, a Nubian slave and member of the Assassini

Pietro, an ex-street child, now a royal page

Prince Frederick zum Bas Friedland, bastard son of Sigismund, ruler of the Holy Roman Empire, one-time suitor for Lady Giulietta and a guest at the court

Late members of the Venetian court

Atilo il Mauros, once adviser to the late Marco III, and head of Venice's secret assassins. Alexa's lover and long-term supporter. Was engaged to the late Lady Desdaio, daughter of Lord Bribanzo

Prince Leopold zum Bas Friedland. Also dead. Until lately leader of the *krieghund*, Emperor Sigismund's werewolf shock troops. (Brother of Prince Frederick)

Dr Hightown Crow, alchemist, astrologer and anatomist to the duke. Using a goose quill he inseminated Giulietta with Alonzo's seed, leaving her with child

Iacopo, once Atilo's servant and member of the Assassini

Captain Towler, mercenary leader in Montenegro

The Three Emperors

Sigismund, Holy Roman emperor, King of Germany, Hungary and Croatia. Wants to add Lombardy and Venice to that list

John V Palaiologos, the Basilius, ruler of the Byzantine Empire (known as the Eastern Roman Empire), also wants Venice. He barely admits Sigismund is an emperor at all

Tamburlaine, Khan of Khans, ruler of the Mongols and newly created emperor of China. The most powerful man in the world and a distant cousin to Duchess Alexa. He regards Europe as a minor irritation

PART 1

"There is special providence in the fall of a sparrow. If it be now, 'tis not to come; if it be not to come, it will be now . . ."

Hamlet, William Shakespeare

1

Austria

The emperor rode ahead on a high-stepping stallion draped with a cloth of gold, and behind him came his flag bearer, the double-headed eagle of the Holy Roman Empire snapping in the winter wind. A small group of carefully selected courtiers followed wrapped tightly in furs against the early snow. Old men riding down a valley towards a troop of younger men who were the future if they lived long enough.

Sigismund of Germany had come to meet his son.

The emperor was in his fifties, long-faced and tired eyed, exhausted by the effort of controlling an empire for which he hadn't provided a proper heir. The boy he approached was a youthful indiscretion. Well, as Frederick was seventeen, perhaps not that youthful on Sigismund's part, but still an indiscretion.

Since he was a bastard, had lost his battle against Venice and was returning with a dispirited army, having gained little glory from his siege of the island city, Frederick wondered why his father bothered to greet him.

At a word from the emperor the courtiers halted, and though they stayed in their saddles they relaxed enough to let their tired mounts feed on the thin Alpine grass of the high meadow. The emperor rode on alone.

Sliding from his horse, Prince Frederick knelt on the damp grass, bowed his head and waited. Only for his father to vault from his saddle with the enthusiasm of a man half his age. "Stand," Sigismund insisted, dragging his son to his feet.

Frederick said, "I apologise. The fault is all mine."

Clapping him on the shoulder, the emperor grinned. "Nicely said. Always take the blame and share the glory. It costs nothing but words, and makes your followers love you." He glanced beyond Frederick at the returning troops. "Sieges are always hard – especially when they fail. You could have done with a proper battle and a few more deaths."

"Your majesty . . .?"

"What did you lose? A half-dozen of your friends, no real soldiers at all. Your troops need comrades to mourn and enemy outrages to make them angry. I'm riding for Bohemia to put down a Waldensian heresy, your army can join mine. There'll be killing, mourning and drinking enough to make any soldier happy."

"I would be honoured to ride with you."

"And use that sword?"

How did he . . .? Frederick shifted uncomfortably and his father smiled.

Sigismund said, "It was well done, a fair exchange. We get the *WolfeSelle*." He nodded at the anonymous-looking blade slung across his son's shoulders. "And we gain proof that her brat is . . ."

"One of us?"

"One of you, certainly." There was slight jealousy in the emperor's voice. One Frederick had noticed before. "So, as I say, a fair exchange. I'll be honest, I never expected you to win."

"Father . . ."

"You stand here before me. The emperor in Constantinople waits to get his son back in a barrel pickled in brandy. You lost well. The Byzantines badly. Venice remains Venice and ready

4

for the taking." Wrapping his arm round his son's shoulders, Sigismund hugged him. A gesture undoubtedly noticed by both the courtiers and Frederick's friends. "Why should I not be happy?"

"I lost."

"Who said you were meant to win?"

"You did." Frederick's voice cracked and he blushed, hoping no courtiers had heard. "You said . . ."

"Whatever I said it's enough Byzantium is damaged. Now, I have another task. You are to return to Venice and woo Lady Giulietta. What you could not make Venice give you through force – and I've been unable to gain through fear – we will make them give us from love. Take your friends and go humbly. In battle, timing is all. So wait for the right moment."

"You want me to win Giulietta's heart?"

"And her other parts," Sigismund said. "Make her like you. Make her love you. Hell." He smiled. "Make her smile. That usually gets them into bed."

Cheers greeted the news of a fresh campaign, rising loud enough to echo from the mountains when Frederick's troops discovered the emperor himself would be leading them. Having appointed a replacement for Frederick, Sigismund ordered them to head up the valley, through the pass and keep moving until they reached the first town on the other side, where they were to billet. He would join them there that evening. His courtiers were to remain with him but keep their distance. He wished for time to say goodbye to his son.

Frederick watched and he listened and he wondered as all this went on around him. Mostly, he wondered why his father thought winning Lady Giulietta di Millioni's heart would be any easier than conquering her city. She was notoriously as stubborn as the city was strange. He watched his own armour and baggage be sent back the way he'd come to wait for him at an inn below.

His friends were gathered in a group, talking quietly. They'd asked as many questions as they dared.

"Now," Sigismund said. "Tell me about the man who gave you the *WolfeSelle*."

"Tycho," Frederick said. "Lady Giulietta's lover."

The emperor saw his son's unease and waited, listening to Frederick's faltering attempt to describe how the battle on Giudecca ended.

"Tell me *exactly* what you saw."

"Flames," Frederick said. "Wings of fire."

"My Moorish astrologer says she beds a djinn, my bishop that he's a devil, my cabalist says a golem of china clay. The Englishman Maître Dee says an elemental fire spirit. What did he look like to you?"

"Competition," Frederick said after a moment's pause.

The emperor laughed. "How long since you've run?"

"Weeks," his son admitted.

"Since you ran as a pack? For the joy of it," Sigismund said firmly. "I mean, how long since you ran as a pack for the joy of it?"

"That day in Wolf Valley when you came to find me."

Sigismund said, "Then run now. Run here where no one can see you. Catch up with your carts when the hunt is finished and take new clothes. But enjoy yourself for today and worry about duty tomorrow."

A run . . .?

The boy stripped quickly, his enthusiasm overwhelming shyness. The others, his friends, realising what was happening, grinned and stripped in their turn. Frederick was the youngest, his body slight, the hair at his groin pale as gold, the hair on his chest so fine as to be near invisible. And then he began to change, and his father, despite having seen what happened half a dozen times before, looked away as his son's flesh rippled and his bones twisted and fur rolled up his body in a wave, closing over the wolf's head. Only his eyes remained the same.

Frederick was not the largest animal in the pack. But he was the only one with silver fur and he was the one who opened his mouth and howled loud enough to echo off the valleys around them. And then, without even glancing at his father, he turned and headed for distant rocks and the pack followed without question, a streaming V of smoke behind their leader as they raced forward, and a stag that had been hiding among the rocks lost its nerve, rose to its feet and ran.

Sigismund sighed. He was emperor of half the Western world and, God-given duty or not, he'd give it all to run with his son.

2

Venice

"So I withdraw from city life for a life better suited to an old solider. I will tend my vines and plough my fields. Repair the walls on my estate in Corfu and have wells dug to water the olives . . ."

Of course you will, Tycho thought.

The Regent's honeyed words had to be borrowed from someone else. An old Roman statesman maybe. They certainly didn't sound like anything Prince Alonzo would have thought up for himself. "I will be taking my wife with me."

Even the sleepiest member of Venice's Council of Ten looked up at that. They all knew the Regent was unmarried and had no children, legitimate or bastard. His sister-in-law's threats to poison any brats at birth saw to that.

"Your wife?" his sister-in-law asked.

"Lady Maria Dolphini . . ." Prince Alonzo smiled at Duchess Alexa, nodded politely to the councillors on their gilded chairs, let his gaze slide over Duke Marco, otherwise known as the Simple, and ignored Tycho entirely. He was only there because Marco insisted on bringing his bodyguard.

"I marry Maria tonight," the Regent said. "With your permission, that is. The archbishop has already given his agreement. I know that I need the Council's seal on this but I imagine no one would deny an old soldier company in his remaining years?"

Alexa snorted but her heart wasn't in it. Tycho could see she was as shocked by this news as the rest of them. And worried, if she had any sense. Alexa liked to keep her enemies close. In banishing her brother-in-law she had, like it or not, given him freedom to move.

"No one objects . . .?"

The Regent was a barrel-chested, broad-shouldered bear of a man, as fond of wine, women and warfare as he was publicly contemptuous of politics. In private, of course, he was as political as the next Venetian and that was very political indeed. Smiling deprecatingly, he took a sip of red wine and pushed his glass firmly away. *Look*, the gesture said. *I'm barely drinking these days.*

Around the small room on the first floor used for meetings of the Ten, old men were shaking their heads. A single chair stood empty, the one used until recently by Lord Atilo, now dead and buried. The Regent was careful not to glance at it just as he was careful not to glance at the boy sprawled on the throne, or the boy's mother beside him. Duke Marco was watching a wasp repeatedly take off and crash-land, its flights short, abrupt and increasingly desperate. "It's d-d-dying . . ."

Alonzo's scowl said he wished Marco would join it.

"Everyone's d-dying these days."

When the duchess looked at her son strangely, he simply nodded to a soft-jowled courtier in a purple doublet twenty years out of date. "I think Lord B-Bribanzo wants to s-speak." The two things, Bribanzo's opening and shutting mouth and Marco's morbid comments, were probably not linked. With Marco it was hard to know. "You w-wish to o-object?"

Lord Bribanzo shook his head fiercely.

"W-what then?"

Bribanzo looked to Alonzo for guidance, caught himself and

pretended he'd been looking at a tapestry of a unicorn on the wall beyond. Marco's brief moments of clarity always caused problems for those used to taking their cues from Alexa or Alonzo; depending which faction they favoured. There was more to Lord Bribanzo's nervousness than this, though. Something in his manner said the hesitation was staged. Alonzo had just accepted defeat. He was withdrawing from public life to his estates in Corfu, one of Venice's many island colonies. This was close to open surrender.

Of course, Alexa had left him little choice. Exile or death had been her offer. Since Tycho had provided the proof that Alonzo was behind a plot to have Alexa murdered, along with Marco and Marco's cousin Lady Giulietta, he was on the list of people Alonzo would like dead. "Get on it it," Alexa said.

"I disapprove of the Regent's decision."

Everyone looked up, openly shocked. Bribanzo was Alonzo's man, his banker. The idea that Lord Bribanzo would publicly disapprove of anything Alonzo wanted was absurd. Lapdogs had more will.

"Y-you d-do?"

"Yes," Bribanzo said fiercely. "It's a waste. Our greatest general retiring to dig his own fields." He sounded as if he really thought Alonzo would dig ditches, tend vines and build drystone walls. He must know Alonzo's bucolic vision was for public consumption – like most of the things Alonzo said.

"Politics bores me, Bribanzo." The Regent's voice was warm and convincingly honest. The qualities that made him loved by his troops and so dangerous to Alexa. Drunk, Alonzo was dangerous. Sober, he was more dangerous still. It had always been thus – to use one of his own expressions.

"My lord, reconsider. For Venice's sake."

"My mind is made up."

"If you're bored with the city . . ."

"Bribanzo. I was born here, the canals are my home. I spoke

Venetian before I could speak Latin or mainland Italian. Listen to the crowd . . ." The Regent paused, a little too theatrically, to let the Council hear the rumble of carts, the singing of gondoliers and the shouts of stallholders on the Riva degli Schiavoni. "That is the sound of my heart beating. This city is my heart. The canals my blood. How could I ever be bored of Venice? The thought is absurd."

Staged, Tycho thought. Both men had rehearsed their lines before the meeting began. If not, then they'd certainly discussed how this should be played.

"Then why . . .?" Bribanzo began.

Alonzo risked a glance at Alexa. A quick, slight glance that suggested complications and things he couldn't say. Questions that only she could answer, not that he expected she ever would.

"I-is this g-going anywhere?" Marco demanded.

"Highness. We have Barbary pirates in the Adriatic. The governor of Paxos has declared himself king. Then there are the Red Crucifers . . ."

Marco looked at his mother, who bent to whisper. "Ahh," he said. "The renegades. I thought I'd lost t-track of a c-colour . . ." He smiled as the Council laughed dutifully. The recognised Priories were the White, who protected pilgrims, and the Black, who extracted sin with torture and oversaw executions. When the local Prior of the White in Montenegro proclaimed himself High Prior of the *Red*, and announced he and his followers would drive heretics from Montenegro, most regarded that as heresy itself. The man might be dead but his knights remained, holding to their new name, their supposed religious mission and the land they should be protecting from Serbian bandits. The Duchy of Montenegro was one of Venice's newer colonies. Not large, but its position across the Adriatic from Sicily made it key to protecting Venetian trade.

"My friend . . . What are you suggesting?" Alonzo asked.

Bribanzo glanced at the other councillors. One of them nodded slightly, and from the sudden stiffening of Alexa's shoulders Tycho knew she'd caught the glance. Alonzo's plot spread wider than both of them thought. *She's worried. Alexa worried is me worried.* Tycho loosened his dagger and Alexa shook her head.

"If you won't stay here, my lord, serve Venice in another capacity. Don't simply retire to your estates. The city can't afford to lose its greatest general."

The Regent shrugged.

"I mean it, my lord." Bribanzo's voice was stronger.

Here it comes.

"So," said Alonzo. "Sail against the Barbary pirates . . . Retake Paxos . . . Defeat the Red Crucifers . . . Which do you want from me?"

"Any of them, my lord." Bribanzo looked to the Council for agreement and received half a dozen nods. Alexa would note who agreed and who kept their counsel. She glanced at her son but Marco seemed too lost in his thoughts to notice a split was appearing.

"Alonzo," she said.

"Yes, my lady?" The Regent sounded innocent.

"I thought you were determined to retire to your estates?"

"That is my dearest wish. But if the Council of Ten still want me to serve my city . . ." There was enough ambiguity in his tone to leave it unclear whether he meant he served the city, or he regarded the city as *his*. He'd made it clear to everyone over the years that he didn't consider it hers. "If the Council want me to serve, how can I refuse? No matter what my enemies say about me . . ." He looked at Tycho this time. "My devotion to Venice is unchanging. My friends already know my friendship is for life. My enemies would be fools to underestimate me . . ."

"*Alonzo.*"

"A man may say goodbye to his friends. Especially when he goes to risk his life for his city. Any Venetian knows this."

"And I'm not Venetian?" Alexa's voice was tight.

12

Alonzo smiled. "As you say . . ."

"S-s-snow." Marco said suddenly. The room stilled as he unfolded spidery legs, abandoned his throne and wandered to the window. He opened an inner shutter, peered through a small circle of bottle glass and sucked his teeth at the darkness beyond. "It's going to s-snow. Look . . ."

Stars that had been high and bright when the meeting began were now shrouded by cloud, and the moon a sullen glow on the far side of a slab of grey. It was cold enough in the chamber to need a brazier in the fireplace, but snow? Snow was rare in Venice. At least flakes that lasted beyond a few days.

"Isn't it, T-Tycho? Y-you've seen snow. D-doesn't it feel like snow to you?"

What's behind that smile?

"M-my uncle will need a big b-blanket, and an army for when he g-goes to M-Montenegro. Well, g-gold to buy an army but in such a good cause. And a n-nice thick coat for M-Maria for when he's not k-keeping her warm in b-bed."

"Montenegro?" Alexa asked.

"He can fight the Red C-Crucifers. He'll l-like that." With this, Marco abandoned his window, wandered to the door, which he opened for himself, and ambled away whistling "Touch Her Teats First", a song usually heard at peasant weddings on the mainland. The meeting broke up immediately. Marco was duke; without him there was no meeting to be had.

"My lord . . ." Bribanzo bowed to Alonzo. "May I offer you my congratulations on your forthcoming marriage? This is unexpected, but welcome."

"Not so much forthcoming, Bribanzo, as immediate. I go to the basilica now. Come with me and be my witness."

Lord Bribanzo looked flattered.

The Regent owed him several thousand gold ducats, and undoubtedly hoped to put off repaying the loan for some while yet. Tycho watched Prince Alonzo and Bribanzo leave together and saw three Council members follow after. Turning, he found Alexa beside him.

"Find my niece," she said, "escort her to the basilica." Seeing Tycho's expression, she added, "Alonzo is a prince of Serenissima, the late duke's brother and the new duke's uncle. She will be there to see him marry, so will Marco, whether they want to or not. We will all be there."

We will all be there . . . Tycho took the words out of the chamber and along a servants' corridor he used to pass discreetly through Ca' Ducale, the Millioni's palace overlooking Piazza San Marco. He'd been born an orphan, and the discovery of that had been a relief, since he hated the bitch he'd believed his mother. Now he had a girl who loved him, who had a baby who loved her. While Alexa, who had every reason to hate him, since he had arrived in Venice with the sole purpose of killing her, included him when she spoke of we.

He was still smiling when he reached Lady Giulietta's door. If they were a few minutes late in arriving and Giulietta seemed a little breathless . . . Well, they were young and what could anyone expect?

3

When the patriarch called San Marco "Europe's most beautiful basilica", he wasn't simply pandering to Venetian pride. By the year of Our Lord 1408 there had been a church on the site of San Marco for six hundred years; admittedly not the same church, and the basilica had been rebuilt, extended, had new domes and new frescos until few could imagine what the original must have looked like, but there had been a church and it had been famously beautiful even back then. Now the wedding congregation stood before a flamboyantly jewelled rood screen, beneath a stern-faced Christ, while a fretted brass censor swung overhead beneath the largest of the five domes. Venice was once a colony of Constantinople, and it showed in the basilica's Eastern architecture.

Lady Giulietta had never doubted it was beautiful, for all it was from here she'd been abducted the night before she left to marry King Janus of Cyprus, a marriage that never happened. Since Janus had been a Black Crucifer and his previous marriage had been *complicated*, she was glad.

"You're safe," Tycho whispered.

"What?"

"You shivered."

Folding her fingers into his, she gripped tight and smiled when he turned to watch her, nodding at the couple before the rood screen to say he should be watching them instead. For once her uncle had discarded his breastplate. His bride huddled inside a huge fur coat against the cold. The coat was made from the pelt of a brown bear, and legend had it that Alonzo stabbed the bear himself. Legend also said he gutted the animal, ate its heart and skinned its carcase, washing its bloody pelt in a stream as clear and cold as ice.

The problem with Uncle Alonzo was that it could be true.

His bravery in battle was renowned and his skills as a general had brought him fame before she was born. Had Uncle Marco not died and his idiot son become duke, Uncle Alonzo would be happily besieging a castle somewhere. It was Aunt Alexa who said Alonzo fought the bear hand to hard. That he hadn't claimed it himself only made Giulietta believe it more. Still, the bearskin made a weird wedding dress. So large and bulky, almost as if Maria was trying to hide something.

Lady Giulietta nudged Tycho. "Don't you think Maria looks . . ."

"Like a girl who needs to get married in a hurry?"

She shushed him. Maria was a few years older than them, so somewhere in her early twenties; the ideal of beauty, heavy breasted and full-hipped, with long hair dyed Venetian-red as tradition demanded. Giulietta's own hair was naturally red, her body slighter and her figure much less arresting. Her aunt always said Giulietta would grow into her looks and she had; although she'd never believed Aunt Alexa back then. For the first time Giulietta could remember she felt like her skin fitted as it was meant to fit. Maria, however, looked bulkier than Giulietta recalled.

If she *was* pregnant then Alonzo leaving for his estates on Corfu made perfect sense. Taking her on campaign less so, but even that was safer than leaving her in Venice for Aunt Alexa to poison.

The rumour of a Grand Canal full of dead fish came from her aunt's earliest years in the city. Whispers said she dropped a single glass vial of poison, barely larger than a child's finger, and every fish in the Canalasso died. Like the story of Alonzo and the bear, Alexa and her vial had gone beyond rumour into legend.

"But what does Uncle Alonzo get out of this?" When Tycho looked round, Giulietta realised she'd said the words aloud. It was obvious what Maria got. She got to be a princess of Serenissima and live in the ducal palace. Well, she would have done if Alonzo weren't being quietly banished. But Maria . . .?

"He gets that," Tycho whispered.

Maria's father dripped gold. *As rich as a Dolphini*, the *cittadini* said. *And as vulgar*, the nobles added under their breath. He was dressed in the gaudy grandeur Giulietta expected. A doublet of scarlet velvet glistened wine-dark in the shadows. His matching cloak was yellow-lined. The gold chain around his neck was thick enough to moor a barge. He stood next to Lord Bribanzo, equally rich if less gaudily dressed. Between them they were richer than the Millioni, and Giulietta's family was the richest in Europe. If Maria produced a son there would be no stopping Lord Dolphini's ambitions. The old man would lavish gold on his princely grandchild and Dolphini money would strengthen Alonzo's position.

"I bet Aunt Alexa asks you to kill her."

"She can't," Tycho said. "It's not allowed." The rules governing his position as Duke's Blade, head of Venice's cadre of assassins, prevented the duchess using the *Assassini* against any member of the Millioni family, just as they prevented the Regent from doing the same. Once married, Maria was untouchable.

"Really?" Giulietta asked. She sighed.

It was not that she wanted Maria dead . . . But she'd always hoped her aunt would one day kill her uncle. Had Venice always been this dark and twisted, this complicated and divided? Was

17

it like this in Milan, Paris and Vienna? Lady Giulietta sucked her teeth, running through the dark reputations of those cities, and decided it probably was. The whole world was like this and Giulietta wished it was better. If she was ruler of Venice it would be different. She'd insist on it.

Up ahead, the patriarch was asking Maria if she married freely. Having been assured she did, he asked Alonzo if he would be faithful to death. His booming boast that he would be faithful to death and beyond was not in the order of service but heads nodded approvingly in the small party around him. Rings were exchanged, the blessing was given and the marriage was done.

This was the shorter service. Without a Mass, without a choir, and without much by way of guests or congregation; but it was done and it was legal. Alonzo il Millioni was married and the young woman beside him was now a Millioni princess and looking slightly stunned by the turn of events.

4

"*No*, I don't want Alonzo killed." Duchess Alexa, Mongol wife of the late duke and mother to Marco the Simpleton, who seemed daily less simple, looked at the restless young man in front of her desk and smiled sympathetically. She'd known his suggestion before he suggested it. This was not magic. She'd want the same if she was Tycho; young, full of life and in love with her niece.

"My lady. Let me do this."

Alexa shook her head.

"Please . . ."

"*Tycho!*" Now her hated brother-in-law was headed for exile she was sole Regent and intended to use the power. Mostly she liked her life; albeit in someone else's city, ruling someone else's people, and having taken a name not her own. But she was dying of old age and a disease ate her insides. She had no time for new complexities. "You will not mention this again."

The boy smouldered like phosphorus dropped into water, his anger so palpable that she sighed. It wasn't that Alexa even objected to him killing her brother-in-law, she simply knew it to be unwise. Pulling a stiletto from his belt, the boy absent-mindedly reached for a sharpening stone.

"Put those away . . ."

He looked up in surprise. "It relaxes me."

The boy's hair was wolf-grey, his cheekbones high and his amber-flecked eyes the most arresting she'd ever seen. He could see perfectly in darkness but the daylight terrified him. Beautiful but flawed, with a hint of danger. What young girl looked for more? Alexa didn't blame her niece for being infatuated, for all she wished it otherwise. "It must be sharp surely?"

Dropping the whetstone into his pocket, Tycho drew the blade across his thumb and watched blood bead in a dark line. Almost as quickly, the cut began to heal. "Sharp enough to solve your problem."

Alexa sighed. Above her city the black sky held faint traces of purple. The canals were quiet, the Venetian crowd still subdued following the recent departure of a Byzantine fleet that had blockaded the lagoon. There was a chill to the night air that had been missing a week earlier. "You know the rules."

"Ignore them. No one will suspect you."

"Of course they will." Her voice was dry. "Everyone will suspect me. What you mean is they won't be able to prove it."

"You aren't worried about letting him go into exile?"

She started to deny it and decided not to bother. Somehow she always ended up telling Tycho the truth. Well, mostly. But then Tycho *had* found her with a map on her desk, outlining Montenegro's territories in red ink. "It's complicated."

The boy ginned. Everything in Venice was.

"I ordered him to take exile. I can hardly complain if he offers to rid the Adriatic of pirates, protect our Schiavoni colonies and defeat a ravening horde of renegade Crucifers, can I? Any one of those would have brought half the Council back to his side, and there's always a chance . . ."

"One of the three might kill him?"

Alexa nodded.

"Don't leave it to chance," Tycho said seriously. "We can make it look natural if you want. Give me the right poison and he can die in his sleep. Think of the solemn service, his weeping new widow, the whole family dressed in black and saying prayers for his soul. You can have sculptors carve a beautiful marble tomb."

"This is about Giulietta, isn't it?"

Of course it was. Her brother-in-law had treated Giulietta abominably. Fathering a son on her as Saracens bred horses, with a goose quill of his own seed, so she could bear an heir for Janus of Cyprus, a king she never married. If she was Tycho she'd want Alonzo dead, too.

"It's not the rules governing the Assassini. I gave my husband my word I'd let his brother live. Marco made me swear this on his deathbed. You think for one minute that if I hadn't . . .?" He'd be dead a hundred times. Dead within the first week. Not killing Alonzo was the hardest thing she'd done. *I took him to my bed*, she thought bitterly. *To protect my child I took him to my bed, and he tried to poison my son anyway.*

How can I break my word now? "Alonzo *will* leave for Montenegro the day after tomorrow. You *will* not kill him. Understand me?"

Tycho bowed.

"Good," Alexa said. "You may go . . ."

She'd considered having Tycho killed and still wondered if it would be the sensible thing for her to do. He was brilliant, beautiful and dangerous. All the things that attracted her niece worried her. But how could she hold his exotic looks against him. Over the years she'd suffered the stares and glances of her late husband's subjects, who'd apparently expected her to have golden eyes or scales. As if the docks at Arzanale and the quaysides on the Canalasso hadn't already been full of Mongols and every other race beside. On her husband's death she adopted the widow's veil, finding relief in the fact that the people she ruled could no longer see her clearly. Her son, however, with his sallow skin and almond eyes they saw clearly enough, and blamed her for his foreignness.

The Venetians were barbarians – backward in their manners, ignorant of the sciences, perversely superstitious – but her marriage had been necessary to seal a trade treaty and her husband proved no worse-tempered than any other man, and more willing to listen to reason than most. In this he'd been like his city. The one thing she could say for the Venetians was that the rest of Europe was worse.

5

"My lord . . ." The tailor was nervous.

Called from his bed by guards and bundled into the palace and up the back stairs to the private quarters, he stood blinking at the lamp just lit for him. Since Tycho could see in the dark the lamp was for the tailor's convenience. "You have made all my clothes."

"It has been an honour, my lord."

The reflex response of a weaker animal in the presence of a stronger. Tycho doubted the tailor realised that, and was surprised to find himself thinking it. A month back, on the island of Giudecca, Tycho had changed to something so beyond human it had altered how he saw the world. That was why he now moved so carefully around Giulietta. He could see fondness in her eyes, fierce love and simple devotion . . . All the feelings he had for her. There was more, though. In the last few weeks, he'd seen awe and that made him uncomfortable. It was awe for something he no longer was and couldn't remember how he became.

The angel, she called it, until he asked her stop.

"I need another suit of clothes."

The man wanted to say, *You had me woken in the middle of*

the night and brought here for that? He had more sense, however. Tycho was now a baron, he was rumoured to be the lover of Lady Giulietta di Millioni. Soon Venice would decide it was time to forget he'd ever been a slave. Besides, he paid well for the tailor's services and if he wanted to order clothes in the middle of the night instead of sending his servant during the day . . .

"Tycho . . .?" Tycho turned to finding Giulietta in the doorway. Seeing he wasn't alone, she huddled her blanket tightly around her and the tailor made himself look away. "Who is this?"

"My tailor. He's making me a doublet."

"You were gone," she said sleepily. "I woke and you were gone."

The tailor's face went very still. Anyone looking would have thought he was lost in his own thoughts but Tycho knew differently. Giulietta had just confirmed that she and Tycho shared a bed and the tailor was wondering how dangerous that was for him to know. That she barely noticed his fright was typical.

She was Millioni.

Tycho loved her and she'd changed since they met but he had no doubt she would remain Millioni to the day she died and the Millioni *were* Venice. At least, they considered themselves and the island city interchangeable. Tycho had *met* the city. A dark and twisted spirit of place so old it barely distinguished one generation from another. He doubted that city even knew the Millioni existed.

"You have new doublets," Giulietta protested.

"I want a white one."

This was so unlikely that Giulietta's blue eyes opened wide, and even the tailor forgot himself and looked up. The whole city knew Tycho wore only black. Black doublet, black hose, black cloak; even his padded codpiece was black.

"It's going to snow . . ."

"Says who?" Giulietta asked.

"Marco, in tonight's meeting."

"That doesn't mean . . ."

"It does," Tycho said. "He's usually right about these things." At that, the tailor's mouth fell open again. "The duke is much better these days," Tycho explained, addressing the tailor directly. "The fever he had this summer brought back his senses . . ."

The fever had been poisoning, and Marco's senses had always been there, hidden behind the twitches and the drooling. Only his stuttering had been real and that was nothing like as bad as everyone thought. Marco's idiocy had been a disguise to protect him from his uncle. Only Tycho and Giulietta knew this. But it wouldn't hurt if the city began to believe Marco was returning to his senses. With his uncle effectively banished and his mother's party stronger than before, now would be a good time for the people to begin trusting him.

"My lord. How soon do you want the outfit?"

"By nightfall tomorrow."

The tailor opened his mouth to protest and shut it. He bowed to Tycho, bowed lower to Lady Giulietta and backed out of the room. A minute later Tycho saw him cross the inner courtyard for the Porta della Carta and say something to the guard who unbolted the smaller door and let him out on to the Piazza San Marco. He'd been escorted to the palace but could find his own way home.

By dawn a layer of snow dusted the piazza's herringbone brick, except around the edge where the boots of the Night Watch had ground it to grey slush. The morning crowd would have done the same to the square if the snow hadn't kept falling. It fell through the morning into the afternoon. It was still falling when darkness set in. At no time did the sun shine warmly enough to melt the snow. When the tailor returned, Tycho had just woken from dreamless sleep to find the Piazza San Marco blanketed white.

"This is good," Tycho said.

The tailor bowed himself from the room, still smiling in grateful relief. He'd cut the doublet in the latest style to end halfway down Tycho's hip and not quite cover the padded cod at the front. With the doublet came white hose and a cloak lined with pale grey silk. The grey and white would mimic snow and shadow for anyone who saw him pass. Not that Tycho expected to be seen.

"Sweet dreams," he told Giulietta, who stirred, and smiled at his kiss; her forehead tasting of salt and rosewater. At the edge of the Molo, which was the little terrace in front of the ducal palace, Tycho discarded the black cloak he'd worn to leave the palace and tucked it behind a statue where it was unlikely to be found, then unfolded the white cloak he carried beneath.

A second later he'd vanished.

White against white and grey against stone, he owned the shadows and they loved him as he flowed along the cold expanse of the Riva degli Schiavoni and turned north out of the wind, taking an alley full of overhanging houses so close they kissed. He chose a route that took him north and let him curl back towards the great houses above Ponte Maggiore. Here Lord Dolphini lived, and Prince Alonzo now slept, in a palace rebuilt and renovated until it was grander than its neighbours.

Tycho stepped into a doorway to let the Night Watch stamp past, their teeth chattering in the cold and their words reduced to sullen and unhappy grunts of disgust. They left a trail of footprints a blind man could follow. Tycho used their tracks for the next half-mile. He was going to kill Alonzo without Alexa's blessing and against her orders. This way no one could hold her responsible.

Two floors up, third window along.

That was where he'd seen Maria Dolphini stare out the night before. Rolling himself over a balustrade crusted with snow, Tycho slid his dagger between the shutters and lifted the latch.

Someone had nailed a blanket against the cold over the window beyond and he opened the window and lifted the blanket aside.

Alonzo's room was in near darkness, with only the sullen glow of almost dead embers in a wide fireplace to light it. His bed was huge and curtained. Tycho imagined the biggest of the guest chambers had been given over to Alonzo and his bride. The room looked too self-importantly grand to be Maria's own. When a board shifted slightly under his feet, he froze, listening for any change in the faint snoring that came from beyond the curtains. Alonzo slept heavily but Maria's breathing was light and nervous. Drawing his dagger, Tycho pulled the curtain aside.

The air inside was hot with sweated bodies and stank of wine, garlic and recent sex. It flowed past him like a history of the hour just gone. Prince Alonzo was sprawled on top of Maria, whose gown was round her hips, one heavy breast bulging sideways where his weight pushed down. She shivered as the air grew colder.

But Alonzo's weight, and his face slumped on to her neck, stopped her turning her head to see what had changed. He was snoring heavily, and her hands were still wrapped uncertainly round his bare shoulders.

The man was utterly defenceless. A single thrust through his back would pierce his heart, a sliced throat would sluice blood on to the woman trapped below him, a stab to his side and he'd take days to die . . .

Alexa would be pleased. Furious, obviously. Tycho would have to deny it, as he'd have to deny it to Giulietta, who'd want him to swear the truth. Except he'd never lied to her and didn't want to start now. So he'd have to tell her the truth and swear her to secrecy. Do it, Tycho told himself. *If you're going to do it. Do it now.*

"Who's there?" The voice was small and frightened.

The inrush of cold air had finished waking Maria Dolphini and Tycho could hear the terror in her voice. She tried to shake

Alonzo awake, but her husband slept too deeply and was too heavy for her shift. A thick fur draped his feet, a blanket half covered his thighs. "Who's there?" she repeated.

"No one," Tycho said. "Sleep safely."

He pulled up the blanket to drape over her naked hip and closed the bed's curtains, crossing the room in a shadow and readjusting the window blanket on his way out, closing the bottle-glass window and the shutters beyond. Although his footprints on the balcony had filled with snow they were still visible. So he swept the snow away with his hand, watching it fall into a heap in the alley below. New snow would cover the balcony floor and balustrade and leave both smooth by morning. A man's height from the ground, he jumped outwards, landing in a run of tracks made by passing rubbish pigs while he was inside. He walked carefully, stepping in the hoofprints of the animals, the rhythm of his feet irregular. Anyone listening would have missed them, being used to footsteps that sounding rhythmic, impatient or hurried and scared.

Lord Atilo had been a brutal master and his methods would have left scars had Tycho's childhood not left them already. The *Assassini* skills and Tycho's own abilities made for a lethal mix. *So why didn't you kill Alonzo?* Tycho asked himself as he made his way back to Ca' Ducale. He'd gone intending to kill his enemy. Intending to kill him and lie to Alexa . . . Instead he'd let the man live.

What had changed his mind? Finding Maria Dolphini awake and scared? Realising he could lie to Alexa but not to the girl he loved, and she was bound to ask? The question was simple but pinning down an answer proved so difficult he'd reached the Molo and collected his cloak from behind the statue before he realised there wasn't one. He'd acted on instinct and against his interests. Life with Alonzo dead would be a whole lot safer.

One thing he did know, though. Maria Dolphini's body might be lush, her hips broad and her breasts large enough to strain the fine wool of her nightgown but he'd seen her half naked and she wasn't pregnant and looked far less bulky than she'd been in the basilica when she married Alonzo.

"Where have you been?" Giulietta asked sleepily.

"Walking in the snow."

"You like snow?" She sounded surprised.

"Hate it." Bjornvin, his childhood town, had been snowbound for months at a time, and since the change – his change – he felt sluggish in the cold. Of course, sluggish to him was still invisibly fast to anyone else. He could feel it, though, in the slowing of his thoughts, a slight lag in his reflexes.

"Come to bed," Giulietta said.

"I thought you were sore?"

"That was earlier." She shifted on her mattress, making space, and Tycho discarded his cloak, and then everything else.

"I'm cold," he warned.

"I don't care." A small shriek when he put his hands on her stomach said she did, just not enough to kick him out of bed or demand he warm his fingers first on the brazier burning in her fireplace. Their lovemaking was slow and lazy, and, when it was over, she slumbered and he lay staring at cracks in her ceiling.

Winter has its advantages, he realised with surprise.

His reflexes might be slower but the nights were far longer and the extra hours made him happy. As dawn approached he left Giulietta sleeping, snuffling softly in her dreams, her baby safe in the next room and a guard outside her door. He still had no answer to his earlier question – at least none that was acceptable. The only possible answer he could think of was that he'd balked because he'd have to kill Maria Dolphini, too. That looked worryingly like conscience. A master of the Assassini with a conscience was no use to anyone.

6

"Did you know," Aunt Alexa asked, "that Lord Dolphini had his palace exorcised against ghosts this morning?"

"Really?" Lady Giulietta examined her fingernails.

Her aunt sat in a red-lacquered palanquin drawn up on the snowy edge of the Riva degli Schiavoni so she could watch her brother-in-law set sail for Montenegro. Out in the dark lagoon his sailors were raising a sail and his oarsmen settling their oars as the anchor chain was wound in. This type of winch was new, based on the Florentine model used for winding crossbows. It used gears, pulleys and different sized drums and lifted the anchor at an impressive rate. The tide was high and the wind fair; they could leave now or wait and lose a day.

The galley was brightly lit and hung with lamps.

Lady Maria Dolphini and her new husband had embarked last, carried to their vessel on a gaudily painted lugger. Lady Maria had worn the bearskin cloak in which she'd married, looking as bulky as she had that day. The Regent wore a new breastplate that flickered and flashed in the flaming torches around him. Lady Maria's father had a palanquin of his own.

Held back by guards, a group of ragged Castellani watched from a dozen paces away. Another crowd, Nicoletti this time, stood on small bridges and narrow *fondamenta* further west. The two main gangs had sworn a truce for the evening. Alonzo was popular with the city's poor, who mistrusted Alexa's Mongol blood and didn't see why her half-Mongol simpleton son should rule when Alonzo could do it better. A position Alonzo did little to deny.

"Exorcised," Alexa repeated. "Against ghosts."

What did Aunt Alexa expect her to say? Tycho was really cold when he came to bed last night, apparently he likes walking in the snow? I'm sure he simply took a turn round the square.

"Don't you find that strange?"

"Find what strange? Giulietta asked.

"That Lady Maria should see a ghost the night before she left with her new husband for our provinces in Montenegro . . ."

"An ill omen."

"No one's seen a ghost there before," the duchess said, ignoring her niece's words. "Strange Maria should see one now." Aunt Alexa wore a veil, as always, and her voice was flat to the point of being bored. All the same, Lady Giulietta could swear Aunt Alexa was looking past her to Tycho beyond.

"All in white," Alexa said.

Tycho went still.

"Yes," said Alexa. "A ghost, all in white, wafted through her window and disappeared just as quickly, having tucked Lady Maria into bed. She asked who it was, little idiot. Seemingly it answered, *no one . . .*"

"A lost soul," Lady Giulietta said.

"So Dolphini's priest thinks. Hence the bell and candles, prayers and incense. Of course, my brother-in-law slept through all of this. So like Uncle Alonzo, don't you think? To be asleep when the gates of hell open for him and close again."

Pity he didn't fall through them. We could be burying him instead of waving goodbye. Aunt Alexa would like that, too.

Her aunt was staring to where lamps on the galley lit Uncle

31

Alonzo against a backdrop of steel-grey clouds and a glowering half-hidden moon. He was good at stage-managing these things. Even Aunt Alexa admitted the only difference between princes and actors was that princes could kill the audience if they misbehaved.

Moonlight reflecting from snow lit the underside of the clouds, which reflected the light back to the snow. The strangeness of this and the thick-falling snow gave the galley and San Maggiore an unworldly look. As if Alonzo was leaving this world for another. Thinking that, Giulietta shivered, and suddenly Lord Dolphini having his palace exorcised didn't seem so strange.

"How much longer do I have to wait?"

"*Giulietta . . .*"

"Sorry." She'd sounded like the girl she used to be; not the new her who would marry Tycho and become Regent one day. "I don't want to leave Leo too long."

"You fuss too much," her aunt scolded.

Most noblewomen left their infants with wet nurses or sent them to mainland estates to be kept out of trouble. Boys left home by the age of seven to join another household if they were noble, to become traders if they were *cittadini*, or be apprenticed if they were poor but lucky. Street children ran ragged in the cold and quickly died.

The thought of ragged children made Giulietta think of Alta Mofacon in the Julian Alps. Her favourite manor perched on the side of a hill and the snow would hit it hard. She hoped her villagers had enough food to last until spring.

"A few minutes," Tycho whispered. "You're doing well."

So she tightened her fingers into his, and stared at the bloody galley and tried to look as if she was worried for her uncle's safety rather than hoping that storms capsized him and waves ground his boat on the rocks. She felt closer to tears than she liked. These days she felt permanently close to tears.

Shock, Tycho called it. She'd asked him shock from what and

he'd just looked at her. They spoke little about had happened on Giudecca before Tycho killed Andronikos, and what they did say was too much.

"Thank the gods," said Alexa. Apparently even her aunt was bored with standing on a cold quayside pretending she was sad to see Uncle Alonzo go. His sail was being angled to catch a wind blowing along the wide expanse of the Giudecca channel; and a kettledrum began its slow beat as oars dipped into the water, and the freemen Venice prided itself on using in its galleys drew their first stroke and Alonzo's war galley shifted slightly. A second then a third stroke were enough to make its movement obvious.

"I hear the storms are bad this time of year," Tycho muttered.

"You're going to have to stop doing that."

"No magic," he said. "I simply watched your face, saw you glance at your uncle's boat, scowl deeply, and knew what you were thinking."

"Knowing what I'm thinking is magic."

"Not when you make it that obvious."

Lady Giulietta folded her fingers tighter into his. On their way back, she hesitated as they approached the Porte della Carta and glanced to the darkened edge of the basilica beyond. The two buildings stood side by side, with the basilica stepped forward and obviously Byzantine in style; while Ca' Ducale, with its pale marble columns, fretted balconies, pink brick and elegant colonnades looked like a Moorish sugar cake. "I'm going to light a candle for my mother."

"Do you want me to wait for you?"

"You go home . . ."

She saw him smile. Her home, maybe, although even that was new. She could remember when she called Ca' Ducale a prison. She watched Tycho turn to find a guard to escort her, but one had already peeled off in anticipation. Of course he had. She was a Millioni princess. "See you later," Tycho said.

Giulietta nodded.

The basilica was empty and her footsteps echoed as she walked under the stern-faced apostles ringing the dome above. The frescos were new and their colours still fresh, and saints watched her as she stopped to ask the Virgin's blessing. Mary's cloak was paler than it had been the first time she knelt there, the night she arrived in Venice as a child, her mother dead, her father still hunting her.

The bright circle of glass stars on a wire that ringed the Madonna's head was now dusty. But she had the same smile, the same kind eyes. Lady Giulietta felt a wave of happiness wash over her. It was here she had met Tycho on the worst night of her life, when the palace felt like a prison and all she wanted was to kill herself – and even that had turned out for the best. The thought of him dropping from the ceiling, strange-eyed and wild-faced, made her smile. Back then she'd been terrified into not taking her life. Now it felt like a warm memory. She glanced apologetically at the Virgin as other warm memories made her blush. "Thank you," Giulietta said.

The stone mother smiled.

7

Alexa's party had won and Alonzo was going into exile. Duke Marco appeared less of an idiot every day, the Byzantine navy that blocked the lagoon, and the German army that had camped on its edge, had left . . . Tycho doubted Frederick's army would have a good time of it in the snows. He didn't envy the Byzantine fleet the storms that would buffet the last of their journey. But those were not his problems.

I have the girl, I have the title, I have the gold . . . Half the nobles in the city envy me. The others want me dead so they can take my place. Why had tightness gripped his chest the moment he entered the palace? Why this dread as he climbed the marble stairs to the Millioni chambers, passing sour-faced dukes staring from paintings, and tapestries exaggerating how great their victories had been? Tycho knew something was wrong the moment he reached the landing.

His jaw ached so fiercely the pain stopped him dead.

As walls and windows, tapestries and a guard outside Leo's nursery fell into sharp focus, his dog teeth threatened to descend and Tycho recognised the smell of Millioni blood tainted with shit and the smell of fear. The guard stepped back as Tycho hurtled towards him.

"My lord . . ."

Leo's nursery was locked.

"There's a new woman tonight, my lord. I heard her lock the door behind her. Perhaps she's embarrassed about feeding?"

"Leo's weaned." Anyway, it wasn't a wet nurse's job to be embarrassed about breastfeeding a baby; it was what she did, fed a child and kept it safe. "Stand back," Tycho ordered. Twisting, he side-kicked the lock.

By the time a second guard came running the door hung on one hinge, Tycho having aimed for a point behind it. The stink of Millioni blood was overwhelming. At least, it was to him. "Get Duchess Alexa . . ."

The new guard froze. Tycho might be noble, Lady Giulietta's lover and rumoured to have powers, but Alexa was sole Regent now Alonzo had sailed. She couldn't simply be sent for.

"She'll have your head if you don't." *Yes, thought that would convince you.* The man ran and the other guard tried to look past Tycho into the blood-splattered room beyond. "Stay back and stay out."

"My lord . . ."

"This is blackest magic."

The guard instantly averted his eyes.

Taking a deep breath, Tycho forced himself inside. Spilt blood, a discarded knife, open shutters to a window with the glass cut out, a grappling iron and a rope still hanging from the sill beyond. A single glance was all it took to know the world had changed. Tonight's nurse had been ripped open and her guts bulged in coils through the edges of the cut. Leo's cradle lay overturned on a carpet that was dark and sticky with blood. Not that. Anything but that.

Tycho upturned the cradle to reveal the dead child beneath.

Very small, very precious, and very broken. Sliced cloth and the pucker of a wound showed where Leo had been stabbed in the heart. Other wounds disfigured the tiny chest. His mouth was open in a silent cry. Tycho felt sick at the sight, raw with grief and riven with unfitting hunger.

Hunger? The thought brought him up short.

The child at his feet was dead, and yet hunger tightened his throat so viciously his teeth threatened to descend. One of them was still alive. Swinging round, Tycho dropped to a crouch beside the nurse. She was young, dark-skinned and on the very edge of death. "Look at me," he ordered.

Dark eyes opened and struggled to focus.

At the far end of the corridor halberds crashed as guards came to attention. The nurse tried to speak but her throat was ruined. A flat-handed strike had been used to silence her. He could read the mute desperation in the woman's eyes. She was desperate to say something. He could feed, of course, take her memories and use what he learnt to hunt down whoever did this. Because he would hunt them down. The cold fury where his heart should be guaranteed it.

Raising his head, Tycho let dog teeth descend, blood filling his throat from where they cut his gums, but he was too late. He felt rather than heard Alexa behind him. "Leo's dead?" she demanded.

Tycho knew he looked strange, crouched over the nurse, his hand over his mouth as if to stop himself vomiting. Alexa had come alone.

"Tell me."

"Yes, my lady."

"I will crucify him between the pillars. I will cut down his bloody olives, destroy his precious villa and sew his land with salt. His name will be cut from public plaques and his portraits burnt."

"Who, my lady?"

"Alonzo. Who else?" The duchess turned so swiftly Tycho had only just looked round when her dagger stabbed the original guard under his chin and pierced his brain. He tottered, dead without knowing it, staggered backwards as she withdrew her blade. Contemptuously, she tumbled his body into the room.

"My lady," Tycho protested.

"You disagree with my actions?"

The guard's smile had been easy and his manner relaxed when Tycho first arrived. Too relaxed? Did Tycho now imagine an uncertainly around the eyes? A slight desperation? "We could have questioned him."

"And learnt what?" Alexa's voice was brutal.

"Whatever he knew, my lady . . ."

"Others will give us that information. Where is my niece?"

"Lighting candles for her mother."

Duchess Alexa froze, and Tycho wondered if even here, even now, so many years after Lady Zoë's murder, the woman who brought up Lady Giulietta could be jealous of the mother who'd never age, never be cross, never be anything other than perfect in her daughter's eyes. "I'll have guards detain her," Alexa said.

"She'll want to see Leo."

"You'd show her this?" Alexa gestured at the window, the nurse bled out on the carpet, the cradle Tycho had righted. Alexa saved Leo's blood-soaked body until last.

"She has a . . ."

" . . . right to be driven mad with grief?"

"My lady."

"I lost a child," Alexa said. "My first son. He died in his cot and I was the one who found him." It was obvious from the flatness of her voice she stood in that room, not here in the doorway of this. "That was hard enough . . ." Nodding at the bloody scene, "This is more than even I could have borne."

"I'll go to her . . ."

"No. You have other work to do."

Alexa will look after her. Walking away from Giulietta's scream was the hardest thing he'd ever done. Not even falling through the circle of flames in Bjornvin or waking, chained naked to the bulkhead of a ship in the Venetian lagoon, with silver shackles burning his skin, came close.

I must keep walking.

In that second he *was* Giulietta and she him. The sound of her anguish echoed inside his head long after it stopped in the hall. He and Giulietta were tied in a way impossible to describe. In a way he wondered if Giulietta even understood. When the screaming was replaced by silence he knew she'd fainted, been drugged or magicked by Alexa into some false peace. By then he was striding towards Misericordia on the city's northern shore . . .

The area was well named. A fierce wind blew into his face and the tramped earth beneath his feet felt slick with compacted snow. Ice crust cracked as he walked through street-wide puddles, and his boots were soaked and his feet numb by the time he reached a square of dark water. A monastery stood on the inlet's far side, its walls black with soot from nearby foundries, which burnt all night with a sombre glow, their fires and furnaces never being allowed to cool. The guard Alexa killed had lived in a narrow tenement between the monastery's wall and the side of a foundry. His wife, Francesca, lived there still.

Francesca was Leo's usual nurse, and, between her falling sick and a new nurse arriving, she'd arranged for Leo to be looked after by the wife of one of the cooks. That Francesca then called a replacement from the mainland worried Alexa. In a city of a hundred thousand, twenty-five out of every thousand died each year and fifty were born; fifteen of which lost their mothers in birth, and twenty-five died within the year . . . The point was that in a city where five thousand gave birth annually there was no shortage of women able to act as wet nurses, nurses and childminders. So why summon one from the mainland?

Letting himself in through the tenement door nobody had bothered to lock, Tycho headed through a squalid hall greasy with the stink of cheap food and poverty, two smells he remembered well, and headed for a door at the back.

"Riccardo?" The voice sounded relieved.

Tycho tapped again. On the door's far side, Francesca lifted a handle and slid the bolt back in its hoops. She'd been waiting anxiously for her man to return, and, since there'd been no sound of her crossing the room, she must have been waiting on the far side of the door. Tycho felt sick at what that told him. And even sicker at what he would do. Having shot the bolt, she began to open the door.

Tycho was inside before she realised, his hand over her mouth as he positioned himself behind her. At most, she'd have seen a white-clad figure flow ghostlike through the half-darkness. Blowing out the cheap candle she clutched, he felt bitter smoke fill his nostrils. When she stopped struggling, he took his hand from her mouth. "You know why I'm here."

"Riccardo?"

"Is dead."

"*No* . . ."

"You know it's true."

She did, too. It was in the slump of her shoulders and sag of her body. For a moment she tensed, glancing longingly at the door, then hope leached from her. "Will they torture me first?"

Had she been able to write she could have made no clearer confession. Although Tycho was uncertain what she confessed to. That she would help murder the baby she nursed felt wrong. "It will be a quick death."

"Thank you . . ."

Such resignation. "How could you agree?"

Francesca opened her mouth and shut it. She had typically Venetian features, wide-cheeked and dark-eyed, with a strong nose. In another life the woman might have been pretty; in this she was cheaply dressed and heavy dugged from years of giving milk to other people's children. Her husband had died quickly. He had no way of knowing his wife would be offered that luxury and had risked her life anyway. "You didn't think you'd be discovered?"

"My husband was always Prince Alonzo's man."

So Alexa had been right. "But you fell ill because your husband told you to? And he changed his shift at Alonzo's orders?"

She shrugged. "My man came and went."

And how would I know which guard shift he pulled? Tycho could read the question in the flatness of her tone. He had a question of his own. "You knew Prince Leo was to be murdered?"

"What?"

"Stabbed through the heart," Tycho said. "Your replacement gutted. The nursery looks like an abattoir and stinks like a mortuary. I found the child you fed lying dead beneath his upturned cot."

Twisting free, she put her hands over her ears, refusing to hear any more.

"*No,*" she whispered. "*No, no.*"

Pulling her hands away, Tycho said. "That wasn't meant to happen?"

"*Of course not.*" Francesca shook her head fiercely. "Prince Alonzo wanted the child with him so that Mongol bitch couldn't corrupt the boy. That's what my husband told me. The Regent wanted to keep Leo safe . . . He's really dead?"

"I saw the body."

"What will happen to my child?"

A slaughter for a slaughter? There were undoubtedly cities and rulers who worked like this. Alexa was more complex and her responses less simple. "He will be looked after. A new family will be found."

It was a half-truth. Leo's body would be buried quietly. The slaughtered nurse would simply disappear. A new room would become Leo's nursery and a new nurse found for the new Leo, who would remain Giulietta's child for as long as it took Alexa to decide what should be done.

"Where is your child?"

"Sleeping." Francesca indicated the darkness behind.

Wooden internal walls, tar paper across the windows, a cheap pine table and two stools. A pile of hay in one corner for a goat brought in from a tiny yard outside. The building would burn readily enough.

"He will be safe," Tycho promised.

"And me . . .?

She was not the cause, Tycho reminded himself. Reaching up, he put his hand to her cheek and turned her face until she faced him. "Look into my eyes," he said. "Look into my eyes and don't look away." Her pupils grew huge and fell out of focus. Her eyelids fluttered as she reached the edge of sleep and he felt her body begin to slump. She would have fallen but he caught her, his dog teeth descending as he bit into the nape of her neck.

As always, the world fell into sharp focus. Had he gone outside the sky would have been blood-red, the stars hard and distant worlds he could freeze into his memory in a single glance. And he would have seen the stars, because they would have been points of heat through the cold of the clouds.

He was Fallen. The reality of that fact he only remembered now. At other times, he knew it in an abstract way. Here and now, with blood in his throat and flames flaring from him in colours the human eye couldn't capture he *understood* what it meant. This world was not his world. These people were not his people. Except for him, he doubted *his people* still existed; although he'd made – by simple accident of blood exchanged – one other who acted like him and had his speed and hungers. Dismissing Rosalyn from his memories, Tycho concentrated on Francesca.

It was a small life but dear.

A childhood on the edge of the Arzanale, with her father a ropemaker and her mother a servant to Lord Roderigo's father. A marriage at thirteen to a man who hardly ever beat her and used brothels only rarely. She had three children still living. A daughter of fourteen, already with child, a twelve-year-old boy apprenticed to the Rope Walk, and the infant still sleeping. Those born in the years between were dead of hunger, illness or bad luck. Her life was familiar in shape. A thousand women within a mile of where she lived would recognise it.

Tycho found no taste of treason.

There was little sense she'd lied to him and the lies she told herself were no more significant than those she told her husband, sins of omission at the most. A small life – now lost through someone else's greed. Lowering her to the ground, Tycho put his fingers to her throat and felt nothing. She'd died because her man betrayed her and a man sent by Alexa killed her. It was a small debt and a high return, and he doubted if what had just happened was fair or even just.

The tenement burnt easily. A jug of the cheapest fish oil tipped on to the straw let him start the flames, and the stool and battered table he stood over the straw caught soon enough. *Take the child*, Alexa said. On his way out, Francesca's infant in his arms, Tycho stood in the hall of the tenement and shouted, *Fire* . . . The one word guaranteed to have Venetians tumbling from their beds.

8

"Come in . . ." Alexa's voice was firm.

Hesitating, Tycho wiped frost from the infant's hair and nodded to the guard on Alexa's door. She had trusted guards, as Alonzo had his. Almost all the guards he'd have expected to find in the corridors were gone, however, and the marble floors echoed with silence. Sent home with orders to say nothing, probably.

Not that they'd know much. The guard on Leo's door was dead, and the other guard had been sent to fetch Alexa before Tycho discovered the baby dead. At worst, there would be rumours of a failed attack, and not even that if Duchess Alexa got her way, and she usually did. "It's done?"

Tycho bowed.

Without another word, Alexa crossed her study to take the shivering child from his arms. She stripped off its rags, turned it over and considered it carefully. Tycho knew what she was thinking. About the right age, about the right colouring; dress it in Maltese lace and give it an ivory teether and few would know the difference from a distance. Giulietta would, of course.

He doubted she'd go near the child Alexa would put in Leo's place.

"She's asleep," Alexa said, answering his question before he could ask. Catching his expression, she added. "Poppy in brandy. It's quick and will keep dulling her pain provided we don't use it for too long." Casually, she stripped off her shawl and wrapped it tightly around the grizzling child, considering the result. "I'm going to . . ." A knock at her door prevented Tycho from discovering what.

"You're back." Tycho said, although it wasn't his place to speak. The Nubian woman in the doorway nodded.

"Obviously."

Tycho was grateful for the smile.

"A job well done," said Alexa, and it took Tycho a second to realise she meant Amelia's job, which should be obvious. Little enough about tonight's events was well done. "She killed the Valois king's physician. Using her . . ." The duchess hesitated. "More unusual skills." Amelia's smile was cat-like. Praise given, Alexa switched subjects. "You've heard the palace rumours?

Amelia shucked herself out of a snow-flecked coat. She wore daggers on both hips and her braids were frosted. "An attack?"

"Yes," Alexa held up Francesca's child. "They almost got Leo."

Tycho glanced at the duchess and held his peace, waiting to discover how Alexa wanted this to unfold. He watched her walk the room with the changeling in her arms, tracing a path across a priceless Persian carpet. The restrained fury of her steps and the preciseness of her route reminded Tycho of one of the panthers in the duke's zoo. In one corner of her room, curled around itself but watchful, was her winged lizard, a gift from the Chinese emperor.

Tycho wondered how far Alexa had made it fly and in what conditions. She used the dragonet as her eyes. If Alexa was holding back from sending *Assassini* after Alonzo she had a reason.

"You will guard this child," Alexa told Amelia.

The Nubian nodded.

"And me," Tycho demanded. "What do I do?"

If Amelia was surprised he spoke so freely it was because the rumours that he was Giulietta's lover hadn't reached her. The fact he wore the duke's ring, which had been relegated to a copy, since a copy had been declared the original, hadn't escaped her, though. The duchess had noticed, too, and Tycho was impressed by her refusal to ask where the ring came from. "You wait for me to tell you."

"How long will Giulietta sleep?"

Alexa's face softened. "Until tomorrow. Do you want to see her?"

"She's not in her chamber?"

"She's in mine. And there she'll stay until I'm happy she won't harm herself."

"Yes," she said, seeing Tycho's shock. "She threatened to kill herself. *First my husband, now my child. Why would I want to live?*"

Because I'm still alive? Wrenching his thoughts from the cut Alexa's words inflicted, Tycho wondered if it was cowardice or common sense that made him change the subject to something safer. "What do you know about the nurse? Apart from the fact she came from the mainland . . ."

"Walk with me," Alexa said.

The family chambers were on the floor below, with government offices on the ground floor below that. The civil service used the *procuratie* buildings along one side of Piazza San Marco, the customs had their own offices on the far side of the Grand Canal and the mint was in a small building next to the campanile. With the guards sent home, Ca' Ducale felt as empty as a drum, their footsteps chiming on cold marble as Alexa led Tycho towards the main stairs.

"The nurse," Tycho reminded her gently.

"I asked Giulietta when the poppy was just beginning its work. She said Francesca recommended her and she was Francesca's cousin. My niece trusted Francesca and took her recommendation. Why wouldn't she?"

"Francesca thought the baby was to be abducted."

"Did she now?" The duchess considered that point. "No doubt her man was loyal to Alonzo. But she was Leo's nurse so she was told Leo would be taken and he was killed instead. What worries you about her replacement?"

Tycho tried to pin down his thoughts.

"Tell me later," Alexa said. "We're here now." She opened the door to her chamber and waved Tycho inside. There was a guard by the window. A sergeant whom Tycho recognised from his time in the palace. A hard-faced man with cropped hair who nodded abruptly and opened the inner door at Alexa's command.

"I'll join you later," Alexa told Tycho.

The guard shut the door behind him. The clothes and rolls of cloth that had filled this tiny wardrobe were piled in one corner, and one of Alexa's servants sat in a chair. She almost tripped as she scrambled to her feet. "My lord . . ."

"Stay there."

Smoke thickened the air from herbs charring on a brazier. A silver goblet was sticky with residue, and Tycho dipped a finger into the tar. His skin sizzled slightly where it touched the silver. *Opium . . .* He knew the taste and the effects, which would last far longer on Giulietta than him. His body sublimated wine, opium and other drugs. The girl he loved was so deep in dreams he doubted she could find the door between worlds even if he called her. So he knelt by the bed, folding her fingers into his and wished he could do more. "Go," said a voice behind him. It was Alexa dismissing the servant.

"You love my niece, don't you?"

"Of course . . ."

"There's no 'of course' about it," Alexa said cuttingly. "Most men want Giulietta for her lands, her fortune. Even the fools have worked out she'll probably be Regent after I die. The clever ones have worked out she might be duchess."

"Marco's dying?"

"We're all dying. Well, most of us." Alexa's voice was dry.

Sometime in the last few months she'd decided she could talk to him freely. Perhaps she hadn't had anyone to talk to since her husband had died – except there had been Lord Atilo, obviously. Tycho's old master had been her lover. The fact she now felt free to talk to Tycho was a compliment. It was also dangerous.

Alexa left a trail of dead. For all he admired the duchess and even in some strange way liked her, he'd be a fool not to fear her. They might be allies for the moment, but who knew how long that would last?

"He's made for another world."

Tycho knew she was talking about her son.

"The black moods take him and . . ." Alexa shrugged. "Who will stop him harming himself when I'm gone?"

"You will live for years yet . . ."

"You think I'm immortal?"

The thought had occurred to him. He knew the duchess was far older than she looked and wore her veil to hide her youth as much as in mourning for the late lamented Marco the Just. One of the few men for whom the words *late* and *lamented* always went together and were meant.

"I have a year at most. Perhaps less."

"My lady . . ."

"Magic, potions and self-control can only do so much." Opening a small alabaster box, Alexa took a handful of herbs and scattered them on the brazier, letting sweet smoke fill the tiny room.

Alta Mofacon . . .

Tycho recognised the scent carried on the previous summer's winds when he'd stayed at Lady Giulietta's manor on the mainland. Lavender, hops and dog rose. Something medicinal hid under it.

"Wherever she is I want my niece happy."

"How long will she be like this?"

Duchess Alexa considered the question. "A week at most. Any

more than this and I risk addicting her. Even that long may be too long."

"And me?" Tycho asked. "What do I do?"

Alexa smiled bleakly. "Sharpen your daggers. You seem to enjoy doing that. Sharpen your daggers and prepare yourself for a trip to Montenegro. You're to kill Alonzo . . . I should have had you do it sooner."

Tycho kept his silence.

9

This should have been when we were happy . . .

The days were short and the nights long, giving him time to enjoy himself and her, had enjoyment been possible, and it should have been. Giulietta should have been laughing at his side as they kicked through the snows in the rose garden at the rear of Ca' Ducale, Leo asleep in his cradle or carried in her arms.

Instead, Tycho killed Alonzo a thousand times.

And in between his moments of rage-crazed fantasy he sharpened his daggers until their edges glittered and their points could pierce boiled hide. Having sharpened them, he oiled them against rust and made sure they slid effortlessly from their sheaths. Then he sharpened them again, and again, until their edges cut almost before touching and the points could make the very air bleed.

No matter how often he did this, in his head he killed Alonzo more.

He gutted him, castrated him, cut his throat, pierced his heart. He burnt him alive, drowned him in a ditch, tossed him over a cliff. All he wanted was Alonzo dead and Giulietta freed from the drugs that kept her misery at bay but took the life from her eyes. Hatred of Alonzo consumed him.

Others couldn't see it but he could from the corner of his eye.

A swirling darkness that isolated him in the cold corridors of Ca'
Ducale. Guards still came to attention; servitors dropped curtsies,
footmen bowed . . . Gestures he barely noticed. No one knew his
position any more. Until others stopped knowing he hardly gave
having one a moment's thought. He loved Giulietta and she loved
him; that was all that mattered. Now he knew the court's reluctant
acceptance had been based on him being Giulietta's lover.

With Giulietta so *ill*, the balance changed.

What worries you about Francesca's replacement?

Alexa's question about the dead nurse troubled Tycho so deeply
he stopped bothering to eat or reply to questions or even return
the nods of those who still greeted him. *What was it that he'd
missed?* Tycho stalked through the gaming rooms without noticing
that silence fell the moment he entered. Courtiers, dozens of
them, they all looked the same to him.

When the answer came to him it came if not by accident then
by chance. On the third night he returned before dawn to find a
red-haired girl in his bed. Alexa had sent her. The duchess thought
he needed company. Despite the young woman's protests Tycho
sent her away. She was back the next night to tell Tycho he could
do anything he wanted with her. Alexa's orders. It was obvious
she had no idea what *anything* meant. Equally obvious, she didn't
need to know to be terrified of whatever it might turn out to be.

"What did Alexa offer you?"

"My father's life."

The man was a forger. Since Venice's trade depended on the
purity of its coin, and a Venetian ducat was welcome anywhere in
the Mediterranean, the city was brutal to those caught forging. Her
father would be blinded and his hands cut off to stop him forging
again. Tycho considered bedding her to still his fury, as Lady
Giulietta had used him to still her grief the night her husband died.

But he didn't trust himself. More to the point, this wasn't the
woman he wanted – but if it was true her father would be blinded
if Tycho rejected her then how could he reject her, or wasn't that

his concern? Alexa's logic was cruel enough for Tycho to decide this was a test, but of what . . .? He was still wondering when he looked up and thought – for a moment – it was Giulietta in his bed.

Tycho said, "Show yourself."

Her hips were a little wider, her buttocks slightly rounder, her teats a little more generous . . . But she was close enough in looks to be mistaken for Giulietta at a very quick glance, or would have been had her hair been natural. The long hair she'd untied was only dyed the red he loved so fiercely.

Tycho shivered.

He felt not elation but the first stirrings of recognition. He wondered briefly what he'd have done had Alexa sent him a natural redhead, a girl closer to Giulietta in looks. Bed her and be done with it? Lose what he'd just found?

"Stand up," he said.

The girl stood naked while he walked around her. He touched her body hair and it was soft as silk where Giulietta's was coarse and wiry. The hair on her head was too fine and smelt wrong. She smelt wrong. He stepped back.

"You don't want me, my lord?" The girl sounded worried.

"Tell Duchess Alexa your debt is paid a dozen times."

She looked at him.

"Go," he said. "Go and talk to whoever you're meant to report to. Be sure to say the debt is paid, and tell your father to find another job, one that doesn't land you on your back in bed with a stranger. If such a thing exists." Girls from her class ended up either married or in brothels, and he'd come to wonder if there was a difference. Giulietta would say not, but Giulietta's anger at where she'd found herself was fierce.

Something had been waiting beyond his shock at discovering Alexa was dying . . . Beyond his fury that the woman he loved lay drugged because the risk of addiction was less than the damage grief might do. Against all logic, Giulietta had adored the child

52

Alonzo's plot had forced on her. Take Leo away and all that was left was her uncle's brutality. Alexa's drugs were there to prevent Giulietta from realising this.

Anger at the unfairness of it all had stopped him finding the answer. Stopping for a moment had let his thoughts settle like water filtering through sand. But first he needed to check that what he suspected was possible.

Leo's former chamber was locked but the key rested in the door. A guard hesitated at the end of the corridor, and, knowing the next door led to Giulietta's original chamber, turned and strode back the way he'd come with the steady steps of someone convincing himself he'd done the right thing. He turned in surprise when Tycho followed him. "Has Leo's room been visited recently?"

"My lord, I wouldn't know."

"Of course you would."

The palace guards knew everything and said nothing. They saw what never happened, heard words that were never spoken. "I believe, my lord, orders are no one visit this corridor. Except us, of course . . ."

"Of course . . ." The palace guard walked every step of every corridor and colonnade every hour. Ca' Ducale might be a confectioner's delight, made from pillars as fine as spun sugar, and every canal and the whole lagoon act as its moat, but that didn't mean the Millioni took risks. They were protected against everything, except, it seemed, themselves.

The nursery was in darkness. It stank of death and dried blood. The carpet had been removed for cleaning or destruction; cleaning, probably. It had been Persian and valuable. The duchess was practical about such things. Little else had been touched. A broken crib, a burnt-out fire, evidence of emptied bowels . . . The tiles had been mopped but dirt stained the mortar between them.

Glass from the window lay in a heap.

In the richer Venetian houses windows were made from small circles of greenish bottle glass fixed into a lattice with lead, rather than oiled paper. The local pebbles could be ground to almost pure silica; the city had a monopoly on soda ash shipped from the Levant, and the glass was justly famous.

Pulling aside a drape and opening the shutters, Tycho let in fresher air. Shards of glass jutted in like the teeth of a lamprey. A neighbouring pane was cracked and Tycho looked more closely. Two chips revealed the bottle glass had been hit from outside. A single chip showed it had been hit from inside as well.

Several things were wrong with that. The first was that the sound of a window breaking would have startled Leo's nurse. *Why didn't you call for help?* The second was obvious. *Who had reason to hit the glass from inside?* No one, unless that's where you already were, and you hit that pane first, found it too tough to crack and tried another instead. *Should have let me have the guard.*

He wished Alexa hadn't simply stabbed the man.

The rope the killers were supposed to have used was still tied to its grappling hook and lay coiled in one corner. Rust flecked on to Tycho's fingers as he hooked the grapple over the window. Slipping out of the window, he lowered himself over the edge and gripped the rope, planning to climb down.

A split second later he was falling.

He kicked off from the wall and turned in mid-air to land knee-deep in snow. The grappling hook remained in place but most of the rope lay coiled in front of him. It was as rotten as the hook was rusted. While most of Venice watched Alonzo's ship sail for Montenegro the killer had entered the nursery by the door. Tycho doubted the nurse killed the child. He didn't discount it but he doubted it. A hundred women in the city would be desperate enough to kill a child if the money was right. The nurse had been brought from the Italian mainland for another reason.

Tycho intended to find out what that was.

10

That thought took him through the palace garden, over a lowish wall and into the garden of the patriarch's little palace next door. Most young men his age probably linked places in the city to kisses taken and kisses given, knee-tremblers in darkened door-ways and perhaps the occasional street fight. He remembered places for people he'd killed or deaths he'd seen or overheard.

Here was where Lord Atilo slit the throat of the last patriarch, and Tycho watched before dodging the dagger Atilo threw after him. Tonight Tycho moved swiftly through the snow-covered garden and over a second wall into an alley beyond. And then, as if a man returning from a tavern, sauntered into St Mark's Square and let himself discreetly through a door into the basilica. He nodded to the stone mother with her halo of glass stars, and stole a candle from a box, lighting it from a wall lamp and gluing it with a blob of wax to the floor at the Virgin's feet.

The crypt was below the altar, down a cold spiral of steps that magnified Tycho's careful tread into giant's footsteps as he descended into a darkness his eyes swallowed and turned to light. A thousand ghosts plucked at the shadows' edge. Here princes and statesmen had lain before they were buried. Because the ground was frozen hard and the attack on Leo was a secret, here lay a small child and the nurse who'd been looking after him.

Ice slicked the wall in a pottery glaze that made the walls look natural, not something built by man. The sluggish water around the island city was gelid, the canals snaking through its heart colder still. Old women were insisting the canals might freeze. It had happened before when they were children. Touching his fingers to the wall, Tycho believed it could happen again.

In a year when the world turned colder, and canals froze in Venice, blizzards smothered a town beyond a huge ocean no dragon-ship had crossed for more than a hundred years . . .

Tycho muttered the words so softly they might have been a prayer for the two cloth-covered bodies on slabs in front of him. They came from a book by Sir John Mandeville's squire; a man who travelled to the world's strangest places, where the dead walked and dragons lived and serpents spoke. It was the story of Bjornvin's fall. The last battle of the Far West Warriors, the Viking conquerors of Vineland, whom Tycho remembered as drunken scum. But he'd been their slave, from a people far older, so he was hardly likely to remember them fondly.

The blizzard almost buried the woman approaching the gates of the last Viking settlement in Vineland. She had walked an ice bridge from Asia. Not this winter. Not even the one before.

She was at Bjornvin's walls before the gate slave saw her. His orders were to admit no one. He would have obeyed, too. But she raised an angelic face framed by black hair. Even at that distance he could see she had amber-flecked eyes.

Without intending, he descended the ladder from the walls, removed the crossbar from the gate and opened it . . .

It was the amber-flecked eyes that made Tycho suspect the woman was his mother. The gate slave who descended the walls was his foster-father. Tycho could remember Bjornvin falling. He was the reason the town fell. He'd not been called Tycho then. He had no idea what he'd been called.

Thorns and wild roses probably grew over its remains; at least he hoped they did. The caribou, foxes and hares would have returned. He doubted even Bjornvin's red-painted enemy, the Skaelingar, remembered it had existed.

Leo's nurse and the dead infant lay under grave sheets on marble slabs that looked like cuts of some fatty meat. He could smell corruption in the air, so faint a trace he doubted anyone else could do the same. It was the corruption he'd expect from a corpse an hour or so dead. Alexa must have had them carried down here quickly. The cold had done the rest.

Pulling back the sheet revealed the naked body of a woman in her middle twenties. Her limbs were frozen as if rigor had set and remained rather than eased as it did naturally. Her skin had the sheen of glass and her flesh the translucence of alabaster. But nothing could make pretty the cut that revealed an icy twist of gut. He found what he wanted below her left teat.

A dagger wound. The blow was perfect.

The blade had slid between ribs and ruptured her heart. *A blow so neat and a gut wound so brutal?* Bending closer, Tycho found a twist of thread in the stab wound and blew on frozen flesh to free it. Red wool from an overgown, bloodied flax from an under-gown beneath. The rip to her gut had no threads and its edges were bloodless and too straight. The original blow had bled her out and eventually killed her. The second was for show. She was already mortally wounded before the second cut was made . . .

"*That way madness lies.*"

"Your highness . . ." Tycho hastily covered the corpse.

Thin as a stick insect and gangly as a spider, Duke Marco stood in the doorway dressed in black. In his hand was a church candle. His doublet could have been Tycho's own. "P-pretty angel," Marco said, sounding for a moment like his idiot self. "So alone. So b-bemused. So unlike the rest of us. It was cruel, you k-know. To d-disappear like that. She thought you were g-gone for ever."

"Lady Giulietta?"

"Who else? She t-told me, you know. About h-how you grew wings of f-fire. And then d-disappeared. She c-cried." Marco's mouth twisted in self-mockery. "I c-cried."

"I had to help Rosalyn . . ."

"Who loved you so f-fiercely she couldn't bear to s-stay in Venice? You learn so m-much as an idiot. People t-talk in front of you. They s-scheme, p-plan, p-plot and lust. After a while you become invisible. But no, I d-didn't learn about her f-from g-gossip. Julie t-told me."

"She gave Rosalyn an estate."

"I know," Marco said simply. "I signed the d-decree . . . *Just write your name here as neatly as you can. Big letters will do.*" His mimicry of his mother was exact. "It's amazing h-how easy it is to w-write M-MARCO for the thousandth t-time if someone is holding your h-hand to h-help you. Did you love her?"

"No," Tycho said firmly. "Only Giulietta."

"Are you s-sure?"

"We were too alike . . ."

Marco nodded at that. "What b-brings you here?"

"This," Tycho said, lifting the woman's cloth. He scraped his nail along the edge of her stab wound, collecting blood that had begun to dry before it was frozen. Without allowing himself to hesitate he tasted it.

Vomit rose in his throat.

He spat at the foulness of its taste and scrubbed the back of his hand against his mouth. When he'd finished spitting, Marco held up his candle and stared at him, fierce intelligence in his eyes. "Well?"

"She has Millioni blood."

"My mother would say that's impossible."

"Highness. I can taste it. She and Giulietta share . . ."

Marco's nod was abrupt and Tycho realised that being told the intricacies of Tycho's and Giulietta's relationship by Giulietta

58

was one thing; having it confirmed by Tycho was another. The duke took a moment to find his thoughts. "There's no doubt?"

"None, highness."

"Well," he said. "She's not Alonzo's. He'd never be able to keep a daughter hidden from my mother. She's obviously not mine. Which makes her my father's . . . You realise this means Alonzo knows more about you than you thought?"

Yes, Tycho did.

"The n-night you found Leo dead. *What h-happened?*"

That was the question. He'd run into the nursery, smelt Millioni blood and *known* Leo was dead. Only, what if he wasn't? What if an imposter, a changeling, was dead in Leo's place? Everything suddenly made sense. The Regent's sudden marriage and willingness to accept exile, his almost perverse enthusiasm for the tasks the Council had set him. How long would Alonzo need to stay away?

Three years, four . . .?

Would anyone really notice if Maria Dolphini's son looked a little more grown up than he should? At five he would be precocious. At nine less so. At thirteen . . . Who would notice? Alonzo could pass Leo off as his son.

A new heir for Venice.

The twisted brilliance was that Leo *was* Alonzo's son. He was Alonzo's son because Alonzo had his niece impregnated with his seed using a goose quill. The late Dr Crow had ensured the seed quickened into a boy.

"Fiendish, isn't it?" Marco said.

Tycho nodded.

"My uncle k-kills my half-sister to make *you* think he'd k-killed my nephew. What a f-family." The duke sounded like he meant it. "We'd b-better look at the other h-half of his t-trick."

Across the infant's chest was a short, slightly ragged scar that had healed at both ends. It was newer than Leo's scar, it had to be. Leo and Giulietta had returned to Venice over six months before and Leo was just over a year old. Was this Dr Crow's work? Tycho wondered. The scar on the imposter was so precise someone had to have examined Leo closely and made drawings.

This was not a new plan.

By now Tycho knew the dead infant was a stranger's child but he still tasted its blood, knowing how vile it would be. Once again he spat, gagged and wiped his mouth. Then pulled up the grave sheet and stood while Marco recited a prayer. "Someone's d-daughter. Someone's s-son," Marco finished, when his prayer was done. "You must tell Giulietta and my mother. Leave me being here out of it."

"Highness?"

"I am my father's ghost. Far less visible than my uncle's ambition or my mother's guilt . . . Like you, I am here and not here. Like you, I live for the shadows." With that, he was gone. A swirl of black cloak, a toss of his head and Marco, duke of Venice and prince of Serenissima, blew out his candle and disappeared into the dark twist of stairs beyond. Tycho suspected he was being mocked.

11

The guard on Alexa's door was unwilling to knock, uncertain if he was allowed to let Tycho do so and afraid of making the wrong decision. No doubt he had a wife, children, and a house that was falling down and in need of repair. Pretty much every man in Venice did. Tycho sighed. "State business."

The words were enough to make the soldier step back.

The duchess was famously unforgiving about being disturbed without satisfactory reason. A servant of Alexa's came to the door, realised it was Tycho who wanted entry and vanished again. A few seconds later the door opened for a second time and the servant slid through it, hastily dressed in a thick cloak.

"The duchess is waiting inside . . ."

Tycho should know the girl's name. He should know the name of all Alexa's staff, but since she called them *you* – and they looked interchangeable, being soft-faced and wide-eyed and scared of him – Tycho hadn't bothered. He knew them by sight. If he was honest, he knew them by smell and the waves of interest and doubt they left in the air as he walked past them.

"Come in then."

Tycho shut the door behind him.

"This had better be good," Alexa said. On her table were maps of the Mediterranean, a jade bowl of water, and what Tycho realised was the duchess's own notebook. A quill pen stood in an inkpot next to it.

"Did your husband have bastards?"

Alexa slapped him. She had to cross the room to do it.

"Is that a yes?"

"Tell me why you ask."

"Because the dead nurse in the crypt is Millioni."

The duchess froze. For a second she might have been ice. Raising both hands, she lifted her veil, and then removed it altogether. "Are you certain?"

"Positive," Tycho said.

He waited for her next question. After a moment, he realised she was still waiting for him to answer the last one. "The nurse was killed so I would think Leo was dead. I can . . ." Wondering how to word it, he realised Alexa probably already knew. "I can recognise Giulietta's blood by . . ." He almost said taste and changed it to smell.

"That night. It was the dead woman's blood you smelt?"

"Yes, my lady." Tycho nodded.

"And the infant?"

"The right age and colouring."

"That was enough to fool you?" She sounded disappointed. Tycho hesitated. Was the *krieghund* scar his secret to tell? Lady Giulietta was convinced her aunt would kill the child if she realised what it represented. That her uncle would do the same. She'd told both it was a splinter wound from the Mamluk battle.

"He has Leo's scar."

"Clever," said Alexa. "You smell the blood and see the scar . . . I should have looked at the child myself." She sucked her teeth. "My fault for growing soft in my old age. I wouldn't let Giulietta look either. You realise," she added, "if Alonzo realises Leo is *krieghund* he'll kill him anyway?"

"*My lady?*"

"I'm not a fool. Prince Frederick's war pack changed sides to come to your aid on Giudecca. You had my orders to kill him but you let him live. He wanted to see my niece before he left Venice. He especially wanted to see her child. Oh, don't be jealous . . . She refused."

"I gave Frederick the wolf sword."

"I know. But that alone wouldn't be enough. So afterwards, when you disappeared and my niece was stamping round like a sulky child refusing to eat or sleep and crying in corners, I started to wonder why Frederick withdrew so easily."

"His war pack was dead."

"His army still existed. The city was hungry and beginning to starve. You gave him the *WolfeSelle*, which saved him from outright disgrace when he got home. But to leave so easily. It took me until you returned to work out what I'd missed."

"You asked Giulietta?"

"I examined Leo. Magic clings to the scar."

"And you let him live, my lady?"

Alexa shrugged. "We were ready to give the city to Emperor Sigismund if we had to. Better that than let the Byzantines have it. This way Venice remains independent for the moment, and a child of Millioni blood inherits the throne for all that a German emperor pulls the strings. Sigismund has no legitimate son as yet. My hope is he makes Frederick his heir. That would make Leo second in line to the imperial throne . . ."

Tycho could see how that might meet with the duchess's approval.

12

The night was chill and Lady Giulietta unhappy at being woken. She wanted poppy, and was put out to be given a sharp-tasting draught of nux vomica instead. Tycho understood. At least he understood sweet dreams were more comforting than being woken, wrapped against the cold and bundled downstairs and through a door between the palace and the basilica. "What must I see for myself?"

The lamp Tycho held stank of fish oil, because all the lamps in Venice stank of fish oil, and its light glittered on glass mosaic and bounced off gold leaf. The rood screen exploded into light as they approached. But Giulietta simply glanced at a fretted brass censor high overhead – as she did every time she visited the cathedral – and her fingers tightened a little on his. Tycho was glad. The passive and drugged young woman of recent weeks was not someone he recognised.

"Down here," he said.

"No . . ." Lady Giulietta pulled away. "Why are you doing this?" The sight of the stairs to the crypt made her turn away.

"Aunt Alexa says you must see for yourself."

The habit of obedience carried Lady Giulietta down the stone spiral. When she halted at the bottom, Tycho put his hands on her thin shoulders and walked her into the chilly room. When she saw the small shroud-covered body, she turned away and would have bolted if he hadn't held her tight. "You can't make me."

"Look closely . . ."

"Why are you doing this?"

Because Alexa says you have to discover the truth for yourself. Because Frederick wanted to see you before he left. Because I'm not as kind as you think I am . . . Tycho sighed. "Because I must." Pulling back the sheet, he lifted his lamp to light the naked infant. "Is this Leo . . .?"

He wanted to say, *This isn't Leo, is it? Look carefully, you'll see it's someone else's child.* But that was the best he could offer. Bending close, she forced herself to look carefully at the small boy, the sharp edges of her face softening as hope melted them. The horror at what Tycho was making her do ebbed, the bitterness left her mouth. Happiness, which went missing when she thought Leo dead, flickered in her eyes, like life returning. He held her then, fighting his own emotions as she sobbed into his shoulder, her body shaking. "I shouldn't be happy."

"Yes, you should."

"Not when . . ." Reaching down, she stroked the dead child's face and flinched at the cold. "How?" She asked, meaning the scar.

"A knife. Maybe a little magic. It's deep enough to make the scar and shallow enough to have healed quickly." The *who* was obvious; although he let her get there herself.

"So Leo is alive?" Her eyes widened as she realised something else. "My Uncle Alonzo has him?"

Nodding, Tycho led her to the second slab. He didn't bother to pull back the shroud this time. "The last duke had a natural daughter by one of his mistresses and kept it from your aunt. The girl was sent to the mainland and Alexa doubts she even knew her parentage."

"Why would he go to this much trouble?"

Tycho found himself on the edge of saying something he'd never put into words for her before. Giulietta knew – how could she not? – he'd drunk her blood the night he spared Prince Leopold's life, having tasted a single drop months before when he found her in the basilica. Since she was too tired to understand how he sensed sound and colours and smell, and he barely understood that himself, and he couldn't bring himself to admit her blood was an addiction, he simply told her different people's blood smelt differently to him. Hers made him drunk. This woman . . .

"There's a family likeness?" See, he knew she was quick.

"She was killed so I'd smell Millioni blood . . . I'd rush into Leo's nursery, smell Millioni blood and see the baby's scar. I'd believe the child was yours."

Picking up the lamp, Tycho edged Giulietta towards the stairs and turned for a final look. A woman and a child killed to tie together a plot Alexa still needed to unpick and he needed to stop. The Millioni left death in their wake. All powerful families did. *Am I worse because I kill face to face?*

Venice had its Blades, other kings and cities had their own assassins, less good in Venice's opinion, and in this the city was right. Atilo had trained his followers well and Tycho was the best of them. He'd failed in this, though. It didn't matter that the child was in Leo's gown, in Leo's cot, and had Leo's scar.

You should have made sure.

"Uncle Alonzo's going to claim Leo for his own, isn't he? That's why he married Maria Dolphini. Why she was bundled in that coat. That's why she went with him when anyone sensible would have stayed at home."

"Yes . . ." It was the only way Leo's abduction made sense. Alonzo couldn't keep the child openly without making an even worse enemy of Alexa. And, while having him killed would have been a decisive and irrevocable decision, and Alonzo liked decisive and irrevocable, he *was* the child's father. Only he could hardly claim parentage of an infant produced under the directions of an alchemist excommunicated by the Pope. But if Alonzo presented the child as Maria's . . .

It was brilliant. As his heir by Maria Dolphini, the daughter of one of the richest and most ambitious nobles in Venice, the child's future was gilded. Alonzo could count on Dolphini money to carry him to the throne. The thought of Maria Dolphini as duchess and her son as heir would guarantee that.

13

Hunger ate at his stomach. Simple hunger, the kind that wanted food not blood, ate at his gut and Tycho realised it was hours since he had eaten. He still wore the clothes he'd thrown on after he sent the forger's daughter away, and a bleak hope had driven him to Leo's nursery looking for certainty.

He found the kitchens lit red from the embers of the fire pit and almost tripped over a sleepy boy crouched beside a bread oven. He almost tripped over the boy because he was looking beyond the oven to where Duke Marco sat at a table scraping black off a burnt pastry he'd taken from a bin. Beside the duke rested a fishing net on a pole, the kind used by children to catch sprats.

"You were l-longer t-than I expected," said Marco, pushing half the pastry across. Tycho was hungry enough to take it and eat.

"Giulietta wanted to talk, highness."

The duke sat with his knees pulled up to his chin and the fingers of his left hand endlessly twisted his curls into tight knots. He was so sleepy his head kept dropping forward and jerking upright. "Of c-course she d-did. I imagine she w-wants you to s-stay here?"

How did he know that? Tycho had imagined Lady Giulietta would want him to fetch Leo back immediately. It had been a shock that she wanted her aunt to send someone else. Alexa said it was the poppy talking.

"You must leave n-now. Before you decide she's right, and my mother agrees to send another in your place. Finish that and go."

"It's almost daylight, highness."

"You'll burst into f-flames without your ointment? Go up in a twist of s-smoke? Turn into a pillar of salt like Lot's w-wife? You've never said w-what would happen."

"I don't know."

"And y-you're afraid to f-find out?" There was little amusement in the duke's smile. "We're alike, you and m-me. Trapped in our little p-prisons. There's a barge waiting by the M-Molo. You'll be protected from the s-sun."

"Lady Giulietta . . ."

"Will wake to f-find you gone. She'll be upset with the w-world and f-furious with you. This will exhaust her less than a couple of d-days spent b-begging you not to go. By the t-time you return the p-poppy will be done. She'll b-be back to the young w-woman you love."

"Yes, highness."

"Take w-whatever you n-need from my t-treasury and stores."

Horses? Weapons? Archers? Tycho ran through what he might need and arrived at an unexpected answer. "Give me Amelia."

"She's y-yours anyway." As head of the Duke's Blade, Tycho controlled the *Assassini* who enforced Venice's will at home, killed her enemies abroad and slaughtered traitors wherever they could be found. That was the official description. Since their battle against the *krieghund* a couple of years before, which saw most of the Blade killed, the most fearsome thing about the Assassini was their name. A fact known only to those who needed to know which, thankfully, was very few.

"Take h-her," said Marco. He hesitated. "Has m-my mother t-told her about . . .?"

Leo being abducted? "No, your highness."

"Keep it that w-way for now. One f-final p-point."

Tycho waited.

"Don't come back if you fail."

If I . . . Tycho felt his stomach tighten.

"My m-mother will be f-furious if you l-leave without her orders. But it's J-Julie who will n-not forgive you." Marco shrugged. "I know her, n-not the way you k-know her b-but well enough and I've k-known her longer. She'll f-find it h-hard enough to f-forgive you for leaving. If you c-come b-back without Leo . . ."

Tycho nodded.

"We make b-bad enemies. And d-dangerous friends."

Marco pushed himself up from the bench using his fishing net as a walking stick and stood unsteadily. He kissed Tycho on both cheeks and sighed. "I'll walk you to the M-Molo, and then f-fetch Amelia. You m-must leave the m-moment she arrives . . . Now, what do you k-know of M-Montenegro?"

"Nothing yet, your highness."

"It's w-wild, cold in winter, filled with mountains and riddled with b-bandits. Those are its b-better points." The duke shrugged. "No doubt m-most empires think their n-newest colonies barbaric. In Montenegro's case it's true. As for the Red Cathedral, it sits on an island in the c-centre of a demon-filled lake. You know I'm d-duke of M-Montenegro?" His smile was sour. "Duke of Venice, duke of M-Montenegro, duke of C-Corfu, and prince of Serenissima. Also k-king of Hungary . . ."

"Highness?"

"Oh, d-don"t worry. Sigismund says he's d-duke of Venice."

Life in Bjornvin had been simpler, Tycho told him. The Vikings hated the Skaelingar and killed them when possible. The Skaelingar tried to wipe the Viking settlements from the face of Vineland. With the fall of Bjornvin they managed it.

"S-sounds blissful," Marco said.

In the corridor, on their way to the Molo gate, the duke's face suddenly twisted, his shoulders hunched and a nervous tic began to drag one corner of his mouth. He clung to his fishing net like a man drowning. For a second, Tycho thought Marco was having a fit and then he heard footsteps behind them.

"Your highness . . ."

"Ah, C-Captain W-Weimer. Out h-hunting b-baby bats? So s-sweet when d-dipped in h-honey. Did you f-find me any?

The crop-haired young officer hesitated. Bowing low, he glanced at Tycho, and then quickly looked away. "Your mother, highness . . ."

"D-drop in on m-me, d-did s-she?"

"I imagine so, your highness."

"Y-y-y-y- . . ." Duke Marco stamped furiously at his inability to get out his words. "Y-you m-may tell her I'm h-hunting b-baby b-bats, lost l-lovers, and m-my f-father's g-ghost." He swept his pole through the air and looked mournfully at the empty net.

"His ghost, highness?"

"Y-you h-haven't s-seen it anywhere?"

Captain Weimer crossed himself. Admitting that he had not, he bowed low and withdrew at a wave of Marco's hand. Weimer was Alexa's new appointment as captain of the palace guard. Alonzo's man was gone.

"This is the p-plan," the duke said.

The other Marco was back.

"Y-you defect to Alonzo . . . T-that's the only way you'll get close enough to get Leo back. My uncle will be expecting y-you. W-who else would my m-mother send? You know they were l-lovers?"

"Highness?"

"Alonzo p-poisoned me as a child, had my father m-murdered and b-bedded my m-mother. I've spent m-most of my life wanting him d-dead." The duke smiled sourly. "But I want Giulietta happy more. If the c-choice is killing my uncle or saving Leo you s-save the child. Understand?"

Tycho nodded. "My page . . ."

"Pietro?"

Tycho was surprised Marco remembered the boy's name. "Yes, highness, Pietro. Can I leave him in your care?"

"Of course." Marco smiled. "I'll give him to Giulietta to remind her of you. You can have him back when you return."

He might have been talking about a pet.

PART 2

"This thing of darkness I acknowledge mine . . ."

The Tempest, William Shakespeare

14

Montenegro

The big cat looked down the white slope from between two twisted fir trees and growled softly in the back of her throat at the sight of soldiers struggling through knee-deep snow. She was sand-coloured, with darker spots and ears that twitched to catch every sound. Her true home was far to the south, where the nights could be this cold but the days far hotter.

The man hunting her belonged to this pack.

She knew that with the certainty she knew many things. That she could outrun their hunter was the least of them. His feet broke the snow, where her paws barely troubled its crust and carried her across gravel streams without breaking thin ice. His arrows had been spent worthlessly and when he reached this spot she would be somewhere else.

For a second she considered attacking the men below. The thought put the smell of blood in her nostrils. Her hackles rose and she bared her teeth to show yellow canines. She could kill half, bowling through them in a flash of claws and ripping teeth, but those left would probably kill her. It was time to return to her lair.

Her path led up through twisted trees into snow-speckled scree above. Here brutal winds stopped the snow from settling. The ice patches were cold beneath her paws and the frozen scree colder, its sharpness lacerating the pads of her feet. They might be too numb to hurt now but they would bleed later.

Below her twisted a road the soldiers would use. Her own route had been more direct and led from a high pass where the air had been clear and so thin her ribs had hurt with every breath. Beyond the pass was a stone fort, larger than those she'd seen in the last few days. Built in the style of the early men – thick walls, heavy crenels, narrow windows – it protected the head of a valley that looked too bleak for anyone to bother protecting. Its walls still stood, for all half the roof had fallen in.

Her job had been to find it if she could.

It was hunger that drove her through the trees and down towards the valley floor on her return journey, until an arrow past her shoulder snapped her wide awake and changed the nature of her hunt. She'd caught a hare in its white winter coat, before staining its fur and the snow red with its blood. The mouthful it provided did little to assuage her hunger. Tomorrow she would have to go out again.

At the mouth of a tunnel dug into a snow bank she halted and hesitated before beginning her change. The air shimmered, making the slate roof of an almost buried shepherd's hut beyond her look like rock seen through running water. There was none of the anguish of a *krieghund* change, no ripping flesh, shifting muscles and cracking bones. Amelia simply became something else. In place of a sandy-hued leopard stood a young Nubian woman, naked against the white of the snows behind her. Tycho had known she was other. Unless he was a fool, he'd known that from the first night they met, beside a frozen canal in the middle of a battle between Venice's street gangs. But Amelia doubted he'd known what form her otherness took.

Climbing into her trews, she struggled into her jerkin and slid her daggers into her belt; her sword she slung over her shoulder, not bothering to buckle the baldric that held it, since she'd take it off again the moment she was inside. When Tycho woke she'd tell him about the soldiers.

Captain Towler was older than he looked and younger than he felt. A tallish man, with broad shoulders and cropped hair, his skull was slightly misshapen from being crushed with a shovel during the siege of Belgrade. He'd been young then and his attacker a woman. His reluctance to kill her had almost cost him his life. It was the last time he let chivalry get in the way of self-preservation. At the sack of M'dina six months later, he grabbed the first woman to jab at him with a spear by the throat and tossed her off the city walls. That was the version he told in taverns, with a whore on his lap and his hand up the skirt of the nearest serving girl.

Naive young English recruit learns war's lessons the hard way. The truth was more ordinary: he'd been clubbed round the head by a German sergeant after starting a bar fight he was too drunk to finish. Five people had known the true story and four were dead. The German he had killed himself weeks later. Of the others, one had died outside Paris, one of plague, the other drowned at sea.

Towler shrugged. His might not be much of a life but it was the only one he had and he wasn't ready to throw it away. He'd been a corporal back then. One of Sir John Hawkwood's finest, and carried two gold coins and five silver wrapped in a rag at his hip. Now he banked with a moneylender in Milan and counted his wealth in tens of gold, and hundreds of silver. If Prince Alonzo Millioni's offer was good – and assuming the world wasn't actually ending – he'd be counting his gold in hundreds and his silver in thousands before next year was out.

That thought made him happy. Well, if not happy then almost content, and if not content then at least willing to battle along a snow-covered dirt road through twisted firs towards a pass through the mountains above. Once he got above the treeline he'd be able to see where the hell he was and move his men out of this damn valley, and into the next most probably. His map was old but not cheap, and said nothing about this many mountains.

Above him the sky was high and clear, lacking the heavy cloud they'd come to expect since Towler's Company landed in Montenegro. Still as cold as a whore's heart, of course. As cold as a whore's heart and unwelcoming as a nun's arse. Of course it was. He'd met a Schiavoni merchant in Ragusa who said the canals in Venice were ice. A French merchant had topped that by saying the river through Paris was solid enough for the king's coach to use it as a road when he fled the starving city. Hedge priests said the world was ending and snow now fell alike on rocks in the far north and southern pastures that had never seen it before. Wolves from Russia were crossing the frozen Baltic into Sweden. Wolves from Sweden were crossing the frozen sea to Denmark. Olive groves in Italy were dying in their thousands. The vines of France were brittle fingers that would never regrow. The world might as well end, because there'd be nothing to feed those left alive when the snows melted.

"Hurry it up," he shouted.

The men-at-arms at the back looked at one another and increased their speed. In a day or so they'd look at one another, shrug and one would give up and the other join him. He'd hung the last two to do that. There was nothing like a good hanging for keeping soldiers cheerful. Obviously he'd hung the two least popular men in his troop. Why make trouble for himself by hanging men people liked?

Morgan and Lyle had been new. Survivors of a troop massacred outside Palermo. He'd hung them naked so his men could watch them dance their way to hell, and both had pumped their seed on to the trampled snow, which everyone knew was good luck. Also, hanging stragglers meant more food for the rest. Towler trusted Prince Alonzo would be grateful for all the hardened men he could get, and a more hardened group than this it would be difficult to find. They'd fought in Italy, Austria, Sicily and France. They'd fought for the Medici boy one year and against him the next. That was the way of free companies. Their kind kept the world safe, and he was proud of it. Captain Towler had no fear of God.

In all his life he'd never eaten meat on a Friday. He said his prayers daily, made confession monthly and gave gold to rebuild any churches he'd been forced to destroy. More than one bishop had assured him he'd be welcomed into heaven when the time came. Which he hoped, trusting in God's mercy, would not be for some years yet.

"Pull them up," he told a soldier squatting by a tree. "Or have your bollocks drop off from cold."

"Like that would make a difference," someone muttered.

Another laughed and the crouching boy blushed.

"Crap your pants if you must," Towler said more gently, knowing the real answer was don't crap or piss at all. But the boy was human in a wind-whipped wilderness that made no allowance for that. *This is the way the world ends . . .* He'd heard a ragged preacher in the town before last say that. Sinners brought this on the rest. God was turning his back on the world.

The preacher was selling misery as enthusiastically as a baker sells hot cakes. Someone called him a liar, someone else said it was true. Towler was glad when the local Watch arrived and his preaching ended in a grunt and a slumping body. Towler had bedded his first whore in weeks that night. Fat and greasy and stinking of garlic and smoke, she swore she wasn't really in the trade. What she lacked in looks she made up for in willingness and he overtipped disgracefully in gratitude. She'd been so shocked she sucked him for free. Perhaps she'd be his last. If he died on these slopes would it be so bad?

"*That's the cold talking,*" Towler muttered. Seeing a man look across, he scowled back. For miles the cold had been telling them to sleep. All any of them had to do was lie down on its white feather bed and the cold would welcome them home. He couldn't remember a winter like it. No one could. Even the old – who usually claimed that what happened to them was bigger, better or worth more – shook their heads at his question. Towler wanted to know. What others had survived could be survived again and lessons learnt earlier used this time, too.

In the last town the priest said a witch was to blame, and the old women said it was the priest's fault for forcing people to abandon the old religion. On the day they marched out, Towler's Company passed the manse burnt out and roofless. An accidental fire, the mayor said. So it might have been, if the priest's front door hadn't been nailed shut, with bars of charred oak still bolted across to stop him from escaping.

In five days they'd reach the Red Cathedral. He'd told his men three for obvious reasons. They had food enough for two and imagined themselves able to do the last day hungry. Tell them they had to survive three days without food and they'd realise they weren't going to arrive at all. Since Towler was refusing to admit that possibility to himself he was hardly going to share it with them. There were days he hated his job, and this was one of them. He should have been at home with his wife and children.

But then, of course, he'd need a wife and children in the first place. Instead he had bastards – because what man didn't – and two or three women who probably considered themselves his wives. Sir John Hawkwood, his first captain, had let his troops travel with camp followers. In the end a much younger Towler had summoned the courage to ask why, since they slowed the troop down, caused fights and stole the stores. *If the worst comes to the worst you can always eat them.* He still didn't know if Sir John had been joking. It was possible he meant every word. *Will we end up eating human flesh?* Captain Towler considered the question and decided it depended on how hungry they got.

"All right, Captain?"

Towler scowled at his sergeant.

"You sighed like you meant it."

He'd been wishing he had a priest along to tell him how much forgiveness of a sin like that would cost. "We need to make camp soon."

His sergeant flicked a glance at the darkening sky. The snow would reflect tonight's full moon, making it light enough for any bandits to find them. The lack of cloud cover also meant it would be colder than ever; what little warmth the world still possessed stolen by eternity. "We'll need a fire."

"Then send men to find wood. Is Evans back yet?"

Evans was their archer, disliked by the sergeant but useful all the same. He could outshoot most men, and a longbow in a forest like this was the difference between life and death for all of them. The last animal Evans killed was a wolf, more bones and sores than ribs. It tasted like week-dead carrion but they ate it all the same and cracked its thicker bones for the marrow. The captain hoped Alonzo had food enough. He'd have a mutiny on his hands if not.

"He's over there, Captain . . ."

The archer looked flustered and scared as he slid and slipped his way downhill towards the road. His long face was red and puffy, his overfull lips taut as he gasped down gulps of air. "Bandits?" Towler demanded.

Evans shook his head and the captain relaxed slightly. The stragglers in his troop had arrived by the time Evans finally caught his breath enough to tell them he'd seen hunting. But, first, the sergeant got his usual insults in.

"Sod *seen*, you Welsh bastard. Did you catch anything?"

When Evans shook his head the sergeant turned away to spit and almost missed the corporal's words. "Saw a cat though . . ."

Wild cats might live this close to the treeline, Captain Towler thought. You could eat cat, he'd done that more than once.

Better than rat, certainly better than wolf. Although even wolf was better than nothing. If there was one cat up here, maybe there were more. Maybe it had a mate and kittens.

"This big." Evans held his hand waist-high.

Towler steered him away from the others, nodding to the sergeant to say he could follow. Evans looked sober enough, and where would he have found spirits this far into a march? The hill villages were deserted and the towns in the valleys where they'd billeted so poor that to find thin beer was a treat. "This big?" The sergeant's voice was a mocking echo of his own.

Evans held his gaze and nodded. "Yellowy with spots," he said. "Ripped a hare right open with a single bite and ran faster than a galloping horse. It dodged my bloody arrow as if it was a feather falling."

"If it was really that big," Towler said, "you're lucky to be alive."

Evans nodded soberly. "Do you think . . .?"

"No, I don't, and nor do you, understand?" Captain Towler watched his Welsh archer join the others, glance nervously back at the captain and begin talking anyway. They were superstitious fools and the last thing Towler needed was his men getting spooked by reports of were-beasts and worse.

It he didn't find them food soon he'd have to give them another hanging. He'd like to start with Evans but the Welshman was too valuable so it would have to be the last recruit. A dark-faced Sicilian who swore his family had never been heathen. No one believed him or much liked him either.

15

"I will *not* go and greet his arrival . . ." Lady Giulietta tried to sound like she meant it, because she did mean it; she was simply having trouble convincing her aunt. "You can't make me."

God, now she sounded like a nine-year-old.

Blinking back tears, she fussed with her shawl so Aunt Alexa wouldn't see how badly her hands were shaking. From the softening of her aunt's expression she'd seen anyway. Now her aunt was going to treat her like a bloody child.

Because you're behaving like one.

She knew it was true. Turning her head, Giulietta stared through the glass to ice on the lagoon. No ship could enter and none leave. That had to be why no message had come from Tycho. He'd have written otherwise, wouldn't he? She knew he would, although she'd probably still rip up his first letter. She was cross enough. Every day she waited for him to write and nothing came. It was . . . *intolerable*.

"Giulietta . . ." Alexa's voice was neutral.

"*What?*" That wasn't how you spoke to the Regent of Venice, even if she was your aunt and you were alone except for Marco. The fact Aunt Alexa's lips barely tightened told Giulietta how worried she was.

"It's the poppy," Alexa said apologetically. "I gave you too much poppy and now your body wants more to stay happy."

"So give me some more."

"I'd like to but I can't . . ." Duchess Alexa shook her head.

"You only gave it to me so you could send Tycho to Montenegro." Lady Giulietta could feel her eyes fill and looked away. She hated feeling like this. She hated being like this. And she wasn't going to go out in the cold to greet Prince Frederick, who shouldn't have been here anyway.

"Tycho leaving like that was as much a surprise to me. He didn't leave Ca' Ducale with my authority."

"I don't believe you. You've never liked him, I know you haven't. That's why you won't sign the decree letting me marry. Now he's going to get killed and Leo will die and you want me to meet . . ." Tears overflowed, and she brushed them away angrily. "I don't even know what he thinks he's doing here. I wouldn't be surprised if you sent for him."

Now she *was* crying openly.

"You doubt Tycho?" Alexa sounded interested.

"Of course I don't doubt Tycho. He saved me in the battle off Cyprus, remember. And in the banqueting hall . . . And when that horrid Byzantine captured me. All he does is bloody save me." Jamming her fists into her eyes, Giulietta turned for the door and froze as strong arms folded around her. She tried to fight them off and then realised it Marco, gripping her tight and stroking her hair.

"Angels f-fly away," he said.

"Then they come back," Giulietta replied fiercely.

Marco smiled at how quickly she'd turned *he'll die* into *he'll be back*. Stroking her cheek he found a tear and dried it with his fingers. "Angels f-fly away, and sometimes they come b-back and sometimes they f-fly away again. That's why t-they're angels . . ." He kissed her cheek. Leaning close, he whispered. "It's my b-bad luck we both love the same b-boy. You were always g-going to win."

84

Lady Giulietta stared at him.

Stepping back, Marco said. "Do this for me . . ."

And Giulietta discovered she'd agreed to greet Prince Frederick after all, which meant the carriage waiting below would be needed, despite her having spent the last half-hour telling her aunt to send it away again. Venice was not really a city of carriages. Gondolas, gondolini and luggers, yes. Handcarts and trestles, even ox-drawn sleds. But the noble used gondolas like everyone else, and anyone rich enough to have a mainland estate kept their carriages there.

"Is this going to be safe?" Giulietta asked.

The carriage was old and someone had hammered steel nails through the rusting hoops of each wheel to help them grip the ice. She imagined the carriage would look ridiculously outdated to Frederick. The bastard son of Sigismund of Germany probably had a dozen gold carriages of his own.

Frederick was her late husband's half-brother, and the closest thing the Emperor Sigismund had to an heir. When Giulietta asked Alexa if that made him her half-brother-in-law, Aunt Alexa looked into her eyes and muttered that the poppy was taking longer to leave her body than expected.

Lady Giulietta had meant the question seriously.

No one in the Venetian court had any idea why Prince Frederick had returned in the middle of winter to a city he'd besieged that autumn. Although it would make him famous in years to come. The man who crossed the Venetian lagoon by carriage in the middle of the worst weather the world had ever known. Assuming the priests and doomsayers weren't right, and this wasn't the end of the world. "Do you think it is?" Giulietta asked, settling herself between her aunt and cousin. "The end of the world, I mean?"

Alexa considered the question carefully, but it was Marco who answered it as they were riding beneath Ponte Maggiore, the huge wooden bridge that linked the banks of the Grand Canal, their wheels squealing and grinding on the ice. The bridge was heaving with sightseers and both embankments were thick with crowds. Since no one but the court yet knew of Frederick's planned arrival, and Giulietta didn't yet know how her aunt knew about that, the carriage on the Canalasso was obviously enough to bring out the crowds. A fair number cheered, their breath rising like smoke in the freezing air. It had been a long time since anyone in Venice cheered her aunt. Now simply showing herself in public seemed enough.

"They're scared," Marco said. "And n-no, this isn't the end of the w-world. At least not yet and p-probably n-never." Even Alexa turned to hear this. "Think about it," he said, with barely a stutter. "Think about what would h-have to change for the w-world to end . . ." He grinned. "You can't g-guess?"

"I'm not good at guessing games." Aunt Alexa smiled and Giulietta wondered what was funny.

"Yes, you are," Marco said. "You just d-don't like g-giving answers in case they're w-wrong. Go on, tell me why the world's not r-ready to end."

She tried, she really tried. Perhaps it was the drugs, perhaps she simply wasn't as clever as Marco. That was more likely. Giulietta was coming to realise there were few people as clever as Marco. He was so clever most people thought him a fool. "I give up," she said.

"One of the kitchen maids is pregnant."

Alexa went still, and then let the breath from her body when her son shook his head, slightly mockingly. His smile said he'd shown little interest in women so far, surely she didn't expect him to change now? The disappointment showed on Alexa's face and Giulietta felt sorry for her.

"How do you know she's pregnant?"

"I asked."

This left unanswered what Marco was doing talking to kitchen maids, but since he was duke, and Alonzo was gone, there was

86

little to stop him from wandering where he liked and talking to whom he liked. Besides, the kitchens were warm, so spending time there probably counted as sensible.

"So is Antonio's wife," Marco added.

"Who's Antonio?"

"The young guard on the Council stairs, the one with the fair hair."

Lady Giulietta had barely registered that there was a new guard, never mind learnt his name, noticed his hair or discovered his wife was pregnant. She imagined there was a purpose to Marco's words and he'd reach it soon.

"Think about it," Marco said impatiently. "Are there midwives in heaven? Will some women in heaven be pregnant for eternity? Are there going to be births, and babies and breast-feeding and nappies? We'll know the world's going to end when women stop getting pregnant."

"Who told you that?" Alexa demanded.

"Worked it out for myself." Marco rewarded himself by raising the leather flap over the side window and sticking his head into the wind like a dog on a barge. The crowds on both banks erupted with excitement and Alexa stopped trying to pull him back inside again.

"He's changing," Giulietta risked saying.

"You've noticed it too?" The duchess's gaze sharpened.

Giulietta wondered what Aunt Alexa would do if she discovered her son's idiocy was a disguise adopted in childhood to protect him from Alonzo, her brother-in-law. Would she blame Uncle Alonzo? Would she decide it was her own fault? Or would she take it out on those who already knew this? Lady Giulietta had no intention of being the one to find out. Only, the question she did ask earned her such a glare she might as well have talked about Marco anyway. All she did was wonder aloud how her aunt knew about Prince Frederick's arrival.

*   *   *

"Which one is he?" Lady Giulietta demanded.

Aunt Alexa looked at her.

"We've never met. Remember?" Giulietta didn't want to revisit the night her lady-in-waiting was killed by an arrow meant for this boy, the night Marco revealed to her that he wasn't the idiot prince his subjects thought. She scanned Germans and saw a large, broad-shouldered young man in a wolf-fur coat looking entirely too pleased with himself. "That one?"

"No," Alexa said. "Over there."

A narrow-shouldered youth was climbing from the last coach and looking nervously around him. He stamped the ice as if three carriages, five horses and a dozen people weren't test enough of its strength. Turning, he noticed Lady Giulietta staring and hesitated. She watched him force himself to approach – and somewhere in the handful of steps between his carriage and where she stood his face changed, losing its nervousness and filling with a terrible sadness.

He stopped, and reached for her hand. Lady Giulietta expected him to kiss it, but he simply held it for a few seconds longer than he should then let it go. He looked as if he wanted to hug her and didn't quite dare. "I'm so sorry," he said. "Really sorry. I know how it feels."

"Your highness?"

"To lose a child . . ."

He should be paying his respects to Duke Marco, or kissing Aunt Alexa's hand, but his eyes were for her and they were brown, intense and bright as cut agate. His face was raw with sadness.

"Who said anything about a child?" Giulietta demanded.

"Our spies say Leo is dead and a substitute takes his place." The boy looked beyond Giulietta to the scowling duchess. "At least, until your aunt decides her next move. It must be brutal having to pretend." His beautiful brown eyes filled with tears. "*Prince Frederick . . .*" The Duchess Alexa stepped forward.

"I was married," Frederick said simply. Maybe he read Giulietta's thoughts that said he was too young to have lost a wife and child. No one had told her this when he was mentioned as one of her suitors. "Your wife died in childbirth?"

"Plague." The prince gulped and Giulietta realised how much it hurt him to talk of it. "I was thirteen and she was fifteen. My father wanted to cement an alliance and . . ."

Yes, Giulietta knew how that worked.

"Annemarie," Frederick said. "We fell in love." His shrug said stranger things had happened. "And she had a child a year after we married."

"A boy?"

"A girl. While I was on campaign, plague swept the castle and both died . . ." This time he did reach for her, although it was to grip her shoulders rather than hug her. "So I know what it feels like. I'm sorry."

"When did this happen?"

"Four years ago."

Four years? Lady Giulietta thought about that. Four years and Frederick was *still* mourning the loss of his wife from an arranged marriage and a child who wasn't even a boy? Behind her, someone stepped forward.

"T-these are d-deep matters."

"I'm sorry . . . I should have . . ."

Duke Marco waved away the young prince's apology. "If I w-was you, I'd h-have wanted to talk to her first, t-too. But you'd better . . ." He smiled and pointed to his mother, who accepted Prince Frederick's bow with a thoughtful expression.

"You understand," she said. "I have no idea what you're talking about?"

"Of course." The prince bowed again to show he did.

"So . . . Accepting that. You came all this way to tell my niece how sorry you were for this thing that we don't accept has happened?"

Prince Frederick hesitated. "I wanted to tell her how sorry I was. That I knew how much it hurts to lose a child. Also, we never got a chance to meet."

"You thought you might try wooing her again?"

The prince looked shocked. "Oh no," he said. "I know she's going to marry Lord Tycho. All Europe knows." He meant the thin sliver of the nobility who cared about such matters.

"But it doesn't hurt to be seen trying?"

He blushed, looked behind him to check his courtiers weren't listening. "It gave me an excuse to leave court. I'm still in disgrace, you know. Although not as much as I could be. Since I returned something my father wanted."

"The *WolfeSelle*."

His shocked expression made Giulietta smile.

"One of the worst kept secrets in the city," Alexa said tartly.

The *WolfeSelle* was the *krieghund*'s totem, an ancient sword revered by the Wolf Brothers and wielded by their leader. It seemed absurd that this should be the shy young man standing in front of Giulietta, but she'd seen him fight in wolf form that night on Giudecca, when Tycho offered to return the *WolfeSelle* if the *krieghund* would join him in rescuing her. They'd fought and mostly died, and Tycho kept his word, returning the blade to the Assassini's oldest enemy. "You were saying," Duchess Alexa murmured. "About being in disgrace?"

"Out of favour might be more accurate. My father is busy besieging heretics in Bohemia. Life on campaign is . . ." Frederick hesitated. "Less fun than it might be. So I thought . . . And I did want to say how sorry I was." His smile faded at the mention of Giulietta's dead child.

Lady Giulietta wondered if she should tell him Leo was still alive.

16

In the hours that followed, Prince Frederick and his small court settled themselves at the Fontego dei Tedeschi, his father's warehouse just below the Rialto Bridge. Rooms were cleared and stables found for the horses. The land on which the warehouse stood was German, according to the rules governing *fondaci*. The land was German and so were the laws applied inside. By the time night fell – which was early, this being the start of winter – Frederick had made the rounds of his men, checking they were housed properly and settled into their chambers.

The last thing Frederick did before retiring was send for one of his men and give him a message for his father. Frederick had let Alexa believe he was here without the emperor's blessing. In fact, he had left court with permission. It was time to make his first report.

"Yes, highness . . ." The man bowed low.

Standing at the window a few minutes later, Frederick watched a young wolf skulk out on to the ice of the Canalasso and disappear into the night. The journey across the snows would be brutal, but his message would arrive. If anyone could clear the distance and arrive safely it was them. They were *krieghund*.

*   *   *

In the same hour, on the far side of the Adriatic Sea, which glittered with white crests on black waves, halfway into a range of mountains that rose for ever, the man named earlier as Lady Giulietta's next husband scowled at the crude walls of that night's shelter and thought about Venice not at all. Tycho was too cold and too hungry and too worried to think about anything other than the yard in which he stood.

The map Marco had provided was crude, but the fort was on it and had always been marked as one of their stops. Everything about the place felt wrong, starting with its shape, which was a quarter-circle of grey stone, built across the narrow head of the valley, with rising cliffs and a slit cave behind. At first Tycho thought the fort must protect a silver mine because what else in this godforsaken country would need protecting? Only the arrow slits faced in both directions, down the valley and into this tiny yard behind. No force big enough to trouble a fort could gather here so why did the arrow slits exist? The other reason the cave couldn't be a silver mine was that the track marks where sleds had been dragged from underground were missing.

The heaviest wall was on this side rather than facing into the valley. The door on the valley side was thick, but the door to the yard thicker still and fat-hinged, with a steel plate set into it through which three dozen arrows could be fired simultaneously from a three-stringed porcupine.

The layout made so little sense that Tycho began to explore. Under the roof a dormitory full of abandoned bedrolls, saddles and curved sabres showed that cavalry had manned the fort until recently. At ground level the empty cupboards in the kitchen showed they'd taken any food with them. And they'd obviously left in a hurry because a half-cooked but now frozen deer carcass rested on an iron spit above a cold fire pit. In the yard someone had killed a horse and flensed its carcase, cutting all the flesh from its bones. Tycho could imagine how hungry cavalry would have to be before they ate their mounts.

A well in the cellar held water sealed with ice that clattered three seconds after Tycho dropped a stone. His second stone was larger, broke the ice and brought Amelia running . . . "Found anything?" she asked.

Tycho shook his head. "You?"

"Well, maybe . . ." she admitted. Amelia was wrapped in furs that stank even in the cold, unless the stink was her and that was possible. "There's burnt-out mage powder on the armoury floor."

That begged two questions. How Amelia recognised mage powder, because he didn't think he would. And what the hell it was doing in a crumbling fort in the pits of nowhere. Mage powder was a mix made by alchemists that burnt so hot it cut steel and so fiercely water couldn't put it out.

"How much?"

Pinching her finger and thumb together, Amelia looked cross when he snorted. "There's also an empty barrel."

The barrel was small, and had been stored inside a bigger one filled with sand. The sides of both were varnished and their bottoms and lids sealed with slugs of tar that took the imprint of Tycho's thumb. Whoever stored the powder had been determined to stop air from getting in and setting it alight. It might take a minute or so before the grains of phosphor sparked, but once the mix was ignited it would be unstoppable. So why had it been opened and emptied?

Pushing open the rear door, Tycho stepped into the small, rocky yard formed by the fort closing off the very head of the valley. Icy slopes rose on both sides and where they joined the slit cave showed dark and daunting. Tycho knew instantly what the soldiers had used the powder for. Flame marks darkened the underside of a cracked ledge high above. Mage powder made a poor explosive, but they'd still tried, and failed, to close the cave.

"Right," he said. "Let's see what they intended to hide."

"No." Amelia grabbed his arm, letting go when he swung

round to face her. He expected her to step back but she stood there shaking her head. The woman was *Assassini* trained, as fast as him and almost as deadly. He thought for a moment that she might be joking, her humour being somewhat strange, but she seemed serious.

"We have no business here."

What has that to do with anything? By definition the *Assassini* went where they had no business. The shadows embraced them and in turn the *Assassini* embraced the shadows. He was simply the logical conclusion to that. A man so in love with darkness he couldn't stand the light. Tycho stopped, shocked by the unexpected insight. *Where had that come from?*

"Gods," he said. "I'll search it myself later."

If he read the fallen rubble right the vanished soldiers had tried to cause a rockslide that would bury the slit cave, but failed. They'd risked handling mage powder, but been too frightened or in too great a hurry to try again and had abandoned a second barrel inside the rear door. The fort's layout finally made sense to him. It was built to protect the valley from whatever was in the cave, not the other way round. Whatever was in there probably knew Tycho and Amelia were here. All the same, he saw no point in attracting attention.

"No fires," he said.

Amelia glared at him. "We'll freeze."

It was so cold they ended up huddled in a bed they found in a small room beyond a dormitory full of soldiers' cots. Both rooms were bleak and made the fort look like a punishment posting. Tycho wondered what the men had done to be sent here. For the captain to live so close to his soldiers also seemed odd until Tycho realised the men would have to be dead before an enemy could reach the inner room.

Dragging a rancid bear's pelt from the bed, Amelia dropped it on the floor in disgust, tied back flyblown bed curtains and looked round for something to replace the stinking bear skin.

Two chests were empty but a third contained blankets so cold one cracked when she shook it. Amelia's breath came in smoky gasps as she laid five blankets over a stained horsehair mattress. "You could have helped."

Tycho put his whetstone back in his pocket and his dagger back in its sheath. "You could have gone into the cave . . ."

Amelia didn't reply. Instead, she shrugged off her cloak and dragged at her boots, which she tossed to the floor. Her sword she put upright against the wall, her daggers on the chest where the blanket had been. She climbed into bed in silence and watched him put aside his own weapons and climb in beside her.

"Against the cold," he said.

"Like it would be anything else."

Lord Atilo had bedded her, whether when she was his slave or his apprentice Tycho was unsure. He imagined she'd kill any man who now tried to take her against her will, but the bonds of ownership or duty had kept his old master safe. She lay stiff as a board beside him for so long he thought she'd fallen to sleep; until finally she sighed, rolled in against him, tightened her arm across his chest, folded her leg over his hip to hold him in place and said sourly, "Now let me sleep. And you do whatever you call whatever you do . . ." A few minutes later, she spoke again in a voice smoky with darkness and age-old mystery. Wherever Tycho was, she was somewhere else.

"I am the moon . . . I am the mistress . . ."

Her words were a whisper in the silence of the snowscape beyond the fort walls. She was saying a prayer, he realised. A prayer addressed to a goddess unknown to him. He remembered that other night, on the edge of a cold *fondamenta* in Venice, when she'd talked of the moon, her mistress; and before he could unpick the memories of their first meeting, darkness took him. He woke to find her still in his arms, her body rigid as wood, one hand jabbing his side.

"*Wake up.*" Her voice was tight.

It couldn't be the next night already? But the colour of the sky beyond a broken shutter was still just this side of midnight rather than early the next, and he'd lost more than an hour to dreamless sleep. Amelia jabbed her hand at him harder. "All right," he said.

He was rising on to his elbow when a sword point touched his throat and he opened his eyes. The man with the blade was filthy, crop-haired and half drunk with exhaustion. "What have we got here, boys?" Behind him soldiers clustered closer and one lifted a freshly lit torch that still smoked and spluttered.

"Pretty boys," the man said. "Pretty boys in bed together." He looked back at his men, gauging their reaction. "You know what that is, don't you? It's a hanging offence."

17

The day began with sun squinting over the distant sandbar at the mouth of the lagoon and lighting a path so bright across the ice that it lit Venice in a glow that made the buildings golden and the icicles sparkle. Above a balcony at the back of Ca' Ducale the sparkling icicles hung like glass bars; as if the cold wanted to cage them and the sun was trying to brighten their prison in compensation.

It was, Lady Giulietta admitted, a strange and beautiful sight for all it was unnerving. Seeing the sun made her happier than she'd been in days, though it did little to melt the icicles and nothing at all to melt the snow that covered the small garden at the back of the palace and turned rose beds into ghostly squares. Looking down on to that garden was where Prince Frederick found her after his morning meeting with her Aunt Alexa.

"Your page told me where you were."

"I don't have a page." As she said this, she saw Tycho's urchin behind Frederick, shuffling his feet and dressed in Millioni scarlet. At Pietro's stricken look, she added, "Not officially, anyway." Gods, when had she started caring about the feelings of street children? When she met Tycho probably, that was when most things changed. For the better? Well, life was less interesting back then, also safer and quieter and a lot less strange.

"The view's better on the other side . . ."

Frederick meant from Ca' Ducale's grandest balcony, the one that looked over the herringbone brick of the *piazzetta* towards a clump of poplars frequented by lovers and thieves and the occasional equestrian needing to tie his horse. Hardly anyone rode in Venice, apart for the Dolphini; and they only did it to show off, and even they weren't stupid enough to ride in this weather. All the same, when they reached the other balcony Giulietta saw a grey horse tethered to a distant tree.

"Mine," said Frederick, following her gaze.

"You like riding?"

"Everyone likes riding."

"I hate it. Everyone sensible hates it." Her father had ridden. The only time Lady Giulietta remembered him smiling was when he was with his horses. She made herself unbunch her fists and felt sweat trickle from under one arm down her ribs inside her dress to soak her waistband. Giulietta hated that his memory could still do this to her. She also knew Frederick was staring.

"I'm going inside."

He nodded absent-mindedly and looked at his horse, his head tipped a little to one side. "Have you done much riding?"

Giulietta ignored his question.

"They're very gentle creatures really."

She opened her mouth to disagree, reddening when he nodded in sudden understanding. "It's not the horses you dislike. It's the people who ride them." Frederick waited for her to say he was wrong and smiled to himself when she didn't. "We're not all bad," was all he said.

"I rode as a child," she admitted. "Well, I was carried."

How could she forget? The sky above Venice was changing from the pale blue of the Virgin's cloak to an azure rich enough to be the sea in a newly painted fresco. It would darken over the afternoon through Persian blue to purple and then black. When

98

she'd been carried as a child the sky had been steel-grey, the mountain wind vicious as a knife as it slid between the rips her father's whip had cut in her clothes. Lord Atilo had placed her in front of him, until the gale made her so tearful he put her behind him and tied her on. Lady Giulietta shivered.

"We should go back inside," Frederick said.

"Not yet . . ."

When he vanished through the arch behind her, Giulietta thought for a second he'd left without bothering to say goodbye. She was preparing to be really offended when he reappeared with a richly embroidered cloak, which he draped carefully around her shoulders against the cold.

"Are you trying to woo me?"

"I'm not that stupid." Frederick's smile was light. "You shivered. I'm simply trying to stop you from freezing . . ." He hesitated, and decided to ask anyway. "Where is Sir Tycho? I'd thought to have seen him by now."

"*Lord* Tycho," Giulietta corrected. "He was made a baron."

Frederick smiled ruefully. "For defeating me? Or for defeating the Byzantines . . .? No, let me guess. For defeating us both."

Giulietta nodded.

"Is it true he was born a slave?"

"Possibly . . ." She hesitated in her turn. Should she discuss this with him? She'd had no one else to discuss anything with since . . . And how could Tycho leave like that in the middle of the night, without even saying goodbye? When she'd asked him not to go? He was probably dead already . . .

A hand touched her shoulder. "You're crying," Frederick said.

"It's the poppy," Giulietta said furiously. "My aunt gave me too much poppy and now I can't stop . . ." She caught his look and shrugged. "Well, it's mostly the poppy. I was thinking about . . . About my lady-in-waiting."

"Lady Eleanor?"

Giulietta was surprised he knew her name. "She made a better lady-in-waiting than I made mistress. We were cousins and I never made enough of that. Now she's gone and I miss her."

He shrugged. "Of course you do. We all need someone to talk to. I miss my brother. Leopold was . . ."

"Brave, funny, handsome, fearless?"

"You loved him, didn't you?"

"It was complicated."

Frederick laughed, the first time she could remember. "Of course it was complicated. With Leopold everything was complicated, his fierce friendships with men who began not certain they liked him and ended up devoted, and his love affairs with women who began by admiring him and ended up unable to bear being in the same room. Yet, you love him still, it seems to me. And he loved you to the end. I wonder what was different?"

He didn't take me to his bed. Well, not for that. They slept enough nights in each other's arms, talking or staring at the ceiling, his hand on her belly in the early days to feel the child who wasn't his kick with life. He even found her the surgeon who cut open her belly when her precious child refused to be born, and sewed her up again with the tail hair from a horse, long after the midwife had given both mother and baby up for dead. Prince Leopold had married her, adopted her child, named Leo his heir and died to save her. But he never once bedded her.

"There's something I have to tell you." Frederick must have heard the seriousness in her voice because his smile faded and he turned towards her. "It's about my son . . ." He opened his mouth to say how sorry he was and shut it when she held up her hand, stilling him. She knew he was sorry. He'd said it several times and meant it every time. "Leo's not dead."

"Giulietta . . ." There was sorrow in Frederick's voice.

He thought her mad with grief, and she couldn't help if her eyes filled with tears, could she? When she turned away, he turned her back and tried to hug her. Her hand slid from his chest to his face as she pushed free, and she froze, appalled he might think she'd hit him on purpose.

"I'm sorry," he said. "I'm sorry."

As he stepped back, she grabbed him and refused to let go. She was crying openly now, fierce sobs that made her face hideous. "It's true," she said. "I promise you. It's true."

Frederick shook his head. He was biting his lip and she realised – with shock – was close to crying himself. "My love," he said, and she pretended not to hear that. "I'm so sorry, but it's not." Pulling her close, he told her life could be horrid but she'd survive. If he could, she could.

And then she cried until she could cry no more.

18

Rough hands reached for Tycho and he tensed until a touch at his side stilled him. Amelia was fully awake and watchful, her fingers tugging at the lace that held her ankle dagger in place.

"Hanging offence," the man holding the sword repeated. He glanced back at his followers and seemed disappointed that they looked less enthusiastic than he expected. "Isn't it, boys? The Pope says so."

When you lived in a world where it was wise to nod when the Pope's name was mentioned you nodded, and so they did. Their captain looked happier as he pulled back the covers and raised his eyebrows at the way Tycho's and Amelia's limbs were twisted together. As if soldiers had never clung together against the cold.

Tycho would have knocked the man's sword aside but for a long-faced archer with an arrow aimed at Amelia's heart. Tycho knew Amelia moved fast, she had were-blood and was *Assassini* trained. The question was what she could survive in the way of wounds. He'd have risked it for himself. Tycho's smile was sour. He'd definitely have risked if for himself.

"Something funny?" their captain asked.

Tycho shrugged.

"Get them up," the man said, and Tycho felt himself dragged from the bed. They reached for Amelia and she froze. For a moment Tycho thought she'd risk the arrow, but she allowed herself to be stood upright, her eyes never leaving the archer's bent bow.

"Right, find me some hanging rope."

A soldier disappeared through the door with one of the lit torches and the narrow chamber lurched into half-darkness. "And find me some more torches," the captain called after him.

A blond, pale-skinned soldier reached for Amelia and rubbed her cheek, checking his thumb afterwards to see if any of the black came away. He scowled when one of the others mockingly did the same, miming surprise at the lack of dye. Amelia accepted their horseplay quietly. Anyone untrained might have thought she was scared but Tycho knew she'd memorised their positions and numbered their weapons, checked the exit and looked for places that could be defended.

Assassini skills stayed with you for life.

The horse-faced archer still had his bow drawn and the soldiers were careful to leave a path between his arrow and her heart. Their captain seemed unnerved by her calmness. "You can't escape," he said.

Amelia smiled. "Nor can you."

The man scowled. "Hurry up and find me some bloody rope."

A couple of others went after the first, their boots slapping on the spiral of stone steps leading to the floor below. The fort was old, built from grey stone that was crumbling with age. The floors were uneven. The ceiling beams split and twisted where broken tiles had let in rain.

A cold wind howled through the arrow slits, twitched at the drawn-back bed curtains and tumbled dust balls across the floor as Tycho made himself wait for the men to return without rope. And they would return without rope because he'd crawled all over the fort and knew better than they did what there was to be found. If they really wanted to hang him their best bet was the cord used to tie back the bed curtains and no one needed to leave the room for that.

How far had these men come – and did they imagine they'd ever reach where they wanted to go? Did he? Tycho no longer knew. He had his reasons for being here. What reason did they have for trudging through snow-filled valleys in the middle of winter? Alexa always said, know what a man wants and you know how to move him. For the duchess, all men were pieces on life's chessboard. And which piece was he? Tycho wondered sourly. He'd thought himself a knight, perhaps a castle in time. But castles and knights were sacrificed and perhaps he'd never been more than a pawn. He wondered this in the time it took for the men to reappear.

"No rope," said the one who'd originally gone looking. Behind him the other two nodded their agreement. One of them held a tar-dipped torch that guttered and smoked so the search hadn't been entirely worthless.

"We could impale them," growled the man who'd rubbed his thumb across Amelia's face. His scowl said he needed to get some self-respect back. "That's what they do round here, isn't it?"

"That's the Seljuks."

"So what? It's not like we've impaled anyone before, is it? We've hung lots. We're always hanging people." He looked round for support.

"You're full of shit," the archer said.

"You wouldn't say that if you weren't holding a bow."

"Well, I am," the archer said. "And you're full of shit. Everyone knows you're full of shit. Heathens impale people. Are we heathens?"

"Two pretty boys. It would be justice."

"She's not a boy," Tycho said.

The archer and the other man stopped glaring at each other and turned to Tycho, who got a split second of their attention

104

before they both turned to examine Amelia, as did every other soldier in the room. "He's wearing a doublet," the archer protested.

"And trews," the man he'd been arguing with said. "And men's boots. And that's not a woman's knife." Dipping forward, he drew Amelia's ankle dagger and stepped quickly back. "Toledo steel, no less."

"Stolen most like."

"Her name's Amelia," Tycho said swiftly.

"Prove it."

"How can I prove a name?"

A jab of the sword was his answer. A trickle of blood rolled down his throat. "Don't get clever."

"Too late," Amelia said.

Her voice was light enough to be a girl's. Alternatively, it could belong to someone not yet a man. Tycho watched their captain realise this. Behind him, his men were beginning to look restless. "Show them," Tycho said. The eyes that met his were hard and flat and impassive in the way only someone fighting for self-control and finding it can manage. He expected Amelia to reveal her teats because that's what most women would have done. Instead she unlaced her trews and dropped them, revealing smoothness beneath. To make the point, she turned a circle.

The ugly-faced archer still had his fingers hooked round the end of his arrow but his bow was only half drawn and pointed nearly floorwards. Even their captain seemed more interested in examining Amelia than keeping his sword level.

One problem had turned into another. Everyone knew that.

"She's better than any hanging." Unnotching his arrow, the archer unstrung his bow and returned his arrow to its quiver without being ordered. Those keeping out of his way pushed forward into the gap.

"Captain goes first," the blond-haired man said.

"Meaning you go second," the archer muttered. This was when

Tycho realised the man who'd checked Amelia's cheek was their sergeant. A sergeant who hated their bowman could be useful.

"Boys . . ." the captain sighed. "There'll be plenty for everyone."

"No," Amelia said. "There won't."

Turning to glare at her, the sergeant said, "Yes, there will . . . A woman dressed in a man's clothes. That's a hanging offence."

"Burning," the archer said.

"So you'd better to be nice to us . . ."

"Yeah," said the archer. "You can begin by unbuttoning your doublet." He glared at the sergeant, daring him to disagree. "In fact, why don't we just take everything off and you can crawl back into bed?" Ignoring the sergeant's barked order to wait his turn, the archer took a step closer and reached for Amelia's buttons.

Two things happened.

She grabbed the man, spun him round and slammed her heel into the back of his knee, dropping him to the floor. A split second later, as she tightened the string of his bow around his neck, Tycho used his elbow to knock up the captain's sword, twist its handle from his grip and bring its point to rest under the man's chin. Amelia scowled and twisted her home-made garrotte a little tighter.

"Nicely done . . ."

She glared, as if asking if he really expected a compliment that thin to make up for what had gone before.

"What's your name?" Tycho demanded of the captain.

"Towler."

"And the name of your company?"

"Towler's Company."

"How original. Amelia, I really think . . ."

She loosened her bowstring slightly and the archer slumped forward, gasping hideously and purple-black in the face. He'd live, most likely. Although he'd be voiceless for a week.

"What's a fine company like yours doing here in the middle of winter?"

The captain looked to see if he was being mocked by having his straggling troop described as fine, decided he was and realised there wasn't much he could do about it. "Prince Alonzo di Millioni has sent out a call for good men . . ."

And you bring him these? "Alonzo?"

"You know him?" Captain Towler sounded doubtful.

"One of my closest friends."

"It's true," Amelia said. "My lord and the prince are so inseparable you could barely fit a knife blade between them."

"Your lord?" Towler seemed bemused by the appearance of a title. "Then perhaps you could put in a good word for us, my lord. I mean, if that's where you and your . . ." The captain hesitated, uncertain how to describe Amelia, who was watching impassively. "Where you and your companion are going."

"You go to fight the Red Crucifers?" Tycho asked.

"*My lord . . .?*" the man said.

Oh gods, thought Tycho, reading the anxiety in Captain Towler's face. The Regent never intended to fight the Red Crucifers at all. He'd gone to command them. Alonzo Millioni was a trained *condottiero*, son-in-law to the richest noble in Venice. Left alone, the Red would decay and be destroyed or destroy themselves. With Alonzo as their master . . . "What title has he taken?"

"Duke of Montenegro."

Of course he had. Half the city-states of Italy would recognise him now, the rest within a year if they bothered to wait at all. Alonzo was Italian and Alexa was Mongol, mother to an idiot son no one expected to rule. As for the Pope . . . All Alonzo had to do was offer to destroy the Serbian heresy, return Montenegro to Catholic rule and establish the Red as a legitimate order swearing allegiance to Rome, and the Pope would be sending him sacred war banners and a personal blessing.

If that happened Alexa would find herself with a civil war. The colonies would declare for Alonzo, Venice would split into feuding noble families and the street gangs would riot. If Alexa was lucky the Castellani would declare for her if the Nicoletti declared for Alonzo, but the chances were the gangs would combine behind Alonzo and the Watch would be unable to keep them under control. Tycho could imagine the city welcoming Alonzo simply because he offered order.

"I'm Lord Tycho bel Angelo. This is Lady Amelia . . ." Beside him, the young Nubian raised her eyebrows at her sudden ennoblement. "You see that post . . ."

Captain Towler nodded.

"Who's your best knife man?"

The captain pointed to his sergeant.

"The centre boss," Tycho told him. "One throw only."

When the man pulled a knife from his belt without first checking with Captain Towler, Tycho smiled to himself. Get the sergeant obeying orders and the men would follow. He needed the man to throw well.

Amelia just needed to throw better.

"Take your time," Tycho suggested.

It was a clean throw, hard enough to kill a man across a tavern, and left the dagger quivering to one side of the boss. The sergeant expected Tycho to throw next and looked shocked when Amelia stepped forward.

Men whistled as her knife slammed into the post just inside the first knife. *Impressive*, Tycho thought. Not the throw, but to beat the man by so little was subtle. The sergeant's rueful grin said he was impressed not offended.

"Brilliant," Tycho said.

"Not *nicely done*?" She turned to the sergeant. "In my country it's the women who wage war."

"You're Amazon?"

"Nubian," Amelia said. "We're worse."

19

A tightly wrapped German noble arrived unexpectedly at the doors of Ca' Ducale an hour after dawn on a proud, high-stepping stallion that snorted, steamed and blew dragon's breath at the cold air. A second grey trotted sedately behind, saddle empty. Sliding from his mount, the man landed with a bump that blew a laugh from his chest, and immediately unwrapped a huge wolf-pelt coat that he draped across his mount's back before turning for the palace doors. That was when the guards on the Porta della Carta realised their visitor was Prince Frederick, and that he'd arrived without courtiers or bodyguards.

"Would you see if Lady Giulietta is home?"

They found his Italian hard to understand, and his stepping from foot to foot against the cold made his accent stranger still. What muddled them, though, was his politeness. "Certainly my lord . . . I mean, your highness."

A guard abandoned his post at the gate – a whipping offence – rather than ring the bell and wait for a messenger. He hurried across the inner courtyard and up steps made treacherous by ice, even though they'd been scraped the previous evening. Prince Frederick watched him go and, after a while, asked if he could come inside. A few minutes after this a door opened on to a gallery above and a young woman strode down the stairs. "Your highness . . ."

"Frederick," he said, smiling.

Lady Giulietta shrugged. "Frederick."

"My lady . . ."

She smiled. A brief flash of amusement.

Meetings between people of their importance were usually arranged in advance. There were protocols in place to agree suitable times and neutral locations, with some clue given in advance as to the reason. "Has something happened?"

"I upset you yesterday."

Giulietta checked to see if the nearest guard was listening. Even a year before she wouldn't have noticed he was there, except in the way she knew wardrobes and cupboards existed. The guard's face was impassive enough to suggest he was. "That doesn't matter."

"Of course it does." He hesitated. "Well, it does to me."

"You'd better come in."

He almost did, and then she saw him find his courage and come to a decision. "I have a better plan." He put his hand under her elbow and turned her towards the door behind them. It was a tentative touch and he looked ready to let her go if she protested. Giulietta's mouth quirked. Beyond the door stood two horses, one high and sleek with a swan-like neck and noble forehead, the other squat and almost shaggy. Her heart sank. Surely he didn't mean . . .

It turned out he did. "Her name's Barrel."

"How does she stay upright?"

Frederick looked at her and Giulietta shrugged. It was an obvious enough question. Everyone in the city kept slipping over. Surely having hooves instead of feet simply made things worse?

"Look . . ." Frederick bent Barrel's leg as easily as a Venetian boy might loop a rope around a gondola post and tie it off. "She won't hurt you . . . See," he said.

110

See what?

When he took her hand and touched her finger to the horse's shoe, Giulietta found herself blushing, damn it. But Frederick was peering at the horseshoe and waiting expectantly, so she ran her finger over ice-cold metal and felt jagged edges beneath her fingers. "There are ridges."

Frederick smiled.

"Chevrons," Giulietta added, naming the heraldic vees sometimes found on shields in battle. "Dozens of them."

"My design. My blacksmith made them."

"You brought your blacksmith?" Lady Giulietta was surprised. Venice was a city of foundries and metalworkers. Actually, it was a city of everything workers, from boiled leather to finest gold.

"And my cook, and armourer, and doctor."

"Why?"

"Well, the cook's obvious . . ." His tone was light, but it was clear he meant it. Until recently he'd been their enemy. Venice was as famous for her poisons as she was for her gilt and glass. He'd be a fool not to bring his own cook and food tasters, and the same applied to his doctor. "Besides, they're my friends."

It seemed unlikely enough to be true. The guards on the Porta della Carta were watching her from the corner of their eyes, and a *cittadino* family on their way home from mass had stopped to stare openly. If she turned round, she'd probably find her aunt staring down from the central balcony. Lady Giulietta had always hated being watched. "I should . . ."

"Yes," Frederick said. "You should."

Before she could protest, he dropped to a crouch and folded his fingers together to make a step. *That's not what I meant at all.* Still, a Schiavoni trader dragging a cart had now joined her audience, stilled by the sight of horses, the lavishness of Frederick's cloak and the realisation that the girl hesitating to mount was Lady Giulietta Millioni. *How did I let him do this to me?* She knew she should be furious, but he looked so anxious that she put her foot in his hands, blushed scarlet as he saw her lower leg in a swirl of skirt, and let herself be boosted up on to a side saddle.

Snow and ice on a high pass through the wintry mountains.

She'd been sitting in front of the grey-bearded Moor, who'd wrapped his cloak around her to keep her warm although he was freezing himself. Inside her cloak, she stank of fear and not washing and having soiled herself, because he refused to stop. At the time she'd thought him unkind. Now she realised Lord Atilo's refusal to stop had probably saved her life. She could remember riding in front. When he tied her behind him, she had been so miserable her memory blanked.

"You all right?"

It was the smell of horses, she realised. The sweet stink that rose from Barrel beneath her. "Bad memories," she said. "I told you I was carried once. A long-time ago when I was still a small child."

"Through the high pass beyond Monfalcone?"

"How do you know about that?"

"Everybody knows."

That didn't make her feel any better. Having checked his own stirrup leathers, Frederick vaulted on to his mount with the ease of someone who had grown up around horses, slid his feet into his stirrups and leant forward to grab her leading rein. Lady Giulietta expected him to turn for Piazza San Marco but he rode instead towards the edge of the Molo, the hooves of his horse ringing loudly on the frozen brick, her own mount sounding muted behind. A moment later they stepped down on to the ice of the lagoon, and a wide expanse of white stretched before her all the way to the sandbanks guarding the lagoon mouth.

Is it *safe* . . .? She kept her question to herself.

Wind had scoured snow from the ice to leave a hard surface that rang like glass as they rode over it. The sky gleamed like turquoise mined in Persia, bright blue without a single flaw. When

112

Giulietta turned to look at the city behind her, she saw Venice glittering and clean, cut from ice and set in a marble sea. The air above the mainland was so clear the high peaks of the Altus showed sharp in the distance, closer than she'd ever seen them.

Frederick grinned. "Beautiful, isn't it?"

"Beautiful," she agreed.

The saddle was awkward beneath her, the stirrups too wide for her feet to stay in place easily, Barrel bumped up and down with every stride; but she didn't mind and it didn't matter. The freedom of being out alone on the ice was all.

He led her out towards the middle of the channel so they passed between the island of San Maggiore, and Castello, the westernmost of the *sestieri*, the districts Venice had been divided into in its earliest days. Then he leant over and looped the leading rein around the top of her saddle.

"I can't . . ."

"Of course you can." Frederick dropped his reins to the neck of his horse, which lowered its mouth to the ice and shook its head crossly at finding nothing worth eating. "Fold them through your fingers like this. And don't pull unless you want Barrel to stop." As they were riding in a straight line and Barrel walked on when she kicked her side at Frederick's suggestion, Giulietta held her reins and did nothing else, because that was what he was doing. To their left was Castello, and to their right, beyond San Maggiore, the bigger island of Giudecca.

He saw her look and nodded grimly.

His friends had died there, more than a dozen. They fought Tycho, and then changed their minds and joined Tycho to rescue her and Leo, and fight the Byzantines. That Frederick was still alive was a miracle. That she was alive was an even greater one. *Why would he come back? Why would he return to a place where something like that had happened?*

"Why are you really here?" she demanded. "I mean, you didn't have to come."

"I know that. But Leopold was my brother, and Leo his son. I know what it's like to lose . . . His face shut down and he stared hard towards the low line of snow-covered sandbanks framing the lagoon. One hand gripped tight on his reins, and his other rubbed crossly at his eyes. That was when Giulietta knew she had to explain. Anything else was unfair. She didn't want to be unfair.

"Listen," she said. "Leo isn't dead . . ."

"*Giulietta.*" He turned then, and she saw the tears streaking his cheeks and dampening the upper edge of his slight moustache. "I know it's hard, God knows, I know it's hard." Reaching across, he grabbed her hand, gripping so tightly her fingers hurt. "But you have to accept . . ."

"*Frederick . . .*"

He let her fingers go.

"Leo isn't dead." She held up her hand. "Just listen, all right. Yes, the infant in Leo's nursery at Ca' Ducale is an impostor. Yes, I know there's a dead baby in the crypt. He's a changeling, too. The real Leo was stolen by Alonzo."

"God's name why?"

"Because he's the child's real father."

The horror on Frederick's face made her redden. "Not like that. His alchemist did what was necessary with a goose quill."

It was his turn to blush. "That's why Tycho isn't here?"

"Yes," Giulietta said. "That's why Tycho isn't here."

"He must be brave." Frederick's voice was matter of fact. "To go into Montenegro alone to try to get him back."

"You wouldn't do it?"

"I would for you," Frederick said firmly. "I'd want to take an army, though."

Me, too, thought Giulietta. And she meant it.

As they rode out towards the mouth of the lagoon, Giulietta told Frederick about Dr Crow and how her own Aunt Alexa abducted her and pretended it was the Mamluks, and how Frederick's brother really abducted her, how she escaped and how Leopold tracked her down again. How he married her and adopted Leo . . .

Underfoot, the ice changed from marble-white to blue, its surface increasingly laced with cracks like flawed alabaster. When Frederick suggested they turn back, Giulietta agreed. She was proud that she paused, and pretended to consider riding on, rather than simply gasping with relief.

"So stunning," said Frederick, looking at her city.

He means it, she realised. His tone was wistful, and yet there was more to it than that. He sounded like someone saying hello and goodbye at the same time. Maybe he intended to go home? He turned, and Lady Giulietta expected him to announce he was leaving the next day or at the end of the week, or however long it would take to make arrangements for his return. Instead, he simply stared at the marbled ice stretching around them like God's own floor and at the snow-covered mountains on the mainland beyond. When he spoke it was softly. "Do you believe the world is ending?"

"Why?" said Giulietta. "Do you?"

He nodded sadly.

"You're wrong." Having explained that the world could only end once all the babies were born, Lady Giulietta added that her aunt's orders instructed that all new pregnancies be reported, and there were more than ever as couples took to their beds against the cold. If the pregnancies did stop . . . Well, he'd still have nine months to repent his sins, which she doubted were huge.

"Alexa's astrologers worked this out?"

"Marco," Giulietta said.

"The duke?" Frederick looked surprised, then doubtful, and finally so thoughtful that Giulietta began to suspect that she shouldn't have said that. He was silent for most of the return journey, only finding his voice when they reached the shore and the brick of the Molo rang under their mounts' hooves. "Thank you."

"For what?"

"For this afternoon. For the ride. For trusting me."

"Are you going to leave now?" Giulietta hesitated. "I mean . . . Now you know about . . .?" She didn't have to say what. It was obvious she meant Leo being alive and Tycho having gone to find him. She expected an instant answer, but Frederick was looking beyond her to where guards had opened the Porta della Carta. The duchess was in the doorway, obviously unable to decide whether to be cross or amused.

"No," Frederick said finally. "I think I'll stay for a while."

"I'd better go inside."

He smiled. "Probably. Here, let me . . ."

Lady Giulietta sat still, while Frederick slid from his saddle and walked round to help her dismount, steadying her as she landed. He'd already told her he'd stable Barrel with his other horses while insisting the fat little pony really was hers.

"One thing," he said. "If Tycho needs help . . . If *you* need help getting your son back, tell me. I'll see what my father can do." Climbing on to his stallion, Frederick reached for Barrel's leading rein and turned for the ice. He would use the Grand Canal as his road. Lady Giulietta watched him go.

20

"My lord Tycho."

Eat, keep the rest, and go . . . Those were the words he wanted to say as he looked at Captain Towler's weather-beaten face and the rat-faced soldiers behind him. Amelia had returned from a run to say a stag and three hinds had come down to the valley floor from the higher slopes, and were scuffing at the snow looking for vegetation beneath. Tycho sent her out again to stampede the animals back up the slope towards the fort and had Towler's archer position himself in the shadows of the entrance arch. The man was good with a bow for all he stank, had sly eyes and was Welsh. Tycho didn't understand why the last of these mattered, but it was the point to which all of the man's companions eventually returned.

The stag died from an arrow to the heart. The largest of the hinds took to her heels with two arrows in her neck and dropped within a quarter of a mile. The others escaped but Tycho doubted they'd live long without the stag to protect them. Amelia gutted one and he gutted the other, Towler's men lining up to drink warm blood from a rusting bucket. And when they found their strength, Tycho sent them from room to room to collect whatever wood they could and began to smoke the meat. He imagined it would taste of the burnt chairs and broken beds they brought him and doubted they'd much care.

"Send my regards to Prince Alonzo."

Looking up at Tycho's words, Amelia busied herself with ripping slivers of meat from a bone boiling in a pot. Tycho scowled. Amelia didn't understand why she and Tycho didn't simply go with them. That was because he'd yet to give her his reasons.

"My lord, tomorrow. You're quite sure you won't . . .?"

"Thank you. We travel best on our own."

"And you still have things to do here?" Captain Towler looked doubtfully round the kitchen of the fort. For a few hours the room had been friendly with hot food and the fug of bodies and the echo of laughter. Here was where most would sleep, filled with grilled venison and warmed by the fire. Tomorrow they would leave and take what remained of the food with them. That was what had Captain Towler thanking Tycho in the first place.

"I have a vigil . . ."

The captain nodded. Vigils were for nobles, like sacred vows and courtly love. He knew the argument was over. He and his men would be going on alone. If Tycho wanted to kneel in the darkness and pray to some saint . . .

Tycho smiled at the man's careful expression, and knew the captain considered himself to have better things to do. "Three days, you reckon?"

Towler nodded.

"Well, I wish you joy of it."

"We'll see you later, my lord. I'm sure of it."

Not if things work out as they should. Tycho clasped hands with the man, feeling calloused skin from a lifetime's wielding a sword. He clapped the captain on the back and wished him a safe journey, which he meant, and promised to meet again in a week or so, which he didn't. Buoyed up by food and the memory of warmth, they would find their way to the Red Cathedral in a few days. If they arrived in daylight, then Tycho would rely on the novelty of their arrival to distract Alonzo's guards that night. And if they arrived at night, so much the better. He would use the distraction of their arrival to find his own way inside.

"Why do I come here?"

Amelia's question had been abrupt, her voice brittle. She'd found him crouched by the rocky slit, as she'd found him the night before, and the night before that, considering its painted lips and the nub of a stone face at the top of the cleft. They both knew what the slit looked like although neither said. Amelia was watchful and her dagger unsheathed. "You've been here for hours."

"Ten minutes at most." Tycho glanced up and realised he lied. The moon's silver sliver had shifted on the horizon. "You should have stayed inside."

Amelia glared at him.

"And why the drawn knife?"

"Because I'm afraid." She didn't even look abashed. "Tycho. What's so special about this cave?"

"Nothing. It's simply a cave." *Small, narrow, damp and sour.* The grit of its entrance as smooth as if raked, but with ochre drawings of twisted bison and fat-breasted women inside to say people had used it in darker times.

How could he possibly know that?

Amelia lifted the flaming torch she held. "You look . . ."

He imagined she was about to say pale, only that was ridiculous because to her he must always look pale. Anyway, anyone would be chilled by the wind that threatened the flames of her torch, especially if wearing his clothes. Amelia was wrapped in a rancid fur found in the fort, her face reduced to a strip of coal-dark skin and her strange violet eyes.

"Don't leave tonight," she said. "Go tomorrow."

Tycho thought about it. For a second he considered saving his strength, but Captain Towler's men would be arriving or might already have arrived at the Red Cathedral, and a warning on the wind was no real warning at all. "You didn't hear anything?"

Amelia squinted, trying not to make it obvious . . .

"Well," he said. "Did you?"

"Hear what? All I've heard is the wind."

That was what Tycho had heard, too, his trouble being it spoke to him. "*Stay or go*," it said, "*you will be dead before morning.*"

Rocky slopes plummeted away on both sides, treacherous with ice, the drop brutal and deadly; unless he really was unable to be killed, in which case he'd lie broken at the bottom until someone found him and tried to prove him wrong.

You're happy, Tycho thought.

The self-mockery cheered him, even as a sudden gust of ice-cold wind almost swept him over the edge, and he had to drop beneath it and hold tight until the gust faded and he could stand again. Between the fort and where he needed to be was no more than a few hours for him, but the route he chose, the quickest one, was along the granite spine of a mountain, into the face of driving snow that stripped humanity from him, until he had no space for doubts, self-pity or self-mockery, and his thoughts became mechanical and remorseless. He was going to get Giulietta's child.

You're going to get Giulietta's child.

In his head the infant didn't even have a name. It wasn't that he was Leo, that this was Leopold's child, that letting Alonzo claim him would clear his way to the throne of Venice. No, he was simply going to get Giulietta's child.

The spine Tycho ran was the ridge between two high valleys in a row of mountains that climbed higher and higher, until finally the ridge began to descend and the wind became less threatening. On his left, the slope dropped to firs so far below they looked like child's toys. A town in the valley bottom was a smudge of dirt on a white background. On his right a frozen lake lay trapped in a valley so steep at one end that only a mountain goat, and possibly Tycho, could climb it, and he'd rather leave it to the goat. The other end had a village on a silt plain that centuries of rain had pushed out into the lake. The closer he got the more miserable the village became; desolate as a beggar's dog, huts crusted like fleas around its wooden church, shutters like scabs on a village hall, mud tracks dirty as ditches. Even from half a mile away, Tycho could sense misery clinging to it like the stink to a midden.

Rising from the lake was the midden itself.

Jagged rocks broke through marbled ice to make a small island occupied by three buildings that filled all the available space. The largest by far was the Red Cathedral, the others were a bell tower and a fortified hall. Originally red, all their walls had faded to ochre, and the sharp roof of the cathedral boasted a cascade of onion domes that looked as if they should have crescents on the top. Ragged patches of gold leaf clung like onion skin, but Tycho could see wood through the peeling primer beneath. Once it had been the high church of the local heresy. Now it was the Red Crucifers' castle, and Prince Alonzo's headquarters in his coming war with Alexa.

And on the ice between the island and the shore, Towler's Company, heads down and shoulders hunched as they pushed themselves on. Undoubtedly, they knew they were watched from the cathedral. Tycho doubted they realised he was watching from up here. As they stumbled forward, the great doors of the cathedral opened . . . At least, a small side door in the great doors did, and a dozen wild-haired archers tumbled through the door into the snow beyond.

Mongols? Tycho wondered. Magyars?

They wore their hair in plaits and stood with the bow-legged gait of those born in the saddle and raised on mare's milk. Something about their watchfulness reminded him of the Skaelingar, the wild warriors who had destroyed his home village. So, a rotting village *and* foreign mercenaries.

Tycho found comfort in this. If Alonzo felt strong he'd settle in the capital and live in luxury. He might claim to miss the life of a simple soldier, and claim it endlessly until fools believed him; but Tycho had seen the prince's lavish feasts close up, drunk the wine Alonzo iced with snow brought down from the Altus. He doubted a rotting wooden cathedral would keep the man content for long. No matter how many barrels of Montenegrin brandy filled that storehouse and local maidens had been rounded up to warm his bed.

Whatever Towler said convinced the man who went out on to the ice to meet them. He nodded, Towler spoke to his company, and they followed him through the parting crowd of archers towards the cathedral door. The wild archers kept their bows bent and their arrows notched. Tycho doubted he expected any different.

Move, Tycho told himself. In the few minutes he'd been watching Towler's arrival his body had chilled and his thoughts slowed. The cold took his strength, though far more subtly than water. *Anyone would think you were afraid.*

The ice spread in front of him, reflecting the moon so that the clouds were lit on both sides and glowed with a sullen fire. Above him were the now familiar constellations of this world. In front, the moonlit sharpness of the Red Cathedral with silhouetted onion domes. Beside that a separate bell tower and a squat hall beneath. As he watched, the hall doors opened and men and carts flooded out and spread around the rocky edge of the island, the night suddenly full of jangling harness and cartwheels squeaking.

Dropping to a crouch, Tycho hugged the ice as four oxen lumbered in his direction, stopping a dozen paces from the island shore. Men in stinking furs tumbled from the back of the wagons, grabbed pickaxes and spread out. In a line, standing a couple of paces apart, they took their orders from a gang boss and raised their pickaxes together, crashing the points into the ice. All around the island, other men did the same. Alonzo was making himself a moat.

Against me? Tycho rejected the idea as arrogance.

Yet what other reason was there? Captain Towler had probably been happy to boast of having met Tycho on his way here. This, it seemed, was Alonzo's response. A hundred men smashing ice until dark water appeared. Within five minutes, fifteen foot of open water stood between the island and the rest of the lake. Job done, the men climbed into their carts and trundled on.

Maybe taunting Alonzo hadn't been so clever . . .

How many cart teams were there? Was there an ice bridge somewhere? And could he find it and cross it unseen before Alonzo's men turned it too to dark water and left him stranded on this side of the ice? He could overtake the carts and hope to find unbroken ice beyond them, or cross here. Neither option impressed him.

Not giving himself time to think, Tycho shrugged himself from his jacket and slipped into the dark moat, feeling bitter cold knock breath from his body. He swam hard, his lungs too tight to breathe, and reached the edge, dragging himself over it and grabbed a breath. He was almost clear of the water when something grabbed his ankle and he felt himself slide backwards, unable to get a grip on the smooth ice.

What the fuck was that?

He kicked hard, connecting with flesh. The grip on his ankle tightened and yanked harder. A moment later, Tycho splashed into the water, slid under and turned to discover what he faced. His attacker was frog-eyed and broad-cheeked, its wide mouth filled with needle-like teeth. Gills frilled both sides of its neck like wounds.

Tycho kicked for its hand and the thing grinned, letting go of Tycho's ankle and boosting his foot upwards with webbed fingers. When Tycho's head smashed into the ice above the world went black, sickness sweeping through him. As the creature hung mockingly out of reach, a subtle change came over its face, and its grin became scarily human. Tycho drew his knife.

The blow to his head left a hangover of giddiness. Smoke-like darkness ate the edges of his vision as the air burnt up in his chest, narrowing the aquarium dark of the world under the ice to a tight circle of light in front of him. He desperately wanted to draw a breath and knew he shouldn't.

Come closer, he thought. *Fight me.*

Tycho goaded the creature with his knife, jabbing as his strength drained and the chill reached his bones. The face in front of him was familiar now, its cheekbones high and nose strong, wolf-grey braids framing a face as white as alabaster. One monster was gone and another had taken its place. Tycho was looking at himself.

Darting forward, the creature grabbed Tycho's knife hand and twisted savagely. It had all of Tycho's speed and strength, which was more than he had. Think, Tycho urged himself. But all he could think was, this is me, as he watched his dagger begin to spin towards the bottom. He was drowning.

The creature blew out its breath and Tycho felt them both sink after the dagger, following it towards the gravel below. The air in his own lungs was gone. He should be dead or already dying but all he felt was numb.

A numbness as bad as that he'd felt the night rip tides caught him in the Venetian lagoon and dragged him under. Finally depositing him on the stone steps at Rialto for a young street rat called Rosalyn to find. She'd thought him already dead and maybe she was right. Who would find him this time? Always assuming this winter ended and the ice melted, and this wasn't the end of the world as more than half the people in Europe claimed. Feeling the creature wrap its arms more tightly around him, Tycho watched it smile as if reading his thoughts.

The lake was darker here but the water warmer, as if some of the last summer's heat had survived. Maybe there was simply a warm spring venting somewhere near, or perhaps he imagined it. The water felt warmer the deeper he was dragged. A normal person would be dead by now, drowned when the last of his breath went skyward in tiny bubbles. Only he wasn't normal, was he? And here was his proof. He was alive when he should be dead.

Fed up with waiting, the creature dragged him close and tried to squeeze air from his lungs. A splatter of bubbles was all Tycho had left. The thing looked worried now, its face less obviously Tycho's own. In dragging Tycho close, it had given him the opening he'd lacked.

My turn, Tycho decided.

Opening his mouth, he bit into the creature's neck and ripped, sour blood mixing with lake water in his mouth. He clung on, gripping tight with the last of his strength as the creature tried to push free, and bit again, spitting flesh into the water. All the while it bled and struggled, and bled some more, until finally it stopped struggling. Tycho held it until it stopped shuddering and then he released it and watched its corpse float gently away, carried by the rising thermal of the hot spring. In death it reverted to its natural form, looking as Tycho first saw it, like a cross between a frog and a dwarf, with needle teeth and webs between its fingers.

The world was roofed in ice. Thick and dark. As strangely jagged and cruel on the underside as it had been marble-smooth on top. If this was the way the world ended, here was where he would remain, locked on the wrong side of an ice wall.

I've failed Giulietta. It was a bad thought to carry for eternity. Gripping the underside of the ice, Tycho dragged himself in one direction, ice slicing his fingers, until he decided he should have reached the makeshift moat by now if he was going to reach it at all, and began pulling himself in the opposite direction. Except how did he know which was right? The strength the creature's blood had given him was going, leaching away into the water. And he faced a deeper fear. What would happen when the sun came up?

All that light through the ice. Would it burn him?

He suspected it might. He'd failed Giulietta, and the sun would fry him through the ice if he didn't free himself soon. Kicking off from the ice, Tycho hit the bottom and crawled on his hands and knees until he reached an incline. The island had to be up ahead, which meant somewhere above was a circle of fine ice or dark water that made up Alonzo's makeshift moat.

He found it eventually, a crackle of ice thin as leaves and brittle as the skim on a puddle, so inconsequential he barely noticed it as he broke through and gasped air, feeling his lungs fill and his heart restart. Above him the sky was high and clear, and the moon bright enough to show him he was back at the moat's outer edge.

Fingers clawing ice, he fought for a grip, found one and dragged himself on to its surface, only for something to grab his ankle before he could fight free of the water. Two things happened at once. Long webbed fingers tightened their grip and began to drag him back, and what he'd thought was a mound of snow reared up, hurtled across open ice and raised a spear, hurling it into his captor.

"Have you any idea how idiotic that was?" Amelia demanded, as she ripped her spear free and bent to drag Tycho to safety. He wanted to answer but the darkness took him before he could reply.

21

As Lady Giulietta entered the family quarters she heard the sound of a harpsichord, its notes rising like birdsong. For an instant, her heart lifted and she forgot Lady Eleanor was dead, remembering a moment later when she found Frederick where her former lady-in-waiting used to sit. "You play?"

"A little," he said, blushing.

Having thought about it, Giulietta remembered Eleanor wishing she could learn to use a sword and decided Frederick should be allowed to have learnt the harpsichord. "I was wondering," she said. "I don't suppose you have news from Montenegro?"

He shook his head and Giulietta's heart sank. It was physical. Her ribs tightened and her stomach knotted, and she felt her eyes fill with tears as she stared at the distant tower of San Maggiore and willed herself not to cry.

Why not? she wanted to shout.

"It's all right," Prince Frederick said.

"No, it's not." She felt his arm go round her and tried to shake free, discovering he was stronger than he looked. After a struggle, she let him hold her, which he did gingerly as if she might break or melt against him. That was how Duke Marco found them a few moments later.

"J-J-Julie's crying."

"She misses Tycho."

"Her angel? Of course she d-does. We all d-do."

"So here you are . . ." If Aunt Alexa wondered why they were grouped by a window seat or noticed her niece was crying, she kept it to herself. Sitting almost sideways to the window, she joined Giulietta in staring over the Giudecca canal at the islands beyond. "This was my husband's favourite seat, and his father's before that. When il Millioni first became duke it was said he'd sit here for hours, looking at the waters . . . Couldn't believe his luck probably. Either that, or he was hiding from assassins."

"*Aunt Alexa.*"

"Oh, come on. You know he stole the throne."

Prince Frederick was on the point of excusing himself, and had got as far as bowing politely before Alexa grabbed his wrist and patted the seat beside her. "All thrones are stolen," she said firmly. "I'm surprised your father hasn't told you this already."

"He says kings are chosen by God." Frederick sounded unhappy to be disagreeing with a woman rumoured to poison those who offended her. "That everyone knows this is true."

"After the event, perhaps. God agrees. If God has anything to do with it at all."

"*My lady . . .*"

"Listen to me," she said. "All of you . . . A good ruler *knows* that thrones are stolen, and can be stolen again, and does good works to assuage the guilt of the first, and bad works to make sure the second never happens. We have our time on earth and then it's done. What we do with those years is our choice." She got to her feet unsteadily, kissed Marco on the forehead, hesitated and did the same to Giulietta. Then she ruffled Frederick's hair.

"I'm glad we had this talk," she said, before shutting the door behind her and leaving them alone in the little corridor with its harpsichord, window seat and rotting tapestries.

"What was that about?" Giulietta's question was for Frederick but it was Marco who answered.

"My m-mother's scared."

"Of what?"

"Of e-everything," Marco replied.

He left shortly afterwards and an awkward silence fell as Frederick wondered what to say to her, leant forward and opened his mouth a couple of times and finally decided to say nothing. Only he couldn't manage that either.

"Should I leave you be?"

They were the same age but sometimes he behaved like a twelve-year-old. She'd met newly arrived pages with stronger self-confidence. He was watching, waiting for her answer. She sighed.

"It's just . . . You look like you want to do some thinking."

About what, for God's sake? She was sick of chasing the same miserable thoughts around her head: where was Tycho, why hadn't he said goodbye, would he really be able to save Leo, what was wrong with Aunt Alexa? And that was before she began on her memories, which were worse than the questions. Uncle Alonzo and his goose quill, Leopold dying, Tycho leaving . . . She should be in the nursery convincing everyone Venice's supposed heir was happy and alive. Instead she avoided the changeling and even her aunt had stopped scolding her for being unable to pretend.

I'm fine, she thought. I'm fine so long as I don't think about . . .

There was her problem. Thinking about Tycho was meant to make her feel better. And when she didn't feel better, being with Frederick and Marco was meant to make her happier. But now she didn't really want to be with anyone. Did that make her a bad person? She knew Frederick was in love with her. She'd like to be able to say, *of course he was*; as if a whole succession of blond German princelings had fallen in love with her. Truth was, until

Tycho men barely looked at her at all. Even Eleanor had stolen more kisses and she was three years younger. Had been, Lady Giulietta reminded herself. Now she lay beneath a marble tomb in San Giovanni e Paolo. Every year Giulietta got older Eleanor would get another year younger than her.

"What are you thinking about?" Frederick asked.

"My old lady-in-waiting."

"Eleanor?" he said. "I know you loved her."

Eleanor never knew that, Giulietta thought sadly. And, anyway, Eleanor loved Rosalyn, Tycho's ragged girl. Always back to Tycho. "Could you ask your father for me again?" she said, biting her lip.

"Always assuming I've asked him already."

I know you have . . . A few days back, after she asked last time, the Night Watch reported a wolf had been seen slinking from the Fontego dei Tedeschi, where Prince Frederick made his base. Two nights later the customs guard swore a wolf crossed from the mainland and was spotted slinking along the Grand Canal. The animal was said to look emaciated and starving. Rumour said one of Frederick's men had recently died. She was cruel, she realised; cruel to ask him to get news of Tycho.

"Maybe I could see if my father's learnt anything new."

So sweet, thought Giulietta, then remembered the night Frederick led a snarling war pack against the Byzantine infantry. They'd ripped heavily armed spearmen to shreds, with Frederick leading. So, not sweet after all – just kind, which she was coming to realise was different. He was two people and his kindness involved not letting them overlap. Maybe all men were like that.

"My father has mages," Frederick was saying. "One of those might . . ."

"Thank you." Giulietta kissed his cheek.

Frederick blushed. "Or you could ask the duchess?"

"*My aunt?*"

"Umm . . ." Frederick took a deep breath. "You must have

130

noticed your aunt knows most things? Things she shouldn't know?"

"She has spies."

"We all have spies," he said. "Your aunt . . ." Frederick hesitated. "Perhaps hers are simply a little better than everyone else's." The boy looked a little thinner than when he arrived, a little more tired. His beard was still just fuzz and he chewed one side of his lip like a child. It was odd to think he'd had a wife and child.

"Tell me about Annemarie," Giulietta said.

He looked so instantly hurt she might have slapped him. "I'm sorry," she said quickly, "it doesn't matter", but Frederick waved her words away. Without realising, he'd hugged his arms to his chest, rocking his shoulders as if to ease a knot in his back. His blue eyes were as bleak as a winter sky.

Will anyone love me that much?

Instantly, she felt ashamed of her selfishness, but couldn't stop herself from worrying at the question. Did Tycho love her that fiercely? If she died would the mere mention of her name fill his face with misery years later? Grief hollowed Frederick's face so brutally she hardly dared look at him.

Standing suddenly, Frederick left the room. Tycho didn't *leave* rooms. He glowered, smouldered and burnt, often all at once. At worst, he vanished in a swirl of his cloak. Frederick simply left as if he'd forgotten to do something or suddenly remembered he'd promised to be elsewhere. Giulietta chewed her nails and wondered when she'd started biting them again. She was pretty sure it was since Frederick arrived and that made no sense at all.

Frederick returned a day later, asked if Giulietta would receive him and was brought up to the window seat where she sat watching the frozen lagoon. He didn't say hello or apologise for leaving so suddenly the previous afternoon, simply sat beside her and started talking as if he'd never been gone.

"After Annemarie died I had to go through her possessions. Well, I could have given the job to my chamberlain. But she was my wife and I loved her. Jewellery went back to her family, as did half of her dowry. Our marriage agreement specified she had to live five years or produce a child."

"Frederick . . ."

"Since the baby died she didn't count."

His voice was flat, whether from shock or mute acceptance Giulietta couldn't tell. Maybe the passing years had numbed his horror. Giulietta suspected it was immature to be shocked – but she felt shocked all the same.

"You know what I found?"

Giulietta shook her head.

"A letter."

From a lover? She wondered what Frederick was trying to tell her.

"She wrote it the week we married. It was to her cousin in Bohemia." Frederick shrugged. "They grew up together. She swore her love for him would never die. Said how much she hated being made to marry me. That she would remember him for ever. The day they swam together at the waterfall was the happiest of her life. She never sent it."

How could he bear to tell her this?

"The priest who was with Annemarie at the end told me she swore she loved me more than she'd ever loved anyone and regretted nothing of her time with me. That she simply wanted me to be happy after she was gone, as she'd been happy during her time with me. So you see . . ."

What? Giulietta wondered.

"We change. We think we don't but we do."

They sat in silence after that, not quite touching in the window seat of a corridor that linked the family rooms and acted as a little withdrawing room when the official nature of the palace became too much. He'd remained dry-eyed and his voice had been level

132

when he spoke to her, but she was sure his cheeks looked thinner and his expression a little more withdrawn. He wore a doublet in the northern style, richly decorated with gold thread, and a chain of gold and enamel links hung around his neck that fell to a little ivory dragon with ruby eyes. She wondered if anyone really saw past the clothes to the boy inside.

"I should go," he said.

"Of course . . ." She stood, embarrassed, wanting to apologise for asking about Annemarie and afraid to make matters worse. So she talked idiocies about the Watch finding it hard to march on ice, and the price of fish now holes had to be cut in the ice, and recut the next day, and how fishermen were complaining they were being turned into sculptors or carpenters.

"Do you have enough food?" he asked suddenly.

She looked up, surprised by his question. "There's enough to feed an army in the storehouses beyond the kitchens."

"I meant the city."

Giulietta flushed with shame. "I don't know," she admitted.

"Maybe your aunt knows. In fact," he said, "I'm sure she does. We had reports she was buying grain last summer. I wouldn't be surprised if she knew the cold was coming." His comment returned her thoughts to what he'd said earlier, about her aunt knowing things other people didn't, even those with their own spies . . . The more Giulietta thought about it the more she realised it was true. Frederick obviously suspected something. She needed to find out what.

"Why don't we take a walk on the ice?"

So, Alexa thought, *which thread to follow now?*

Of course, there were always two threads, do this or do that. Two threads for every single second of every single minute of every life: and there were self-created flaws in those threads, the things you did half well, the things you did intentionally badly, the things you did too early (usually less critical than the things you left too late). Of such was life woven until death stilled the loom.

Those were not the threads Alexa meant, although she knew she was watching her niece wrestle with the simplest of girlish questions. Who do I want to be? Whom do I love? Is it wise? The question troubling Alexa was which thread would keep Venice safest? Tycho's or Frederick's.

Sigismund's bastard had been right.

She'd been buying grain for months. All the same, there would be food riots eventually, because hunger already ate at the poor. But they would arrive later and be less serious than in other cities. Her subjects might not like eating bread when they were used to fish, they might accuse her of having cupboards full of figs and cheese, but the point was, they ate.

Swirling her fingers through the water in her jade bowl, Duchess Alexa gave the two youngsters on the ice back their privacy. Frederick would tell Giulietta about Alexa seeing at a distance, for all that how she did it was still unknown. Her niece would be drawn a little bit closer to him and he would become a little bit more confident around her, which was good.

The boy needed confidence. At least, he needed it if Giulietta was to fall properly in love with him. So far, neither had the wit to realise this was what was happening. Having felt close to Frederick, Giulietta would feel guilty, which would make her angry. Anger would make her realise that if her aunt could see at a distance, she could discover where Tycho was, and Alexa could expect a knock at the door.

22

Somehow he was back in the fort, in the upper chamber, with its wooden bed and rotting fur, under a familiar ceiling, whose stains mapped worlds he didn't recognise where meltwater dripped through the roof above.

"How did I get here?"

"I carried you." Amelia turned for the door and Tycho saw a bloody bandage around her shoulder. "Bastard to kill," she said, seeing his surprise. "And bastard you for being that stupid." The quietness with which she shut the door was more contemptuous than any slam.

Well, I deserved that.

He thought sombrely of the climb out of the cathedral valley and the wind-swept saddleback of mountain he'd been so impressed with himself for navigating, the ice and ravines and slippery paths between that valley and this, the final tight twist of stairs between the hall below and this chamber, and wondered why he'd ever dared think he was the best the *Assassini* had to offer.

The thought remained with him.

After a while he realised he owed Amelia an apology. He hadn't seen beyond her sex and her skin and her past as Lord

135

Atilo's ex-slave, apprentice and deadly plaything. Maybe that was how Duchess Alexa thought of him? As an exotic toy . . .

"I'm sorry," he said, when she returned.

Walking to the bed, she felt his brow and pulled down one eyelid to peer into his eye. He knew he was being mocked and probably deserved it. "Are you hungry? she asked finally.

Tycho glanced at her bloody bandage.

"Not even if you ordered me to bleed myself."

She shut the door with a bang and they both knew that was an improvement on the time before. An hour later she was back, head down and frost whitening her eyebrows. In one hand she held a dead rabbit and in the other a live one; both wore their winter coats. "I wasn't sure which you'd prefer?"

Her eyes were a challenge.

He had never said he needed blood, nor had he ever suggested he was anything other than human, and yet she'd read correctly his hunger and now brought him both live and dead food. Given the weakness in his limbs it was an easy choice. He pointed at the live one.

"You died," she said.

"Again . . .?"

She raised her eyebrows.

"I died the night I arrived in Venice. Well, I think I did. As Rosalyn dragged me up the water steps I felt my heart start again."

"Yes," Amelia said. "That would be a clue."

She handed him the kicking rabbit and grimaced as he raised it to his mouth, thin blood trickling down his chin as he took away the lake creature's foul taste. Carcase drained, Tycho offered it back in case she wanted the meat.

"Gross," she said. Pulling flint and tinder from inside her coat, she produced twigs she'd bundled tight with an old bowstring, and, dropping to a squat, lit a fire right in the middle of the floor and skinned both rabbits by cutting once around the neck and ripping their pelts inside out.

136

"Some of us," she said, "are civilised."

He grinned ruefully, and later ate slivers of roast rabbit that were somewhere between raw and cooked and more pink than they should be. It took him a while to realise she was waiting for him to ask why she'd disobeyed his command to stay where she was. So he asked. She had orders of her own she told him, from Duke Marco. She was to keep Tycho safe, if possible. "Thank you," he said, which surprised her as much as his apology.

"Were you expecting vodyanoi?"

Tycho paused, the final scraps of rabbit halfway to his mouth. "Was I expecting what?"

"Water demons."

"That's what they were?"

"Where you find vodyanoi you find domovoi, house demons."

And I thought Alonzo was absurd to have his men smash up the ice to make a moat . . . It looked as if the Regent's defences were better than Duchess Alexa had suspected. Somewhere between that thought and the stringy shreds of rabbit meat stuck in his back teeth, Tycho came up with a plan no more absurd than any other and substantially better than throwing himself in a lake full of water demons. As he picked his teeth with a splinter of wood and licked grease from his fingers, he ran through the plan looking for flaws before explaining what he had in mind.

"Why don't we just kill him?" Amelia asked.

"No, we have to get inside the castle," he started to say, then remembered she didn't know Alonzo had Leo. Amelia thought they were there simply to kill the man. "Alexa told me to . . ."

Amelia's face tightened. She had orders from Marco he hadn't known about. Now she understood that he, in turn, had orders that had been kept from her. Why would either of them imagine it might be different? Tycho returned to his plan. It was the rabbits that gave him his idea. That, and knowing Alonzo's passion for hunting. All the joy of blood and battle with none of the danger. The Regent would undoubtedly ride out early and return late, and the winter days meant Tycho would have an hour at each end to hunt the man down. Boredom would drive Alonzo from his cathedral and darkness would deliver him to Amelia and Tycho. All they had to do was watch and wait. "He'll be better tempered if the hunt is good," Amelia said.

"And worse if the day goes badly."

"Then we'd better make sure it begins and ends well."

They ran the rocky spine between valleys, the wind less cruel this time, and found a cave high above the village, with the Red Cathedral beyond. Tycho left her there, going to the edge of a small cliff to keep watch. On their second day of running the ridge and keeping watch, torches flared far below and a party of horsemen began to gather in front of the cathedral. It was more luck than he deserved.

A few moments later, when he went to check on Amelia she was already tightly wrapped in her cloak and fast asleep at the back of the cave. He scratched the sign for prey sighted into the rock and returned to his watch; the beginning and end of the day were his and the daylight hours hers.

Finding a five-point stag in a high valley, Tycho harried the beast through the narrow gap of a pass and down to where firs rose at the start of the treeline. Their trunks were twisted and old, half banked with snow and awkwardly angled from a life fighting the winds. They would survive the winter, though, which was more than the stag would have done. Its ribs jutted like bare twigs and its hips were hollows of starvation. Alonzo would still be grateful for the kill, and his men grateful for whatever meat his butchers extracted from its carcase. A snow rabbit crossed his path and Tycho let it go.

Wild pigs were in the lower valley, huddled in the dark spaces beneath the forest, where the snow had settled on top of the trees to create a hidden world where pine needles stank of urine as his feet kicked rotting scabs from the forest floor. He left the sows where he found them, circling an elderly one-tusked boar. Alonzo's hounds would scent them easily enough.

In a narrow cave covered with more paintings of animals and stick-like hunters he found a huge bear sleeping on a litter of dry bracken it had collected for bedding. Rotting meat decayed in one corner, and white bones said the bear's ancestors had used the cave for generations. Tycho left the great beast sleeping.

A wolf provided better prey. Tycho saw it climbing towards the pass he'd used earlier, and it saw him and began to hunt, calling for its brothers with a triumphant howl he hoped the Regent would also hear. The pack chased Tycho down a gully, certain they could tire him, until he brought them to where Alonzo's men would ride. He left them in a burst of speed, rocks slippery under his feet as he ran a line of boulders tossed down by giants in older times. With luck, frustration would make the wolves reckless enough to risk attacking one of Alonzo's outriders, and the Regent would have outrage to add to whatever else the hunt brought. Alonzo loved outrage.

His part done, Tycho shook Amelia awake, slumped on to the floor of the cave and slept in turn until a shake woke him again. The night sky was snow-bright and Amelia was looking pleased with herself. "A good day?" he asked.

She grinned. "The wolves were yours?"

"Alonzo liked them?"

"They killed his squire. His hunters killed five of them. Alonzo accounting for the biggest. He also took an old stag, two bucks and a hind. That probably clears the entire valley of deer in this direction."

"Anything else?"

"Wild pigs to provide meat for the kitchens. A farmer's daughter to provide warmth for his bed. We go down there now?"

"Yes," Tycho said. "And swear loyalty to Alonzo."

"What?" Amelia looked shocked.

"It's necessary."

"This is pretend, right?"

"I will make the full oath . . ."

"And me? Am I expected to do the same? I know you have private orders. But I thought we were here to kill him."

"You misunderstand. I'm offering him the Assassini."

With the Assassini came her, and everyone else in Venice's guild of assassins who'd survived the battle against the *krieghund* two years earlier. True, less than a fifth remained, but it was their reputation that convinced cities to offer tribute, and made foreign princes sign treaties they disliked. "You're giving him Venice."

"It's not even your city."

"It's the only one I've got," she said flatly. "It's where I did most of my growing up. I pledged my loyalty to the Lion of St Mark when I took the Assassini oath."

"You're keeping that oath."

She shook her head.

"We must move," he said. "Or the Regent will end the hunt before we can reach him. Run with me, and I'll tell you why we're doing this." He owed her that at least.

A dozen courtiers followed Alonzo. Three wild pigs and a one-tusked boar with balls the size of oranges hung behind four different saddles. A thin-hipped stag was lashed on a litter behind another, and half a dozen hastily skinned wolf pelts dripped blood and unnerved the horses across whose backs they'd been tossed.

Flaming torches threw shadows on the forest as the hunt broke cover, laughing and shouting now the chase was done. It was obvious to Tycho that they'd been drinking and were happy with how the day had gone. Not only good sport, but also meat for those in the cathedral. Tempers would be calmer and arguments fewer in the days to come. Alonzo in particular looked pleased with himself.

"Those wolves, Roderigo . . ."

"You were magnificent, my lord."

He shook the praise away and nodded all the same, his hand reaching over to pat the rolled fur behind Lord Roderigo's saddle. The space behind his own was filled with a villager's blonde daughter. She looked thin and hungry, and scared at where she found herself. Tycho wondered how Lady Maria, the Regent's new wife, would feel and realised that didn't matter. Maybe she expected her husband to take other women; perhaps she was even grateful.

Tycho was tempted to step in front of the Regent's mount simply to see it shy and watch Alonzo fight to get the beast back under control. But that would make the Regent mislay his grin and his good temper and what came next would be harder. So he fell back to the open space between the treeline and the village.

The hounds saw them first. As they howled, a huntsman raced forward hoping for one final chase to close the day and saw Tycho and Amelia blocking the way. His whip sang and Amelia's hand flicked up to catch the lash. Stepping aside, she forced the red-faced man to ride a tight circle to avoid having the whip ripped from his hands. The hunt laughed and slowed, stopping mere paces away.

"My lord Regent," Amelia said.

Around them, men Tycho didn't recognise lifted their torches to see who this woman was who could recognise their master in the near dark. Light spilled on to Tycho's face and Roderigo spurred his horse forward. "Wait," Tycho said.

Amelia was reaching for her daggers.

"My lord," said Tycho, "I would speak with the Regent."

"Who is it, Roderigo?"

"Alexa's pet, and Atilo's black woman."

The Regent rode so close his mount nearly trampled both as he grabbed a torch from a servant and thrust it towards their faces. "Gods," he said. "One black as sin. The other white as a virgin."

"You know them, my lord?" a thickset man asked.

"All too well," Alonzo said. That he didn't simply tell Roderigo to kill them showed how successful the hunt had been. His admiring courtiers, the fresh meat they'd collected, the wild ride across frozen slopes and through dark forests were what kept Alonzo from giving the order. That could change. With Alonzo it could always change. "Sent you to kill me, did she, Tycho?"

"Yes, my lord. But she doesn't know why I'm really here."

The Regent's eyes narrowed. "Why are you here?"

"My lord, if we could . . .?" He nodded at a gentle slope near the edge of the lake and the Regent hesitated. If Tycho was here to kill him then separating him from his followers was a good start.

"I have no secrets from such good friends."

The courtiers preened at the flattery. Were they so simple? Tycho wondered. Or was it some court tradition where they pretended Alonzo's flattery lifted their hearts and Alonzo pretended to believe them. Life in Bjornvin had been simpler. Lord Eric's nobles were either in favour or out of favour, and those too out of favour ended with Lord Eric's knife in their guts. "My lord, these are matters of state. Such as my late master dealt with."

This was as close as Tycho dared go to suggesting this was Assassini business. Only the Regents and the Council of Ten knew the name of the head of the Assassini. Even Lord Roderigo didn't know; or, if he did, he shouldn't and Alonzo had broken his vows of secrecy.

"Really?" Alonzo demanded.

Tycho unslung his sword, unbuckled his dagger and dropped his weapons into the snow, stepping away from them. "Really, my lord."

Raising his hand commandingly, as if an entire army needed to be told to stay where it was, Alonzo slid from his mount. "The black bitch stays there. Your responsibility, Roderigo. Come on then . . ." The Regent stalked towards the shore, although Tycho noticed he kept his hand on his dagger the entire way.

"Alexa sent you to negotiate?"

"No, my lord."

"The Council then?"

"I am here for me."

"For you? And yet this is Assassini business?"

Tycho bowed slightly. He knew the Regent had taken Leo as surely as he knew he'd had a surrogate killed to fool everyone into thinking Leo was dead. And Alexa was sure Alonzo was behind Marco's poisoning, and the attempts on Lady Giulietta's life. All it would take was a blow to the throat, or a twist of the head brutal enough to break his spine.

Tycho would have failed in his mission.

"My lord, may I speak freely?"

Although he kept his hand on his dagger, Alonzo heard something in the question that made him relax a little; self-interest probably, he'd recognise that. Nodding towards the cathedral's black silhouette, he said, "Impressive, isn't it?"

"Yes, my lord. But it isn't Venice."

"Impregnable, too."

"My lord, an army could cross this." Stamping, Tycho felt his heel jar as it hit rock-hard ice. Tycho was right: an army could march from here to the island near the lake's far edge.

"You haven't been out there yet?"

Tycho shook his head.

He could feel the Regent watching him. "We smash the ice," Alonzo said. "To make a moat. The moat contains monsters." He glanced at the peaks around them. "The whole bloody country contains monsters. You should feel at home."

"I don't intend to stay. Neither do you."

Alonzo tipped his head to one side. An almost self-mocking expression entered his face. "Go on," he said. "Don't stop now."

"My lord, it's obvious. This is simply a stage to let you claim

Venice. Montenegro gives you a land base and silver mines. There are ports on the coast where Roderigo can collect taxes. The farmers' sons can provide you with an army, whether they want to or not. And their daughters can fill your bed." He nodded to where the village girl still sat behind Alonzo's saddle, little more than a child. "But this is not Venice. I've tasted the food here. Rats wouldn't eat in this country. You don't strike me as a man to settle for second best."

"This sounds dangerously like treason."

"My lord, Marco Polo making his dukedom hereditary would have been treason if he'd failed. Success made it glorious."

"Are you offering me loyalty?"

"Yes, my lord."

"*You . . .?*"

"Once you offered me your friendship."

"You betrayed me."

"No, my lord. You threw me aside when Lady Giulietta refused to marry me as we planned. You transferred your patronage to Iacopo, my known enemy. Yes, I killed him in a fit of anger but any man might do that . . ." Indeed, the Regent had once slaughtered an entire *fondak* of Mamluks because he thought they were behind his niece's abduction.

"How is her child?"

"Getting so fat you'd barely recognise him."

Prince Alonzo shot a sideways glance that was almost amused.

"And Lady Maria?" Tycho asked in his turn. "This isolation must be hard for a young heiress more used to Venice's glories."

"She's pregnant." Alonzo paused, and Tycho realised he was meant to congratulate the man, which he did. "Heavily pregnant. She keeps to her room."

"My lord, I'm offering you the Blade."

The Regent looked at him. He stared into Tycho's face, though the darkness must have reduced it to shadow, and then he turned and stamped his way to where Lord Roderigo stood, cutting him out of the crowd and leading him aside. The argument was fierce, and Alonzo returned with a scowl on in his face. "It's a trick," he said. "You must think I'm stupid."

"No trick," Tycho promised. "No trick at all, my lord."

"Then prove it. Perform a task."

"Whatever you ask."

"You swear that?"

"I swear it."

"Good." Alonzo smiled. "Kill Alexa. Bring me proof."

23

The duchess sat with her son in one of the kitchens. The staff were neither told to stay nor go, but had chosen to leave and Alexa let them. In truth, she barely noticed, being too busy sautéing snails in a hot pan.

"Your favourite," Alexa said. She watched her son sniff the air, grin at the smell of garlic and butter, and look puzzled. *How*, he obviously wondered, *did Mother find snails in midwinter?* She let him wonder. Lifting a lid, Alexa spooned half the snails on to a platter for him and loaded half on to another for her.

"Eat," she said, handing him a pin.

The duke dug happily into a hot shell and chewed, even closing his eyes to savour the garlic as he'd done as a child, before his *illness*. The word tasted sour and she winkled out a snail and chewed the taste away. Marco was already swallowing his second and reaching for a third, grinning at his burnt fingers. That, too, reminded her of his childhood. He'd always mixed contemplation with sudden awkward enthusiasms. Snails would become his new favourite.

"This one's a-alive," he said holding up a shell.

"Really?" Before he could ask how an uncooked snail got into the pot she slid in a question of her own. "How would you get it out?"

Marco dug with his pin and the snail shrivelled, retreating behind the turns in its shell until the pin couldn't reach.

"You could stamp on it," Alexa suggested.

"All that b-broken shell."

"Indeed." Lifting the pot's lid, she helped herself to a little more melted butter and diced garlic, and was about to replace the lid when Marco shook his head. Grinning, he dropped his live snail into the sizzling liquid. "Finish mine," Alexa said, "while you're waiting."

And so we teach our young. Well, so she taught Marco. One live snail among those already cooked. Had he understood the lesson? With Marco it was hard to know . . . "D-done," he said, scooping the snail from the pot.

"Good boy. Tomorrow I'll have someone take you skating."

"On the b-big ice?"

"The canal behind the palace," she said and watched his face. She'd love to let him skate on the lagoon, however many guards it took, and however many times he fell over; since, not having skated before, most Venetians were clumsy . . . But that would take everyone's eyes off Frederick and Giulietta, and Alexa had her own reasons for wanting the public to watch them.

A cobbler in San Croce made himself rich by persuading a metalworker to fashion blades that could be nailed directly to the soles of sturdy boots. The cobbler then left a pair at the palace door for Lady Giulietta, and a pair outside the Fontego dei Tedeschi for Prince Frederick, with whom the whole city knew she'd been walking on the ice.

Bone skates had been used for ever.

Well, as far as Giulietta knew. A chamberlain so old his eyes were sightless and his voice a whisper remembered metal skates from the last time the canals froze, but those had been tied on and were blunt enough for their owners to need poles to push themselves along. To nail the blades directly to the boots was genius. Aunt Alexa had all but ordered Giulietta to try them out.

Within two days the cobbler had more orders than he could meet. Other cobblers suddenly found themselves busy, and the Duchess Alexa gave dispensation for a foundry to relight its furnace and burn precious fuel turning out blades by the hundred. "She's brilliant," Prince Frederick said.

He'd just turned an almost brutal figure of eight that sprayed ice and brought him back to where Lady Giulietta stood, unsteadily leaning on a stick and well aware he'd long ago abandoned his own. With blades this sharp you didn't need to pole yourself along so those watching – and there were more people than she liked watching – knew she needed it for balance. "Who's brilliant?"

"Your aunt. Now, take my hand."

"*Leopold.*"

Frederick scowled and she blushed furiously. "*Frederick,*" she said. "Sorry, that was really stupid. I know . . ."

"I'm Frederick?"

She nodded dumbly.

"It's all right," he said. "Now, drop your stick."

He was holding out his hand and a hundred people were staring, and she knew she was blushing harder than ever, so she reached hastily for his fingers and gripped the impossibly soft leather of his gloves.

"You're cold," he said.

Her fingernails were almost blue.

"Wear these." He was pulling off a glove before she could refuse. The surprise was that they fitted. "Small hands," he explained, matching his fingers to hers. "I say . . . Are you all right?"

"My page is watching."

Prince Frederick let go of her fingers. "Sorry," he said. "I forget how to behave sometimes. That's why I like . . ." He chewed the corner of his lip, having apparently decided against what he intended to say.

"You like what?"

"Being with my friends. It's more natural."

"Natural?" she asked. Catching the amusement in his eyes, she realised too late he meant the *krieghund*, he liked being with his kind. That was a discussion she felt unready to have. Certainly here, watched by every layabout in Venice. "Tell me," she said. "Why is my aunt brilliant?"

He grinned at her change of topic, and grinned again when she discarded her stick. She felt him take her shoulders and turn her to look at the scene behind them. A thousand people, possibly more, thronged the ice. Stalls lined the edge of the Riva degli Schiavoni. Skaters, and those who'd been walking on the ice in studded boots, formed queues to buy hot bread and warm pies. The smell of roasting meat wafting over the ice from where an ox roasted over a fire pit on the quay.

"Other cities are rioting," he said.

Are they now? Aunt Alexa had mentioned nothing about that.

"Farms are being sacked in Lombardy, and granaries broken into all across Germany. Warehouses in Milan have been gutted and burnt. My father's had to burn the leaders of a peasant rebellion and hang a hundred of their followers. And what is Venice doing? Holding an ice party . . ."

"You've had fresh news from your father?"

Frederick's face went still.

He must have heard the hope in my voice. "About Leo, I mean?"

Instantly, she felt guilty. She should have said, *about Leo and Tycho.* But it was kinder to let Frederick think her worry was about Leo alone. Looking up, she expected Frederick's face to have relaxed. If anything, he looked unhappier than he had done before. "*You've heard something about Leo . . .*"

He shook his head.

Thank God, she couldn't stand that.

"Nothing about Leo, my lady. There are rumours Lady Maria is pregnant enough to keep to her room." It took Giulietta a moment to realise he meant Maria Dolphini. "If you're right, they'll introduce Leo as her son soon . . ."

"What else?"

"My lady . . .?"

He was too fond of her for such formality. "Your highness, what other news have you received? What aren't you telling me?"

"You know what rumours are like." In her experience rumours were almost always right. He obviously read the anger in her eyes because he sighed. "I'm not saying it's true. And you're not going to like it."

"Obviously," she said tightly.

"An unconfirmed report says Lord Tycho has sworn loyalty to the Regent, that he has offered Alonzo the Blade."

"You knew Tycho was Duke's Blade?"

"No," said Frederick. "But I do now. Until a second ago it was simply rumour."

Lady Giulietta glared at him. "Impossible," she said. "Tycho would never betray me . . . He'd never betray Marco. He belongs to Alexa. He *knows* how much I hate my uncle."

"Everyone knows how much you hate your uncle. No one knows why. Although there are rumours about that as well."

"Of course there are. There are always rumours. You said yourself they're usually wrong. And that one's wrong, too." Gathering her cloak, Giulietta turned for the shoreline. "Take me home."

As they were approaching the Porta della Carta, just before the guards came to attention, Frederick said. "Ask your aunt the truth of it. She has a way of knowing these things. She can tell you if it's untrue."

"It's a lie," Giulietta said firmly.

She went inside without saying goodbye, dismissed Pietro to wherever he went when dismissed and made straight for her chamber, where she locked the door behind her and curled into a ball on her bed, letting the sobs take her. The afternoon had been going so well until Frederick ruined it. She hated Venice. She hated Frederick, too.

24

The sound of Lady Giulietta's tantrum brought Marco from his chamber to find Pietro crouched across her doorway. "Y-you shouldn't be here."

The boy scrambled to his feet. He was thin and tousled-haired, still a child. Better fed, however, than when Marco first spared his life. Finding his courage, the boy said, "Lord Tycho . . ."

"Said you s-should l-look after her?"

Tycho's page nodded.

"Then, of c-course, you m-must."

Turning the corner into this conversation, Duchess Alexa smiled. It was exactly what she expected Marco to say. He seemed so much clearer about what was going on around him since his uncle had gone. It would be terrible to discover Marco's idiocy . . .

I'm not even going to finish that thought. Alexa had always prided herself on facing difficult truths head on, but tonight was different. Neither her son nor Pietro knew how different, and how could she tell them? "What is he doing here?" she demanded.

The page choked on his answer.

"H-he's with me," said Marco, earning a glance so grateful Alexa knew the duke had a follower for life.

"In that case . . ." Alexa ruffled the child's hair.

The boy would remember that, too. No matter how old he grew or what he became in later life he would remember the night the duke of Venice lied for him, and the duke's fearsome mother ruffled his hair. Of such tiny memories were lives made.

The night was so cold that frost bloomed inside the glass, and all the fire did was fill the corridor with smoke and make their clothes smell.

"You must to bed," she told Marco. "Tomorrow will be a hard day, take my word for it." Leaning forward, she kissed him, whispering *sorry* as her mouth touched his ear. Let him decide what for. Going to Alonzo's bed had been a mistake. Not realising Alonzo would take the act as proof they'd formed an alliance and kill her husband was a worse one.

"I'm glad you're getting better."

Marco's eyes went huge as he considered this. His father had been a simple man. His nickname *the Just* a tribute to his ability to see everything as black or white. She doubted her son had ever seen the world in anything except complex shades of grey. She'd come to realise he'd seen too much.

"Bed now," she insisted.

Leaning forward, he kissed her back. He was intuitive enough to know something was wrong and discreet enough not to ask what, although he would know soon enough. Sighing, Alexa watched her son return to his room, humming some ditty about icy hearts and frosted thighs. It was a plea to reluctant maids to give what they held dear, since the world was ending and what use were honour and virginity now . . . Half the young men in the city were singing it. Where did he learn these things given that some days he barely left his room?

"Sit by the window," she told the boy.

The first time Alexa knocked Giulietta didn't hear. At least, her sobbing didn't stop or her sniffing change pitch. So Alexa knocked harder and heard Giulietta groan, "Go away."

She was seventeen, Alexa reminded herself. At seventeen, she'd been as unhappy as this, that was the truth of it. Some girls were born happy and remained so through their storm years – the late Lady Desdaio, for example – but Alexa had not been one of them and neither was her niece.

"Giulietta . . ."

"I said go away."

At which Alexa knocked hard enough to make her knuckles hurt, and loudly enough to have two guards come running. In a final act of kindness she decided to give them their lives, although she doubted they'd understand this was what she'd done or believe it of her. "Leave," she said. "Do not return."

They hesitated.

"Did you hear me?"

The men glanced at each other, some thought passing in a flicker, and they bowed, leaving quickly and not glancing back. They would report her order to their sergeant who would wake their lieutenant, who would wake Captain Weimer, who now commanded the palace guard. That would take time, which was good because she needed time. Only a little of it to be sure, because that was all she had left anyway. Just enough to do what needed to be done. Knocking harder, Alexa heard sudden silence and imagined Giulietta was wondering if she dared tell her aunt to go away a third time.

Alexa was the duchess. Sole Regent now Alonzo was gone.

When the bolt on the door shot back, Alexa felt almost sorry that her niece had surrendered so easily. Childhood obedience was a hard habit to break and one she would need to break if she was to rule well. Being impressed because people were older, because they were male, because they were impressed with themselves made a bad foundation for choosing friends and a worse one for choosing advisers. Her niece would be surrounded with flatterers. Alexa just wished there was a way to make the next few days easier for the young woman now opening her door, the scowl on her face sulky enough to suit a twelve-year-old.

"May I come in?"

Giulietta looked surprised.

So Alexa waited until her niece stepped back, opened the door a little further and waved her aunt inside. A brazier burnt in the corner, and one window was wide open. She knew she should say something about wasting coal but couldn't bring herself to. Giulietta would discover how little was left in her own time.

"Are you all right?" Giulietta said.

Alexa smiled sadly. "I should be asking you that but I already know the answer." Reaching forward, she wiped a half-dried tear from Giulietta's face. "What did Frederick say to you?"

"How do you know it was Frederick?"

"Who else would it be?"

"He said that Tycho had offered his loyalty to Uncle Alonzo. To Uncle Alonzo. How could Frederick even imagine . . . He said he'd offered him the Blade."

"It's true."

Lady Giulietta froze.

"I've had those reports, too." The duchess hesitated, torn between being lying and the truth, between being harsh and being kind. She was happy to lie on matters of state but tried not to lie to her own family unless necessary. Who knew what was kind where Giulietta was concerned? Her pretty if vapid mother killed, her father a monster. Her late husband only happy to bed boys. As for her would-be second husband, he was another problem altogether. And then there was Frederick.

She saw no problem with Giulietta being in love with two people at once. Men did that all the time. She'd loved Marco, and loved Lord Atilo. The Regent had been a mistake. Her going to his bed a simple attempt to protect her son. Looking up, the duchess realised her niece was still waiting for her to speak. "Your uncle and Tycho met in a forest near the Red Cathedral."

"*You knew?*" Giulietta looked as if she'd been slapped.

"Look at strange objects from all sides before deciding what they are."

"That was one of my uncle's sayings." She meant Marco the Just.

"Exactly. Tycho might have his reasons."

"Oh, he's got his reasons all right. He leaves without telling me and then I discover he's changed sides. *I'm never going to get Leo back.*"

"Listen to me . . ." Alexa's voice was so sharp Giulietta stiffened and Alexa sighed. *This is impossible . . . I've made her too like me*, Alexa realised. Saying goodbye to Marco had been simple. A kiss, a *sorry*, he'd know she'd loved him. In the red-haired girl standing in front of her, Alexa saw herself. Her hair was the wrong colour, her skin too olive, her eyes had those strange Western folds. She was scrawny where Alexa had been lithe, her hips sharp against her nightgown, but staring from those pale eyes . . . She'd proved, to her own satisfaction, it was who brought the child up, not who the parents were, that mattered.

"I have always loved you," Alexa said.

Giulietta looked stunned.

"As much as if you were my own daughter. If I could have made you my daughter I would have done. Marco wouldn't allow it." She smiled sourly. "He said it would turn the Arsenalotti and the Nicoletti against you. They would say it was because I wanted to train you in poisons and witchcraft."

Wide eyes watched Alexa.

Oh, you'll remember this night. For the wrong reasons at first, and later, if Alexa was lucky, for the right ones. That would make a difference in the years to come. She needed the girl to be a good Regent, to continue doing the things Alexa had always done; smoothing the way to treaties and removing obstacles when necessary. So many threads for Alexa to tie off, so little time left for tying.

"You were a difficult child."

Giulietta smiled.

"That you're proud of it is just one of the reasons you remind me of me." Yes, she thought that would surprise Giulietta. "I've tried to teach you what you need to know."

"Tycho asked if you'd trained me."

"In what?"

Giulietta coloured. "I thought he meant *the arts of love*. They say . . ."

"Of course they do." Alexa was meant to have kept the late duke enslaved and in her power with unspeakable skills. As if a man like Marco couldn't simply fall in love with his wife once the wedding and bedding were done. Marco could recognise good advice, even when it came from a woman and a foreigner. "What *did* he mean?"

"Shielding my thoughts, I think."

"Of course I taught you," Alexa said. "How could you survive in this cesspit if you couldn't shield your thoughts? How could anyone survive? Some lessons you don't learn by sitting at a desk with books in front of you. In fact, most lessons that matter you don't learn like that." Leaning forward, Alexa kissed her niece on both cheeks and then on the forehead. "Sleep well, my dear."

"And you," Giulietta said.

"I intend to . . ."

The corridor outside was empty of guards so Alexa guessed the sergeant was still trying to wake the lieutenant or the lieutenant wake the captain. Either way, no one saw her climb the stairs to where Tycho's page waited by her study door. "What's your name again?"

"Pietro, my lady."

"Stay there." Vanishing inside, Alexa returned with a lizard the height of a small cat, although longer. The boy's eyes widened as the creature turned its baleful orange gaze on him and ruffled its neck frill in irritation. A second later, it spread leathery wings and Pietro gasped. "He's just showing off," said Alexa, as she put the dragonet into the boy's arms. "You'll find he does that a lot. Now, touch your forehead to his."

The boy shook his head.

"*Pietro* . . ."

He flushed, torn between two fears.

"It's how they make friends," she said, which was close to the truth in that it wasn't exactly a lie, more a massive simplification. "Do it now."

The boy put his head to the dragon's and flinched.

"His name's *dracul*, which means little dragon in my mother's language. He's yours," she added. "Tell Duke Marco I said that. He's yours to keep." She ushered the page along the corridor and told him to sit with the dragonet in the window seat overlooking the Molo. "If anybody asks you have orders from me to sit there. In a while dracul will grow restless and want to fly. You will wait for his return."

"Will he want to fly every night?"

She smiled at his mixture of wonder and worry. "Only tonight," she promised. "He has one last job for me. After that he belongs only to you." She patted the boy's shoulder, scratched dracul under his chin and left them there. How old was he? Nine, ten . . .? She doubted the boy was eleven. With those born into poverty it was hard to tell. Old enough to be a reliable witness, though. And she'd made him invaluable; she hoped Lord Tycho appreciated the gesture. Pietro would become the duke's eyes for as long as the dragonet lived, and they lived for a very long time. He would be the perfect spy.

It was time, or as close as made no difference.

Afraid? Of course she was. Who wouldn't be? Alexa poured rainwater from a silver jug into her jade bowl with as much care and solemnity as if conducting a final tea ceremony, and she was proud of how little her fingers shook and how steadily she poured. Closing her eyes, she concentrated on what she wanted to see, pinned the figure in her mind and waited. It was a while before she heard the scratch of a knife at her window.

"Come in," she said. "It's unlocked."

25

"My lady . . ." Tycho swept a low bow.

So little had changed, he thought, looking round Alexa's study. She sat – where he'd expected to find her, if he found her awake – at her desk, with that bowl in front of her. He watched her sweep her fingers across the water inside and smile. Having dried her fingers, she covered the bowl with a cloth and settled back, studying Tycho carefully. She said, "You're thinner. I wouldn't have thought that possible. Have you been eating?"

He stared at her.

"You could feed now."

"My lady . . ."

"Call me Alexa. If you can't call me Alexa now . . . Not that it's my name. But I've learnt to answer to it like some exotic pet."

It was as if she knew why he was here, Tycho realised. He would need something of hers, drenched in blood. Her dress would be distinctive enough. If he talked fast and moved faster, he'd have a week and maybe more to make his peace with Alonzo, trick his way into the Red Cathedral and steal back Lady Giulietta's child before the news that Alexa still lived reached him.

"It won't work."

"My lady . . ."

"I know what you're thinking. It shows in your eyes. Sometimes you forget to shield your thoughts. Usually when you're upset or worried. Like now."

"I need a favour."

"No. You need to kill me."

"That's not why . . ."

"Why you're here? It should be. You're the Blade. Your job is to keep the city safe. You think anything less than my death will convince Alonzo? He has spies in this court. We need to do this properly."

"A blood-splattered dress . . ."

"Will not be enough. Do you want Leo to die?" She smiled sourly. "You think that's unfair? When have I ever had the luxury of being fair? The Millioni became my family when I married Marco and I will protect them, even from themselves. This city *needs* Leo. Do you know why?"

Tycho shook his head.

"Because every throne needs an heir. There is nothing more dangerous to thrones than no heir to sit in them. It scares the loyal and tempts traitors." Alexa sucked her teeth. "I've known it make traitors of the loyal. My son will not produce an heir so Giulietta's son must do instead. Find me Prince Leo di Millioni and bring him back. It's harder for traitors to kill two princes than one."

"Have you considered restoring the Republic?"

"That's what Giulietta wants? Of course she does, she's young and romantic, she thinks herself a rebel. She'll grow out of it. People rule or are ruled, those are the choices."

"I don't want to rule. Simply not be ruled."

"Tycho . . . You're not normal."

He took a chair without asking and examined the woman opposite. She was as beautiful as the last time he saw her without her veil, with an ageless face and flawless skin. Her eyes were deep brown and bright, but there was a tiredness to her smile and she held his gaze with effort.

Tycho stared at Alexa and realisation dawned.

She smiled at his surprise, and for a second he saw, amongst the tiredness and the lines that sickness had etched on her face, pleasure at a plan coming together as intended. "Yes," she said. "I pushed Alonzo to this point."

"Why, my lady?"

"I'm dying . . . We're all dying, obviously, I'm just doing it rather faster than I was, and you're doing it a little more slowly than everybody else. I have a year if I want to draw things out. Six months if I let it take me. Two years ago you came to kill me. Now finish the job. Did anyone see you?"

Tycho shook his head.

"You're sure?"

Of course I am . . . The streets and frozen canal behind the palace had been silent, the fierce cold of the night had done what Watch captains only achieved in their dreams – cleared the city of whores, revellers and robbers. The palace guard had been so cold they simply stared at their feet.

"Quite sure," Tycho said.

"You need to look up more."

Pushing himself out of his chair, Tycho went to the window and let in the cold as he opened the shutters. A patch of darkness swept circles in front of the slender stars, showing darker still when it bisected a sliver of cloud.

"Remember my dragonet?"

He remembered it right enough. The little lizard had been waiting at the house Alexa gave him, starving seemingly. Now he suspected dracul was just greedy. It had taken Tycho a while to realise the dragonet acted as her eyes. Abandoning the dragonet to its high circling, Tycho closed the shutters and turned to find Alexa had removed the cloth from her jade bowl.

"Take this with you."

"What is it?"

"The most valuable thing in Venice."

Tycho glanced at the translucent bowl and thought of the *pala d'oro*, San Marco's gold and jewelled altar screen with its two thousand precious stones and painting of Christ in Majesty. Nothing in Europe was more sacred or precious. So Giulietta said. He came closer. "Stare into it," Alexa ordered.

And see what? Clear water in limpid stone?

"Close your eyes, think of what you most want to see and open them again." The duchess's voice was almost matter of fact enough to make him ignore the enamelled dagger she was taking from a drawer and placing in front of her. "Close them then. Now open them."

Opening his eyes, Tycho saw Giulietta naked.

He glanced up to discover Alexa was still turning the dagger over in her fingers. "Exquisite," she said. When Tycho returned his gaze to the bowl, Giulietta had put on a nightgown and a lady-in-waiting Tycho didn't recognise was tying the ribbons at her neck.

"It shows what you want to see. Occasionally, if you're lucky, it shows what you need to see. Now, we've wasted enough time. You know what comes next . . ." Her hand trembled as she offered him the knife.

"I have daggers of my own."

"Of course you do. But Marco gave me this when we were married. The city's finest armourer made it. Can you imagine the outrage . . .?"

Tycho's mouth opened.

"The duchess killed *with her own knife*. Take the dagger with you and give it to Alonzo, with my blood still on the blade." She held up her hand to show the wedding ring Marco had placed on her finger. "And take this."

"My lady."

"Do it," Alexa said fiercely. "The cities will talk of nothing else. Even if you arrive before the news, outrage will follow so closely it could be your shadow. Alonzo will embrace you like a brother." Taking his hand, she folded his fingers round the enamel of the handle and put the point to her breast. Her hand trembled only slightly.

Tycho said, "What do I tell Giulietta?"

"Try the truth. She's had little enough of that in her life."

"My lady . . ."

"You've seen my niece as naked as the day she was born, if not as innocent. She will forgive you."

"And if she doesn't?"

"Then she will have to forget you . . . Those are the options. One final thing, you must drink my blood." Her eyes narrowed at his reluctance. "You think what I know isn't worth learning?"

He stabbed then, seeing her eyes widen. Grating across a rib, his blade reached her heart and touched muscle.

"*Murder*," she screamed.

Hot blood spurted across Tycho's fingers as his blade came free with a disgusting sucking noise. She dropped and he followed, drinking straight from the wound as her fingers gripped his hair, holding him against her. Feet pounded along the corridor outside.

A guard hammered on the door and kept hammering, Alexa having bolted it earlier. She was unconscious and close to death as Tycho crawled across her and tried to remove the ring from her finger. She must have known he'd need to saw it off. He turned, her finger in his hand, as the door smashed open and a guard howled at him to stop. Behind the man stood Pietro, mouth open and face white with shock. He looked from Alexa to where Tycho crouched and his face crumpled.

"Don't move," the guard shouted.

Tycho threw himself backwards through the window, landed clumsily in the garden below and ran for a tree he remembered climbing once before. He jumped from the tree to a wall, a narrow canal flashing below him as he leapt for a roof beyond. An arrow and then another followed . . . They were shooting at shadows for the sake of it. He could hear yells from inside. More shouting in the courtyard beyond.

How could you make me do that?

Tears streamed down Tycho's face and soured his throat, as salt as Alexa's blood and filled with as much sorrow. Her memories were his, and though some already faded like half-remembered dreams, others bedded in where they were needed. He had Mongol, a language he'd barely recognised as words before. Poisons and potions, schematics of more plots than he could imagine. Alonzo had been behind most of them; and Tycho was just one of a long line of assassins who'd failed to kill her until she let him.

He should have realised he was not the first. The most desperate perhaps, possibly the most expensive for Alonzo to arrange, but not the first, second or third . . . That the assassin before him had been a Persian turned from his faith at vast expense told Tycho all he needed to know. He had been Alonzo's last throw.

After Tycho, Alonzo changed tactics.

Around Tycho the street hunkered down in silence, little knowing the clamour and outrage the next few hours would bring. The windows stared blind and dark, the locked doors were silent mouths and sealed lips. And he sobbed as he ran, unsure what he was sobbing for, unless it was the memory of Alexa's unforgiving courage, the shock of what she'd asked him to do. Streets became shoreline and then the ice of the lagoon, and still he ran. Where the sea became too salt and restless to freeze the lagoon ended in a ragged frill of rotten ice. The small lugger that had delivered him to the ice shelf waited off the ledge, a merchant ship waiting beyond that.

Alonzo's letters had smoothed the way. In some weird manner, Tycho's demand for gold and letters allowing him to commandeer a Montenegrin ship had convinced the Regent he was serious, that he would do what Alonzo demanded. Without that, Tycho would never have been allowed to leave the clearing, while Alonzo put Amelia into Lord Roderigo's care and the rest of Alonzo's courtiers looked on wondering what they were watching.

A sailor on the lugger lifted his lamp and swore at the blood on Tycho's hands and his tear-streaked face. Tycho tossed him Alexa's jade bowl. "What's this?" the man demanded.

"The most valuable thing in Venice."

26

Lady Giulietta knew she should have put a wrap over her night-gown, but it was more than this that made the guards refuse to meet her eyes. Faces tight, they looked as if they wanted to hurry past. "I said, what's happened?"

"Giulietta."

The voice came from behind. Her name without hesitation or stutter. Turning, she saw Marco flanked by guards with torches. His face was pale and his gaze serious. It took her a moment to realise he was dressed.

"You couldn't sleep?"

"It's almost as if she knew," he said.

Who knew? Knew what? Giulietta's fingers tightened into fists as her cousin turned for a window to stare at snowflakes falling from a grey, dark sky. On either side of him, guards came to a standstill. "But how could she know?" Answering, "This was my mother. How could she not know?"

"Marco . . . *What's happened?*"

Then she knew because a slight body was carried from Alexa's study on a bier. Although a blanket covered it, blood had soaked through grey wool to leave a crimson stain where her heart would be. "*Don't . . .*" Marco shouted. His words came too late to stop Giulietta from lifting the blanket away.

So beautiful . . . Aunt Alexa looked asleep.

Lady Giulietta couldn't help dragging the blanket down to reveal her aunt's wound. And though Marco came to stand beside her, he let her touch her finger to the blood-soaked tear in Alexa's gown. "I'm so sorry," she said.

"Me too." Marco's arm went round her, and she leant her head into his shoulder. "Now, let them d-do their job . . ." He moved her back and one of his guards replaced the blanket before the bier was carried away. "I've told them to t-take her to the crypt." Marco's eyes were unreadable. "Many more b-bodies and we'll have to stack them somewhere else."

Shock. This has to be the shock talking. "Who did this?"

"That can wait. First I must s-secure the city." Gesturing to Captain Weimer, he called the man closer. "Wake the Ten, tell them they're n-needed now. Accept no excuses, everyone is to attend."

The captain was surprised at Marco's crispness. This was not the duke he or his officers knew. This duke was already glaring beyond him to palace guards crowding the stairs as they fought to present themselves.

"Weimer."

He seemed shocked Marco knew his name.

"Throw a c-cordon round Ca' Ducale. Put archers on the roof and wrap them warm, they're no used to me half d-dead from cold. Have a fire lit in the s-smaller state room, if anyone comes from the embassies p-put them there. Have them g-given wine and f-food, water and food for the Mamluks and Moors. Send a m-messenger to let me know."

"Yes, highness."

The duke headed for the stairs down which his mother's body had just vanished and his bodyguard hurried after. "If shock can make fools of men," Lady Giulietta said to Captain Weimer, who stared after them.

"It can make men of . . ." He didn't dare finish his sentence.

"He was brilliant as a child, my aunt said."

Captain Weimer nodded, and Giulietta left him pondering as she hurried after Marco, who was in a corridor below ordering braziers be lit in the council room and letters sent to other princes informing them his mother was dead. She wondered how Marco expected the letters to be carried in his weather and realised he regarded this as a problem for the head of his messenger service. Mostly she wondered how he could be so *calm*.

You're not a child. You're not a child. She repeated the words every time she felt tears. She *would not* cry into front of all of these people. But a life without Aunt Alexa . . .

"Follow me," Marco said.

Giulietta obeyed without question.

Three guards stood in a side room, with Tycho's page hunched on a seat with her aunt's lizard on his lap. The boy looked frozen with horror and the guards nervous. The dragonet merely glared balefully. "So," Marco said to the senior guard. "Tell me again why you weren't guarding my m-mother's door."

"She dismissed us, your highness."

"Dismissed you?"

"The duchess ordered us to leave. She said that if we were questioned about this we were to say it was her direct command."

"If you were questioned . . .?"

"Yes, highness."

Marco considered the point, and Giulietta watched him assess the man who spoke. Typically Venetian, with curling black hair, and the strong nose and full lips seen mostly in the west of the city. He looked Castellano and his accent confirmed it. He would have a family, wife and children. He would have been chosen carefully and had no reason to lie. If he said Aunt Alexa dismissed him . . .

"And then?"

168

"I heard the duchess scream *murder* . . ."

Giulietta dug her nails into her hands. How could Marco *bear* this? She wanted to vomit, and he just stood there impassively. Like a prince, she thought. Like his mother. He watched, considered and listened the way Alexa said a prince should behave. The way Giulietta had never been able to behave herself.

"So you d-disobeyed her order to stay away?"

The guard obviously hadn't thought of it that way.

"I would have d-done the same," Marco said.

Relief flooded the man's face and those either side of him relaxed slightly. "The door was locked, highness. So we broke it down, we were desperate." There was truth to his words, and he moved carefully, like a man who'd bruised his shoulder. One of the others had cuts on his hands.

"Go on." Marco said. "Spare no d-detail."

The man swallowed. "The duchess was on the floor, dead already. There was blood all around her, and her hand . . ." He hesitated. "He was hacking off her ring finger with a knife."

"Who was?" Giulietta demanded, feeling violently sick.

Marco raised his hand to silence her. "There are three of you. Why d-didn't you arrest him?"

"Highness, he threw himself through the window."

"It's three floors up. He'd have b-broken something."

The man Marco spoke to glanced at Giulietta, whose throat soured. *No*, she thought. *No* . . . She knew instantly what he wanted to say, opened her mouth to stop him from saying it and shook her head.

"Highness." The man gulped. "It was Lord Tycho."

"That's not true." Giulietta knew her voice was loud. "Make him take it back. Tycho would never . . ." She grabbed her cousin's arm. "You must believe me. The man's lying. He has it wrong. It was someone disguised as Tycho."

"Who survived a d-drop from a third-floor window?"

"Magic," Giulietta insisted. "Someone made to look like him

and given his . . . powers. He's in Montenegro. How could he possibly be here?"

"My love . . ."

"*It can't be him.*" She sounded desperate, even to herself.

"My lady . . ." Pietro, Tycho's page, stood with Aunt Alexa's winged lizard in his arms like an ungainly cat.

"What are you doing with dracul?"

"He's mine." Pietro took a breath. "I mean, the duchess said I was to have him. That he was mine now." Pietro rested his head against the dragonet's forehead and his expression when he lifted his head away was bleak. He looked as sick as she felt. "My master did this." His words were a whisper. "It was him."

"Pietro . . ."

"*Why would he do this?*"

"Return to your d-duties," Duke Marco told the guards.

Giulietta wanted to accuse the boy of lying. Ask him how he dared betray the man who freed him from prison, ended his life as a street rat and made him his own page. Pietro would be dead if not for Tycho. Dead, or starving in a gutter. But the boy's face was hollow with guilt and horror, and she knew he'd asked himself those questions already. "Speak," Marco said.

The boy gulped and held the dragonet tighter. "I saw Lord Tycho in the window, before he threw himself to the ground. Dracul saw more, he saw him arrive and followed when he left. He was met on the edge of the ice by a boat that rowed to a ship further out. The sailors sank the boat."

How could he know these things? Why didn't Marco ask how he knew? "I suppose the lizard talks to you?"

"We share thoughts," Pietro mumbled.

Marco looked intrigued. "Think c-carefully. You share, or you k-know dracul's?" This new Marco was scary, so icily measured Giulietta wondered if he'd even loved his mother.

"I know his thoughts," Pietro said finally. "Except they're not *thoughts*. I see what he has seen but he doesn't understand it and I do."

"Let me." Taking the winged lizard, Marco put his forehead to the creature's skull and trembled. His face was unreadable when he gave dracul back. "Clearly it only w-works for you."

Pietro bit his lip.

"Now t-tell me again how you come to have my m-mother's gift from the Khan?" The boy repeated his story of sitting outside Lady Giulietta's door listening to her sob, and how the duchess sent him away. Giulietta wasn't sure which surprised her most. The boy being there in the first place, or Alexa not being furious to find a page wandering the family floor . . .

"And later," Pietro said, "she brought me the dragon."

"*She brought you the dragon?*" Giulietta said.

"She told me to put my head to his, my lady. Then took the beast away as he had one last task to perform for her."

Marco looked very thoughtful indeed.

27

Horns blew and scared away any quarry not already gone to ground. The early morning hunting party that rode out from the Red Cathedral had gone in search of sport and food. The sport was all Alonzo's men talked about, their voices warmed by pre-dawn goblets of hot wine mixed with honey and strong local brandy, but it was food they needed and only a fool would think the hunting had been good.

Luckily there were enough fools among Alonzo's followers to make the silence of those who understood how desperate things were look like distemper or a hangover. From his vantage point, Tycho watched a dozen men ride out of the dark forest towards the village and frozen lake beyond.

Alonzo led them. But close behind, holding a flaming brand and grinning widely, was a thickset man, wrapped in a lavish fox fur that glowed smoky red in the light from the torch he held. *A local princeling?* Too neatly barbered and too well dressed. And unless that cloak's curing was very good indeed the fur must stink enough to have told the prey they were coming. So either it was cured, or the man with the oiled beard was too important for Alonzo to offend. Tycho wondered if he'd seen the man before and decided not.

Lord Roderigo rode a horse's length behind, looking unhappy to find himself relegated to a lesser place. As for those who followed, few were Venetian, most Montenegrin or renegade Crucifer. These last looked a little wilder, talked a little louder and had clearly drunk deeper than their companions. Their noise was such that the man with Alonzo looked back in irritation. His glare stilled them into silence.

Interesting, Tycho thought.

Standing, Tycho shook snow from his cloak and waited for one of them to see him. It was a local huntsman, who brought a life's experience of looking for prey in the half-dark of dawns and twilights. The man spurred his horse forward, drew closer to Prince Alonzo and pointed . . .

"You're back."

"Obviously, my lord."

The Regent flushed and Tycho cursed inwardly. He needed to learn to hold his tongue around this man. Without Alonzo's blessing he would never find his way past the demons in the makeshift moat. "I've brought you gifts." Unbuckling a satchel at his side, Tycho produced a cloth-wrapped parcel and revealed Alexa's bowl.

"What is that meant to be?"

"The most valuable thing in Venice."

Alonzo scowled, obviously wondering if Tycho was mocking him. He refused to take the bowl from Tycho's hands. "And then there's this." Tycho held up a blood-stained knife. "Recognise it, my lord? And finally, this . . ." He dropped a ringed finger into the bowl, hearing it clink as metal hit stone. "I'm sure you recognise that."

This time Alonzo took the bowl and held it carefully, his eyes drawn to the severed finger, although it was the dried blood on Alexa's dagger that made him dismount and draw closer. "Tell me everything."

"She died bravely once she realised she had to die." That at least was true. Tycho hoped Alexa's ghost would forgive him what followed. "She offered me gold, your highness. Gold, titles and Giulietta's hand. A place on the Council of Ten, and a place on the throne beside Lady Giulietta when the time came."

"What did you do?"

"Killed her anyway."

The Regent glanced to where Lord Roderigo sat, watching intently. Then he looked at the fox-furred man, realised he looked amused, and scowled. "I don't believe you," he said. "It's a trick."

For the next two days, Tycho remained locked in a circular cell. His prison walls were wood, and curved out towards the waist and in at the top. The room stank of decay and bird shit, mould and something feral. Endless scratching like scrabbling fingers came from outside, and Tycho realised he was imprisoned in one of the dozen or more onion domes decorating the cathedral's roof. The scrabbling had to be crows or other large carrion birds.

The space inside was big enough to hold ten, but he had it to himself. To make sure he remained secure the hatch had been nailed shut. A hundred wild-haired and high-cheeked tribesmen had watched Tycho enter with the Regent and his Byzantine companion. Because that's who the fox-furred man turned out to be. A Byzantine duke called Tiresias who looked surprised and then impressed when told Tycho's name. The Regent himself had led Tycho through crowds of renegade Crucifers, and up a twist of stairs, along a rotting gallery to a makeshift set of stairs to a landing made from planks nailed between two beams.

Smoke filled the air from a central fire as he was led to his cell. Braziers stood in a ring around the cathedral walls, with split logs and broken planks piled high to keep the fires burning. The air was stale from two hundred unwashed soldiers, their faces red from wine and made redder by the flicker of torches. It had been like passing through hell.

At the end of his second day, the nails were dragged from the lengths of wood fixing his trapdoor in place and Alonzo stood on the landing below. "We're still waiting," he said. "If you're lying, you'll die. If you're not . . ." Alonzo shrugged. "We'll unnail the hatch again." A scuffle behind Alonzo only stopped when a naked woman was dragged forward, ordered to put her foot into the step a soldier made by joining his hands, and boosted through the hatch into his onion dome.

"Have some company," Alonzo said.

It was the farmer's daughter from the night Tycho was sent to kill Alexa. Her face was bruised so badly one eye was closed. She looked terrified and pissed herself when a guard slammed the hatch and began nailing it shut.

"Not in here," she begged. "Not in here."

As Tycho reached for her, she began to scream. Outside the door, the soldier with the hammer jeered when Tycho slammed his hand over her mouth and her yells were cut short. She was younger than he remembered, with small pink-tipped teats and wide hips. Although she'd been stripped, the guards had tossed her rags after her. "Dress," Tycho ordered. Then he remembered she couldn't see in the dark, so he reached for her skirt and put it in her hand. "Put that on and hurry."

"You don't want me?" *Everyone else has taken me*, her voice said. Half the men and all the knights had raped her, no doubt.

"I want you dressed."

"*Domovoi*," she said, voice flat. "*Domovoi . . .*"

"No," Tycho said. "I'm not a monster."

"You don't understand. Up here is where the domovoi live. Hundreds of them . . ." She looked round, as if expecting to see demons in the darkness. All Tycho could see was rotting wood and stained walls. Telling her that did little to put her mind at ease. After a few minutes she subsided into mutters and the occasional sob, and shortly after that Tycho forgot that she was there at all.

* * *

How long had Alexa known she was dying? That was the question Tycho wanted to unpick, although why it should matter was another question altogether. Was Alexa heroic or cowardly to make Tycho end her life?

Sinking back against a strangely sloping wall, he pulled up his knees, wrapped his arms around them and rested his chin on his knees as he examined every memory he'd taken from her. She'd been five when her husband came to his throne, a small girl in another country, unaware Venice even existed. She'd been eleven when the marriage was arranged, twelve when it was consummated, fifteen when she had her first child and not from lack of trying. It died, as did the one after, and the one after that, and the one after that.

It took Marco sending his brother on a year-long campaign in the south for a child of hers to live. She was twenty-three and pathetically grateful his subjects no longer had barrenness or dead babies as a reason to hate her. She studied poisons in the years that followed, although she learnt antidotes first. Simple magic after that, deeper magic later.

Hugging his knees, Tycho considered what this new knowledge brought him. Little he hadn't worked out for himself. Most of Venice's policy had been made on the fly, actions and reactions, strategies born of disaster, tactics shaped by mistakes. Much of what looked intentional was simply accident, only inevitable in hindsight. After a while, Tycho realised the farmer's daughter had come to crouch beside him. She froze when he reached for her, but shuffled closer and after a while he felt her settle against his shoulder.

"Sleep now," Tycho ordered.

But she wanted to say something. Tycho waited while she opened her mouth half a dozen times and swallowed her words before sitting back defeated. Now she was cross with herself. "You can tell me," he promised. Part of it was cynical: he wanted news of Amelia. A farmer's daughter, passed from soldier to soldier, would have heard more than those abusing her realised.

She said, "Domovoi."

Sighing, Tycho asked his question anyway. The black woman was somewhere. The answers drew another sigh and a fresh order that she should sleep. It was an hour before exhaustion took her and she slumped against his shoulder. Another hour and a dead arm before he let her slip sideways, cradling her head and stroking her hair as he might stroke a cat.

As her breathing slowed, and she lost herself to dreamless sleep, he bent for her wrist and bit tenderly, warm blood filling his mouth. He warmed his bones with a single gulp, just enough to clear his mind of Alexa. Having fed, he gave the girl a drop of his blood in return. Not enough to turn her, as Rosalyn turned, but enough to lend her strength and help her heal. A second drop he smoothed across the worst of the bruising on her face, touching her one place else before he woke her. "What's your name?"

"What is it to you?"

Tycho grinned. That was more like it.

"I'm Tycho," he said. "I live in Venice with a girl called Giulietta."

"You're not *Romaioi*?" She scowled like someone tricked. "They said that a . . ."

"I saw him when I arrived. He's older and has an oiled beard. They called him Tiresias and his cloak stinks. It's fox fur. You didn't see him?"

She shook her head.

The Romaioi were Byzantine aristocrats who traced their descent from the Romans and ruled the Greeks and Seljuks who peopled an empire that still styled itself as Eastern Roman, for all the Rome-based half of the empire had fallen a thousand years before. "So," Tycho repeated. "What's your name?"

Melina was fifteen, and her father had owned the only mill in the valley, which had belonged to his father and his father before that. She sobbed when she mentioned her mother. This told Tycho all he needed to know and he let her cry herself out against his shoulder. She talked and he listened for the rest of that day, her chatter broken only when bodily need won over modesty and Melina vanished to the far side of the dome to pee on bare boards. An hour later, to great embarrassment, she returned there to empty her bowels.

We're animals, Tycho thought. A day into darkness and already she was returning to her spore. Well, she was an animal, though one with a soul if her priests were to be believed. What he was, was an altogether more difficult question.

The second day was stranger. Scratching from beyond the wooden walls woke him from death-like sleep. The roof beyond sounded alive with scuttling and scurrying, scratching and clawing, as whatever was out there fought to find a way in. Melina huddled at his side, hands over her ears.

"Rats," Tycho told her.

"Domovoi," she insisted.

Melina did what wounded animals did and curled around her misery and fear, dozing fitfully until real sleep took her. On the third day, things changed.

"Wake," he told Melina.

"What's happening?"

"They're about to open the trapdoor."

She scrambled to her feet and stood behind him as a claw hammer was forced under nail heads and wood screamed as the nail withdrew. Alonzo stood below, with Roderigo beside him, holding a burning torch.

"You've been banished," Alonzo announced. "All *good Venetians* are to kill you on sight. The Council have offered five thousand gold ducats for your head. You are stripped of your titles and your name has been struck from the books. The Pope has been asked to excommunicate you." He handed up a goblet of wine. "You really did it," he said. "You killed the Mongol bitch."

Lord Roderigo's face was unreadable.

Taking the goblet, Tycho stared at the liquid in the bowl. He put it down without tasting. "What are domovoi?" he demanded.

Alonzo turned to a renegade Crucifer behind him. The man muttered something in broken Latin. Roderigo answered first. "He says monsters, like you."

28

They met in the corridor with the window seat and sat together, saying little and staring at an old tapestry of a unicorn resting its head on the lap of a virgin. It had looked so sweet when she was a girl. Now Giulietta knew what happened to the Maid, and what happened to the unicorn, too. It was killed, and its horn sawn off and sold. Her cousin, who sat beside her turning a letter over in his hands, had half a dozen unicorn horns in his cabinet of curiosities. She'd reached her first bleed before it occurred to her how sad that was.

A unicorn tapestry, a brazier against the cold, mice behind the panelling and a harpsichord untouched since Frederick last played it. Giulietta wished she'd learnt to play properly, but she'd never got beyond her scales and was too embarrassed and too sad to play, so she sat and waited.

Marco hadn't exactly summoned her; more sent a note saying he was sure she knew there was a Council meeting that afternoon, and it would be kind if she could spare him a few minutes first. It was the gentleness of his rebuke that shocked her out of her misery. So she'd splashed cold water on her face, changed her clothes, brushed her hair for the first time in a week and gone to find him.

She almost wished she hadn't.

Lady Giulietta was now Regent, she knew she was Regent, it was just . . . *Oh God, it was just what, you idiot? You thought you wouldn't have to take the meeting? You thought you'd just sit in your room issuing orders and sulking? You really thought they'd let Marco take the meeting himself?*

"I'm sorry," she said.

Marco shrugged her apology away. "You should r-read this."

She expected the letter to be from his mother. Instead it was from the long-dead Marco Polo, il Millioni himself. The words were simple. The more Millioni sat on the throne of Venice the more inevitable it would seem. "You hold the throne because the people believe you hold the throne. Without this belief you have no throne to hold."

"Like f-fire-eaters," Marco said.

"Like . . .?" Giulietta was puzzled.

"We think fire-eating's d-dangerous and throw them coins for their bravery. How many dead fire-eaters have you h-heard about?"

"None," she admitted honestly.

"Exactly," he said. "Fishermen drown every w-week but who's impressed by fishermen? We b-buy their fish. Do we throw them coins for their b-bravery? Maybe we should." Marco smiled. "Come on," he said. "Let's g-get this over."

It was hard to know what outraged Lord Bribanzo most. That Lady Giulietta gave permission for the emperor's bastard to stand at the back of a meeting of the Council of Ten or that she was the new Regent and in a position to make that decision. She suspected he didn't know himself.

For once Marco sat upright and paid attention. Everyone in the room noticed this. Her cousin walked a tricky line between acting his old idiot and not admitting he'd always been sane. With Alonzo banished and his mother dead, Giulietta knew he itched to take control of the meeting and wished she knew what he would do differently.

The news from the world outside was worrying. Alonzo had offered homage to the Byzantine Empire in return for their emperor's recognition of his claim to be duke of Venice, prince of Serenissima and duke of Montenegro. The tensions inside the city following Alexa's murder were worse.

"My lords . . ."

"*This is unworkable.*" Bribanzo barely bothered to pretend he was addressing the throne. "With respect, Lady Giulietta is barely old enough to know her own mind never mind decide for others."

Lady Giulietta knew her own thoughts well enough. Anyone who began with *with respect* was being rude; and being rude to her, and ignoring Marco, showed a worrying confidence on his part. She wondered how many others felt the same.

"W-what are you s-suggesting?"

Trust her cousin to cut to the heart of things.

Lord Bribanzo looked round the small chamber. Alonzo's throne stood empty, Lord Atilo's chair had not been filled on his death, and two other chairs were also empty, their owners apparently too ill to attend. Those two would go along with whatever the majority decided but wanted to avoid the taint of having decided themselves.

"My lords, Venice needs to be strong."

Here it comes, thought Giulietta, digging her nails hard into the palms of her hands. The pain made her focus and she rested her hands carefully on her knees. She would not show anger or fear – that much she'd learnt from Aunt Alexa. The Regent's job was to appear impassive and be above common weakness. Bribanzo was rich, and until the death of his daughter Desdaio he'd been ambitious, but he was gutless. What he wanted fought with his cowardice until even the mildest Council member began to look irritated by his hesitation. Leaning forward, Giulietta said, "My lord Bribanzo. You had something to say?"

At the back of the room, Frederick smiled. He must have realised she was pretending to be her aunt. Bribanzo's fat face hardened.

"We need a strong duke . . ." That was close to treason unless he trod carefully. It turned out he'd chosen his steps with extreme care. From the nodding heads around Bribanzo, he'd talked this through with friends, unless they simply agreed, which was more worrying still.

"Is this leading somewhere?"

"Yes, my lady. You now act for Duke Marco? Is that right?"

Lady Giulietta nodded. That was a simple way of looking at her responsibilities, but not wrong. She made decisions because Marco was unable to make them for himself, and when she gave orders they were in his name.

"Then you can abdicate on his behalf."

"*Why would I do that . . .?*"

Lord Bribanzo sat back smugly, leaving Giulietta furious, mostly with herself. What was the use of pretending to be Aunt Alexa if she stopped at the critical point? She should have held her peace, been seen to think carefully before she spoke. Bribanzo's smile worried her.

"My lady," he said. "Venice needs a strong head and experience. With respect . . . You are seventeen and the duke has neither a strong head nor experience in matters of state."

"This is treason," Giulietta said.

"Not at all, my lady. I'm suggesting you abdicate on his behalf and the Council approach Prince Alonzo and offer the throne once held by his brother. Everyone knows the prince is experienced." A couple of the Council smirked.

Typical, she thought. *At a time like this they're thinking of his other conquests.*

"W-we will t-think about it."

Lady Giulietta turned, shocked at the words from beside her. Marco's face was still and his eyes guarded. He could have been thinking about murder or the weather. *That is how I should have been.*

"This meeting is at an end," she said firmly.

She saw Bribanzo glance at his friends and noted who they were. Lords Dolphini and Corte. Since Dolphini was now Alonzo's father-in-law and this would make his daughter duchess of Venice that was scarcely a surprise; and Corte came from one of the oldest families in Venice, famous for its hatred of foreigners and the late duchess in particular. That put him on Alonzo's side. Marco's enemies were rich and established. She realised, a second later, they were her enemies, too.

"We r-risk civil w-war." Marco said it the moment the door shut behind the last councillor. "The C-Castellani will side with m-my uncle. Possibly the N-Nicoletti too. He will carry m-most of the *cittadini* with a p-promise of lower t-taxes and freer t-trade. We'll k-keep the nobles and stallholders."

"Cousin," Frederick said. "There's another problem." He was no more Marco's cousin than Lady Giulietta's. It was a politeness between princes. Marco smiled to say he was listening. Frederick could speak. "My father . . ."

"Y-yes," Marco said. His voice dry. "I c-can imagine."

Sigismund would never let the Basilius claim Venice. He would move against the Byzantine emperor, and the war Duchess Alexa had spent so long trying to prevent would happen anyway. Of course, if Leo ever inherited the Venetian throne then Sigismund would effectively gain Venice and the Basilius might feel compelled to react. But he was old and had yet to choose an heir, and, if Venice was lucky, his sons and grandsons would fight among themselves.

"Why did you say you'd think about abdicating?"

"To b-buy time, obviously." He smiled. "So much is n-not what it seems. I'd have thought you both k-knew that by now."

"You have a plan? Frederick asked.

"I have s-several."

29

Upstairs on the internal balcony of the Red Cathedral Maria Dolphini screamed for hours, jagged shrieks of pain that regularly silenced those dining below. One of them, her husband, tried to visit more than once and was publicly thrown out by the local midwife. So he sat in front of untouched food and called for wine, although he drank less than usual, and certainly less than he pretended. And Tycho doubted any midwife could have kept Alonzo from his wife's birthing chamber had he really wanted to enter. The balcony was open-sided and renegade Crucifers watched Lady Dolphini's maids hurry back and forth with bowls of hot water.

Maria di Millioni, Tycho reminded himself.

She was Princess Maria di Millioni. If Alonzo had his way, she'd become duchess of Venice and sit beside him on the ducal throne. Their son – the boy being born, who was born already and over a year old – would take the throne after Alonzo, and was his son in truth, for all Maria would have to lie. Tycho wondered what Alonzo had offered the local midwife, and his wife's maids, for going through with this charade. Unless letting them keep their lives was reward enough.

Alonzo would need to keep Leo hidden for a few months, if

185

not longer; even supposedly monastic knights and heathen archers could tell the difference between a newborn and an infant. A particularly long scream had Alonzo emptying his goblet and shouting even louder for wine.

"Gods," he said. "And I thought war was brutal."

The next scream ended in the wail of a child, and Tycho immediately wondered how they'd kept Leo quiet these past few weeks. But around him men were rising to their feet to toast Alonzo, and he hurriedly joined them.

"Congratulations, your highness," Roderigo said.

Alonzo said. "Not so fast. It might have a cunny."

Someone laughed and he pulled a face. "It's happened to better men than me. Better go and check its bits, I suppose." He strode away and took the stairs with surprising ease for someone supposedly so drunk. A moment later he appeared on the balcony and shouted, "Balls and a prick . . ."

As a cheer went up he vanished inside again.

"She wants to rest," he said, when he returned. "She deserves to rest. I'll let her be for a few days and see how she does after that." He might have been talking about a horse or his falcon. His voice proud, but leaving no doubt both woman and child belonged to him as much as his horse did. The man was grinning as he returned to his seat and demanded more wine. And why not? That little charade with the screaming would bring him the throne.

Tycho said. "You must be relieved."

Alonzo squinted at him suspiciously.

"Birth can be a tricky time for a woman."

"And for a man," Alonzo said, emptying his goblet and grabbing a hunk of bread, which he chewed like a man who'd just realised he was hungry. "You wouldn't believe how bad-tempered she was by the end."

"With carrying the child?"

"What else?" Alonzo demanded crossly.

"Indeed," Tycho said. "What else. Highness, the Nubian woman who was with me when I first arrived . . ."

"I sent her south with Tiresias."

"Why? Highness?"

Alonzo looked surprised. "He wanted her."

And is probably already dead from greed, Tycho thought, wondering how long Amelia had waited before killing the Byzantine duke. She'd have to slaughter his servants, too, to make her escape, unless she made do with disabling them. Somehow that didn't sound like Amelia.

The evening passed, as most did in the Red Cathedral, with drinking and laughter and the occasional fight. They were an army waiting for battle. But it was an army made of three parts, none that perfect a fit. Tycho thought this as he watched the renegade Crucifers wander outside alone to use the privies, or drag serving girls outside to use them instead. The wild archers kept to themselves. They ate Alonzo's food but refused his drink and ignored the women. And where the Crucifers used their weapons only in drunken anger, the archers trained daily with their bows, firing and retrieving their arrows for hour after hour. When not practising their archery they tended their horses, which they treated with greater kindness than they showed each other. The last part of Alonzo's forces was his immediate followers. Venetians, like the man now walking determinedly towards Tycho.

Lord Roderigo looked out of place among the wild archers and renegade knights who crowded the cathedral floor around them. Of course, empires were conquered with men like these and Roderigo knew that, but he looked as uncomfortable as any Venetian noble dumped in a rotting church on an island in the middle of nowhere with two hundred men who hadn't washed for a month. Tycho knew his being there made it worse.

"Enjoying yourself?" Roderigo demanded.

"As much as you, I'm certain."

Scowling, Roderigo snapped his fingers at a serving girl, who came scurrying. He'd never be so coarse back home so maybe the crudeness of those around him was rubbing off or he was too drunk to care. When he slapped her arse as she left Tycho knew it was the latter. "That bitch is really dead?"

Tycho nodded. He hoped his face was impassive.

"I want to hear you say it," Roderigo said. "Say it."

"She's dead."

"How? Tell me that. How did you get past her witchcraft?"

"She was old," Tycho said. "Her magic was mostly gossip and rumour. Maybe she could see a little in the future and I don't doubt she knew her poisons . . ."

"She was a witch," Roderigo muttered. "His highness should have had her burnt. The Pope would have loved us then. Anyway, Alonzo was always the real duke."

So was history rewritten. If Alonzo succeeded, then Marco the Simple's brief reign would become a glitch in the city's glorious history. A weak pretender, unfit to rule, put on the throne by his scheming mother and removed by the rightful heir. Looking up, Tycho realised he'd missed something. "I'm sorry . . .?"

"Venetians won't stand for Giulietta being Regent, and Frederick as co-Regent would only make it worse. They'll turn out in their thousands to welcome Alonzo home."

Frederick as co-Regent?

The man opposite wore a smile that said his mention of Frederick was intended to hit home. "Haven't you heard? Alonzo's had news from Bribanzo in the city. Frederick sits in the Council meetings now. They were friends before, apparently. But now . . . Alexa's death, you know. It brought them together."

Tycho's mouth filled with bile.

"Going somewhere?"

He'd stood without realising. "I need the privies," Tycho said shortly. He hoped Roderigo was drunk enough to take several minutes to realise he wasn't coming back. In the centre of the floor, a hulking renegade and an archer circled, stripped to the waist, with knives in one hand and their other wrists tied. The archer was female, her teats tiny, her torso hard as oak and dark as walnut. She was grinning at the blood running from a cut on her opponent's shoulder.

"Five gold on the woman . . ." Tycho found no takers.

Heading for the balcony, he passed between a knight who was smiling and a servitor who wasn't. Her protest that she was a maiden followed Tycho up the stairs; as did the ex-Crucifer's promise to change that. By tomorrow she'd need another tune to sing. Reaching Maria Dolphini's door, Tycho knocked heavily.

"Who's there?"

"His highness sent me."

On the far side of the door a bolt slid in its clasp, then another and another, three in all. The door opened slightly. The eyes of the midwife widened as a knife touched her throat. "Who is it?" someone asked

Tycho put his finger to his lips.

The midwife backed herself into the room and Tycho eased the door shut, then reached behind him to fasten the bolts. He was planning to slide their handles into their safety slots when he had a better idea. Gripping, he twisted hard and metal sheared. The other two handles followed and he dropped the broken bits on the floor.

"What was that?" The voice was querulous, spiteful.

"Nothing, my lady . . ." The midwife's eyes never left the dagger in Tycho's hand and when he pointed at a chair she sat without protest. Ripping her scarf in two, he used half to tie her hands, and stuffed the rest into her mouth to gag her; then, feeling guilty, smashed his dagger's hilt into her skull, high above her hairline. Knocking her out now might stop Alonzo killing her later.

"*I said*, what was that?"

An inner door opened and Tycho flowed through, finding

himself face to face with Maria Dolphini. She looked older than he remembered, her hair faded to a dull blonde and her eyes puffy. The room was shrouded in hangings and piled with cushions, the air hot from a brazier in the corner. Maria covered her breast and Tycho realised she'd been trying to feed the child. He expected her to yell; instead she grabbed a fruit knife from a table and stood in front of the cot. "You," she said, her voice hoarse from all the screaming earlier.

Tycho nodded.

"You were the ghost."

He nodded again – remembering the night he went to Ca' Dolphini intending to kill Alonzo, and found Alonzo snoring and Maria Dolphini pinned beneath him. Her wedding night if he remembered right. Life would be much simpler if he'd done what he'd gone to do, instead of trying to do what was right. "The incense and bells didn't work," he said. "So here I am again."

"You're not harming my baby."

Tycho looked at her. There was such determination in her eyes, and a fierce love that made her grip the knife harder.

"Did you really think you'd get away with it?"

"With what?" Maria demanded.

"Stealing Giulietta's child."

"He's mine," she said fiercely. "My child. My son. She never deserved him. I can be a better mother. Alonzo told me how the little whore crawled into his bed when he was drunk and he didn't realise it was her. He was half asleep and thought it was me." Maria believed it.

Tycho looked for doubt, for a flicker of shame that said she knew she lied but found only certainty and a fierce determination. "How did you keep Leo quiet?"

"His name's Little Alonzo."

"How did you keep him quiet?"

"A gag." For the first time she looked uncertain. "On the ship we used a gag. His father said it was the only way. Here . . ."

She gestured around her, giving Tycho a hundred chances to take the knife. "Those help. A dozen carpets overlapped around the walls, nailed direct to the wood beneath rather than hung on poles in the usual fashion. The floor, too, was thick with carpet. "And he had a pacifier, silver and ivory. We bought it before we left."

"The screaming?" asked Tycho. "All that screaming while you were meant to be giving birth? Everyone could hear that."

"We left the doors open, obviously."

"My lady . . ."

"You can't. I won't let you."

Knocking aside her knife, he slammed the hilt of his dagger into her temple and caught her before she dropped, feeling a heavy breast against his hand. He doubted much here was Maria's choice. Giulietta said rich women had even less choice than poor ones. She was wrong. He'd lived in Bjornvin, and survived Venice's night streets, where the Rosalyns of this world had so little choice Giulietta wouldn't have recognised their lives as living.

Leo slept fitfully, dressed in a gown that was grey with dirt. Beneath it was another, with another beneath that. In keeping the child warm Maria Dolphini had probably saved its life. How many times would Alonzo have to look at the scar before he realised it was a *krieghund* mark and not a shrapnel wound from the battle off Cyprus? Unless Alonzo needed the child alive more than he would want a *krieghund* dead . . . As Tycho debated the question, he searched for the source of the slight breeze he could feel. The faintest whisper of night air.

A shuttered window behind a wall hanging was sealed with oil paper, which made it old since most cathedrals could afford glass even in minor rooms. With the carpet rolled and tied with a strip of Maria's gown it was easy enough to cut free the oil paper, which the wind swirled away. A window sill jutted over a wall that looked too sheer to climb.

There's no such thing. Atilo had told him often enough. The old man's words, and his death, stayed with Tycho, and not simply because Tycho delivered the blow. *Finish it, always slick the blade sideways.*

Atilo's last words had been a lesson.

Tycho stripped Leo, wrapped him in a fur and tied it tight with a ribbon ripped from Maria's dress. "Here we go," he told the child, before preparing to lash the bundle to his back. Leo just stared at him. Crouching carefully on the window sill, Tycho yanked the strip of cloth to unroll the wall hanging. *Nothing says magic like a locked room.* Another of Atilo's maxims.

A body in a locked room creates fear. Just as something stolen from a room still locked suggests a demon is involved and no further investigation is needed or wise. Although Tycho would not achieve that he hoped to unsettle Alonzo's followers. *Time to move.* Feeling with his toes, he found a gap between staves and braced, then lowered himself slowly over the edge. As Tycho did a shadow raced out of the darkness and hit hard, trying to knock him from the wall. Long fingers reaching for his eyes, legs hooked around him to double his weight.

Domovoi.

He tasted blood fouler than sewage. The shadow howled in his ear and its thumb half found Tycho's eye socket, pressing until the night sky exploded. Tycho spat finger to the dirt below. Leo's terrified wail gave the creature new focus.

"No you fucking don't."

Long fingers grasped for the bundle on Tycho's back. Still hanging one-handed from the sill, he grabbed the thing's wrist and bit to the bone, chewing sinew and ripping arteries that spat foul-tasting blood. Up close, the domovoi stank. Scales covered its body and its face was reptilian, the eyes cold and lidless. As thin lips drew back to reveal needle teeth, Tycho smashed his elbow into its mouth, breaking teeth and ripping his flesh. It jerked back, and he dropped his hand to his dagger, unsheathing it and driving it into the creature's side.

He twisted the blade viciously. The domovoi wailed, unlocked its legs and tried fighting free. But Tycho simply ripped his dagger from its side and cut its throat, watching it fall away into darkness and thud to the dirt below.

The shadows around him quivered in outrage.

What he thought was darkness began to flow towards him from all directions as dozen of domovoi descended on him, drawn by their fellow's death and Leo's thin cry. In the few seconds before they struck, he thought of Giulietta and felt only despair at failing her so completely.

30

"You loved your aunt?"

For once the new Regent didn't say the first thing that came into her head, or what she thought Frederick wanted to hear, or even what she thought Frederick didn't want to hear simply because she was feeling difficult.

"And feared her," Giulietta admitted.

Frederick waited. He was like Leopold in that. Leopold regularly outwaited her, looking thoughtful and considerate, as if simply waiting politely. With Leopold you knew it was intentional. It was never quite manipulation. All the same, Leopold could lighten her mood with a kind word or force a quarrel with a cruel one. Frederick seemed less calculating.

She was comparing the half-brothers a lot these days. Maybe it was that they shared smiles and a dancing, slightly dangerous laughter in their eyes. She loved Tycho. But each day made her more grateful for Frederick's companionship in a world shrunk by ice to a window seat in a passageway, with doors at both ends and a unicorn tapestry. And if she was cold, hiding here with her braziers and her glass windows and wood panelling, how were the rest of the city coping, huddled in their own frozen, tiny worlds? They must be even colder. Although she wasn't sure that was possible. She was to-the-bone cold, cold to her soul, and Frederick was her warmth in the wilderness. There, she'd dared think it.

"If you haven't lost someone close to you . . ." She flushed, feeling mortified when he touched her hand to say it was all right. Of course he'd lost someone close to him. He'd lost his wife and his child, and she'd done what she promised herself she'd stop doing – speaking without thinking.

"It's all right," he insisted.

"I shouldn't be so bloody thoughtless . . ."

"You're not." He smiled. "If anything, you think too much." He pulled a deeply serious face, and smiled when she did. "That's more like it." Slicking condensation from the window with his finger, he wiped it on his doublet. The world beyond was as white as it had been the day before, and the day before that. The flat expanse of Venetian lagoon stretched away in unmoving marble, and he peered harder as if looking for evidence that something had changed.

When he turned back, Giulietta knew he'd been steeling himself to say something. Only every time he tried to say it his lips twisted and his mouth twitched to one side. It seemed there was a lot he wanted to say.

"My father has . . ."

Frederick stopped, and Lady Giulietta was sure she heard scratching behind a tapestry. Mice perhaps, if the palace cats had left any alive.

"Are you hungry?" Frederick asked unexpectedly.

She shook her head.

"It's just . . . we have food in the *fondaco*."

Have you now? Every house in the city had been told to hand a list of its stores to the captain of the local sistiere, the six districts of Venice. Being German-owned and counting as foreign soil, Frederick's *fondaco* was excused the food census. Her spies said the Mamluks had grain and the French salted meat. The spy she sent to the Fontego dei Tedeschi never returned.

"We didn't kill him."

Gods, was she really so transparent?

"What did you do to him?"

"Fed him," Frederick said with a shrug. "Gave him warmer clothes, hot wine. Told him he'd need to wait until I'd talked to you. After that, he could go home."

"You fed him out of kindness?"

The young prince looked uncomfortable. "And to see how hungry he was. The answer was very hungry. Too hungry to worry that the food might be poisoned or we might be grooming him to commit treason . . . Our spies say the grain Alexa bought is almost gone, and half the city is starving. That most of the street children are dead. If you need our stores, they're yours."

"*What?*"

"We have pickled herring and salted beef, wizened apples and dry pork, also cheese and mutton."

"And you do *this* out of kindness?"

"My father is impressed by our friendship . . ."

She looked at him in shock, but he kept his face impassive until she glared hard enough to have him grinning. "You fear him?"

"And love him," said Frederick, reversing her earlier reply.

"Then thank you," Giulietta said. The cold showed no sign of lifting and the ice covering the lagoon was hard as granite. Holes sawn and drilled for fishing filled overnight and had to be drilled again. Although no snow had fallen for a week it still covered the island city and smothered the mainland. The Alps stood so sharp against the blue sky they looked close enough to pluck. As Regent she needed to appear confident, which was hard when the city's supplies were dwindling, and listing stores, although essential, would have told everyone how bad the situation was.

"You will put my offer to the old men?"

She nodded. "Speaking of which . . ."

"You should go. And this time I'm not invited . . ." Frederick shrugged. "I understand. If I were the Council I wouldn't invite me either." As she stood, he made himself say what he'd tried to say earlier. "My father has placed spies in Alonzo's camp."

Giulietta froze. "How does he . . .?" She realised Frederick's spy probably used carrier pigeons. Everyone knew they could fly hundreds of miles without resting. Pigeons were so important, the first thing Tamburlaine did when besieging a city was order his bowmen to kill every pigeon they saw.

"He can talk across distances. Well, his archer can. Towler can probably get you news if you want. News of . . ."

"Leo?" she said, and watched him smile in gratitude.

At the start of the stairs, Lady Giulietta hesitated, and hesitated again at the top, only turning back when she actually reached the door of Aunt Alexa's study. Her study now; her desk, her portraits of the staring Millioni, her box of poisons . . . "Forgotten something," she told a guard, wondering why she bothered to lie or even explain herself at all. Time was she'd barely have noticed him.

Outside the door, she stopped as she realised Marco had beaten her to it, and now sat where she'd sat in the window seat. "You d-don't m-mind me being here?" she heard him ask Frederick.

"It's your palace."

"M-more's the pity," Marco muttered. "You've b-been with my c-cousin?"

"She's preparing for Council."

"It will b-be a hard m-meeting."

Marco was right in that. The old men were split on accepting Lady Giulietta as Regent or asking Alonzo to return. Her marriage to Frederick's brother and Frederick's friendship counted against her.

"She'll manage," said Frederick. He seemed to mean this seriously, Giulietta realised, stepping back from the door. I should leave, she told herself. It's wrong to listen at doors. God knows, that habit had got her whipped enough as a child. But how else did you discover what was going on? She stepped back a little further, knowing her hovering there no longer looked like hesitation to the guard, if he was looking her way, which he probably was.

"Poor c-child," Marco said. "She's friendless, p-powerless and scared. Of c-course, she's not as f-friendless as she thinks, is she? Nor as p-powerless. And Giulietta scared is still braver than most. She would have m-made me a good wife if I was the m-marrying kind. My mother wanted that once. Of course, my m-mother wanted all sorts of impossible things . . ."

The duke turned to the window to wipe away condensation as Frederick had done earlier. He too stared at the lagoon beyond as if looking for changes. The parties on the ice were over. The gaiety gone. The poor fiercely hungry, the rich scared they would soon be the same. "Don't h-hurt her."

"I don't want to hurt her."

"She'll find that attractive," Marco said. "Well, I'm told girls find that attractive eventually. You love her?"

"Beyond life."

Lady Giulietta climbed the stairs to her study, let herself in and sat at her aunt's old desk, her feet resting on her aunt's poison chest, the words she'd just heard going round her head. *Beyond life . . .* Frederick would never have dared say it to Giulietta's face. Putting her notes in order, she carried them to her room and dressed in a daze, accepting a black velvet gown. She scolded the maid who said black velvet set off Giulietta's hair, pointing out she was in mourning for her aunt and her hair was irrelevant. But her heart wasn't in it, and the girl, who looked about eleven, was so crestfallen she began sniffling. So Giulietta hugged her quickly, told her not to be so silly, and waited patiently for the child to brush the shaved velvet and lace up Giulietta's shoes.

Only then did Lady Giulietta return to the corridor, her determination to play fair and let them hear her coming strengthening as she reach the first door. Behind it, Marco sounded agitated. So agitated that she pushed her way in. Her cousin was hopping from foot to foot in excitement. "A r-rat," he said. "I know a r-rat when I s-smell one." Dragging free his dagger, he ran at the tapestry and stabbed viciously for the unicorn's eye, driving his blade home.

"F-for the p-pot. A r-rat for the p-pot."

Ripping his dagger free, he stepped back and something slumped forward as blood began to stain the canvas and the tapestry prevented that something from falling. Anguished gurgling came from behind the cloth.

Marco grinned at Giulietta. "Just in t-time."

She looked from the blood on his stiletto to the lumpy tapestry and the shuddering shape behind. "Your highness . . ."

"C-c-congratulate m-me, t-then."

"Well done," Frederick said. He took the dagger gently from Marco's fingers and led him away from the tapestry, through the door Giulietta had just used to enter and out to the landing beyond. She heard him talking to a guard, and the guard reply as if Frederick had a right to be giving him orders.

"He's going to rest," Frederick said on his return.

"We should . . ." Of course they should. From the moment Marco stabbed the tapestry it was obvious they'd have to see who he'd killed. She just knew she wasn't going to like the answer.

"Bribanzo," said Frederick, letting the body slump at his feet. The old man lay in a puddle of blood, his fat face smoothed into blandness by death. All of the avarice and scheming now gone. "Giulietta, may I get my men?"

She stared at him blankly.

"I have men in the *piazzetta*. May I summon them?"

"Of course," she said hastily. If anyone queries their presence say you're acting on my orders . . ." His smile was quizzical enough to make her wonder what she'd said. "And send me the guard outside. If he's back from putting Marco to bed."

The guard looked nervous when Frederick returned with three broad-shouldered Germans, wrapped in horse blankets like barbarians. When Frederick told him to step outside, he looked to his mistress for permission.

"Do it," she said.

Frederick smiled. "Moritz, check the window in that room."

A bearded young man disappeared into the family archives and pulled open two shutters, wrestled at the fastenings that freed the glass. Cold air blasted into the archive as he lowered the glass to the floor. "Your highness?"

"Do it," Frederick said.

Lifting Lord Bribanzo, the man carried him to the window and tossed him out before Giulietta could object. She tried not to wince as Bribanzo thudded to the ground below.

Frederick said, "Now the mess." Between them, his men wiped blood from the corridor floor using horse blankets, rolled up the priceless unicorn tapestry and wrapped it inside a blanket. "You'll need another wall hanging to hide that," Frederick said, pointing to the now exposed alcove. "Bribanzo died in a street stabbing. Understand? Long before he reached here."

Somewhere outside a horse clip-clopped into the distance, its hooves sharp on the ice that glazed the herringbone brick below. At a nod from their master, Frederick's men stuffed the last blanket inside the others, slung bundles over their shoulders like woodcutters and headed for the door

"I thought my cousin was better."

"My lady . . ."

"He was *meant* to be better."

"Giulietta . . . He just killed the man calling for his abdication. The banker funding his uncle's treason. Are those the actions of an idiot?"

"No," she said sadly. "They're the actions of a Millioni."

31

They'd come at him from all sides, the domovoi . . .

Quickly, very quickly, he realised he could fight them or concentrate on climbing down the side of the Red Cathedral. He could fight them or concentrate on keeping Leo safe. At best, he could do two of those things. There was no way that he could manage all three.

He died a dozen times in the descent from Lady Maria's window, flesh ripped from his face and neck, ribs broken and remade. His fear was a gaping hole that would swallow him if he dared look back at it. Laughing and sobbing, he descended through the flames of his own pain, hoping to find himself burnt clean on the other side. A nightmare touched the ground and crossed the ice in front of the Red Cathedral in slow, bloody footsteps, leaving a trail of dead behind.

Flesh was gone from his face, one eye pulped to egg white dripping down a cheek that was shiny with bone. His neck was a patchwork where needle-like teeth had ripped away his skin. Blood, and a thin clear liquid, dripped from his wounds until his body began its healing mechanisms. That experience as brutally painful as the battle that injured him.

It was said – at least it was said by Giulietta's priests – that your sins found you out. As Tycho left the ice and stepped on to the shore he wondered what he'd done to deserve that, and, thinking about what he had done, wondered if there was more pain to come or if he'd settled the score. He was too tired, too cold and too close to simply giving up to bother trying to hide his tracks. But at least his footsteps were no longer bloody as he stamped his way through the village and headed for the forest beyond. They'd come at him from all sides, the domovoi.

Maybe he really did deserve this. Punishment for something he'd done, or, even worse, for something he was going to do. He tried not to think about either possibility. Although he couldn't shake the feeling that this was somehow deserved. A price that had to be paid. When the walking turned to clambering over boulders, he clambered. When it turned to climbing, he climbed. One day became another.

He knew where he was and wondered at himself for returning.

Behind him, on the slopes leading up to the fort, pursuers hesitated and slowed, a few of them stopping, only to move again at a snapped order. With his own breath scalding his lungs and his heart hammering inside his ribs, Tycho knew only that he had to keep climbing. Much as he wanted to turn and fight, keeping Leo alive was more important. What was the point of any of this if he failed in that?

Scrabbling over treacherous rocks, he climbed towards a door left open because he'd left it open. The squat walls of the fort reared above him, guarding whatever it was they guarded. Venetian bowmen fought from inside castles or improvised barricades of sharpened stakes. These were mounted archers, men who could ride into battle firing forward, fire sideways as they passed and twist round to fire behind them as they galloped away.

Clambering over a boulder, Tycho found a dead wolf on the far side, too frozen to stink and too starved to count as food. He kept climbing, the scree beneath his feet glued in place by ice and sharp as running on razors. The fort would provide immediate protection. Longer term, something better would be needed.

The fort had too many rooms and too many ways in for him to keep Leo safe from stray arrows, thrown knives and swinging swords. Because the responsibility of keeping Leo safe terrified him. He'd survived wounds that killed others. But Leo . . .? Only Leo's whimpers told him the child was still alive.

What you love makes you weak.

He understood Atilo's maxim now. Only people like Giulietta believed that what you loved made you strong. The thought almost stopped Tycho in his tracks before common sense and a stray arrow had him scrabbling the last few paces to throw himself through the fort door and barge it shut behind him, hinges screaming with ice and rust. Clumsily, he lifted an iron crossbar from the dirt, losing skin from his fingers to the frost as he dropped it into place.

Roderigo's men would have to force the door, scale the walls or clamber through an upper window, those being the only windows there were. Racing up the guard stairs, Tycho stepped on to the windswept battlements and took his first clear look at the men who'd been tracking him for two days. A hundred wild-haired archers, two renegade Crucifers and Lord Roderigo.

Roderigo's mount was struggling up the final slope, torn between fear of the icy scree under its hooves and its master's flailing whip. His two lieutenants were having equal trouble. Only the archers moved fluidly. Streaming between boulders and flowing over the scree as if born from wolves and raised in the snow.

"Up there," Roderigo cried.

Tycho had run at night and hidden in the day, and his pursuers had used the dead time to catch up, tracking him easily. A fresh fall of snow had sealed his fate. Even with the finest Assassini skills, it was impossible for a limping man to carry a child across virgin snow without leaving tracks. And the scree, the slope, and fear of hurting Leo, stopped him running as fast as he wanted.

What you love makes you weaker.

The previous night he doubled back to kill the man he thought their tracker, having left Leo under the shelter of a rock. He swirled out of the darkness in the seconds of safety offered by a cloud and sprayed blood across snow without even stopping to feed. He'd swerved, jinked and danced his way back to the tree-line as arrows followed. It made no difference. Tonight, he woke to smell horses on the wind and hear the distant jangle of bridles.

"Sorry about that," he told the infant.

It snivelled and whimpered and he wondered how cold it could get without dying. The fact it was blue was a bad sign. Leo, he thought. Not it. Leo, Giulietta's son. The reason he stood here while they scurried below. Without a ram or wood to start a fire the gate would hold them until Roderigo lost patience and ordered his men to scale the walls or climb the valley's end and try to enter that way.

But first, it seemed, Roderigo intended to try talking.

A makeshift white flag was being raised and Roderigo spurred his mount forward under its protection, his lieutenants slightly behind and to either side like a double shadow. "Surrender the child," Roderigo shouted.

Tycho remained silent.

"Princess Maria told us of your brutality."

I let her live, Tycho thought. She gagged Leo on the voyage and I let her live. Where was the brutality in that?

"His highness offers you a fair trial in return for his son's safe return."

The wind whipped and the white flag snapped, and Tycho used the seconds to count the archers and examine the killing ground in front of the fort.

"Are you really such a monster?" Roderigo shouted.

Depends how you look at it.

Everything always depended on how you looked at it. Tycho didn't doubt Alonzo thought himself the hero, and Roderigo thought himself the hero's faithful captain. Leaving Roderigo standing there, Tycho carried Leo below and began putting together the two parts of his plan. "Do you like the idea? he asked the infant.

It snivelled. That was pretty much its answer to everything.

"I'll take that as a yes. I don't suppose you'd like to help me move this?"

It simply looked at him, so he balanced it on the giant crossbow, which was still strung with its three dozen arrows in place. "Hold on," he said and, pushing open the fort's rear door, wondered if he had time to move the porcupine. Until trying to shift the crossbow told him the real question: had he the strength?

Sinews popped as he tried to get the porcupine moving and he was close to accepting defeat when one wheel shifted and he found his grip and the porcupine began moving through the fort's rear doors, until Tycho used its own momentum to swing it round to face the way it came. Stepping back, he looked at the parapet above the yard and realised the crossbow was far enough inside the arch's tunnel to be hidden from anyone above. The tunnel was so deep a dozen soldiers could have stood on the iron grating of its murder holes and poured a river of boiling oil on to those below.

"Had I a dozen men," he told Leo. "And fire to heat the oil, or indeed any oil. What I do have though . . ." he carried the child into the armoury, "is mage powder. And that we need for the front." The powder was inside a small barrel hidden inside a bigger barrel, sealed with a circular slug of pitch. Silvery specks glittered on its surface. These burnt to the touch the way silver did, except these hurt everyone.

"You stay here," Tycho said.

He put the infant with its back to the crenellation and was grateful the wind was in the right direction for what he wanted to do. It howled from behind him as he looked down on a tangle of archers standing in front of the gate arguing. One barged it, another hissed at him. Lord Roderigo stood several paces away, looking increasingly impatient. None of them glanced up.

Why would they?

A fierce gust gave Tycho what he needed and carried the powder over the edge, into quieter air that dropped it gently on to those below. A man looked up as the first drifting grains rained down, and took a face full of stinging powder. It crusted his hair and coated his jacket like scurf.

"Up there," another shouted. An arrow hissed past Tycho and then the man who released it was clawing at his own face as falling powder filled his eyes. A second archer was doing the same.

BURN, Tycho thought.

It was over in a moment. Mage fire burnt to the bone and beyond. It burnt to the soul. Screaming men staggered back, frantically brushing at their jerkins, which simply glued burning phosphor to their hands. Once started, mage fire could not be put out with water. A man tried to dig beneath the snow for earth to quench the flames but the ground was frozen too hard to help him.

A few of those who took the powder were still alive enough to scream when Tycho grabbed Leo and abandoned the battlements, spun his way down twisting stairs and exited into the guardroom where the porcupine once stood. Shutting the double doors with a slam that rattled the fort as if it was trying to awake, he jammed a rock under the middle to stop Roderigo's men from forcing their way through.

Whatever was in the cave frightened the wild archers beyond the walls. If they made their way into the fort – and they would – it would take them the coming day to search the building properly. By nightfall they should have found their courage to enter the yard. He hoped their fear of the cave would stop them coming further. The crude steps up to the slit in the rocks were treacherous with ice. The top step littered with offerings, from fox skulls and bloody rags to the bones of a raven. Tycho hesitated on the edge of entering, and then stepped inside to be met by a gust of rank air. "My lord of light," it hissed. "Welcome home."

Tycho wrapped his arms round Leo.

The air chuckled.

32

"Tell me it's not true . . ."

Lady Giulietta's voice was shrill enough to make a guard turn. The man caught Prince Frederick's eye and flushed. His stare when he looked straight ahead would have drilled walls. It was unwise to interfere in the quarrel of princes, especially when one was female and close to tears.

"My lady . . ."

"Either go. Or tell me it's not true."

Standing, Frederick bowed clumsily. "I'd better take my leave."

"Don't come back," Giulietta shouted. "Never ever. You're banished from this court. You too . . ." She pointed at the guard. "Not banished," she said furiously, seeing his shock. "I mean, go. Now."

Having hesitated for the briefest moment, the guard trooped from the little corridor on the upper floor with its new tapestry and window seat over the Molo. Here was where she had once discovered her cousin Marco poisoned, that afternoon when Aunt Alexa was still alive. Now Marco was in prison.

Except you didn't put reigning dukes in prison, so he was secure in his chamber on her orders. That was what she'd decided. That he was to be secured. Even at his worst under Alexa he'd never been locked away for more than a few days, and now he was there until she decided differently. Two bolts and two guards made sure no one tried to let him out.

She was lonely, scared and needed to talk to someone. The old patriarch would have done. Unfortunately, Theodore was dead and so was Aunt Alexa, and Marco was mad again, and Tycho wasn't here and Frederick was a traitor.

"Go," she shouted.

"Listen to me," Frederick begged.

"So you can tell me more lies? I bet all those things you said about Annemarie weren't true either."

She'd never seen anyone go white with anger before. Frederick bowed again, and this time he meant it. She watched him walk backwards to the door. Since he was a prince in his own right this was unnecessary and she wondered if it was mockery, but his pale blue eyes showed only cold fury.

"I never even liked you," Giulietta said.

He bit his lip. "You did," he said. "That's the problem."

Frederick shut the door carefully and she heard his footsteps in the corridor. They stopped when she opened the door and slammed it hard behind him. The loud silence that followed was broken by the sound of his heels on the stairs and, later still, a jangle of harness in the *piazzetta*.

She should call the Council.

Only then she'd have to admit to telling Frederick secrets and they trusted her little enough as it was. Her aunt they had mistrusted because she was Mongol, Giulietta they mistrusted because she was young. At least, they whispered that that was their reason. Their real reason was simpler. She was a woman in command of a council filled with old men.

If she told them Frederick had tricked her into friendship, they'd remove her and replace her with Alonzo, who was a man, obviously. A famous general, which was even better. And he was probably going to win anyway. The Byzantine emperor had acknowledged Alonzo as rightful duke of Venice. That was what Frederick had arrived to tell her. But she'd been too furious to listen. He didn't even deny it.

His father had sent him.

Sigismund had ordered Frederick to make friends. Every word he'd said to her was false. She couldn't trust him any more than she'd been able to trust Tycho. Ca' Ducale was freezing, its tapestries stiff with cold, the marble tiles of its open colonnades glazed with frost. Individual rooms were warm but ice had entered its fabric and its soul. She and the palace suited each other.

Three thrones waited, with one larger than the others.

Alexa was dead, and Alonzo banished and Marco confined to his room on her orders for murdering a councillor in cold blood; for all the city had been told Bribanzo died in a street stabbing. Half that city thought she had no right to be Regent anyway. What if Uncle Alonzo simply decided to return? Would the palace guard obey her if she ordered them to defend her? Would the militia bands flock to her banner or line up along the Riva degli Schiavoni to cheer Alonzo's barge as it drew alongside?

Slouched in Marco's seat, Giulietta stared at the shields on the panelled walls and wondered how different life would have been if she were a boy. Or if she'd been someone else entirely. Someone other than a Millioni. Marco the Just had sat where she sat. The thought of Aunt Alexa's husband made her sit straighter.

Il Millioni himself had sat here the day he claimed the throne and abolished five centuries of elected rule. She'd wanted to return to the Republic and that would never happen now. She'd wanted many things, from a happy childhood to marriage to Tycho, and the first hadn't happened and the second never would . . . Tycho had betrayed her, too. His love was ambition.

It was the only reason for what he'd done. He'd been the first to worm his way into her heart; made her want him and offered to protect her and become a father to Leo. And then what happened? He left when she begged him to stay, offering his loyalty to the man who . . . She couldn't even bear to finish that thought.

Even worse than this he had returned to kill Aunt Alexa. And now Frederick – who was meant to be her friend – had not only tricked her into friendship, but also destroyed what little hope she had left. Lord Bribanzo had died with two scrolls in his belt. One said Frederick was here on the orders of his father. The other that Maria Dolphini had given birth to a child. Alonzo had a son, an heir to take his name and follow after him. Bribanzo was to challenge Giulietta on whether she believed the child was Alonzo's . . .

Of course it was. He'd stolen Leo and was passing him off as Maria's child. The second part of Alonzo's challenge was more brutal still. He stated his belief that the boy in the nursery upstairs, where she could hardly bear to go, was an impostor, which he was. And that a dead infant answering Leo's description was hidden in the crypt of the basilica, which it was. He challenged her, on oath, to say that he lied.

Her uncle had won.

When the Council heard the news they would replace her and Alonzo would sail home with Tycho at his side. Frederick would abandon her. Not that he'd ever really loved her. She'd be back to who she always was. Someone's cousin, someone's niece, someone's plaything. A thought so horrific occurred to her that she nearly pissed herself. What if Alonzo had promised her to Tycho? What if she got the marriage she'd once wanted to a man who betrayed her at the command of a man who'd done worse? She would never forgive what her uncle had done the night an abbess and a hedge witch held her down so Dr Crow could impregnate her on his orders.

She loved Leo, but the nature of his getting tortured her.

Walking to the door, Lady Giulietta shouted for a messenger and sent him for the new master of the Assassini, an anonymous man who'd returned a month earlier from Vienna to find his city changed. He was master because Giulietta had stripped Tycho of that title. She waited impatiently for his arrival.

"My lady?"

"Find a hedge witch called Mistress Scarlet and the Abbess of San Loyola, kill them both before nightfall, bring me proof . . ."

He risked a glance and bowed.

The door shut behind him with a whisper and it was done. She'd condemned two people to death. Lady Giulietta would have made it three but doubted he'd obey. Asking the master of the Assassini to add her to his list might be an order too far.

Aunt Alexa's poisons chest sat beside Giulietta's desk, as it had sat beside that desk from the time Alexa first arrived in the city as a child and asked for a room of her own. No servant had dared move it or even dust it. A thin film covered its surface, except for two patches where Giulietta had taken to using it as a footstool.

The saddest thing about the study for Giulietta was not that Aunt Alexa had died here, it was her aunt's dead pots of flowers and withered bushes. Alexa grew them to provide fruit for her giant bat, Nero, which would eat nothing else, coming from Egypt where that was what bats ate. After Nero died, Alexa kept the plants alive anyway, having braziers brought in day and night to keep them warm when the snows came. With her death the braziers stopped being brought and the plants died. There was probably a lesson in that somewhere.

Pulling back her scissor chair, Giulietta sat at her desk, found a sheet of velum and a quill and reached for the ink with shaking hands. When she discovered the ink was dry she gave up all thought of writing a note. What would she have said anyway?

The bottle was one of the smallest. *Dracul's tears* read its label.

A crude glass vial with a cork stopper sealed with wax. Her aunt had medicines arranged by potency and it had taken

Giulietta a while to work out the meaning of the coloured waxes sealing her poisons. Red meant death. Only this bottle was in the next row. Its wax was purple. Breaking the seal, Giulietta hesitated.

Self-murder was a sin. She would ask God to take account of what had been done to her already when he decided what should be done to her in the afterlife for what she was about to do.

Lady Giulietta crossed herself.

She said the Lord's Prayer, the Creed and Ave Maria, because those were the prayers she knew by heart without even having to think about them. After the last *Amen* came the poison.

33

You're giving me the child?

That was the last thing Tycho intended.

At the thought, the foul breeze through the cave laughed. It was sour and old and carried putrid memories of someone he wasn't. The black flames and cavernous ceilings of the memory were not his. Tycho managed five paces into the cave before the stink forced him to a stop. The cave walls were soft, spongy and warm to the touch. As narrow inside as the entrance suggested without.

Leo was crying, pitiful whoops as he struggled for air. Tycho wished he knew how to help the child. But his own head was filled with dreams of a mother who died so he could be born. Impossible dreams. She was beautiful, distant and cold, with the same amber-flecked eyes. She walked in daylight and Tycho wondered why, if that was true, he now lived in darkness. Except why should dreams be true? "Sleep," the voice said. "Or whatever it is you do."

"The child . . ."

"Will not die while it is here."

He woke to putrid warmth on a bed of white fibrous rot like albino body hair. A tendril of tree root had wrapped itself round his ankle and proved harder than he expected to snap. Leo lay beside him, eyes closed and curled into a shivering ball. The voice had told the truth. The child was alive, although only just. Picking him up, Tycho staggered to the entrance.

"What do you think?" Tycho asked.

Apparently the infant thought nothing. At least, nothing worth more than a snuffle. The day was dying and the coming night his only chance of ending this. Fear of the cave, or the need to search the fort thoroughly, meant Roderigo's men had yet to force the yard door. On one side of the valley beyond the fort the sides were black, on the other they were purple, and he saw the lines where they joined the sky with frightening clarity.

"Planet," Tycho said. "Planet, star, asteroid . . ."

The child showed little interest in his astronomy lesson. Above the cave's mouth the sky glittered with the objects Tycho offered the boy, while the moon cast a tallow glow across what showed of the giant crossbow, which stood undisturbed. Tycho imagined that meant the rock he'd jammed beneath the doors was still there. If there was a guard on the battlements he was sleeping, bad at his job or simply too afraid to do it properly.

"Remember how the wild archers hesitated in front of the fort?"

Leo didn't but Tycho did. Only Lord Roderigo's fury had driven them on. They were already afraid. Brave men, naturally brave men, made weak by what they feared. *What you love makes you weaker* . . . Tycho wiped away the thought and wished it would stay banished. Maybe they were right to be afraid. Maybe he should be more afraid than he was. From inside came the noise of men talking. Tycho listened harder. Hearing the jangle of bridles on the far side of the fort.

"Leaving or arriving?" Tycho asked.

Leo kept his answer to himself. But Tycho thought it must be someone leaving, a message for Alonzo perhaps saying his quarry had gone to ground.

"Do you want to be part of what happens next . . . No? Probably wise. Princes shouldn't be involved in things like this. Better put you back in the cave then."

The jangle of harness receded and Tycho let the fort settle before striding to the rear door and hammering hard as if demanding entry. As if he was not the man who'd barred the door. Inside the talking stopped. A moment's utter silence gave Tycho his own ragged heartbeat.

The fools should have rushed to the murder holes in the tunnel roof above and dropped stones or fired arrows through its rusting grating. Instead they erupted into shouts of outrage. So Tycho hammered again, louder and harder, furiously insistent. He could sense men gathering on the far side of the door. Bows being strung and arrows slotted to their strings. Maybe they expected him to open the door.

In case any dawdled, Tycho hammered one final time before retreating to yank the porcupine's lever. Three strings released with a twang, the giant bow straightened and thirty-six steel-tipped arrows, matched exactly to the steel holes in the door that would have let them fire out, hissed inwards.

Screaming began.

So much blood . . . The thought followed him up the fortress wall and along the top. The single sentry listening to the screaming below never heard his death coming. Tycho broke his neck with a single twist and fed briefly.

A tiny life made of rapes and murder. Tents, ragged ponies, hours in the saddle. Years in the wrong country, speaking someone else's language and vowing devotion to lords to whom he owed no loyalty. Tycho tossed him over the edge, hearing his body thud to cold dirt below.

He was at the bottom of the guard steps before any realised. The distance between battlements and hall closed in a second. He stood on the edge of *turning*, his reflexes razor and his nerves tight. The nearest archer opened his mouth to raise the alarm and died. Tycho killed fast, but the wild-haired man beyond had time to yell before Tycho broke his neck. Around him, men drew swords or slotted arrows on to their strings. "Kill him," Roderigo shouted.

Now there was a refrain Tycho had heard before. He grinned, and was still grinning when an arrow hit his shoulder and ripped straight through. Looking up showed Tycho archers on a balcony above. As if they'd been waiting for his attention, the rest released their arrows. Half missed, the other half spiked him like a saint in one of Marco's paintings. The archers lowered their bows, waiting for Tycho to drop as the room wavered around him and blackness edged his sight.

To their disbelief Tycho refused to fall.

Instead he flowed up the wall, spiny with arrows, rolled himself with difficulty over the balcony's edge and dropped as half a dozen archers fired. Rising fast, he ripped two arrows from his chest and returned them to their owners. The world slowing as he spun, jabbing and slashing with steel-tipped arrows until blood sprayed, the air grew drunk on red mist and he no longer had arrows in his body.

"Kill him," Roderigo screamed.

"You kill me," Tycho shouted. "Unless you're too scared?"

He vaulted from the balcony and landed in a crouch, drawing the sword that hung from his shoulder as he stood. "Did he tell you I was human?" Tycho stared at the fur-jacketed archers who surrounded him. "Is that what he told you? Is that what you think you've been hunting?" He drew the sword across his forearm, holding it out so they could see black blood well and begin to slow, the cut crusting and the flesh around it begin to heal. They muttered among themselves.

Roderigo's expression said he knew he was losing them.

"He's afraid," Tycho said. "That's why he needs you to fight me instead."

The words drew growls from the tribesmen worthy of a dog

pack disputing ownership of a bone. Several of them lowered their swords or bows. Then, somehow, they reached a silent agreement and they stepped back, leaving Roderigo standing in the middle of a circle. He could fight or lose them for ever.

That knowledge showed in Roderigo's eyes.

With it returned the courage that had seen Roderigo through many battles, or so Tycho had been told. The man would win, or die here. Tycho intended to make sure he died. "You killed the monks at San Lazar."

Roderigo opened his mouth to deny it and swallowed, unwilling to risk facing God with a lie on his lips.

"You set the barrels of powder. Your sergeant lit the fuse."

"He died well?" Roderigo's expression softened at the mention of Temujin.

"Cursing his father for abandoning his mother and promising to screw his first love into the dirt of the afterlife. She died of plague before he could grow tired of her. Of course he died well."

An archer with high cheekbones and grey beard muttered something. As one, those in the crowd of men around Tycho and Roderigo holding bows sheathed them and drew their swords to join the others in forming a circle. Retreat too far or too fast and a sword point would pierce you. Roderigo grinned. "His highness has offered fifty thousand ducats for your head. I'm going to enjoy collecting."

Tycho said, "Strike the first blow."

"Why?" Roderigo demanded.

"I don't want anyone saying you weren't ready."

Roderigo snorted. Raising his sword high, he held the position as he returned Tycho's gaze. What Tycho knew about swordplay he'd learnt from Atilo, whereas Roderigo had a lifetime's practical experience. Both men held three-quarter swords suited to fighting in Venetian alleys or indoors. *You're faster*, Tycho told himself. *You're stronger. You're the better man.*

There was a time he'd have believed it.

He fell back on Atilo's training. Taking the position, he waited. When you don't know what to do, do nothing. He kept his eyes on Roderigo's, and it was Roderigo's eyes that betrayed the man. As Roderigo feinted in one direction, his gaze flicked in another and Tycho blocked the blow, sparks jumping from their blades and the clash of steel echoing off the stone walls.

The fight was quick and brutal after that, and Roderigo nearly made good his promise when Tycho slipped on blood and rolled backwards as Roderigo's blade came crashing down to smash a flagstone. Tycho took a face full of granite chips from the blow that stuck to the sweat on his face. He climbed unsteadily to his feet, blocking Roderigo's next blow.

The cold slowed Tycho down. What feeding had given him, his arrow wounds and the cold had stolen. He needed to kill Roderigo; either that, or fight free of the wild archers in a circle around him, save Leo from the cold and hunger that were undoubtedly killing him and escape. But the real battle was with himself. All the battles that really mattered were with yourself.

Stepping back, Tycho flinched as a sword pricked his shoulder. The wild tribesmen grinned at his surprise. Lord Roderigo was also smiling. He was taller and broader, more experienced in battle and held the slightly longer sword. *But he's not me*, Tycho reminded himself. *And this battle's not over.*

"You should have surrendered," Roderigo mocked.

Tycho slashed furiously. Roderigo's retreat gave Tycho space to launch another blow that was blocked in turn. The two men stepped back from each other and Roderigo raised his sword high. For here he could strike to either side or straight down. The position let him block, while offering blows that would take Tycho off at the leg. Around them the wild soldiers fell silent, having decided the fight was nearing its end. All anyone could hear was wind along the valley and the drumming of a shutter somewhere above.

"Afraid?" Roderigo asked.

"Tired of this," Tycho said. It wasn't the answer Roderigo expected. The ex-Dogana captain had his legs apart to steady himself. His sword at the balance point to let him take its weight. If Tycho stepped back another pace he'd spear himself on the sword wall. If that happened he might as well let Roderigo take his head.

Tycho watched Roderigo's eyes.

In the final moment, they narrowed and flicked to one side and Tycho read the warning in their movement and caught Roderigo's blade on his, feeling both blades shatter. One clattered to the ground, the other scythed into the crowd and ripped a man open at the hip.

"Shit," said Roderigo, grabbing for his dagger.

Tycho was already moving. Having launched forward, he dropped and slid feet first between Roderigo's legs, slashing upward with his broken blade. Roderigo screamed like a gelded horse as blood spurted from his groin. By then, Tycho had rolled sideways, climbed to his knees and sliced the man's hamstrings.

Turning for the rear doors of the fort, Tycho felt rather than saw the wild soldiers move aside to let him through. He stepped over the bodies of those killed by the porcupine, opened the rear door enough to slip through and shut it behind him. Up ahead he could see the slit in the cliff and the steps that led to it.

The wild archers let him go without protest.

A few minutes later he felt rather than heard them go. They left their dead unburied and their captain castrated on the fortress floor. If they had any sense they'd find a new captain and a different war.

34

"Prince Frederick, this is not fitting . . ."

The chamberlain's voice was distant and disapproving. The man was the oldest of the servants at Ca' Ducale. Marco the Just had lately been knighted when he joined the palace staff. Serving the Millioni had been his life. An emperor's bastard wanting to stand guard over the body of his late master's niece . . .

Nothing in a long life of studying etiquette and court ritual told him what to do. He wished Duchess Alexa were alive. At least Lady Giulietta imagined he did. He sounded like he wished something.

"She's alive," Frederick said.

"Your highness . . ."

"I'm telling you. Giulietta lives."

"She has been examined by the best doctors. She has neither heartbeat nor reflexes. Her eyes do not react to the light."

"Her body is uncorrupted."

"The vitality of youth and the sanctity of a life well lived. She will be buried tomorrow . . ." The chamberlain caught himself. However much he obviously wished that to be true, the ground was too hard for burial. He amended his words to "She will be taken to the crypt tomorrow to await burial."

"I saw her breathe."

"I'm sorry, your highness."

"Just now. I'm telling you. I saw her breathe."

"The doctor held a mirror to her mouth and nose. The glass remained clear and unfogged. I'm afraid . . ."

"He should have held it there for longer," Frederick said fiercely. "You must summon him now so he can try again. I'll wait here." His voice fierce. "I'm not moving. You'd better understand that."

The chamberlain sighed.

It was a sigh of half-surrender. In demanding the return of the court doctor Frederick had earned himself the right to hold vigil over her body. Lady Giulietta listened to the chamberlain explain politely, because this was the Emperor Sigismund's bastard, and it paid to be polite, that the doctor could not be sent for twice. Her death had already been recorded in the Golden Book and the warrant announcing it sealed with the great seal of Venice, which showed the winged Lion of St Mark holding the shield of the Millioni. Sadly, tragically, Lady Giulietta was dead.

"You're wrong," Frederick said.

The chamberlain left muttering some commonplace about the harshness of death and the kindness of time. And, dare he say it, how much harder the young found the thought of death than those of his age. Then he shut the door of the great hall behind him and left Frederick to his grief.

The old tales of souls remaining chained to their bodies for three days had to be true because Giulietta felt inside her body and yet not. Her fingers would not move when she flexed them. Her tongue refused to frame words. Her eyes would not open. And her heartbeat was slower than time. Either she was dead, or this was the subtlest of her aunt's poisons. Though Frederick said he saw her breathe she wondered if it were true.

"I'm so sorry," she heard Frederick say.

For what? Giulietta wondered.

"I should have said . . ."

The bier on which her coffin rested creaked as he knelt beside her and though she floated without feeling she guessed he'd taken her hand. Her guess proved right, when he said, "So cold, your fingers . . ."

Perhaps she was dead after all?

"I should have told you my father sent me. I wanted to tell you from the moment we met. You looked so cross at having to meet me and every bit as beautiful as Leopold boasted."

Leopold had thought her beautiful? He'd written to say that? She'd known the half-brothers wrote to each other but not what their letters said.

"I'm sorry Leopold died and Leo was stolen. I'm sorry Tycho left you and changed sides. I shouldn't be . . . Because it let us be friends, but being friends wasn't enough, was it? Most of all," he said, "I'm sorry I caused this."

She heard a sob.

"My father told me to make you fall in love with me – and all that happened was I fell in love with you instead." His voice choked, and Giulietta could imagine his bitten lip and tearful face. "I know my being here is based on a lie. But the rest is true. I know what it's like to lose someone you love. I know what it's like to lose a child. To want to be dead."

He was weeping openly, she realised.

"If Leo's alive I'll find him for you, I swear it. And I'll kill Alonzo." He hiccuped. "For all the good that will do."

Through his sobs, she heard the words of the Creed, then the words of the Pater Noster and finally those of the Ave Maria. She thought it odd and touching the prayers he spoke from instinct were those she'd said before poisoning herself. The prayers you learnt in childhood and knew by heart.

It's not your fault, she tried to say.

Frederick was sniffling and swallowing, and sounded so much

like a young man trying to pull himself together she wanted to smile. Her aunt had called him *that boy*. But he was more than that. He was *krieghund* for a start. Having banished the tremors from his voice, Frederick began to tell her about his childhood in Austria, about meeting and marrying Annemarie. How proud he'd been she was having a child. They'd gone to bed the night before he rode out. His first campaign. She'd sat in the darkness above him, all soft curves and full of life. He'd never told anyone that but he could tell Giulietta because . . .

That produced another sob.

He'd ridden home so proud and found his father waiting at the edge of the estate. Frederick had known instantly something was wrong. The emperor's presence said that. For weeks Frederick begged the plague to take him, too.

The finest marble, and the best sculptors worked on her tomb. His brother rode halfway across Austria to be with him. Leopold sat beside his bed at night to stop him harming himself. He helped interview Italian sculptors. Annemarie's finished likeness was so perfect it could have been her sleeping. His daughter lay beside her, eyes closed and a smile on her tiny mouth. Angels guarded Annemarie's head and stood at her feet. It was a work of art. Unlike any tomb before it.

Sounds beautiful, Giulietta thought.

"I took one look and never returned."

It seemed the church still enjoyed Frederick's patronage: he had masses said monthly for Annemarie's soul and lilies placed on her tomb every year. The closest he came to returning was with his pack, when they left the high valley and their usual hunting grounds and descended to the edge of the churchyard one summer night. He was talking about his Wolf Brothers, Giulietta realised. She'd thought them war monsters. He made it sound as if they were really wolves.

"And then I met you . . ." His voice broke, like the newly bearded youth he was. "Leopold had written but I thought he exaggerated. He said I would love you and teased me that he'd got there first. Leopold could be cruel like that. It was unthinking cruelty. All his cruelty was unthinking."

And his kindness . . .

You had to give Leopold that. His kindness was as instinctive as his cruelty. With her, though, he'd been thoughtful. Although Giulietta still didn't understand what made him kind to her when he was so brutal to so many of Aunt Alexa's ladies-in-waiting. He'd bedded more than half and treated them all disgustingly, while leaving her unbedded and being unfailingly kind. They were a strange family.

Mind you, who were the Millioni to talk?

35

"Where is he?"

Voices laughed in the warm darkness.

Tycho drew his sword. "Give me the child."

"Or what, highness? You'll slice the air to shreds?" The voice was mocking, slightly bitchy. Like one of the eunuchs in the palace of a Mamluk sultan. *Had he ever been in the palace of a Mamluk sultan?*

A creature came out of the cave's darkness in a halo of sullen light. Its face was narrow and nose slightly hooked; weirdly narrow eyes were made stranger by slightly pointed ears. Chest hair gave way to goat fur at the hips, with the greying fur thickening towards the hooves. It was the testicles Tycho really noticed, grotesquely large, hanging like grapefruit beneath a child's penis.

The creature sketched a mocking bow. "After all this time," it said. "You finally deign to visit us . . ."

"You know me?"

"Highness, the whole world knows you . . ." It smirked. "Well, knows your mother. Although perhaps that should be knows her sire. Such a cruel decision to visit the sins of the fathers on the children, although I can see the attraction."

Tycho had no idea what the creature was talking about.

Actually, he had no idea what it was or how it could have stepped out of darkness when he could see through darkness and all that lay beyond was rock at the end of the narrow cave. The creature made a show of looking around it.

"What are you after?"

"Just checking you haven't split yourself into three, highness. Kept the best bit of yourself safe, given a lesser bit for sacrifice and slipped a sliver into some flying creature. Say a dove?" It shrugged. "No, of course, that's taken. A bat, perhaps?"

Tycho raised his sword.

"Now now," the creature said. "Let's not be hasty."

"Give me the child," Tycho demanded.

"You left him here. Anything left here is mine. You know the rules. Ask them. They'll tell you." The creature scowled. "Few enough people leave us live presents any more."

Out of the darkness came others. A centaur, once powerfully built but now sunken around the chest. A dryad with tired eyes and peeling skin, wilting ivy in her hair. A naiad, wearing pond-weed and holding a double-handled jug with a broken side. A faun came last. In her arms was Giulietta's son.

"Give me Leo . . ."

"So that's his name. Thank you." The creature turned to the faun and said, "His name's Leo." She nodded as if Tycho had never spoken and whispered in the infant's ear. She began to raise Leo to her teat.

"*No*," Tycho said.

"He's ours. You left him."

"I didn't leave him with you."

"Yes, you did. You just didn't know it."

"I will kill you." Tycho's voice was hard. "All of you."

"This modern world is grey and old, and what remains to thee of us? If we could be killed don't you think we'd already be dead?"

There were faces behind the faces he could see. Shadowy glares and even sympathy. A boy so graceful his beauty could light the night edged forward, only to be cuffed back by a thickset black-smith. Lady Giulietta would have known who they were, these tired gods and fallen heroes.

"Where am I?"

"The womb of the world. Well, that's what the polite ones call it. The new ones, the ones who came after. We're in the world's cunt. The slit of the elder goddess. A Sybil lived here for a thousand years. Always the same, always changing. Kings came, and princes, demigods and heroes. Always the questions, always the misunderstood answers. Ask us a question. Any question. I promise we will answer."

"Who am I?"

The creature rubbed its hands. "Ah," it said. "An oldie but a goodie. I like that. *Who am I?* So simple to ask. So easy to misunderstand the answer. Has it occurred to you that your fear of daylight is simply that, a fear? As false and unreal as your memories before Venice? That you are ordinary?"

"Are you saying that's true?"

The creature stared at him. "In any situation the simplest answer is usually the right one."

"Are you saying it's true?"

"Not at all. I'm saying you should have considered it."

Tycho caught a memory then and wondered if it was his.

"It might as well be. If not this you, then the yous that came before."

Ahead of him was cold space and stars in different shapes in a darker deeper sky that contained swirling discs that trailed the fluorescent wakes of a million maybe worlds. He could feel wings, visible and invisible, spreading to catch particles of light that lifted him above the disc and carried him through a void of the earliest days of creation. He was a god. One of hundreds, one of thousands.

Split into warring camps and his faction was losing, had already lost to the larger, to the stronger, to the brighter. Most of his troop

228

was falling through a rift into a different darkness beyond. His generals hurled from the high heavens, the others simply following blindly after.

He should go after them.

They were his, where they went was where he belonged. All the same, he hesitated on the edge of going, refusing to accept blind obedience was necessary. There were others who hovered on the edge of doubt. A few, a handful, condemned to fall and yet refusing. In the darkness of a coalescing outer rim there was suddenly light and a pinprick of a sun and half a dozen, depending on how you counted them, worlds slung like beads around it.

It was a small sun.

A meagre and narrow collection of possible worlds. Small worlds around a small sun on the thin edge of a ring smaller and meaner than those around it. He accepted the choice all the same. Spreading wings to catch the light and stepping off into the darkness, he fell, but gently . . .

"Was that me?" Tycho demanded.

"Like enough to make no difference."

"It makes a difference to me," Tycho said crossly.

"The Sibyls were the same. Always protesting they were different. Always identical in every way . . ." The goat-heeled creature plucked at the air and pulled two fat candles into being. "If I light this from that is it the same flame?" He tossed away the fattest candle and produced a thinner one from the air. "And if I light this from that? And this, and this . . .?" The candles got smaller. The flame remained.

And in the light of the candle the cave walls faded and the space around them expanded until the walls were distant and growing ever more so as Tycho stared. Everything seemed to be rushing away from everything else and the darkness had a red tint that reminded him of embers.

"Where am I?"

"Look around you. Where do you think you are?"

There was water where there hadn't been water. A wide and lapping expanse of dark water that began at his feet and stretched to a distant black bank. The air smelt of brimstone. When he looked there was another expanse of water behind him, equally wide and growing wider. Tycho now stood on an island between lakes of darkness. Looking closer, he saw the ripples were ghostly faces, more than he could count in a hundred years, open-mouthed and hollow-eyed. Faces that recanted their sins and begged forgiveness in never-ending pleas.

"Not my afterlife," Tycho said. The lords of Bjornvin had believed in the eternal drinking halls where warriors feasted. The rest, the serfs and the slaves, feared reincarnation and hoped for nothing. A long endless nothing in which they rotted and were forgotten and became one with the earth. If not his afterlife, then whose?

"Leo is dying?"

"Half dead already."

"Then give him to me and let me go."

"No." The female faun's voice was high, jealous. She folded her arms tightly around Leo. "He's mine. I want him. He promised."

"He had no right."

"I had every right. You left him with me."

"You know that's untrue." Tycho glanced behind him, looking for a way out, but saw only dark water and ripples that swore never to sin again. The lake was viscid, slow-moving. He had no idea what would happen if he grabbed Leo and swam for safety, assuming there was any to be found, but he doubted Leo could survive much more ill treatment. Grinning, the creature said, "What will you give me in exchange?"

"What do you want?"

"That's not the way it works. You offer me something."

Tycho looked into the spiteful eyes of the tired creature in front of him. Its narrow face gave nothing away. It was passive, unmoving. As if any greatness its owner once possessed had faded centuries ago.

"I'll give my life," Tycho said. "Let me take the child to his mother and I'll return when it is done. You have my word."

"Predictable. But heartfelt."

The faun holding Leo scowled and that gave Tycho hope. She obviously believed there was something Tycho could offer. But what?

"Killing you doesn't interest me," the creature said.

"My freedom . . ." He'd been a slave once and would be again if that were the price. The creature looked at him thoughtfully. Dark, inhuman eyes examined Tycho's face as wisps of colour trickled into his mind, Giulietta in white, her face still as stone. A blond boy Tycho recognised as Frederick knelt beside her.

"But what if you could only save one? Which would it be?"

Tycho felt cold. "I don't need to save Giulietta," he said. "She doesn't need saving. It's Leo who needs saving. You said so yourself."

"But suppose she did?"

"I'd save both."

"Then the price would be even greater. We don't know you can pay the first, never mind the second, or is it the other way round?" The slyness of its voice and the smirk on its face said the creature was playing to the ragbag of immortals around them. "What would you give to save *her*?"

"I'll give up being me," Tycho said. "I'll give up my powers. My healing, my strength, my speed. All the things that make me other."

The goat-heeled creature walked the edge of the river and dipped both of its hands into the water, the face of a child rippling to nothing as it trapped water between crooked fingers and lifted its hands free.

"Take," it said. "Drink."

Tycho dipped his head and sipped. It tasted as river water

should taste. Neither sweet nor brackish, but fresh and familiar. "That's it?" he said. "I've changed?"

The creature shook its head. "Did I agree that was the price? You looked thirsty so I offered you water." It smirked. "I wanted to see if you were ready to negotiate." *And in doing so, you showed me that you were.*

"Name your price," Tycho said.

"It doesn't work like that."

"It does this time," Tycho said firmly. "That's exactly how it's going to work." A hardening of the creature's expression reminded Tycho of something Alexa once said. Those who'd once been powerful were more dangerous than those who still were. Being diminished by circumstance made you cling harder to what little you still had. The rule applied to people and cities, kingdoms and empires.

"First the mother, then." The creature jerked its chin at Giulietta. "What do you expect me to take for her?"

"My life."

It sighed. "We've been through this. I don't want your life. What use would you be to us dead?"

"Make me a counter-offer then."

"Your death, highness. We'll take your death."

Tycho looked at him. There was nothing human in the creature's smile. It was old and cold, immortal enough to make him shiver. He knew he would hate what came next. The question was whether he'd accept it.

"I don't understand."

"Why should that matter to me? Still, because I'm feeling kind . . ." Behind him, the diminished smirked. "If I take your life, you die. If I take your death, you live . . ."

"For ever?" Tycho asked.

"What would be the point otherwise?"

He would become like them, diminished and unable to die. No matter where he found himself or what was done to him

232

there would be no escape. No salvation either. The woman he loved would grow old. She talked of souls. The incorruptible part of being human, only freed when the body died. If he never died, his soul would never go free. If he had one and today he doubted it.

"I accept," Tycho said.

"Of course you do." The creature smiled wide enough to show yellowing teeth. "And the baby," it said. "Do you want to make me an offer . . .? Or shall I just tell you an acceptable price for its life?"

Tycho nodded.

"You'll like this one. Well, perhaps like's the wrong word. But I'm sure you'll appreciate the subtlety. The price for Leo living is you give up his mother for ever."

It couldn't possibly . . .

Eyes cold as ice watched Tycho battle himself. In a second, Tycho condemned Leo to death and saw Giulietta with another child, his child. All of them growing older together. Except Tycho wouldn't grow older. In the next second he unravelled the decision. He thought of Giulietta, who lay corpse-like on a slab in his mind, and Leo gurgling in the arms of the faun. Tycho wanted to die but he'd given that away already. The knot in his chest tightened and tears scalded his eyes.

The goat-heeled god nodded. "You agree?"

"Yes," said Tycho, but he was shaking his head.

"Which is it?"

"Leo lives." His words were a whisper, his throat so tight he could barely speak and so salt his tears tasted like blood. "I wish to speak to the child's mother. Give me that at least."

"Speak then, highness. She will hear you."

"You have a fever," Tycho said.

"Tycho?"

"Yes," he said. "Me."

"You abandoned me." Her voice trembled.

"I've found Leo and he's safe. I'm bringing him back to you."

"*Alexa*," Giulietta said suddenly. She sounded scared. "You murdered Alexa and changed sides. You're lying to me about Leo."

"She ordered me to kill her."

"She what?"

"The *Assassini* kill when ordered. Alexa's death was her final order. She was determined to make Alonzo believe I'd changed sides. She was dying, Giulietta. She chose it. I simply obeyed."

"Leo's really safe?"

"He's safe and Roderigo's dead. He came after me with wild soldiers but I killed him and half of them. Alonzo will be furious."

"So much excitement," the creature muttered.

"Who's that?" asked Giulietta, suddenly sounding nervous.

"No one who matters," Tycho said.

"Good . . . Where are you now?"

"Montenegro."

"Where in Montenegro?"

"The cunt of the elder goddess."

"Typical," she said with a sniff.

As his sense of Giulietta faded, Tycho turned to find the faun in tears next to him, Leo clutched to her chest. Lifting the infant from her arms, he hugged Leo close, feeling the child snuffle against him. Where Leo had been pale he was now pink. The snot blocking his nose and the filth crusting his eyes were gone. "One question, highness," the faun said shyly.

"I'm not a highness."

She shrugged. "This form you took, this world to which you exiled yourself . . . What were you looking for that you became this?"

Tycho thought back to his memories of the beginning, which was not really his beginning, any more than he was the *you* she addressed. He thought of the warring gods and the battle for heaven, and had his answer. Some had fallen and some had not, and some had ended here. His mother had crossed half the world looking for it. Maybe her father had done the same, and his father, and so on.

"Forgiveness," Tycho said.

When he woke he was curled on the mossy floor of the cave with Leo asleep in his arms. He would have liked to dismiss his dreams, but Leo was healthy and bright-eyed, and Tycho could feel hot tears on his own cheeks. In his hands was the grave ribbon from Giulietta's hair.

36

Lady Giulietta refused to allow her ladies-in-waiting their miracle. She'd fallen into a fever and the doctor who thought her dead was wrong . . . She'd allow him his life as an act of charity but he was banished from Venice on the understanding he spoke to no one about this and never returned. Her aunt would have killed the man. That was Alexa. She was her own person.

"Fetch back the chamberlain, tell Marco's physician I'll be visiting Marco later, so no sedatives, and send Prince Frederick a message asking him to visit at his earliest convenience . . ." Her lady-in-waiting curtsied and withdrew without daring to look Lady Giulietta in the face. None of them dared look her in the face they were all so certain she'd returned from the dead. It would wear off. Well, either it would wear off or she'd replace the lot of them. The missing hair ribbon was a puzzle, though.

They'd found her alive but still in deepest sleep.

She'd told the chamberlain someone had obviously stolen the ribbon from her hair. He'd have been more likely to believe her had the door of the great chamber not been locked after Frederick left. Alexa would have known what to say.

Chances were Marco would know, too.

"A sweet angel t-took your r-ribbon."

She'd barely made it through his door when he answered the question she'd yet to ask. Behind her, two guards stiffened and she knew they were listening and were too shocked to hide the fact.

"Tell me t-that isn't t-true?" Marco was smiling, and his eyes flicked beyond her shoulder to the guards. "A b-beautiful angel t-took your ribbon and k-kissed you on the brow and s-said, God himself was r-returning you to h-health . . ."

"You can go," Lady Giulietta told the guards.

As the door shut, Marco grinned. "So much b-better than talk of d-demons. Within half an h-hour the whole city will k-know an angel came to earth to m-mop your brow and still your f-fever. And took only a h-hair ribbon as his r-reward. How sweet is t-that . . ."

"*Marco . . .*"

"Allow them their little m-miracle and they'll stop l-looking for a big one." He smiled at her. "P-people have been t-talking about n-nothing else all morning. I knew you'd be c-coming to see m-me." Marco patted the seat beside him, as if she had reverted to being a child. Instead of how it really was back then – her always seeming older and him seeming little more than a fool.

"Now, the p-poison. Tell me why you d-did something that s-stupid."

By noon, everyone in the city knew that prayer, God and Lady Giulietta's innate virtue had saved her from the severest of fevers, and that Lord Bribanzo's death, until lately thought a robbery gone wrong, had been at the hands of the Assassini on the orders of Duke Marco himself. The duke having firm proof that Bribanzo had turned traitor. Almost as bad, he'd been funding the ex-Regent, who had allied himself with the Red Crucifers and was threatening Venice.

The rumour that an angel mopped Giulietta's brow and healed

her with a kiss lost ground to the wonder of Duke Marco appearing in public on the Piazza San Marco, in control of his twitching and so poised that he talked to shocked onlookers with almost no stuttering at all. It was widely agreed the Millioni were blessed.

When Prince Frederick presented himself at the Porta della Carta, his entire entourage behind him and all wearing breast-plates, the rumours really started. Venice was allying itself with Sigismund. The prince was engaged to Giulietta. He brought demands from his father. She'd called him to banish him.

The truth never made it to the streets. He came to apologise and tell her he was leaving Venice. He didn't even get a quarter of a way through his apology before she told him to shut up and stop being so bloody formal. Their friendship returned more or less to normal after that; which meant he remained embarrassed and occasionally tongue-tied, and she tried not to tease him too much.

"I thought . . ." He hesitated. "I thought you'd want me to go. I should have said my father sent me. I should have told you m . . ." His hesitation this time was even longer. "I should have told you many things."

"You did," Giulietta said.

He looked happier but no less puzzled.

Rumour mongers visited taverns and rookeries to trim the gossip according to Marco's orders, which reached the rumour mongers through so many levels of secret whispers that few realised where they originated. Venice was not allying with Sigismund (which would cause problems with Byzantium). However, Lady Giulietta and Prince Frederick were firm friends. After the tragic death of his wife and child, even Emperor Sigismund would be glad the boy was coming out of himself.

No one talked of Alexa's will because few knew of it and those who did were too shocked to mention it elsewhere. Pietro produced it, still tied with a ribbon and sealed with Alexa's own seal. He'd brought it to the map room where Marco, Lady Giulietta and Frederick were peering at a fresco of the countries bordering the Adriatic Sea. Marco had just said something.

"The elder goddess cleft?" Frederick asked.

Lady Giulietta blushed.

"The world's cunt," said Marco. He looked at his cousin. "That's what it's called. That's what everyone calls it."

"You know where it is?"

He smiled, pulling a small book from the shelves. He was about to open it when he noticed Pietro in the doorway. "Your page," he said.

"I don't have a . . ." Giulietta stopped.

Pietro bowed clumsily. At least half his clumsiness was because he didn't want to dislodge the dragonet draped around his neck. Given the sharpness of the little lizard's claws and the tenacity with which it clung that was a wise move. "The duchess told me to give you this."

"What is it?" Frederick demanded.

Pietro shrugged, realised that was rude and muttered, "Don't know, sir."

Lady Giulietta waved the boy into the room. "Did she say when you were to give it to us?"

"*Sometime later*," Pietro said.

Marco laughed loudly. "S-so like her." He took the scroll and raised his eyebrows at the seal. It had Chinese characters inside a square. At least Giulietta thought that's what they were. She wondered why Marco didn't banish Pietro and wondered if she should do it herself. The question was answered when Marco ordered the page to sit quietly in the corner with his dragonet.

"It's h-hungry?" Marco asked.

"It's always hungry, sir."

Marco laughed. Returning to the scroll, he freed its ribbon and unrolled the parchment, his eyes skimming line after line of his mother's writing. At the end of it, he sighed. "She was r-rich

in her own r-right, I should have realised . . . All those oppor-
tunities to influence my f-father, all those d-decisions to be made
in Council when she was co-R-Regent. And my f-father gave her
land when they m-married."

"It concerns personal matters?" Frederick was asking if he
should go. Giulietta noticed him chew his lip as he waited for
her cousin to reply.

"Nothing my m-mother did was p-purely personal."
Frederick nodded.

"She leaves m-money to me. That lizard and the r-rank of
armiger to the b-boy. She leaves Giulietta a m-mansion in Corte
di M-Mmillioni, plus its contents. A h-house I d-didn't even
know she owned. She leaves L-Leo vineyards on the m-mainland.
You, she leaves her h-horses."

"Me?" Frederick said.

"A s-stud south of Milan. She thinks you'll l-like it . . ." Marco
hesitated. "Tycho becomes a c-count, and gets her silver m-mines
in M-Montenegro. She thinks h-he'll appreciate the irony."
Frederick looked at Giulietta, who looked at the floor.

"When did she give you this?" Marco demanded.

"The night she was . . . The night she . . ."

"G-gave you the dragonet?" The duke realised the boy didn't
know that Tycho, who had been his old master, was acting on
orders. Abandoning the book he'd taken from the shelves, Marco
went to crouch in front of the boy. They spoke quietly and
Pietro's face changed as Giulietta watched. By the end he was
wide-eyed and wondering, half in tears and half smiling as if the
weight of the world had been lifted from his thin shoulders,
which it had.

How did her cousin know how to do that?

"So," Marco said. "We can t-take it she wrote this k-knowing
she was going to d-die. It r-really is her last will. H-her expression of intent." He lowered his voice, and Giulietta realised he
was trying to avoid being overheard by Pietro.

"She wants Alonzo d-dead."

"I should leave," Frederick said.

"N-no," said Marco, "you should s-stay. Alonzo has signed a t-treaty with Byzantium agreeing an alliance once he t-takes my throne. This is their emperor's revenge for Tycho k-killing his son."

"Rosalyn killed Nikolaos," Giulietta said flatly.

"Did s-she?" Marco looked surprised.

Frederick nodded. "I was there. The wild girl killed Prince Nikolaos and Tycho killed Lord Andronikos . . . So, this means war?"

Marco shrugged. "What other choice do we have?"

37

A declaration of war concentrates the mind. So it's said.

Well . . . So Marco insisted it was said. Lady Giulietta was less sure. It certainly changed the city's view of Marco, though. Those who'd cursed her cousin's name a week earlier vied with each other to be the most patriotic. Within an hour of the war against Alonzo being announced the first drunk had been arrested for celebrating too hard, and a street fight between the Nicoletti and the Castellani had to be broken up, after both gangs accused each other of supporting the traitorous Alonzo and lacking true faith in Marco the Great.

That all it took to have *the Simple* replaced with *the Great* was go to war with his own uncle, Marco professed to find amusing. If he'd known it was that easy, he told Giulietta, he'd have done it years ago. She knew this was a lie, but Frederick grinned at the truth of it. And they all took a turn around the Piazza San Marco so the gathering crowds could see what they'd be fighting for.

In the fever of the city's drunken self-regard, Marco being half-Mongol suddenly became unimportant and his decision to go to war in the middle of the coldest winter anyone could remember hailed as brilliance. When, Giulietta thought, it was probably the most stupid thing he'd done – for all she couldn't see an alternative.

The city's joy was helped by a final emptying of grain from the state granaries and the release of barrels of salt mutton and thin beer from Frederick's own warehouses. So much of all three flooded the market that prices plummeted to the point where even poor households could afford to store food. Parties started up on the Grand Canal and skates – consigned to cupboards – broken out again as the poor, the *cittadini* and the noble mixed on the ice.

Marco asked for and received volunteers in their thousands. Men with military experience were separated from those without. The toughest of the Nicoletti and Castellani street thugs were corralled into auxiliary bands and put under the command of seasoned sergeants. The state armoury was opened; swords, helmets, straw-stuffed leather jerkins and breastplates issued, each one imprinted with the X-strike of the Council of Ten.

Names were entered on lists, and lists of companies collected into a roster that was presented to Marco himself. The duke would be leading his army. Some of the city's earliest dukes had fought in battle. None of them had been stuttering simpletons, although at least one had been blind and another crippled. In recent years the Millioni had relied on mercenaries for their foreign campaigns.

Marco intended to change that.

His war galleys were still anchored off the edge of the lagoon, where the ice could not close around their wooden hulls and crush them. Some of the fleet had been rowed from Arzanale through cracking ice at the start of the freeze, when Duchess Alexa realised how fierce the cold was going to be. Half the City Watch, most of the palace guard and all the customs men had volunteered for battle. Marco told his commanders to accept all recruits.

When it was suggested – gently and politely – that this would leave his city open to disorder, he'd pointed out there was no trade for the customs to tax, and anyone worth murdering would be elsewhere. All the same, he issued a proclamation stating that disorder in time of war was treason, punishable by death, and his law would be strictly enforced. No one dared ask who'd be enforcing this. Since the city guard had all volunteered.

His points made, Marco made Roderigo's replacement as Captain of the Dogana his infantry commander, gave Captain Weimer, the new captain of the palace guard, control of the cavalry, and appointed two Watch captains as their lieutenants. The only serious argument happened in private, out of sight of the Council and the new commanders. Before it happened, Frederick gave Giulietta a present, although the argument was not between Frederick and Giulietta, but between Giulietta and her cousin, the duke.

She was shocked at how certain Marco was of his rights as duke. He was shocked at her declaration of independence from Venice and her statement that as a zum Friedland princess and landowner in Schiavoni she reserved the right to think for herself. For a moment, with Marco refusing to back down and Giulietta refusing to relinquish power as Regent, it looked as if the war might not happen.

But first, of course, Frederick had to give Giulietta her present.

Four of his men carried wooden crates into her study on the third floor of Ca' Ducale, watched – because everything in the long, narrow room was watched – by sour-faced Millioni dukes staring down from the walls.

"Put the crates on the floor and leave," Frederick told his men, who arranged the boxes in a line rather than stacking them. Each box had Giulietta's arms branded into the lid, she realised with a shock. Bowing to her, then to their master, the soldiers trooped silently outside. It took about a second before they started talking among themselves and Frederick grinned ruefully.

"*Krieghund?*" Giulietta asked.

"Every one of them," he answered. He'd brought his entire pack to Venice. He'd told her of Wolf Valley, of their runs in the Alpine meadows of the high slopes. She wondered his friends could bear to be caged in a city this crowded.

"You're going with Marco?"

Frederick raised his eyebrows and she blushed. Of course he was. The treaty Alonzo had signed with Byzantium was as close to a declaration of war as either empire had dared in fifty years. He said, "I've written to my father, telling him you know he sent me. I've also told him it's my choice to accompany Marco on this campaign and no fault lies with Venice if I die."

Lady Giulietta doubted his father would pay much attention. Having lost his elder son off Cyprus in a battle between the Venetian and Mamluk fleets, a letter from Frederick wouldn't be enough to calm his anger if his remaining son died. All the same, she nodded as if she thought that might work.

"And you?" Frederick asked. "Are you going?"

"What do you think?" Lady Giulietta couldn't keep the bitterness out of her voice. "I'm a woman. Or hadn't you noticed?"

He glanced at the low neck of her fur-edged dress.

"That's rude," she said crossly. When Frederick grinned she knew he was teasing. Her overgown was Alexa's and twenty years old, cut low at the front when styles had been a little bolder. The undergown was thin white wool.

"So," Frederick said. "Are you . . .? Going, I mean?"

"I've told you . . ."

His smile was knowing.

"What?" demanded Giulietta, feeling her stomach lurch and wondering who had betrayed her. She'd been so careful. How could he possibly know? She was on the edge of pleading for his silence when he told her he knew her. She was planning to board one of the ships and reveal herself to Marco after they'd left Venice.

"Do that," Frederick said, "and he'll only put you ashore at Ragusa."

"I'm a zum Friedland princess."

"Also Regent. Which is why you need to approach this head-on." He dropped to a crouch beside a crate and wrestled free its lid, which stuck because it was fitted rather than because it was nailed on. Straw spilled across the floor, filling her study with the faint smell of summer. Digging his hands under the straw packing, Frederick pulled out a white breastplate, scattering more straw around him. "I had to guess the chest size . . ." He held it out to her.

Lady Giulietta took it gingerly.

In Italy the description *white armour* meant armour without decoration. This was truly white. As perfect as if freshly painted but hard to the touch. A slight ridge bisected the breastplate and the steel curved gently rather than sharply towards the sides. He'd guessed the size of her breasts and guessed generously. That made her smile. Since, even after Leo, she doubted they'd trouble an armourer's skill. She could probably have fitted into a boy's armour if she tried.

"*Champlevé*," Frederick said.

He meant the white enamel. *Champlevé* was new, expensive and required talent to do well. Turning the breastplate over, Giulietta realised she'd never seen armour designed for a woman before. Although, of course, there were ballads about wives donning their dead husbands' armour to defend the family castle or take revenge on his enemies. Frederick was now wrestling with another box.

"Here's the next bit." He held it up proudly.

The overlapping white scales of a metal skirt shaped to cover her hips and rise at the front to let her to ride astride like a man. She asked what he imagined she'd wear under it. The answer turned out to be in the third box. "It's light," she said, taking the undershirt of mail.

"Star iron. We keep a collection."

It seemed the *krieghund* sought fragments of broken stars and hoarded them until new armour was needed. Then the dark and twisted lumps were added to molten steel, along with the charred skull of a wolf and a rusty nail. The resulting steel could be beaten so thin it had half the weight of ordinary plate.

She doubted Frederick should be telling her Wolf Brother secrets but thanked him all the same. He seemed so proud of his clan's cleverness. After the mail shirt came an open-faced helmet, vambraces for her arms, thigh guards and knee guards and a pair of half-gauntlets.

The second-to-last crate contained white leather trews, a white jerkin, padded inside with folds of fabric, and gloves to fit in the half-gauntlets; all the sizes looked right, and it felt strange to realise Frederick had been watching her more carefully than she knew. Holding up the white leather doublet, she smiled.

"Try it on," he suggested.

She shook her head, looked at the breastplate and hesitated . . . Her undergown was decent and it wasn't as if she planned to put on full armour. She didn't even need to put on the doublet to see if the breastplate fitted. Dropping the fur-lined *houppelande* from her shoulders, she stepped out of Alexa's old gown, realising too late her undergown was thinner than she remembered.

"Let me help," Frederick said quickly.

The metal was cold on her chest, the shoulder plates so hard at the edge of her upper arms that she shook her head. The vambraces chafed her wrists but she left them in place. The armour scalloping her hips was as heavy as a weighted belt. She and Frederick looked at the thigh guards and decided simultaneously that buckling them on might be a step too far.

"Now this," Frederick said. He opened a crate longer and thinner than the others and she knew before he dipped his hands into the straw what it held. She'd fought with sticks as a child, and Aunt Alexa had insisted she learn to handle a dagger, but she'd never studied swordplay or watched a tournament. Uncle Alonzo liked his jousts, and that was reason enough to despise them.

It was a three-quarter sword, maybe slightly smaller.

"Let me show you how to hold it."

Frederick stood behind her and his breath was warm on her neck as he put his arms around her and folded her fingers around the wire-wound hilt. The inside of his elbow brushed her breast where her breastplate scooped low and would be hidden beneath shoulder armour. Neither of them seemed to notice. Well, he didn't. So she held her peace as well.

"Now lift it so . . ."

She struggled to raise the sword above her head. The weapon was heavier than she expected for all it was in the newest fashion and smaller than the swords old men used. Frederick stood right behind her now. She could feel him bump slightly against her back and buttocks. He noticed her unease because he stepped back and she almost let the sword fall down.

"Find its balance point."

He was behind her again but careful not to touch anything except her hands, which he moved slightly up so the sword was exactly above her head.

"Keep it like that . . ."

Stepping round her, he drew his own sword and she recognised the *WolfeSelle* with a shiver. The *krieghund* totem had a new handle. That was why she hadn't recognised it when sheathed.

"Only until Leo is old enough," Frederick said.

Giulietta's lips twisted. Frederick was guarding the blade until Leo came of age and assumed command of the Wolf Brothers. She had her own opinions about that. What made her eyes well up was simpler.

"We'll find him," Frederick promised. "I swear." He looked at the sword trembling in her upraised arms and smiled. "Now strike down to one side. Don't tell me which. I'll show you a block."

"Ready?" she asked.

He grinned. "Always . . . Make it a real blow."

She swung her sword to the left as hard as she could – but he was there first, sparks exploding from their blades and the clang of steel so loud it deafened both as it echoed from the study walls. Her door smashed open and the man on guard rushed in, his halberd levelled and his face torn between fear and duty. He froze, obviously shocked. Whether at her in armour, the fact she was wearing only her undergown, or that she held a sword was harder to tell. "Sorry," Giulietta said. "I'm having a lesson."

"My lady, I'm so sorry. I didn't . . ."

"Of course you didn't." She waved him and his apology from her room. "We'd better practise elsewhere," she told Frederick.

"We'll practise on board." He appeared serious.

"Frederick, Marco will never . . ."

"Demand it. You're still the Regent, remember? Why do you think I had this made for you? I don't expect you to fight," he added hurriedly. "But you should have armour and I thought white would suit you."

Lady Giulietta put down her sword and let him unbuckle her armour, his fingers touching her side as he removed the metal skirt scalloping her hips. She blushed and he seemed not to notice. "I'm your squire," he said, putting the armour back into its boxes. The last to be packed was her open-faced helmet.

"People need to see you."

She wasn't sure if he was making a general point or meant Marco's followers needed to see her face. It turned out he meant the second. He had an idea for refining why Venice was going to war. It involved telling the truth. At least, a version of the truth closer to the real truth than the one currently being told. Having spent her life surrounded by those who dealt in lies and half-lies and held the truth close like hidden cards, she liked it. She liked it very much indeed. For a start, it meant she'd have the changeling in the nursery quietly fostered and forgotten. Only a few knew Alexa had put the nursemaid's infant in the slaughtered child's place, and they would keep silent.

Calling for a messenger, Lady Giulietta dictated a proclamation that ignored the dead baby put in Leo's place and simplified what had happened to something the city could understand and accept. The traitor Alonzo had stolen Leo, her son and Venice's heir. The army of Venice was going to get him back.

By nightfall, those who hadn't already enlisted were thronging the Piazza San Marco demanding that they too be allowed to fight. No man between fourteen and sixty saw why he should be left behind. Marco was furious about the proclamation, but there was little he could do. He tried to tell Giulietta she couldn't come. Giulietta replied that she was Regent; without her permission he couldn't go at all. His going depended on her going. Leo was hers. She would go.

Giulietta won.

38

And on the other side of the Adriatic Sea, in a strange fort built into the head of a high valley, the infant they argued about slept in a stronghold doorway, wrapped in rancid furs, while the man neither Giulietta nor Marco mentioned hacked the heads from dead archers and spiked them on spears arranged in a row. Their bodies he dragged through the stronghold and up stone steps to leave at the mouth of a cave – in case those who lived inside could use them. The weather was so cold that neither the bodies nor their glassy-eyed heads rotted.

Roderigo's corpse he impaled for his part on the night Tycho was captured in a silver net on Duchess Alexa's orders. Under the tallow light of a cruel moon, he put Roderigo right in the middle of the line he'd arranged as a warning to anyone foolish enough to approach the walls. And as he wrestled the spear upright, and dropped its end into the hole he'd stabbed and twisted into frozen earth, he considered what the creature in the cave had said. It could all be lies, of course. Even that strange almost-memory of angels fighting and falling could be a lie. Perhaps he simply wanted it to be untrue . . .

Although those in the cave left him untouched, he knew they watched, unless that was the elder goddess herself. Tycho suspected she was too old and too powerful to bother with lesser immortals any more.

Leo was walking now.

That was new. At least, he thought it was. He hadn't paid the infant much attention except as an extension of Giulietta but he was pretty certain the walking was new and hoped she'd be pleased. He knew she would pass this way soon. He'd told her where he was and that he had Leo. If she didn't come for him she'd come for the child. He was as certain of this as he was that the ice would soon thaw. So he slept his days in the armoury, which was windowless and had a door it was easy to bar, and woke each dusk to find the child sitting by him, looking thoughtful or puzzled, or whatever that strange Millioni expression was meant to be. He fed the infant on scraps collected from the satchels of the wild archers and wondered endlessly whether the goat-heeled creature had lied.

"What do you think?"

Leo didn't care. Maybe he thought they should wait there for his mother.

"Do you?" Tycho asked. The child burped and Tycho decided that was probably a *stay here* vote. He could almost hear Giulietta like a single note at the edge of his mind. Her name was written each night across the sky in stars. He had no doubt she was coming. He hardly dared imagine how she'd managed that. "She'll be here soon." Something he'd been promising for days.

How would they greet each other? Would she see the guilt in his eyes?

Tycho knew he was behaving like a child and felt shamed without knowing why. Inside his head was a cold darkness that stared back implacably, daring him to venture deeper. He'd thought everyone had that. Pulling a whetstone from his pocket, he drew his sword and dragged the stone along its edge, grinding away the jagged notches put there by his fight with Roderigo. As he did, he tried to still the fears in his head and realised that no whetstone existed to smooth out the notches in his soul . . .

So, you think you have one after all?

A soul? Maybe not, but Giulietta thought he did. He'd arrived in Venice without memories, only to regain fragments when near drowning washed his amnesia away, and Rosalyn, the ragged girl who pulled him from the canal, had been certain it was more than near drowning. He'd been dead when she spotted him floating by the stone steps at Rialto and dragged him ashore. How many times could one person die and still keep a soul?

"All right, all right," Tycho said.

Leo was grizzling again. Keeping the toddler shit free and fed was a full-time occupation. The child had re-embraced life with a fierce hunger, lungs of steel and the ability to slime food scraps at both ends.

Leo grinned as Tycho picked him up.

"Yeah," Tycho said. "Your father was a monster, too." Pulling a chunk of stale bread from his pocket, Tycho tore off a mouthful, bit into an even harder sliver of ewe's cheese and began to chew. The pulp he spat into his hand he gave the child, who ate it greedily. "I hope you appreciate it," he said.

The child with Giulietta's eyes looked up at him.

Tycho doubted he would forget Giulietta. Any more than he'd forget Afrior, the girl who died at the gates of Bjornvin and who he'd thought his sister, with all the bloody complication that caused. First Afrior, now this . . . With a shock, Tycho realised letting Leo go would be almost as hard as parting with Giulietta, and that would be unbearable. Heartbreaking, if he believed for a moment he had any heart left to break.

"Shit," he said. "You probably won't even realise I'm gone."

Or was here at all. That was the brutal bit. To sacrifice and not be remembered, walk away and not be able to say why. Because how could Tycho say what he'd need to say to explain why this was happening . . .

Things change.

Well, he could hardly deny that. And some things, he thought bitterly, remain the same. Dawn was coming and Giulietta so close he could taste her on the last of the night wind. When daylight came he would hide. As he would have to hide every day between now and eternity if the creature from the cave told the truth. Time enough to get rich and powerful, if he could be bothered. For a fleeting moment, he fantasised about being the next Tamburlaine, and building an empire across time as well as distance. An immortal emperor of a never-dying empire . . . An endless succession of empresses beautiful enough to make him forget Giulietta. She'd become that young Italian woman with the red hair whose name he couldn't remember, except that he'd always remember it. He knew himself too well.

After he carried Leo into the fort and up the guard steps to the battlements, the cold winds sweeping up the valley blew his fantasies away. He might change his name and build another life but he had no wish to rule for the sake of it. If he really had all of time as his playground he'd find better things to do with it. But that could come later; first he needed to do the impossible . . . Return Leo and lie to the woman he loved.

"You keep what you've seen to yourself," he told the infant.

Leo grinned.

The army marched between the white slopes of the valley and the ground under their feet was so hard it might have been stone. Weeks of freezing weather had turned the snow solid, while furious winds along the valley floor had scoured away any drifting snow that might have softened it.

They took the simplest route and kept to the lowest valleys and would have taken another two days to reach the fort had Tycho not brought Leo to meet them. There were more men than Tycho expected. Although he was not to know – and only discovered later – that Marco had used a quarter of those who accompanied him to secure the port and garrison towns along the way, having already sent half his men to the capital with orders to take it peacefully if possible, bloodily if not. The old Montenegrin aristocracy had used the feud between Marco and Alonzo to declare their own independence. Marco needed to secure the capital for Venice. He intended to besiege Alonzo's headquarters himself.

So the men marched through wisps of drifting snow, heads down, one foot placed stolidly in front of the other, becoming simply an army, that great unthinking creature on the move. The creature had walked in daylight, slept fitfully, moved again under the light of a tallow moon – and would soon sleep again, before moving on. In years to come armies would grow but for now ten thousand was large and fifteen thousand immense. And though Marco had brought somewhere between these numbers, he'd divided his forces so often that fifteen hundred marched unknowing towards where Tycho waited.

Well, most marched: two hundred knights rode at the column's head and a dozen outriders protected each flank. It was one of the outriders who noticed Tycho framed against the dawn. He shouted a warning that had his companions falling into battle order. Tycho hated them for ending this part of his life.

The early sun flared like flame on his shoulders.

He might as well have stood with his back to the mouth of hell. His clothes felt on fire, but his jacket had nothing to fear. His flesh was the only thing likely to burn. But he had chosen a spot where they would see him and see him they had. Stepping now into shadow, Tycho blew out his breath in gratitude. Leo looked untroubled. Down in the valley, however, the column scrabbled like a kicked-over ants' nest. At an order, a dozen archers broke from the column and strung their bows, notching arrows and judging distances as they watched him descend.

"I have Prince Leo," Tycho shouted.

He lifted the giggling child high above his head and relied on the last of the moon and the first of the sun to let them see the prince was happy and unharmed. One of the archers recognised Tycho's wolf-grey braids and a roar of outrage went up. *Outlaw, kill him* and *bastard*. Still they hesitated, watching as he stalked towards them. Tycho was wanted for Alexa's murder and could hardly claim he hadn't killed her. But Prince Leo clung to him and a safe shot was impossible.

"Suppose I should thank you," Tycho muttered.

Leo burbled.

"H-h-hold . . ." The order came from the column's front where a knight in the purple, white and gold of Venice whirled his mount and cantered towards the archers, flanked by a knight in gilded armour and another in white plate. "L-let the g-grievous angel approach."

"I have Leo, your highness."

Tycho lifted the princeling and the knight in white plate spurred his mount, causing the man in gilded armour to shout a warning. Scree shifted and the white-armoured rider dragged at his horse's head to stop it sliding on the slope.

"Give him to me . . ."

It couldn't be, and yet Tycho knew it was.

Lady Giulietta sat armoured and astride a panting warhorse, reins folded into one hand, her other hand reaching towards her son. Tycho wondered sadly why he'd expected anything else. He'd been proud of her from the moment they met. Her fierce intelligence, the quiet fury with which she met life full-on. It was only seeing her now that made him realise how utterly desperate she must have been the night she knelt before the stone mother and tried to take her own life.

The knight in gilded armour spurred his mount forward and Lady Giulietta turned to smile . . . Instantly, Tycho wanted to kill him. He wanted to pull his guts through a slit in his stomach. The wave of jealousy shocked him. "We haven't really met," the knight said. The young man's expression was guarded.

Swallowing his fury, Tycho recognised Frederick, Leopold's

brother. In Frederick, Tycho saw echoes of Leopold, who'd begun as Tycho's enemy and ended as his friend. This man, however, was no friend.

"Your highness . . ."

"Lord Tycho."

"Hello, angel." Duke Marco grinned.

Tycho bowed. "Your mother . . ."

"I k-know," said Marco. "Killed by B-Byzantine assassins. Hideous. I'm so sorry you were blamed unjustly." He edged his mount forward, putting himself between Tycho and the others, and them between him and the archers. "Well," he said quietly. "I can h-hardly say you're the head of m-my *Assassini* and my m-mother ordered her own d-death, can I . . .? Now, put J-Julie out of her m-misery."

Stepping round Marco's horse, Tycho lifted the child. His fingers touched the metal at her gauntlet and he missed the spark that usually flared between them. "My lady . . . Your son."

"T-thank him," Marco said. "He g-got your son back."

Lady Giulietta dipped her head.

Then she was hugging Leo, her steel-clad arms tight around the child and her face pushed to his and she was sobbing as if her heart was broken, although Tycho knew it was mended.

"Thank you," she said. Leopold nodded and Tycho's hackles rose.

Who was he to join in Lady Giulietta's thanks?

"R-ride with me," Marco ordered.

"Your highness, I have no mount."

The duke clapped his hands and a bearded groom cantered forward with one of Marco's spare mounts. The animal was already saddled.

"I'm bad at riding, highness."

"You're afraid?"

"Only of appearing a fool in front of Giulietta."

Marco smiled sympathetically. "I"m rubbish at r-riding," he

confided. "It's best to let the animal do all the w-work and simply p-pretend you know what you're d-doing without doing anything. Much like being a prince . . . Come, we'll both p-pretend we know what we're d-doing. D-don"t worry," he added. "I know we need to g-get you under cover before the sun r-rises."

39

She didn't see Tycho that evening or the next. Lady Giulietta wasn't sure if he was avoiding her or she was avoiding him. Even Frederick seemed unsettled by the blackness of her mood. She clung to Leo, afraid that he'd forgotten her. And when he grinned and said mama, she cried. But still the darkness and the doubts remained, and within an hour she was examining every inch of his body, afraid he'd taken a fever or been hurt in some way. But all he did was gurgle and grin and regard her search as a great game, and by the end she had to admit there wasn't a single bruise.

Tycho had looked after him well.

The day after that Marco's army negotiated the last of the passes and Giulietta stood beside her cousin looking down at the valley with the Red Cathedral in the middle of its lake. A cathedral, a separate bell tower and a squat hall. The buildings were stranger than she expected, more exotic. They didn't look Christian to her at all. The lake itself was long and thin, and the village small and mean. She wanted to be out of the wind as much as the others, but the shiver that caught her had nothing to do with the cold.

He's down there . . . She gave him a name, cross with herself for being a coward, *Uncle Alonzo*. Although *Alonzo di Millioni* would do. She hated that they belonged to the same family. That someone in her family could do what he'd done to her . . . Had her inseminated, made her bear his child and then stolen the baby from her. *Not your fault*, she thought, looking at Leo clutched in her arms. Never your fault . . .

"We should m-move."

Looking up, she realised the entire army was waiting for her. Well, Marco was, and that was the same. "Sorry."

"You should t-talk to T-Tycho."

"*Marco.*"

"The l-longer you p-put it off the w-worse it will get."

Remounting, Marco waited for her to do the same, and together they rode on with Frederick following them like an unhappy shadow and Tycho hidden wherever her cousin kept him hidden during the day. They rode down the valley and into the village, and the villagers were too cowed by the cold and their hunger to do more than come out of their houses and stare. The Red Crucifers, then Alonzo, then Marco . . . She doubted it made any difference to them who was ruining their lives.

Marco set up his camp beside the village on the fan-shaped alluvial plain formed by dirt and grit brought down from the high mountains around them. It was hardscrabble ground that jutted into a narrow and unforgiving lake. Their surroundings suffered the villagers to exist but treated them too harshly to encourage them to increase in number. The rows of graves with rotting wooden headboards and the occasional rusting iron one were proof of that.

The duke apologised to the villagers for what was about to happen, and then he had his soldiers raid their larders, search their straw for hidden food or weapons, round up what was left of their herds, slaughter the few remaining chickens and rip down their log houses for kindling, firewood and logs that could be used to make palisades. The newly homeless he conscripted into his army, housing them under canvas or blankets like the rest of his men.

Hunters became pathfinders or archers, farm labourers dug latrines, the blacksmith joined the armourers, and the wise women were ordered to help with the sick. The rest were given simple spears, shown how to hold them and told to die well. Since they'd lived on the edge of hunger their entire lives, and those lives had been spent on the shore of a bleak upland lake in the shadow of a rotting wooden cathedral, this surprised them not at all.

"Do you think he has men watching? Giulietta asked.

"Obviously," Frederick said. Seeing her scowl, he shrugged apologetically. "I mean, wouldn't you?" He jerked his chin towards the building rising from the ice at the far end of the lake. Walls of rock rose high behind it and to both sides. The marble-white ice provided the only approach. The village was the gateway.

It would be a strange siege. The route from the coast was too rugged and Marco had marched the column too fast for them to drag catapults or timber to build siege towers or the supplies needed to dig tunnels. But why would he need them? He already knew no huge stone walls stood in their way. The cathedral was made from old staves that should burn easily if he could get close enough. His siege engines were individual archers, flaming arrows were what he intended to use to bring the walls down. The ice, he told his officers, was an added bonus. All that water frozen solid so it couldn't be used to put out the fires.

He intended to follow Julius Caesar's siege of Alesia, although obviously Marco had far fewer men and he didn't need to build a *circumvallation* around the cathedral, since the mountains created their own containing wall, nor did he need to dig a ditch round the cathedral and fill it was water, since Alonzo had thoughtfully done that for him with the makeshift moat, whose ice he had broken each day. Marco would, however, be using the other parts of Caesar's original plan.

Frederick said, "Captain Weimer is horrified."

"I'm not surprised." Giulietta smiled sourly. "Basing your siege on dusty scrolls. Who'd be that idiotic? Apart from my cousin, obviously."

"Weimer told him no plan survived contact with the enemy."

"What did Marco say to that?"

"The damn b-battle would d-damn well do what it was t-told."

Giulietta laughed and one of Frederick's staff turned to stare, then hastily looked away and busied himself with the buckles of his saddle. She knew the *krieghund* were watching her almost as closely as they were watching their master. Three names were being muttered among the knights and *krieghund*, and swallowed into silence the moment she appeared. Hers was the first, Frederick's the second. It was the third that made everyone uneasy. She still had to talk to Tycho.

I'm not afraid of him, she told herself, then sighed at the lie. Even Marco seemed afraid of this new version, who glowered at her from across the camp and turned away the one time she summoned the nerve to talk to him. She'd always been a little afraid, for all she believed he meant it when he said he'd never hurt her. Except, of course, he had, and badly. That night at Ca' Zum Friedland when he *fed* . . .

It had nearly killed her. And the dreams it left had lasted over a year.

Night after night she woke bolt upright and in tears; one moment asleep, the next wide awake and so knotted up her heart thudded and she had to fight herself for breath. Leopold had soothed her, stroking her hair and drying her tears, his arms around her until she slept again. Sometimes she'd wake and find him still holding her. That was why she'd been so furious at what happened with Tycho on the deck of the *San Marco* the night Leopold died. She should have still hated him. For months she told herself she did hate him.

It was complicated and about to get more so. She didn't hate Tycho but he definitely made her uneasy in a way Frederick didn't. *Shit . . .* Giulietta stopped, appalled. She'd just linked Frederick and Tycho in the same thought. She was pretty sure that was the first time she'd compared them.

"Are you all right?" Frederick asked.

"No," said Giulietta. "I'm not." She turned on her heels and headed for her tent, knowing that Frederick and his whole staff were staring after her. *You should go back and apologise. No, you should find Tycho and talk . . .* Lady Giulietta ignored both her suggestions. She was arrogant enough to believe Frederick would keep. As for Tycho, if she waited long enough he'd come looking for her.

Snapping awake from dreamless sleep, Tycho looked for Leo and remembered – too late to stop his hand from reaching out – that Leo was Giulietta's responsibility now. It took Tycho another second to remember he was in Marco's baggage wagon, safe under canvas but cold as stone. The brutal weather was slowing his thoughts as surely as it slowed his reflexes.

Stilling himself, Tycho listened.

The sound of horses returning, from hunting probably. The clang of a blacksmith and the hammering of a carpenter, the rasp of a two-man saw and the grind of a sharpening wheel. The noise of a camp settling for the night. He already knew Marco's archers slept in a ramshackle village church that was saved from being stripped for timber after the duke discovered the village boasted a priest and services were still held there. When he asked their religion, the priest took care to ask Marco his first. As it happened, Marco was open enough not to mind if the man was Orthodox or Catholic, so long as he didn't follow a heresy. The man swore he didn't and never had. If he objected to Marco's archers billeting in the church he hid it well.

I should stir, Tycho thought.

It was time for him to walk the lines and check the pickets, make sure the sentries were awake, and go beyond the lines to kill any men Alonzo sent to spy on them. All tasks he undertook willingly without mentioning them to others. But first . . . If Giulietta could not bring herself to talk to him he would have to talk to her. *You might have rescued Leo but you killed her Aunt Alexa*, Tycho reminded himself. *The woman who was her mother in all but name.* Maybe he would walk the lines and check the pickets first.

When the canvas cover of Duke Marco's baggage cart drew back, the soldiers guarding it looked straight ahead and kept looking straight ahead as Tycho rolled himself out of it and landed lightly on his feet.

He could feel their gaze as he headed for the pickets, changed his mind and turned for Prince Frederick's tent, marked by its double-eagle pennant, changed his mind again and headed for Lady Giulietta's instead. He agreed with their whispers that Marco bringing his cousin was plain odd, the fact she wore armour and rode astride like a man was just wrong, and that whatever was going on with those three – meaning Tycho, Frederick and Giulietta – was a bloody mess. He also agreed the Millioni were a law to themselves. He thought their final rhetorical question – who were they to judge? – a wise one.

Sentries let Tycho pass and said nothing.

Duke Marco clasped hands with this man, the one who was supposed to have killed his mother, until it turned out that was someone else. The emperor's bastard gripped his shoulders and clapped him on the back, and if both found the gestures forced, they let it go. Lady Giulietta cast more glances in his direction than a besotted fifteen-year-old at the first boy to kiss her, looking away when he looked back.

It seemed a mistake had been made and Duchess Alexa killed by Byzantine assassins. Assassins sent by those who'd now signed a treaty to give the traitor Alonzo his nephew's throne. Since

Marco said it was true it must be true. But when Tycho smiled men still looked away.

The seams of Giulietta's tent were sewn, thick thread parting under Tycho's knife to let him slip through the gap, unbuckle his shoulder harness and put his sword carefully on the ground-sheet, followed by his daggers. He did this slowly to give Giulietta time to wake. Although, when he turned to see her sitting upright in her cot he knew she'd half been expecting him. "Light a lamp," he suggested.

She shook her head and red curls brushed her shoulders. She obviously remembered his night vision because she suddenly closed her gown at the neck, hiding the soft upper slope of her breasts and the slight valley between.

"How's Leo?"

"Tired, filthy, hungry . . . Glad to be home."

Maybe home really was where your mother was. How would Tycho know? Come to that, how would she know either? All the same, Tycho was happy for Leo and certain the infant deserved far better than his first year of life had offered. Giulietta didn't suggest that he come closer so Tycho stayed where he was, dropping to a crouch and hugging his knees to his chest. "How have you been?"

"How do you think?"

The sudden anger in her voice shocked him. "Upset?" he said, knowing that would barely come close to describing how she felt.

"You should have told me."

Tycho could say told you what? He could make excuses or lie but he'd always told her the truth and now would be a bad time to change that. Instead he nodded, realised his nod was too dark to see, and said, "You're right. I should. I'm sorry I didn't."

"Why didn't you?"

The question was brutal, but it was a kindness. "Your Aunt Alexa ordered me not to," he said, grateful to be allowed to explain.

"It was her plan that you should change sides?"

Tycho hesitated. "Your cousin Marco's idea," he said. "Alexa said I was to leave immediately without upsetting you with long goodbyes. Marco came up with the idea of changing sides."

"Alexa knew about that?"

"I doubt it," Tycho said honestly. "Later, when I returned . . ."

"She ordered her own death?"

"Yes," Tycho said.

"Of course she did," said Giulietta bitterly. "Only my aunt could order her own death as a power play . . . My God, Marco *knew*." She sounded shocked. "When he declared you an outlaw and put a price on your head he *knew* you'd been obeying his mother's orders."

"I think he worked it out." The size of the reward Marco offered for Tycho's death helped convince Prince Alonzo he'd changed sides. Without it, Alonzo might have killed him and been done with it. "Another thing . . . Your aunt was dying. I don't know if she told you that?"

Giulietta went very still.

"She was being eaten up inside." Tycho kept his voice flat. "I gave her a quick death in place of a painful one. She was tired, and she believed it was time for you and Marco to take over. Giulietta . . ." He was going to tell her something he shouldn't know. Without mentioning how he knew. "She couldn't bear for you to see her die. She couldn't bear for Marco to have to watch her fight the pain."

"You swear this?"

"Yes," Tycho said. "I swear it. Only her skill with drugs kept her alive and it was a battle she was losing. She chose to make her death mean something."

Moving Leo to the other side of her cot carefully so he didn't wake, she patted the bed beside her, and Tycho pulled himself up from the floor and sat where she said. She smelt warm and salty, her breath tasting of thyme as he turned her head to kiss her and her lips softened.

"This is a bad idea," she said.

"Terrible." He kissed her slowly with his hands by his sides and this time she turned her head and fixed her lips on his and he knew she kissed from choice. She was the one to lift a hand to his face and stroke, before wrapping her fingers into his hair to hold him still. Her next kiss was deeper. When he put his hand to her breast, she smiled and moved her elbow to allow him room. Her breasts were fuller than when they first met.

"Gently," she protested.

Grinning, he dipped his head and suckled her, her fingers twisting into his hair as she pulled him against her. They slid down on to the cot and he let Giulietta shift him so her mouth could reach his as she folded her leg over his and tightened, grinding herself into him. She came with a gasp and a sob-like laugh.

They lay like that for a while until the sound of her breath was replaced by noise from the camp outside. Sentries changing watch, crackling fires, low talk and nervous laughter. Men had been sharpening swords all evening, checking their armour and quietly saying their prayers. Horses lamed crossing the high pass, and there had been several, had been slaughtered, butchered and eaten. What little wine had been carried was drunk.

The silence beyond the tent was the silence of an army gathering its breath before battle. Frost crackled underfoot and boots broke ice over a puddle a hundred paces away. Someone was circling her tent nervously. Tycho could hear it over the camp's heartbeat and the restless waiting of the men around him. Marco was the first Millioni duke to take himself to war and Tycho hoped victory would be his reward. He prayed for it.

He, Tycho, who believed in no gods . . . Not even the goat-heeled fool who'd stolen his future, prayed to Giulietta's god – in whom he definitely didn't believe – to give victory to the cousin of this girl who was leaving him, whether she knew it or not. Maybe she was expecting him to rage at how things had changed and he might have done if not for the price the creature in the cave extracted for Leo's life. He would have raged and killed and fought. He would have used the bonds between them. Bonds that would always exist unless he . . . Rolling out of bed, he reached for his leather pocket and scrabbled inside. "Still there," he said, his fingers closing around a scrap of paper in the bottom. "Thought I'd lost something."

"What?" Lady Giulietta demanded.

"Peacock's eyes."

She sighed but still moved over when he returned to the cot, and settled her face against his fingers when he reached for her cheek. "I missed you," she said. "I really missed you. You have no idea how badly."

"And then you discovered you could do without me."

She froze and Tycho knew she was waiting for him to say more. Only, what else was there? That was the truth. He'd gone, and she'd realised she *could* live without him. Trying to kill herself was about losing Leo. She'd been able to bear Tycho's absence and what she believed was his betrayal. It was hearing Alonzo had claimed Leo that tipped her over the edge. Well, so Marco said.

"I died . . ." Her voice told him how hard she found that to say.

"You nearly died. If you'd died you wouldn't be here and Leo wouldn't be asleep beside you."

"I took Aunt Alexa's fiercest poison."

"Marco says it was probably designed to paralyse so thoroughly everyone thinks the victim is dead. Useful for kidnapping, he reckons. There's a fish in China. You cut out the liver . . ."

"How does he know that?"

"He reads," Tycho said. "He reads a lot."

Giulietta obviously decided this was a version of the truth she could accept. Her muscles relaxed and her breathing steadied and she snuffled her face into her pillow as he stroked her hair, and kept stroking until he was certain she was asleep. Then he stood, buckled on his daggers and slung his sword over his shoulder without bothering to buckle his baldric.

"Maybe we'll talk later," he told her sleeping form. "Maybe not. Who knows how the battle will go? But you should know I love you."

It was so much easier to say when she wasn't awake to hear it.

"Things change – but that remains."

He smelt the oil in her unwashed hair when he bent to kiss her. Inhaling the salt warmth of her body and seeing what he was giving up in the curves of a sleepy smile. *What did you expect? A throne and the girl you loved?* Tomorrow would be hard for everyone. Difficult, bloody and complex.

Of such days myths were born.

The stars above the camp were high and bright, the constellations clear and increasingly familiar after a couple of years in this strange world. The moon was behind cloud and Tycho dipped his head in homage to Amelia's goddess, wondering where the Nubian was.

On her way to the far south and home? Already returning to Venice? Or out there somewhere, watching? He wouldn't put that past her. He didn't include Amelia's goddess in those he didn't believe in. Tycho liked deities he could see and he could see the moon even when she was hidden.

Tycho made himself wait for the footsteps that drew near and then faltered, turned away and came back again. "Can't sleep?" he asked.

Prince Frederick jumped as if ambushed.

"Always hard to sleep the night before a battle," Tycho said. "Well, I find it hard. You might be better?"

Frederick shook his head. "You think tomorrow?"

269

"Yes," Tycho assured him.

"I'm glad," Frederick said. "I find waiting . . ."

"Everyone does. Come dawn Marco's archers will loose their fire arrows and what choice will Alonzo have? Come out and fight or stay inside and burn."

"Fire arrows?"

"What else? I won't be able to join you until darkness falls."

"If the battle takes that long . . ."

If it doesn't, Tycho thought, *you'll have lost.*

Numbers meant little enough in a battle like this. The Red Crucifers might be outnumbered but they were hardened soldiers, while half of Marco's army were recent recruits, simply there to be killed. The Nicoletti and Castellani would die well for their duke – but they *would* die. The battle would turn on the bravery of Marco's knights and archers, and Alonzo had knights and archers of his own. If the Red Cathedral were stone Alonzo could simply wait his besiegers out, watching them starve while his men hid inside. But it was wood and Marco's secret plan involved fire arrows. Tycho was surprised Frederick hadn't worked it out for himself.

If Alonzo could keep them from his walls he could drag this out for days. The Venetian forces had brought little enough food and found almost nothing in the village when they arrived. If Tycho were Alonzo he'd do everything to drive Marco's archers back. If he were Marco he'd go for a fast and bloody victory.

"Remind Marco to tell his men to stay away from the moat."

"Why?" Frederick asked.

"There are monsters in the water."

"Why don't you remind him?"

Tycho glanced to the east and knew dawn was close, the night had passed beyond the black-thread moment and he would soon need to hide. Giulietta's life was in her own and this boy's hands. "Ever been in a real battle?"

"Skirmishes only. Why?"

"Afraid to die?"

"After Annemarie died it was all I wanted. Now," he glanced at Giulietta's tent, "I want to live."

Serves me right for asking. "A simpleton duke, a raw boy and a man so brave he's afraid of daylight. What damsel could hope for braver champions?"

Frederick shot him an uncertain glance.

"Ignore me," Tycho said. "She does."

Frederick nodded doubtfully. He looked young for his seventeen years and scared at where he found himself. Tycho had to remind himself this was a *krieghund.* No, with Leopold's death, this was *the krieghund,* and his follower would die to the last man at his orders. "You'll carry the *WolfeSelle*?"

"You think I should?"

"You're the master of the Wolf Brothers. Until Leo is big enough the sword is yours to carry in battle. Of course you should . . . I saw Giulietta."

The prince looked at him.

"We talked," Tycho said. "Things change." He left the boy standing there and made a rapid circle of Marco's camp, judging its defences. Not a single sentry saw him. Tycho didn't expect them to.

40

"How do you extract a s-snail from his s-shell?"

Lady Giulietta looked at her cousin, wondering if it was a riddle or a serious question. "Marco?"

"If you use a p-pin he hides. Of course, you can s-stamp on h-him, b-but then you have lots of p-pieces of shell." Marco grinned. "*You c-cook him.* M-mother taught me that."

"But then it won't be alive."

"Not b-by the end," Marco agreed, freeing his sword. "Now, y-you must let the men see you." He gripped Giulietta's reins and walked his horse forward so they rode a dozen paces in front of the army as it began to move. Prince Frederick immediately kicked his spurs and positioned himself on her other side.

"Ahh," Marco said. "Her faithful hound."

Frederick scowled. The *WolfeSelle* had a new handle of white leather wound with gold wire and a scabbard decorated with nielloed flowers. But that, a battered hunting horn and simple trews, was all he wore.

"No armour, I s-see."

"I fight better like this."

"F-feeling wolfish today, are we?"

"Your highness, if I might have a word with Lady Giulietta . . .?"

"I don't k-know." Marco looked at Giulietta. "M-might he?"

She edged her horse to one side by pulling slightly on the reins and kicking on the side she wanted to turn, looking up to find Frederick smiling his approval at her skill.

"I wanted you to have this," he said.

Dropping his hand to his hip, Frederick lifted the hunting horn to free its lanyard and offered it to her. The horn was dented around its rim and its mountings were so tarnished the silver was smoky black. Instinct made her glance back and she saw his men watching her.

"What is it?"

"It belonged to Roland."

The name meant little to her.

"*Roncesvalles?*" Frederick said. "Roland turns back the Saracens at the pass and saves France from becoming Moorish?" He seemed surprised he needed to tell her the story. "It arrived from my father just before we left."

"What happens if I blow?"

"The paladins wake from under the hill."

"Really?" Giulietta had heard of the paladins.

"So it's said." Frederick shrugged. "No one has sounded it for five hundred years. No one has dared."

"Why me?" Giulietta demanded.

"Because Leo is heir to the Wolf Brothers. If his life is in danger *you* must blow it and the paladins will come. You will need a circle of fire from which they can ride. Without the circle . . ."

"You're giving me this because I'm Leo's mother?"

"Because I love you."

Serves me right for asking, Giulietta decided. Frederick was waiting for a reply, and when he realised she didn't know what to say, he leant forward and carefully put the cord around her neck, making sure the battered hunting horn hung neatly at her side.

"That's pretty," Marco said.

"Roland's horn."

His eyes widened and he grinned into the wind. Marco looked good in armour, his thin shoulders widened by boastful shoulder plates, his chest broader than in real life. Had his mother been alive she'd have been surprised at how like his father he looked. "W-what are y-you thinking?"

"You could be your father."

Marco's mouth twisted. "I imagine that's m-meant as a c-compliment." He looked to see if Frederick was listening, but the princeling was staring at the onion domes of the cathedral. These were tarnished, one or two of them askew, but the afternoon sun still glinted on what was left of their gilt. "You k-know why you must let my soldiers s-see you?"

"Because they came to get Leo back?"

Her child was with a nurse back at camp. Four of Frederick's *krieghund* guarded him and a dozen of Marco's best infantry.

"B-because you will r-rule after me."

"Marco . . ."

He smiled. "There, I've said the unsayable. Everyone says my m-mind is weak. Well, my b-body is w-worse. My joints ache, my chest is t-tight, my eyes not as g-good as they should be. Alonzo tried to p-poison me before I was b-born."

"*What?*" Giulietta was shocked.

"That was when my m-mother started taking her daily d-doses of a d-dozen different p-poisons . . . I came into the w-world with the antidotes already in my b-blood. He tried n-next when I was s-small. And this summer."

"The plum . . .?"

Marco nodded.

"Why did you eat it?"

"I like p-plums."

Looking at her cousin, Giulietta knew his mind was keen – often fiendishly so – but his thoughts were unlike other peoples.

That he liked plums and the colour purple was enough to make him risk poison. Aunt Alexa should be congratulated for keeping him alive this long.

"How about y-you?" Marco asked.

Lady Giulietta looked at him.

"Still yearning after p-poisoned fruit? Or . . ." Marco smiled at where Frederick was reciting a battle prayer, "p-perhaps you want something s-safer? Well, r-relatively speaking . . ."

Giulietta blushed.

"Doing right is h-hard. Sometimes it simply t-turns out to be what w-works. Others times, what c-causes least h-harm. Truth now. Do you r-really want a r-republic?"

"You think it's a bad idea?"

"I think it's a d-dreadful idea. Look at the M-Medicis. All that v-vote rigging and influence buying. All those m-murders and p-poisonings. At least V-Venetians know where they stand . . ."

"Which is fine," Giulietta said tartly. "Unless it's on the scaffold, without appeal and without knowing why they're there."

Marco laughed. Behind them, knights were smiling grimly and captains encouraging their men. The duke's good humour carried the first wave out to the island. The first wave being Marco's knights, fifty archers in wagons dragged by horses specially shod for the task, and spearmen who were expected to walk for themselves. A final cart was loaded with barrels and planking.

Ahead of them the Red Cathedral waited on its island.

Not a single sentry could be seen on the balustrade circling the bell tower that stood slightly apart from the bulk of the cathedral, no guards stood positioned on the sharply sloping roof beneath its cascade of onion domes, the great doors were shut and the rocks in front of the church looked deserted. The moat Tycho had warned Frederick about wore a thin crackle of ice.

"You don't think it's deserted?" Frederick asked.

"W-where w-would they g-go?" Marco demanded. "H-how would they g-get past us? No, they're in there all r-right." He glanced round and saw a troop of locals who'd been conscripted into their own company of archers. "P-put the bridge in p-place and s-send those m-men across first."

The archers looked terrified at being singled out.

Lady Giulietta didn't blame them. The cathedral looked ominous and darkly silent. She wished Tycho was here and immediately blushed guiltily because Frederick nudged his mount closer as if reading her fear. One of the archers was arguing with a Venetian sergeant. After a second, the sergeant went to talk to his captain. This was strange enough to make Marco jig his reins.

"C-come with m-me."

Marco's horse edged forward and Giulietta followed, Frederick kicking his mount to a slow amble behind her. Marco sighed.

"Yes. Your s-shadow can c-come too . . . Right, w-what's going on?"

The captain was so horrified to be addressed directly by the duke that his mouth opened and shut wordlessly and it was his sergeant who answered. "The heathen wants to talk to you, sir."

"They're E-Eastern C-Christians."

The sergeant shrugged. "Don't sound very Christian to me, sir. Sounds distinctly heathen. If you'll forgive me."

"Talk," Marco ordered.

The archer glanced at the cathedral, glanced at Marco and then looked desperately at his companions. It was an older man who stepped forward and bowed. It took Giulietta a moment to recognise him as the village priest. He addressed Marco in Latin and spoke slowly as if trying to remember the language.

"May we speak alone?" he said.

"This is my cousin. This is her friend. You may speak in front of them."

Maybe the priest knew he would probably die that day, perhaps he was simply too desperate to worry about manners or maybe he simply didn't care. "Fine," he said, "keep your devil dog and your demon's whore. It won't help you if you try to burn the Red Cathedral. Kill the scum inside by all means, kill them and sodomise their dead bodies . . . But if you try to harm the cathedral its protectors will destroy you." The man spat and those behind them who didn't speak Latin and were too far away to hear anyway realised he'd insulted their duke.

Marco smiled. "T-tell me about these p-protectors."

"Hell will open and demons come through."

"Heaven using h-hell to p-protect a r-rotting cathedral stolen by t-traitors? Isn't that a little s-strange?" Marco looked at the captain. "Get the bridge into p-place over the m-moat and send in the archers. This m-man will l-light the arrows."

"I refuse," the priest said.

"I'll b-burn your c-church in the village if you d-do. And put all the r-remaining villagers inside it f-first." Giulietta couldn't tell if this was simply a threat or if her cousin meant it. "Besides," Marco said, "if you h-hate us that much I'd think you'd be delighted to see us d-destroyed."

"Why hasn't Alonzo come out?" Giulietta whispered.

Frederick shrugged. "Maybe he thinks the walls will protect him."

Leaning across, Marco said, "T-too exposed." He nodded at the wide expanse of ice around the moat. "We h-have more archers. Your lover s-saw to that." He smiled sweetly when Giulietta glanced at Frederick, who scowled.

Up ahead, sappers rolled barrels to the edge of the cracked ice, lashed them into a double row using rope hoops already in place, and pushed them in. Two roof beams from a broken house came next, long enough to stretch across the moat, and the sappers lashed them tight to support the whole. Planks ripped from the side of a house came last. "Will it hold?" Giulietta asked.

"Let's find out," Frederick said.

The villagers shuffled forward under the glare of the Venetian sergeant and strung their hunting bows. At a barked command, they slotted arrows wrapped with naphtha-soaked bandages on to their strings and the bearded priest, scowling furiously, took the flaming torch he was offered. Together, archers, priest and sergeant crossed the creaking bridge, stopped at the sergeant's shouted order, and raised their bows towards the walls. The priest ambled down the line lighting arrows.

"Release them."

A ragged cheer went up from Marco's troops as the volley rose high and dropped towards the cathedral. A few stuck, the rest dropping away to fizzle out on the rocks below. "And again," Marco ordered.

The villagers notched new fire arrows and the priest shuffled forward with his flaming brand, glancing nervously towards the cathedral. The air was unusually still for so far out on the ice, and the valley quiet. Not even the sound of a distant bird broke the silence. "Get on with it," the sergeant shouted.

The priest lit the arrows and the men released their bowstrings.

This time the army watched in silence the arc the arrows made as they flamed into the clear blue sky and then fell towards the cathedral's wooden walls. A few more stuck this time and the sergeant grinned. The villagers fitted new arrows without being ordered, moving like dead men or puppets, not looking at each other or at their priest, simply replenishing their bows and waiting.

"I don't like it," Frederick whispered.

Although the air hung heavy there were no thunderclouds in the sky and no sign of a storm on the horizon. Giulietta nodded her agreement. It was too quiet and she felt exposed out here, as if the mountains were watching. "What's that?" she demanded. The crack sounded as loud as the absent thunder, and she looked at the ice below her horse's hooves to check it was still firm. Others were looking around for the source of the noise.

278

"Light those arrows," Marco ordered.

The bearded priest shambled forward, the flaming torch in his hand, and was readying to light the first arrow when the sergeant yelled a warning. The priest spun faster than seemed possible for such a big man, looking every which way but up, and that was how he found himself standing headless, before toppling sideways to stain the ice a vivid red. A ragged shadow dropped his head and it landed with a thud, rolling along the ice like a ball.

Turning, Giulietta spewed noisily.

"What the f-fuck was t-that?"

"Not sure," Frederick said. "But there's another." He pointed to an onion dome on the cathedral. "See it?"

"M-my eyes aren't that g-good."

"Can y-you s-see it?" Marco asked Giulietta.

"Looks like a bird with the head of a lizard," she said.

"Like big b-bats?"

"Not really. More like gargoyles."

"Does it matter?" Frederick asked, as Marco summoned an officer and told him to make the archers fire another volley.

"Of course it d-does. If I don't know what they l-look like h-how can I work out w-what they are? If I don't k-know what they are h-how can I d-defeat them? Pity Tycho's n-not here. He's g-good at things like t-this."

"He's good at most things," Frederick said bitterly.

Giulietta leant across and touched his wrist. With a scowl, he shook her off and withdrew. Since this involved making his mount walk backwards she was almost as impressed as she was irritated.

"You n-need to choose," Marco said.

"*Marco . . .*"

"I'm s-serious. Which do you l-love?"

She thought about it. "Both, if I'm honest."

"I was a-afraid of that." He nodded to an officer, who said

something to the sergeant, who shouted an order. The villagers notched new arrows and the sergeant took a fresh torch.

"W-wait . . ." Marco ordered. It seemed he wanted a line of Venetian bowmen behind the villagers. They, too, should have naphtha-tipped arrows – but their job was to kill whatever it was before it could kill the sergeant.

Weirdly brilliant, thought Giulietta, seeing her cousin wide-eyed and excited by his own plan. *But not really in the same world as the rest of us.* She watched as Venetian archers hurried over the barrel bridge and drew up in a line. The officer went after them and took a lighted torch for himself.

"When y-you're r-ready."

As the first line raised their bows, a swirl of light-swallowing darkness detached itself from the cathedral roof and the sergeant and officer ran down the double line of bowmen lighting arrows.

"F-first line, f-fire." Arrows rose and fell towards the cathedral, but everyone except the second line of archers was watching Marco, who was squirming with excitement. "S-second line, f-fire." His bowmen had their arrows in the air before Marco finished the order.

The beast swirled away at the last second.

A fire arrow passed through its wing, tearing a ragged hole in black leather. Another struck its chest and the creature screamed.

"B-bring it d-down."

Archers scrambled to obey Marco's order almost before he spoke it.

Two more arrows found the creature as it turned away and flapped its wings frantically, trying to climb high enough to make it home. The beast had almost reached the island before it faltered, twisted in the air and fell.

"Mine," Frederick shouted. Spurring his mount across the barrel bridge, he raced for where the creature struggled to get airborne and five *krieghund* followed, their swords already drawn.

"Such c-children."

Giulietta didn't doubt that half the *krieghund* were older than him.

"Oh h-hell," Marco swore suddenly. Half a dozen black shapes appeared on the cathedral roof and swooped towards Frederick and his followers.

"Watch," Giulietta said.

Suddenly crouching on his saddle, Frederick leapt for the flapping blackness overhead and began his change in mid-air. It was so brutal Giulietta looked away as his scream echoed from the mountains, and she found herself overcome with nausea all over again.

"Oh G-God," Marco said.

Frederick hit the creature full-on, his twisted hands clawing its head as he found his grip and twisted hard enough to break its neck. He dropped back into his saddle, grabbed the reins of his terrified mount, holding it steady with brute force while he drew the *WolfeSelle* from a scabbard on the saddle. Then he vaulted from his horse, strode to where creature he'd originally been after flapped and struggled on the ice and beheaded it.

"He's trying to impress you."

Lady Giulietta didn't bother to say he was succeeding.

Unslinging the ash and buffalo-horn bow bequeathed her by Alexa, Giulietta put her knees to her horse to spur it forward, dipped for an arrow from the quiver by her knee and turned for the bridge.

"G-Giulietta, you c-can't . . ."

For a moment, she thought Marco had grabbed her bridle and opened her mouth to shout in protest, but he snatched the Lion of St Mark from its carrier and thrust the flagpole at her. She showed him her bow.

"Fire y-your d-damn arrow . . ."

Fingers releasing, she let her arrow fly, slammed her bow back into its open-topped case and grabbed the battle flag. *The Lion.* Her throat was tight and tears filled her eyes. She wanted to

281

sneer at herself for the sudden sentimentality but felt only awe as she lifted the flag higher.

"That's it," Marco shouted.

Archers were cheering around her.

Marco's knights had gone from standing to a trot and from a trot to a light canter as she and Marco led them across the barrel bridge. Officers were shouting orders but she had no idea what they were and cared even less. She, Lady Giulietta di Millioni, was carrying the great flag into battle beside the duke himself. It was an act from which legends were made. Up ahead, the *krieghund* sprang at the shadow things as archers began aiming for the walls, with archers behind them aiming for any creatures that appeared above. Young boys dashed between the archers, lighting fire arrows from their flaming brands.

A couple of Frederick's followers lay dead, half-naked boys dressed in bloodied rags where they'd reverted to human form. Giulietta looked frantically for their master. He was a hundred paces away, gripping the *WolfeSelle* in hands that looked too twisted to hold it, his mouth open in a high and ferocious howl, his sex erect and his fur shimmering in a sudden cold wind as he cut the last of the flapping black creatures from the sky.

What was it with the erect sex? They all did it on changing. She wondered if it was the nature of the change or their lust for battle. Catching her glance, Marco grinned. "Not quite as s-safe as you t-thought?"

She scowled at him. "Find your own monster."

"Every time I d-do you take him f-first." She had a feeling he meant that. Dragging his reins, her cousin swerved to shout some order at an officer half a dozen paces away. The man peeled off and she saw him drop back.

"We n-need m-more archers."

Enemy forces were appearing along the roofline of the cathedral, the first of Alonzo's followers she'd seen. They began dousing the arrows stuck into the walls below them. At first she thought they used water then realised it was sand. Behind her came the rattle of carts and the clank of bridles. She heard a cart reach the barrel bridge and stop. The driver, with the thick accent of a Nicoletto, told the archers to walk the rest. Giulietta thought him wise.

Bowmen pushed through a gap in the cavalry and began to range in a line until someone shouted at them to make it two lines, one behind the other. Boys ran along their length lighting the naphtha rags on the arrows. From this close it was hard to miss and a wave of arrows rose to fall on wooden walls. Some stuck fast and were smothered by buckets of sand dropped from overhead.

Enemy crossbowmen on the bell tower raised their weapons and bolts hurtled towards the Venetian army, falling a dozen paces short. Swinging round, one of the Venetians dropped his trews and farted at the enemy while his friends cheered.

"Back into line," their sergeant shouted.

A sudden crack of thunder killed the laughter and those who'd just arrived looked around, puzzled by the lack of storm clouds. Marco and Giulietta were staring at shadows popping into existence on the Red Cathedral's roof, fifty where there had been five before. They crawled and tumbled and found their feet and tried their wings.

"Warn the c-captains," Marco told a messenger.

The man galloped away, halting at each troop to tell them what was happening, until he was so far round the island that Giulietta lost sight of him as he disappeared behind the cathedral. Within a few minutes he was back, his circle completed. Still the shadows gathered.

"M-magic," Marco said.

Giulietta thought he sounded worried. "Frederick's magic."

"He's *k-krieghund*." Marco made it sound something else. Maybe it was, but Lady Giulietta didn't see why.

"Tycho then."

"Who k-knows what he is, p-poor b-boy." The duke chewed his lip as he watched the slopes of the roof become buried under restless shadows. The creatures looked strange and ancient. As if they came straight from hell or belonged to the world in a rawer age. "My m-mother would k-know."

"How to defeat them?"

"W-what they are," Marco sighed. "D-defeating them is s-simple." Giulietta stared at him. "We s-shoot them full of f-flaming arrows and your wolfie f-friends rip off their h-heads. We just need them to d-die faster than we d-do – and h-hope we have some p-people left to k-kill Uncle Alonzo at the end."

Giulietta laughed, she couldn't help it.

Knights looked across and sat a little straighter, archers muttered something appreciative and probably obscene. Unquestionably obscene, since they glanced from her to Frederick, who stood near naked and still in his *krieghund* form, quite as tumescent as when he first changed. She'd expected battles to be fierce and disorientating. Full of ferocious fighting, screams, cowardice and feats of bravery. When she said this to Marco, he smiled at her sadly. "My l-love," he said, "the b-battle h-hasn't even begun."

41

All around the cathedral, a hundred paces from the edge of the island, archers stood on the ice in two ranks, with their bows drawn and point-heavy fire arrows waiting for a flame. The flame boys were nervous, the fate of the priest having spread.

In front of the cathedral Marco raised his sword.

As it swept down, flame bearers ran the first and second ranks, crouching low as leathery shapes rose from the cathedral roof. A boy near Giulietta died. There were other deaths, dozens of others, but his was the one she saw. He went down as a shadow fell on him and bowled him backwards.

"Kill," a sergeant shouted.

Around her archers released arrows into the screaming mass, pin-cushioning the boy as well as the winged creature. Vomit rose in Lady Giulietta's throat. There was nothing glorious about this. No heroism in turning a boy into a screaming pillar of fire, even if it did kill his attacker. The screams ended almost as soon as they began. "V-vocal chords." Marco stood beside her.

"What?"

He tapped his throat. "They b-burn."

The facts her cousin produced scared her. "Don't you care?" she demanded, nodding at the boy. The flag felt like a dead weight in her hand and she handed it to its original bearer, who'd become her desperate shadow.

"I c-can't afford to c-care. All that m-matters is we're w-winning."

"We are?"

The first rows were loosing fire arrows at the wooden walls of the cathedral, while those behind them aimed at the monsters overhead. When a black wing came near Marco, a *krieghund* leapt, hitting it in mid-air before it could strike. The fight was brutal, fierce and bloody, but the *krieghund* won. But for every creature tumbling to earth, stuck with still-flaming arrows, knights, archers or *krieghund* died.

"Watch out," Marco shouted.

Giulietta threw up her arm and a *thing* clanged off her vambrace, wheeling clumsily in mid-air to launch another attack. She vaguely realised she'd shat herself. She grabbed her bow, hands shaking, and a *krieghund* roared past, leaping for the beast. Its claws swept up and ripped the *thing* open, tumbling guts to the ground. The black winged thing was dead before it hit the ice. That didn't stop the *krieghund* stamping on its neck and kicking it hard.

"He really d-does love you, d-doesn't he."

Frederick? Gods, was that really . . .

"You k-know how unusual it is for a *k-krieghund* to think and f-fight at the same time? Mostly they're m-mindless." Marco paused. "Well, that's what my m-mother said. M-maybe it's a lie."

"Over there," said Giulietta. One of the winged creatures flailed at the flames licking its side and fought to reach its home. It landed with a crash on the roof and she realised Marco was smiling. "You intended that all along?"

"I hoped. Injured animals r-return to their lairs. You k-know what Lord Atilo once t-told me? *To f-find out where your enemy l-lives, s-stab him and f-follow him home* . . . Aim for the b-beasts," Marco bellowed.

Enough creatures returned for their funeral pyres to lick the sides of the onion domes. And though Alonzo's men had been doing their best to douse the arrows that flamed against the cathedral walls they could do little about the steep roof; too many fire arrows now jutted from the walls for them all to be smothered.

It was a slow and bloody business. Marco was getting his wish, however. Fire ate at the Red Cathedral and arrows flamed from too many places for the building to survive. The wood was old and still dry from last summer, the falls of snow having spared the walls the drenching rains would have brought. Black wings returned in flames to a roof that was already ablaze. New creatures that popped into existence found themselves burning before they could find their wings.

Around her, knights settled back to watch, while sergeants arranged their men in tighter rows and counted the dead, of which there were dozens. *Hundreds,* Giulietta corrected herself. *Maybe a thousand.* What she could see would be repeated all round the island. The archers stood in ragged groups, checking their bows and finding their breath. Boys ran the barrel bridge fetching arrows. The biggest of the carts had been deemed too heavy to cross. Up among the onion domes of the cathedral the screaming was savage, not even animal in any sense she understood. Marco's zoo back home held every animal in the world, and had even included a unicorn when she was young, but she'd seen nothing like these. "What are they?"

"N-no idea. B-but I want one to examine a-afterwards."

Lady Giulietta decided to be happy Marco thought there would be an afterwards . . . She looked at the darkening sky and wondered if the battle would last all night. Mostly she wondered why her uncle skulked in his cathedral rather than coming out to fight. The fact worried her. He was a famous strategist; if he decided to stay inside skulking then he had his reasons. Maybe Marco was wrong about there being an afterwards. Giulietta bit her lip.

"C-come on," Marco said, "t-tell me."

"It doesn"t matter . . ."

"F-Frederick's over there s-seeing to his m-men."

"It's not that." She knew where Frederick was. He'd resumed his human form and was delivering comfort and the *coup de grâce* to those of his followers too wounded to save. He slid the blade between their ribs himself; you couldn't say that for many princes.

"Tycho, then. You're w-worried about Tycho."

Her cousin was wrong, she hadn't thought about him from the moment the first fire arrow was loosed until now. Maybe that itself was worrying? She should have been wondering where he was, except she knew: under an awning back at the camp and an hour from waking, to judge from the sky. It shocked her how readily she'd come to accept his world was the reverse of hers.

His day, her night. Her night, his day.

Above her, the darkening sky was empty. No clouds, no birds, no raggedy winged creatures trying to kill her. There were broken bodies on the ice. Castellani and Nicoletti were working together to collect the corpses of their friends. The companies of archers were now being reformed into smaller companies made of strangers from companies that had been destroyed.

Lady Giulietta could smell her own shit, feel it under her. Her bowels had voided completely and her guts were hollow. This was war. Dead bodies in ugly piles, and imploring men with their intestines on the ice before them. A soldier crouched, head in hands, quietly shaking. She wanted to cry.

"N-not now," Marco said.

The great doors of the cathedral were shifting. Vast and old and carved when this was a sacred site and long before it was corrupted and turned and finally claimed by the Red Crucifers, the doors swung back to reveal darkness.

Only a nave behind, Giulietta reminded herself.

For a second there was total silence and only the threat of the open doors, with every member of Marco's army on this side of the island frozen, and those on the ice inside the moat on the far side stilled by the rest's silence.

"H-here they c-come," Marco shouted.

Frederick appeared beside Giulietta's bridle with a dozen of his *krieghund* behind him. All were stripped to the waist, barefoot and clutching weapons. They obviously had orders to protect her. Alonzo's banner came first. He had a duke's coronet above his arms. A ducal crown topped the pole from which his banner flew. A white flag below it indicated he wanted to parlay.

"What do we do?" Giulietta asked.

"We t-talk," Marco said. "We h-have no choice." The rules of treaty were strict and Venice would be damned in the mouths of ten thousand strangers if they were ignored. "You'll r-ride with m-me?"

"Me?" Giulietta asked.

"Of course," said Marco. Frederick stepped closer and it was obvious he wanted to be included. "And the emperor's favoured s-son."

"His only son," Frederick said.

"The only one h-he acknowledges, c-certainly."

An emperor's bastard was still impressive, Giulietta thought. As Frederick's bloodstained hands reached for her bridle, and her mount tried to shy but couldn't match the strength in Frederick's arms, she saw him watching her. His eyes golden and fiercely intelligent within a not-quite human face.

"Let's get this over with," she said.

"Alexa's idiot, Alexa's echo and Sigismund's attack dog . . ."

"Y-you called us h-here t-to insult us?"

Alonzo grinned. His beard was oiled and his cloak edged at the bottom with a band of imperial purple to which he had no right. The coat of arms on his shield matched Marco's own. Any herald would have known both men claimed the throne. "Why are *you* here then?

"H-here p-parlaying? Or do you m-mean *h-here*?" Marco swept an arc with his hand that embraced the lake and the mountains, and by extension everything and everyone in it . . . "In this g-garden of d-delights, this p-paradise?"

Alonzo sighed.

"I'm h-here to k-kill you, obviously," Marco said.

Alonzo's bark of laughter was fierce.

"I'm p-parlaying b-because those are the r-rules. Y-you can g-get away w-with anything if you're s-seen to obey the r-rules . . . Trying to m-murder your n-nephew, f-fucking your b-brother's wife, b-betraying your family . . ."

His uncle's face tightened.

Marco's stammer was worse than Giulietta remembered it being in weeks and she wondered if he was pretending or if the broad-shouldered man in front of him really did make him that nervous.

"This is my offer," Alonzo said. "Withdraw, abdicate and accept exile and I'll let you live. Let her live, too," he said, pointing at Giulietta. "Even your pet dog if you want to include him in the deal. But you return my son."

"Y-your c-castle is b-burning . . ."

Alonzo looked at the smouldering walls above him. The cathedral was huge, the bell tower impressive and the hall squat and toad-like, but all were wooden and dangerously dry for all it was winter. "I was bored with it anyway . . ."

"It c-can be your f-funeral pyre."

"And you'll never get Leo," Giulietta said furiously. "You can tell that to the Dolphini milch cow you married."

Alonzo glared. "She hung herself. I have your white-skinned freak to thank for that." Giulietta felt his hatred follow her back to their lines. Although, when she turned, her uncle was gone. The great door of the cathedral still stood open and there was movement in the darkness behind.

"N-now," said Marco. "Now the real battle b-begins."

42

They were losing from the first minute. Marco's infantry might have been enthusiastic, but they were mostly half trained and exhausted from marching from the port where they landed up the valleys and into the mountains. He had archers, but those still alive were exhausted from loosing their fire arrows. He had trained knights, members of his palace guard and enough Nicoletti and Castellani spearmen to give Venice an entirely new generation of widows. He had Frederick's *krieghund*. He even had the poor bastard villagers whose houses he'd chopped up for firewood.

Alonzo had less. But Alonzo had better.

The Crucifers, renegade or not, had trained in war since childhood, giving up their names and families to follow the sword. He had the other half of the wild tribe of archers Tycho had faced at the fort. He had his reputation as a warlord.

She should have known it was all going too easily. Lady Giulietta had trouble keeping track of how the battle developed, but she knew exactly how it began. Her uncle came charging through the huge double doors, clattered his mount down black rocks on to the marbled ice and beheaded the first *krieghund* to charge him. The *krieghund* leapt for Alonzo, who swung viciously, removing its head before stabbing the next *krieghund* in the chest and riding over it.

The cloak slid from Frederick's shoulders as flesh ripped, and he dropped to a crouch, racing forward before she could object.

"L-let him g-go," Marco said.

"Your cousin's right, my lady . . ."

Turning, she found Tycho at her side. His eyes were huge in the twilight and he kept his face twisted from the last of the sun. He'd called her *my lady* ever since he returned Leo. Why, she wondered, did he find her name so hard to say?

"Where's your son?"

"Back at the camp."

"That's where you should be."

"Because I'm a woman?" She glared down at him.

"Because if he's captured all this becomes worthless . . ." Tycho gestured at Marco's cavalry riding to meet Alonzo's charge. They clashed so fiercely the noise was deafening. Swords slashed and spike axes split plate, and, as Marco's knights broke free to regroup, Alonzo's wild archers rode in from the side, squat bows releasing armour-piercing arrows that dropped half Marco's men. A second volley disabled more and Alonzo's knights turned to charge the Venetian spearmen.

One man lost his nerve. He dropped his spear and Alonzo himself swerved into the gap, riding right over him. Two renegade Crucifers followed, killing spearmen either side and widening the gap. The rest of Alonzo's knights flowed through. The Venetians fought fiercely, hooking their spears into the armour of Alonzo's knights. A dozen Red Crucifers were gaffed from their wounded horses and died with daggers in their eye slits, daggers between breastplate and hip armour, daggers into the groin. But the wall was broken and one renegade Crucifer after another headed for where they could see fighting.

The wild archers turned their shaggy ponies and charged at Marco's bowmen, releasing arrow after arrow until the air was thick as rain with shafts. Having ridden straight through, they turned to keep shooting even as they rode away.

"We should help," Giulietta said.

Marco shook his head. "W-we'd should s-stay h-here. We c-can't afford to l-lose our advantage."

She looked around her. *What advantage?*

"We g-guard the b-barrel bridge. How else c-can Alonzo l-leave?"

Having ridden through the middle of Marco's spearmen, Alonzo's cavalry were fanning out behind to turn and attack the infantry from the rear. The moat cut in the ice off the island's edge limited everyone's space. The distance from moat to edge was a hundred and fifty paces, two hundred at most.

"How does anyone know what's going on?"

"They don't," Tycho told her sharply. He bowed to her cousin. "My orders, your highness?"

"Tycho. W-what are t-those?"

"Your highness, my eyes . . ."

Giulietta squinted into the last of the sunlight to see a writhing blackness on the bell tower walls. The bulk of the cathedral was in flames, but the bell tower was freestanding and stood slightly apart. The wall nearest the cathedral would ignite in time but for the moment it just smouldered. "Creatures," she said. "No wings this time." As she watched, the blackness thickened.

"The c-cathedral p-protects itself . . ."

When she turned back, Tycho was staring at her. His gaze flicked to Marco and something grim entered his eyes. "You must retreat, highness."

"Tycho," Giulietta said.

"They're domovoi . . . House demons."

"We killed the winged ones." She couldn't believe he wanted Marco to run away. God knows, she wanted to run away. But she was a young woman. No one but her thought she should be here anyway. Well, Frederick did . . .

"T-this is b-bad?"

"Very bad, highness."

Wheeling his horse, Marco grabbed Giulietta's reins and dragged her after him. After a moment's shock, Captain Weimer and Marco's knights followed.

I saw your death . . . Always, he worked out too late what he should have said. *I saw death in your face and in the skull beneath your skin.* The warnings were rarer now, rarer than when he first found himself in this world, but that one had been too brutal for him to miss.

As Marco and Lady Giulietta rode for the barrel bridge, Tycho jumped on to an overturned cart and stared around him. Renegade Crucifers were still trampling Venetian light infantry, bloody circles showing where knights twisted round, hacking down on heads, or the shields of those who raised them in time.

Each spearman wore mail under a padded jacket. Simple leg armour protected each man's leading leg, and a light shield with a spiked boss had two loops on the other side; one hooked inside the elbow, the other was the handle. Each spear had an armoured shaft and a fierce spike at the business end, with a crossbar that was axe one side and armour-piercing spike the other. It was a fine weapon for hooking into joints in plate armour or jabbing through mail. And the spearmen retreated when threatened and stepped forward again when the knights turned away.

The battle had become something living that consumed everything it touched. If a crowd could become a mob, then an army mid-battle was a crowd turned to something far more dangerous. It looked as if it would kill until it could kill no more and die of hunger only with the last of the dead.

Tycho tried to swallow the numbers in a single glance but the situation changed faster than ink dropped into swirling water. And all the time that pulsing mass dripped down the bell tower walls. Tycho knew the Venetian forces didn't realise it. He wondered if Alonzo's troops did.

"*Frederick.*" His shout was so loud Alonzo himself turned.

"Traitor . . ." The ex-Regent pointed his sword, somewhere between a warning and a threat that he would see Tycho dead. Ignoring him, Tycho watched a *krieghund* break away from gutting a wild archer and lollop towards him. The beast ripped arrows from its flesh as it ran. When Frederick leapt up to stand beside Tycho he was halfway human. "What do you want?"

"See those?" Tycho demanded.

"See what?" Blood dripped into Frederick's eyes from a cut on his forehead and his near-naked body was shaking with exhaustion and cold. *Krieghund* he was powerful, human he was weak again. He squinted in the direction Tycho pointed. It was obvious he was too tired to concentrate.

"Don't go away."

Time slowed and Tycho found himself stepping over corpses and sliding between individual fights as he negotiated the crawling hell of the battle on the ice. A Venetian stabbed at an enemy foot soldier and withdrew his spear, blood drops like pearls stringing the air. He stabbed at the soldier beyond and his first victim, already fallen, slashed the Venetian's ankles below his shield.

The spearman lowered his shield in shock and died when a wild archer's arrow split his mail, blossoming blood as the arrow passed through his lungs and cut his heart in two. Tycho caught the man's falling spear and threw it, skewering the archer and knocking him from his wild pony.

A hundred paces ahead, a Venetian dodged his attacker and stepped straight into Tycho's path. Breath whooshed from his body, he looked briefly shocked to have hit something he didn't know was there. He died when his attacker swung an axe at his back, gaffing him like a fish. Tycho killed the attacker and as many of the slow-moving enemy as stood between him and the black rocks ahead. He ripped his way up the bell tower, hit the nearest creature full-on and let both of them fall. Dragging the thing back to the ice, where the others seemed reluctant to follow, he bit hard into its leathery neck, spitting blood so vile it burned his mouth.

"Well," Frederick said. "That was impressive."

His voice was sour enough to make Tycho wonder if he meant it. Tossing the thing at Frederick's feet, he said, "See it now?"

"Domovoi," Frederick said. "House demons."

"You recognise them?"

"My father keeps some," Frederick said. He raised his head and howled. Instantly, his followers broke from their individual battles and headed towards him. They fought their way through the melee, killing those who objected, but sparing any who stepped aside or turned and ran. Within a moment they stood around the tumbled cart, and behind their own line, while the battle went on without them.

They looked at the battered domovoi in silence and Tycho realised they knew what it was and had probably seen one before. At Frederick's nod they looked towards the bell tower and their faces paled. "The duke needs to be told," Frederick said. "What we do next is his decision."

"There are too many to fight," a *krieghund* said. He flushed. "I mean, there are too many to fight and win. I'm happy to fight them." The beast's face was neither human nor wolf, but something raw and in-between. The blood on his jaws was not from the enemy, it leached from unhealed skin.

"Still his decision," Frederick said.

Tycho said, "Help him make the right one." Both Frederick and the *krieghund* who'd spoken turned to him. "If those attack, the infantry are already dead."

"That's brutal," said Frederick.

Tycho replied, "War is brutal."

Although he scowled, Frederick didn't disagree. Staring

towards the smouldering bell tower, he said. "They're still appearing."

"Do you think Alonzo has a mage?"

"I doubt it," Frederick said. "They're being summoned by the bell tower, perhaps by the island itself."

"And we've set fire to their home."

Frederick nodded grimly. "Let's destroy the bridge and fall back."

"Your highness . . ." It was the *krieghund* who'd spoken earlier. "We may be too late." Marco, his staff officers and his knights were advancing along the lake, their battle flag held high and personal pennants waving.

"Idiot," Frederick said.

It was the first rude word Tycho had heard him say about a man most of Europe thought unfit to rule himself never mind an empire as big as Serenissima. The Venetian knights slowed for the barrel bridge, clattered across it in two and broke into a canter that became a gallop within a dozen paces. Marco had decided to charge his uncle. It was magnificent, and stupid. A rolling front of horseflesh and steel, lances lowered and swords loosened, crashed into the side of Alonzo's cavalry, which was regrouping. The noise knocked snow from the sides of the valley and set avalanches sliding.

Alonzo's cavalry were tired and Marco's fresh.

But his were hardened soldiers and Marco's formed from the sons of nobles and *cittadini*, with a smattering of tried officers to stiffen their spine. They clashed and the Venetians rode straight through. Shouting, they turned and, buoyed by their own excitement, attacked again. Swords swung and hacked, shields came up and knights were knocked from their saddles and trampled by their own animals. The animal that was the battle became more deadly and more vicious.

Maybe the smoke finally drove the domovoi down to ground level and on to the black rocks of the island, perhaps it was the stink of blood or the noise of the cavalry clashing. They skittered on the water's edge, touching the ice as if its solidness was unexpected. A wild archer turned, saw them and loosed an arrow that caught one in the throat. The horseman next to him raised his own bow and did the same. The domovoi clicked their high inhuman protest. Finding the ice solid, they flowed on to it and began to spread out. A moment later the killing began.

43

"Tycho, you c-can't . . ."

"Watch me." Tycho dragged Marco's horse out of the melee. "Has Giulietta gone back to the camp?"

"She's over t-there."

Tycho saw a slight figure in white armour draw her bow and put an arrow into a wild archer on a pony who was aiming at someone else. It hit his leg but was enough to make him miss. A Nicoletto stabbed him, which saved Tycho from having to do it. "Don't move," he told Marco.

Flowing across the ice, Tycho grabbed Giulietta's bridle and ducked as she swung her bow as if it were a sword. "Me," he said, wondering if that made it any better. Her face was strained and she looked close to tears.

"I soiled myself," she said.

"Half the field have soiled themselves. There are more important things to worry about, like keeping Leo alive . . ." Yes, he thought that would concentrate her mind. She followed him to where Marco sat scowling. Before they could reach him, Captain Weimer rode up and saluted. They arrived just in time to hear the captain say, "Your highness, we face a worse enemy."

Having killed their first attackers, the domovoi had armed

themselves with swords taken from the dead and were hacking their way through shields, crushing helmets with maces, stabbing with whichever end of a spear was at hand. Every man to die gave them another weapon and they killed indiscriminately, making no distinction between Alonzo's and Marco's forces.

"W-what are t-they?" Marco demanded.

"Demons," Tycho said.

"Then we s-stay and f-fight."

"Your highness . . ." Captain Weimer hesitated.

"We're C-Christians," Marco said. "W-we're m-meant to f-fight demons."

"I'm not sure it's meant to be this literal," muttered Frederick, sliding himself alongside Giulietta's horse so that he held the other side of her bridle. A high scream filled the air and was chopped off. "Highness, with respect, we should retreat. We don't have the weapons."

"I have this," said Giulietta. In her hand was a hunting horn. "It's Roland's," she told Tycho. "It summons the paladins through a circle of flame."

"Where did you get it?"

"From me," Frederick said.

Tycho ignored him. "Where will you get your circle of fire?"

"There." Frederick pointed at the castle. Turning to Giulietta, he said, "My lady, sound the horn."

"That thing is yours?"

"You'd rather die than accept my help?"

I can't die, Tycho almost replied. She could, though, and Leo . . .

"It belongs to my son," Giulietta said. "It belongs to Leo because he's going to be head of the *krieghund*."

Marco froze . . . So did the nobles around him.

"Y-you shouldn't s-say things l-like that."

"It's the truth," she said fiercely. "Leopold was *krieghund* and so is my son. Leo will lead the Wolf Brothers." She nodded to the sword slung across Frederick's back. "That's the *WolfeSelle*, it belongs to him, too. Isn't that right? Doesn't it belong to Leo?"

Frederick nodded.

Away to the edge of the circle of ice around the cathedral a man threw himself on to the makeshift moat, the crackle ice almost holding as he ran for the safety of the frozen lake on the other side, only to plunge through at the last second. His cry of shock at the coldness of the water turning to screams as webbed hands rose to reach for him and began to tear.

Giulietta vomited.

"Sound the damn horn," Tycho said.

Lady Giulietta wiped her lips and blew a thin note like a child's bugle. The note was stronger the second time. Lowering the horn, she waited expectantly. The entire cathedral blazed, flames billowing through ruptured windows and blown-out doors. Burning domes gave the building a devil's crown of fire. The sides of the valley were molten red. Yet this was a cathedral; it was like watching what was once part of heaven be destroyed by the fires of hell.

"Three times," Frederick insisted. "Try again."

Hurriedly, she raised the battered hunting horn. Her third call rang high and clear and was loud enough to still the battle for a second. That is, the domovoi stopped killing Venetians and renegades for the briefest of moments; both sides having huddled together to face the more brutal enemy.

"T-there . . ." Marco"s face was exultant in the firelight.

Out of the Red Cathedral's burning doorway rode a knight in armour so old it belonged on the slab of an ancient tomb. Embers exploded beneath his horse's hooves, smoke rose from his shoulders, the paladin's tattered cloak wore the flames he had ridden through. Behind him rode others.

Giulietta crossed herself.

"S-so b-beautiful," Marco whispered.

The paladins swept on to the ice to hit the domovoi from the rear, clearing a path with their swords. They rode down Marco's and Alonzo's men alike as they turned and charged again, hacking ferociously and leaving domovoi broken behind them. Their horses were heavily armoured, the metal points of their toes turned down in exaggerated spikes. Marco was smiling as if visited by angels.

Captain Weimer came hurrying up with a question.

Marco shook his head. "T-they are the p-paladins. Who would d-dare offer them aid?" The fighting was spectacular in its fury. The paladins were remorseless and brutal and their enemy driven to fight by some instinct that didn't allow retreat or surrender . . . The paladins killed and the domovoi died, and the inner circle of ice that had been the domovoi's killing ground became their cage. And the spearmen and the knights, the renegade Crucifers and the wild archers, all those mortals who thought the world belonged to them, scrambled out of the way when the fighting came too close, and watched it happen. Slowly, surely, the paladins halved the number of domovoi and then halved it again.

When it came, the end was unexpected. A domovoi jumped for a paladin, missed its leap and impaled itself on his horse's spiked faceplate. The creature was carried a dozen paces still hacking with its stolen sword until the paladin beheaded it, twisted half out of his saddle and kicked it free with curved steel toes. Tycho was the only one to see it happen.

As the paladin began to settle back another domovoi leapt for him and the impact was enough to knock the paladin from his saddle. He landed with a crash that was followed by an echoing boom like the cry of some monster. "What was that?" Giulietta demanded.

Tycho already knew. It was the sound Bjornvin's lakes made at the end of winter when the ice cracked. It seemed the wild archers recognised it, too. A handful began heading for Marco and the barrel bridge behind him.

"Protect the duke," Captain Weimer shouted.

"P-protect Lady G-Giulietta." Marco's counter-order was firm. He loosened the handle of his sword and turned his mount towards the wild archers, and then he looked back at his men. "Ready?"

"Where are you going?"

Marco looked at Lady Giulietta. "To k-kill Alonzo, obviously."

"Your highness," Tycho said. "Wait."

"For w-what?"

For the prickling in the back of my neck to turn into something solid, for what is happening to finish . . . A dozen paladins faced two hundred domovoi who'd found their purpose and moved as one as they crowded the paladins' horses, sacrificing themselves beneath thrashing hooves to slow the beasts. The paladins still fought furiously but they were driven back towards the island by weight of numbers.

"Why d-don't the p-paladins attack again?"

"They're trying, highness. Look."

Domovoi hung from their arms, rendering their weapons useless. Those stabbed with daggers grabbed their attackers' wrists, blades still inside them to stop the paladins from stabbing others. In humans it would have been heroic, in domovoi it was terrifying. Throwing itself under a horse's hooves, a domovoi was crushed as the animal fell, throwing its rider on to ice that cracked loudly. Horse and armoured rider fell through and Tycho realised in horror that the heat from the flames had rotted the ice at the island's edge. Ice cracked again and another paladin followed, taking the domovoi that swarmed over him. His mount flailed desperately, trying to clamber free until webbed fingers and the weight of its own armour dragged it under.

"W-we should h-help them."

Tycho grabbed Marco to stop him spurring his horse. A dozen courtiers dropped their hands to their swords, and Marco scowled.

"D-don't be f-fools. H-he'll kill the lot of you."

Tycho let Marco's arm go.

"C-can't you h-help them?"

"Not without abandoning you, and my place is here."

"At m-my cousin's side?"

"At your side. At Leo's side. Yes, at hers, too."

Prince Frederick looked offended on Lady Giulietta's behalf. At the island's edge another paladin toppled and then another. They struggled furiously, no longer battling, simply struggling to fight free.

One of Alonzo's captains kept staring over and Tycho wondered if he intended to attack Marco. But then he recognised Towler, who waited until Prince Frederick noticed him, and then Towler turned, snapped out an order and together his company charged the domovoi. Before they did, Towler raised his sword in ironic salute.

"F-friend?" Marco asked.

"One of my father's men."

"Your f-father has spies in m-my uncle's c-camp?"

"Of course. Just as you and your uncle have spies in his."

Inspired by Captain Towler's charge spearmen from Alonzo's and Marco's troops turned on the remaining domovoi. But it was too late to save the paladins, who continued to fall through the ice, taking domovoi with them.

Marco said, "I c-can't believe I'm seeing this. The d-death of a l-legend . . ."

"They won't die," Tycho said. He wasn't sure how he knew and had no intention of getting into a discussion about death, knights sleeping under hills and those who entered this world through rings of fire. But the paladins had died to a man at Roncesvalles. Yet here they were again.

A bit like him really.

44

Marco turned from the battle before the last of paladins died, or whatever happened after they fell through the ice. He decided not to gather his spearmen together or order a coordinated withdrawal. The last thing he did before riding for his camp on the lake's edge was order the destruction of the barrel bridge. This trapped his troops with Alonzo's own inside the moat.

He had a right to that decision.

"S-so," Marco said later. "Why d-did I do t-that?"

He was talking to Lady Giulietta, who'd been looking back at the burning cathedral as they rode through the ruined village and headed up the valley side on the road that led to the pass over the mountains.

She shrugged.

"G-Giulietta?"

"Because you're a c-c-coward?"

One of Marco's courtiers gasped and Marco grinned. "Fair g-guess," he said. "But w-wrong. T-try again."

Head down to watch her mare pick a way across a rocky fall that littered the road with scree, Giulietta thought about Marco's question as Tycho watched from where he rode slightly behind. Frederick rode ahead. Only two horses could ride abreast on the narrow road and Marco had claimed the space beside her. Behind Marco came his knights, what remained of Frederick's *krieghund* and those who'd been guarding the lakeside camp.

"W-well?" Marco demanded.

"Don't try to turn your cowardice into a guessing game."

"Those c-creatures are d-dead, the p-paladins are g-gone . . . The thin ice in the m-moat will soon be h-hard enough for people to w-walk. But, m-most importantly, Alonzo won't attack the m-men we left. Not n-now."

"*What?*" She sounded genuinely puzzled.

"He'll l-look for m-me and d-discover I'm gone. He won't r-risk his remaining t-troops in a b-battle for no reason. He's too g-good a soldier."

"He's going to come after us?"

"Of c-course h-he's going to c-come after us. What d-do you expect?" Marco sounded almost happy about it. Either that, or he hoped to steady those around him. His knights had to know how desperate things were. The ex-Regent might spare what was left of the archers and spearmen. The flipside of that coin was that the Nicoletti and Castellani who made up most of those forces would feel no duty to attack him. Leaving him free to track Marco if that was what he wanted.

Tycho nudged his mount slightly forward.

"You t-think w-we should h-hurry?"

"Yes, highness."

"You're p-probably right."

They rode until dawn, higher and higher. The air thinned, and the wind rose when they climbed above the treeline, their horses steaming with sweat as the beasts fought for each step. Far below, the cathedral burnt bright enough to redden the mountainsides until the coming day paled the effect to elegant pink.

"C-cover yourself," Marco ordered Tycho.

"Highness, leave me here."

Instead the duke ordered that Tycho be tied to his own saddle and hidden by horse blankets until his soul returned. "You d-don't sleep," he said. "N-not like we d-do. You abandon your b-body. W-well, so I'm t-told."

Giulietta blushed.

Frederick just looked hurt.

When he woke, Tycho knew instantly something was wrong. His group was too quiet, the atmosphere too strained. He shook his head free from the horse blanket covering him and found his wrists lashed beneath his mount's neck and the animal led by Marco himself. "Shush . . ." Marco whispered.

Leaning across, the duke pulled at a knot and Tycho's hands came free. He reached back to check his sword was loose in its scabbard. Frederick looked tight-faced, his followers watchful. Captain Weimer pale but resolute. Giulietta's thumb was in Leo's mouth to keep him quiet. She looked terrified.

"*Alonzo . . .?*"

Marco raised a finger to his lips.

Fire flamed the mountain ridge behind him and Tycho realised he'd woken to the very last of the daylight. The peaks burnt so bright he turned back to the track and had to close his eyes. There were riders on the mountain below them. Their mounts stumbled on the rocks and steamed with exhaustion, but they kept coming. Perhaps twice as many men as in Marco's party. With Frederick's *krieghund* and Captain Weimer's troops they should be able to set an ambush. Tycho wondered what the other problem was.

Frederick pointed to the cliff above.

Shadows flickered along the moonlit top, fleeting and mostly visible out of the corner of his eye. They were swift and silent and kept easy pace with those using the treacherous track below. The clear sky and almost full moon made Marco's party easier to see. Dropping back, Tycho found Captain Weimer. "How long?"

"Less than an hour, my lord. I thought it an ambush, but . . ."

Whoever held the high ground, they were fresh enough to move at speed, and they could stop or slow Marco's progress enough to let Alonzo catch up if that was their aim. They had done neither. "Bandits?"

"If we're lucky."

"Can we outrun Alonzo?"

"Not without abandoning those on foot."

"Then do it," said Tycho, shocked the captain hadn't done so already. The infantry could make a stand and hold Alonzo back long enough for Marco and Giulietta to ride ahead and find safety.

"The duke forbids it."

"Of course he does. Bloody idiot."

Marco turned and smiled, almost as if he knew he was the subject of their whispered discussion.

"Then we must all make a stand."

Captain Weimer nodded. "My thoughts. Unfortunately, it's not my choice."

"Have you suggested it?"

The captain looked at him strangely. "I've been doing so all day. His highness said no decision could be made until you woke. Well, you're awake, so perhaps you should go talk to him . . ." The man turned away, lost in his crossness at nobles and aristocrats who refused to fight wars properly.

They had nine horses, four knights, two princes, a future duchess of Venice if she lived that long, an infant of less than eighteen months, nine *krieghund* sworn to defend the infant to the death, ten light infantry, Captain Weimer, who made up for in experience what he lacked in numbers, and Tycho.

He could become a demon. He could become an angel.

In recent years, in the middle of battle, he had become both. But here and now, watching the cliff top and worrying about the prickling at the back of his neck, with Giulietta and Marco having a hissed argument, he felt only sad it had come to this. When Frederick fell back, looking nervous, Tycho simply nodded . . .

"What are our chances?"

"Bleak. Unless you have a brilliant idea?"

"You're meant to be the strategist, the man who pulls victory from defeat and work miracles . . ."

I am? "Not me," Tycho said. He doubted he was a man at all.

"Who will win that?" Frederick meant the other battle, the one being fought up ahead in furious whispers between Duke Marco and Lady Giulietta as they hurried their mounts forward.

"Marco, obviously. He has less to lose."

"His life? His dukedom?"

"Giulietta has Leo. Her own life and you . . ." Tycho had to grab Frederick's bridle to keep him moving. The look in the princeling's eyes was unreadable as he stared at the couple riding in front of them. Leaving Frederick to his thoughts, Tycho edged his horse forward. There was barely room for two animals to ride abreast and he had to nudge Marco's horse before the duke noticed him.

"Well," Tycho whispered. "Is it decided?"

"You stay out of this," Giulietta hissed.

"It's d-decided," Marco said. "My c-cousin and Leo will t-take the horses and ride ahead. We will stay h-here to buy them t-time. If we g-get lucky and k-kill Alonzo . . ." He shrugged. "Well, we'll just h-have to catch them up."

Lady Giulietta opened her mouth to object.

"It's d-decided."

"You're *the duke*," she said.

"And you're the n-next d-duchess."

"That's just a label," she said furiously. "It doesn't mean anything."

Marco smiled at her. "S-see," he said. "You're learning. You could even r-reintroduce your b-beloved republic if you w-want to cause r-real chaos. Now let us d-dismount and you can t-take two of the knights, and all the horses. With replacements you c-can d-definitely outride h-him. We'll m-make s-sure of it."

"Frederick should go with her," Tycho said.

They both turned round to look at him.

"I'd t-thought of s-sending you."

"Frederick and the *krieghund*," Tycho said firmly. "They will die to protect her, and even if they wouldn't, they'd die to protect Leo."

"S-so would y-you."

"There are more of them."

Marco looked at him sadly. "You've d-decided t-then?"

"Don't worry," Tycho told Giulietta. "We'll deal with Alonzo and catch you up afterwards. Wait for us at Castelnuovo." He named the port where they'd landed. The one the locals called Sveti Stefan.

"Tycho . . ."

"If I may . . .?" Tycho said.

Marco edged his horse forward to let Tycho take his place alongside Giulietta. Reaching across, Tycho took her hand and she closed her mailed fingers on his. *She's changed and so have you . . . I can do this*, Tycho told himself. *I can say goodbye well enough to let her ride away.*

Giulietta had tears in her eyes.

Tycho felt his own spill over and tightened his fingers, not trusting himself to speak. When he looked up, Giulietta was staring at him.

"I didn't know you could cry."

Tycho let go her hand and reined in his mount, falling back until he was next to Frederick. "You're to go with Giulietta," he told the princeling.

"I'll stay and fight . . ."

"Those are Marco's orders. You take the *krieghund* and the horses and ride for the coast as fast as you can. We do everything we can to buy Giulietta and her son time."

"This is suicide." Frederick looked to where Lady Giulietta sat stiff-backed next to her cousin. "Does she realise you'll all die?"

"I've told her we'll meet at Sveti Stefan."

"And she believed you?"

Personally, Tycho doubted it.

45

"Y-you could h-have gone with h-her . . ."

"No, highness, I couldn't."

Marco sighed and glanced up the track towards the pass through which Lady Giulietta, her son and the *krieghund* had vanished. The cliff rose high on one side of the track and dropped into a ravine on the other. It was just wide enough for six spearmen to block the way. Those behind could stab and slice, and provide weight for the shield wall in front.

Although Marco's remaining knights had the best armour, without mounts to carry them they were near useless and were already shedding what plate they could. It was the infantry who would meet Alonzo's charge. Marco had chosen the battlefield carefully. About twelve paces down the track was a tight bend round a rocky spur. This, Marco announced, was to prevent Alonzo from being able to charge at speed.

It would take two days for Giulietta to reach the coast, possibly three . . . The longer they could hold Alonzo the better chance she'd have. They had the kink in the road and the narrowness of the path on their side. Prince Alonzo had greater numbers and cavalry on his. "W-what are you t-thinking?"

"Your uncle will hate our position."

"You w-would have m-made a good g-general."

The thought was so absurd that Tycho grinned in self-mockery, then realised the duke was serious. "Highness . . ."

"What else would you d-do?"

Tycho looked at men locking shields. "Nothing."

"J-just thought I'd c-check . . . It's t-thawing," Marco added.

Late winter sun and daytime warmth had set runnels sliding down rocks to create a stream below. The temperature was still above freezing because pockets of snow trapped in the cliff face kept dripping and the track was slushy underfoot.

"S-should m-make it easier for G-Giulietta."

Tycho nodded, not knowing if it was even true.

They heard Alonzo's men long before they climbed the track and turned the tight bend around the promontory, stopping suddenly at the sight of the shield wall. As the lead horse shied, another skidded on the slush and Alonzo nearly lost a knight as the heavily armoured man fought to control his beast.

Horses, Tycho thought.

They were Alonzo's strength and his weakness.

"Shoot their mounts," Tycho shouted. The only two archers in Marco's troop looked to the duke for guidance.

"D-do it," he said decisively. And they pushed forward . . . The shield wall opened while Alonzo's two knights were still deciding what to do and the bowmen aimed and released. Both missed.

Grabbing a bow, Tycho slotted an arrow and let go, drawing and releasing another arrow while the first was still in the air. He was already slotting a third when his first target reared, presenting its neck to the arrow he was about to release. It fell with Tycho's arrow in its throat, although what killed it was sliding over the track's crumbling edge and hitting rocks below.

Its rider screamed once on the way down.

The second knight was fighting his wounded mount as Tycho put another arrow into the poor creature's flank, jerking the horse round so it slammed the knight into the rock face. It took the swearing man longer than it should to cut his animal's throat. Infantry pushed their way through to retrieve the heavily armoured knight and barge his dying mount over the edge.

Tycho used the moment to unleash more arrows. A sergeant went down with one through his eye and a horse shied from a strike to its chest, but that was when Tycho's luck ran out. His next arrow flopped to the dirt as the bow cracked and the tension went out of its string.

Stepping back, Tycho let the shield wall close around him.

Two knights edged forward on Alonzo's orders and lowered their lances. One wore a battle axe at his hip, the other had a great sword. It seemed unlikely they'd thought about how much space they'd need to wield either.

"Brace the wall," Captain Weimer shouted.

One of Marco's foot soldiers suddenly stood tall and hurled his precious spear as if it was a common javelin. It arced through the air as Captain Weimer cursed, and struck the leading horse in the chest, sending it stumbling.

The animal next to it shied in panic and threw its rider.

"Open the wall," Captain Weimer howled. He sprinted for the fallen knight and swung his spike axe one-handed through the man's helmet, kicking the man's head to work the axe free. He swung at the other knight, missed and put his axe into the horse's neck, ripping it free and retreating through the shield wall. He punched the offending soldier on his way past.

"N-nicely d-done," Marco said.

The captain grinned. "Thank you, highness."

Dead horses and high ground – those could be Marco's weapons. Dead horses, high ground and the tight bend in the track. The sergeant Alonzo sent to dispatch the screaming mount finally landed a killing blow but couldn't drive the animal over the cliff before it bled out. Both armies could hear Alonzo's fury. The prince wasn't discreet in his anger.

314

"W-well done," Marco said. "We c-can do t-this."

Maybe he really was mad enough to believe it. Alonzo had ridden ahead, which was obviously why he had mostly knights with him, but his army would be following behind and they far outnumbered Marco's group. Everyone but Marco knew death was merely a matter of time.

"W-what will m-my uncle do n-now?"

"Unhorse his light cavalry," Captain Weimer said. "Use them as foot soldiers."

And so it proved. A group of mercenaries advanced with their shields held high as they edged carefully between dead horses. They wore breastplates and open-faced helmets and looked utterly professional. Raising their shields, they advanced in step.

"*Tortuca*," Captain Weimer shouted.

As the front row of Marco's men steadied their shields, Tycho took his place in the second row beside Captain Weimer. The men behind them had shields that they raised against spears or arrows from above. It was a formation as old as Venice itself, possibly older.

Shield met shield as the mercenaries slammed into Marco's wall. The men in Marco's tortuca dug their boots in, steadied themselves and punched with their shields, hoping to hear air whoosh from those they faced. A mercenary stumbled, and his immediate opponent stabbed for the gap. His sword slid off armour and entered a man's neck, jutting right through for a moment until he withdrew his blade in a spray of blood. The enemy wall roared in fury.

The mercenary's comrades closed the gap as he fell.

"Well done, lad," Captain Weimer roared. Quietly, he muttered, "They're pushing us back." Tycho already realised that. The small group protecting Marco gave ground slowly as extra men joined the back of Alonzo's own tortuca.

"We can't hold them for long enough," Captain Weimer

whispered. Tycho's answer was lost as the captain roared, "That's it, lads. Push harder, we're going to march right over them."

Those at the front of Marco's tortuca pushed and grunted, reversing their grips to stab down over shields, while those behind jabbed with spears when they could. One man risked a glance over the wall and took a sword through the eye. Tycho grabbed his drooping shield, stepped into the gap and stabbed the man's attacker. Dropping to a crouch, he slashed another across the ankle. These men had wives and children, maybe even mothers, but he welcomed their screams all the same.

"You've done this before, sir."

He punched his shield into an enemy who tried to push him, heard breath burst from the man's body and slammed the bottom of his shield down on the man's foot, jerking it upwards to catch him under his chin. "I learn fast."

"Nah . . ." The man shook his head doggedly. "You've done this before."

Not at Bjornvin, Tycho thought. In Bjornvin, slaves couldn't even own knives. "I'm going out here. Close the gap after me."

"If you do," said his neighbour, "we'll all die." His tone said he realised there was little to choose between nobles, children and idiots . . . None the less, he'd rather the idiot next to him keep his place. Tycho remained where he was rather than break the shield wall. Those behind him provided the shields that made a roof against spears, while those in his line held fast against the brutal weight of numbers pushing them and those at the very back dug in their heels, fought the slush and strained to hold those in front. Together they made a metal and flesh monster, solid on the outside and fear-filled, stinking and desperate within. All they could do was retreat and keep retreating as slowly as possible.

Marco was muttering to himself, a stuttery two-way conversation about how strange life was and how death was going to be even stranger. He didn't seem upset at the thought, simply resigned. Captain Weimer was beside him. The man would die to protect the duke, probably sooner rather than later.

At least their weight of numbers made Alonzo's men careless.

Marco's group kept their shields high and took heart from enemy screams every time their blades bit home or spears found their mark. The smell of blood was overpowering, the stench of voided bowels even worse. The grinding of shields hurt Tycho's ears until he hated the noise and his sharp hearing. He fought, he pushed back and slammed his shield into the enemy in front. Around him, tired men were facing thoughts of death. Flat, unwelcome thoughts. They stared death in the face and death scowled back. They would die on a mountain road, frozen and hungry, and surrounded by the clash of steel, the gasps of exhausted men . . .

What am I missing? Tycho thought.

In the unexpected silence of both sides suddenly falling quiet he found it and knew it had been there before, time and again, calling to him and waiting on his answer. *The high call of a goshawk.* Shivers ran down his back. On the wind came a second call, so clear he almost froze in shock. *Did he want help?*

Of course he wanted help, and badly. Tycho risked a glance above the shield wall, blocked a thrusting blade and slashed at the fingers of his attacker, hearing the man swear and not caring, because he was already sending a high answering call of his own.

"W-what's-that?"

"Assassini business."

A shadow dropped from the cliffs on to the rear of the tortuca, ran its brief length and leapt on to Alonzo's tortuca, ripped up a roofing shield and broke the neck of the soldier beneath. Howling with excitement, it lunged for another man.

A patter of bare feet on Marco's tortuca turned to a torrent. Screaming began as Alonzo's shield wall fell apart. Standing straight, Tycho watched ragged darkness wash over Alonzo's front line and take down his men.

"Charge the traitorous bastards," Captain Weimer yelled.

"No," Tycho's voice was fierce. "Stand firm."

"T-Tycho. W-what is it?"

"Our sins returned to haunt us."

Marco stared at the ragged children backlit by stars. They were mostly female and dressed in rags that did little to hide their scrawny bodies and even less to keep out the wind. Lacking Tycho's vision, Marco couldn't see the blood running down their chins or the baby white dog teeth with which they tore out the throats of their victims. He just heard screams and saw bodies falling. The children killed the horses cleanly but they fed on anything human.

"S-some s-sins," Marco said.

Tycho nodded grimly. He heard footsteps and turned. On the dark road behind him stood two women. One he'd expected to see, the other he hadn't. She was Nubian, with braided hair that ended in silver thimbles. Her companion was almost a girl, dressed in a tattered gown that had once belonged to Eleanor, Lady Giulietta's dead lady-in-waiting. "Hold Alonzo," she barked.

Her followers swarmed round the prince.

"Your highness," Amelia said. "Apologies for our lateness."

Marco smiled at the Nubian. "You t-timed your entrance p-perfectly. N-now, introduce m-me to your interesting f-friend . . ."

"We've met," the ragged girl said.

"This is Lady Rosalyn of the Carpathians."

"Greetings, my lady . . . And t-those? Marco gestured at the urchins, a few of whom still crouched over shuddering bodies. Some formed the circle that kept Alonzo secure. Behind those were more urchins, silently blocking the path against retreat, had there been any of Alonzo's followers left alive to do so.

"My children," Rosalyn said proudly.

"S-such a big f-family for one so y-young." Marco smiled at Tycho. "And s-such interesting p-parents . . ."

A few of the children came to stand around their mistress. The rest guarded the road or kept Alonzo penned as she'd ordered, although they glanced over jealously. One of the urchins with Rosalyn, smaller than the rest, laid her head against Rosalyn's hip and Rosalyn hugged her briefly. There was something lost in the child's face. "Your little brother is fine," Tycho said.

Fierce eyes fixed on him. "You promise?"

It seemed she remembered Pietro, who got his sister back from the grave only to lose her again. "He's Lady Giulietta's page."

"She treats him well?"

"Yes, my lady."

"Then she can live. That one, however . . ." Rosalyn pointed to where Prince Alonzo stood. "He dies."

"H-he m-must be t-tried."

"Then killed?" she asked contemptuously.

Marco looked rueful. Tycho imagined that was exactly what he wanted. The men behind Marco waited on his orders. Rosalyn waited on his next words and her wild brood waited on her reaction. Amelia stood still, her face impassive. Tycho had a bad feeling about this.

"Some s-sort of t-trial is n-necessary . . ."

"Due process," Alonzo said. "The Venetian way."

"If you give m-me your p-parole," Marco said. "If you s-surrender your s-sword and g-give me your p-promise you won't t-try to escape we won't t-tie you up."

"Your highness." Captain Weimer sounded worried.

"I refuse," Alonzo said.

"To give your w-word?"

"To surrender my sword. You declared me a traitor. I declare you lie. I demand the right to judicial battle."

Tycho looked at Captain Weimer.

"Trial by combat," the captain muttered.

Stepping forward, Tycho drew his sword. "I am the duke's champion."

"You?" Alonzo snorted. "The freak will fight for the fool?"

Tycho held his gaze until the ex-Regent looked away. "I'll have your head if it's what's on offer. Although a goose quill through the heart is what you deserve."

Alonzo flushed. "No champions. I will fight Marco if he dares face me. If not, then I declare him a coward and my innocence is proved." He looked slowly round his accusers. "This is the law. You know this is the law."

"I accept." Marco didn't even stutter. When Captain Weimer opened his mouth to argue the duke held up a hand forbidding it. He was in armour already and had his sword at his side. Both men wore helmets, breastplates and vambraces. Though it would be hard to argue one was better armed, the difference in size and strength was obvious and huge. "I h-have the c-choice of w-weapons."

Prince Alonzo nodded.

"We already fight *alla m-macchia*."

"On common ground," Captain Weimer muttered. Tycho nodded his thanks.

"But the s-slope h-here is uneven."

"I cede you the high ground." Alonzo was impatient.

"I r-refuse to accept. We will f-fight somewhere l-level."

"Up there, highness," Amelia said. "Next to a waterfall, with a shepherd's hut empty in ruins." She saw Tycho's surprise and muttered, "We had time to examine it, God knows." She glanced at Rosalyn and he wondered what she wasn't saying.

Marco smiled. "T-that s-sounds ideal."

"He can't mean to fight him?" Captain Weimer asked. The captain dropped back to walk beside Tycho, who had a gaggle of urchins around him, but was watching Marco and Rosalyn walk side by side ahead. The duke was chatting politely like someone taking an afternoon walk.

It was obvious to Tycho that every last urchin in Rosalyn's wild brood could see almost as well in the dark as he could.

She'd created the army he'd failed to produce for Alexa – wild and fierce and under a single person's control. And Marco walked beside her as if doing anything except go to his death.

"T-this is n-nice," he said.

The passing place for carts was as level as Amelia had promised. Except for a handful of tracks in the thawing earth it was also smooth. A waterfall cascaded from high above into a pool below that bubbled with dark water. Marco walked to its edge and peered down. He whistled.

"Satisfied?" Alonzo demanded.

"V-very impressive." Marco turned to Amelia. "T-thank y-you." He made it sound as if she'd levelled the ground herself and carved him a pool into which water could fall. "I'll h-have a p-proper look afterwards."

"He must have a plan," Captain Weimer whispered. "My lord, tell me the duke has a plan . . ."

Possibly, thought Tycho. Although it might not be what those around him called a plan. He sighed when Marco began to remove his helmet.

"It's h-heavy," the duke explained.

Alonzo grinned. "I hope you don't expect me to remove mine?"

"Oh n-no," Marco said. "It suits y-you." He looked around and spotted the small axe hanging on Captain Weimer's belt. Its armour-piercing spike was dark with dried blood. "We'll f-fight with t-those."

His uncle looked disgusted.

It made sense though. A wrist loop secured the handle to stop it being dropped, the head was reasonably light and the spike fierce enough to puncture plate. With a weapon like that, speed was as valuable as strength. One of Marco's foot soldiers handed Alonzo his own axe with a bow, then stepped back and stared straight ahead. If the ex-Regent won he might well become the next duke. The Nicoletti, Arsenalotti and Castellani liked their politics simple. A victorious Alonzo outranked an untried Giulietta.

"W-when you're r-ready."

Alonzo flushed at the implied insult.

His answer was brutal. He simply charged at Marco and swung the spike axe at his head. The duke dropped under the blow, tripped on a cart rut and rolled away from a second swing. Standing, he then waited while Alonzo wrestled his axe from the hard dirt. "Should have counter-attacked," Captain Weimer complained.

Tycho could only agree.

Alonzo made the next attack as well. A fierce swing that would have spiked Marco through the heart if he hadn't twisted away, his uncle's axe squealing down the side of his breastplate.

"Close," the captain said.

Way too close . . . And Tycho suspected Alonzo would be launching all the attacks. Working his way round those watching the fight, Tycho hurried to where Amelia stood next to Rosalyn.

"My lady," he said to Rosalyn.

The ragged girl looked to see if she was being mocked.

"If you don't mind, I'd like to talk to . . ." He nodded at Amelia, who glanced at Marco, who was backing away from Alonzo. There was a frightening intensity to Amelia's gaze. Like Tycho, she was forcing herself not to intervene.

"Go ahead," Rosalyn said.

"I have a message for Lady Giulietta."

Beside Amelia, Rosalyn's expression froze and Tycho knew she was listening. "Tell my lady I have the right to name my successor as head of . . ."

A gasp made them both start. Marco was rolling across muddy ground away from Alonzo, as his uncle slammed his axe into the dirt and ripped it free. Scrambling to his feet, Marco swung a wild blow that almost landed.

Both men stepped back.

"As head of the Assassini," Tycho said hurriedly, "I can name my successor. I name you."

322

"My lord, there has never been a . . ."

"Doesn't matter if there's never been a female head. Remind her there's never been a ruling duchess, either. With her there will be."

"Alonzo?"

"Dies tonight, one way or the other."

Amelia's eyes widened as she realised what Tycho was saying. Anyone who won a trial by combat was proved innocent. If Tycho killed Alonzo it would be judged pure revenge and he'd be judged to have murdered an innocent man. There would be no stepping back from this.

"That's it?" Rosalyn interrupted. "That's Giulietta's message?"

"Yes, my lady."

"Gods," she said. "You're still a fool."

On the patch of flat ground provided by the passing place, Marco and Alonzo were circling slowly, their breath coming in jagged gasps. Each circle brought Marco closer and closer to the edge of the waterfall. So close he could slip over the edge and tumble into the pool far below at any moment. "You die here," Alonzo said.

"You f-fucked my m-mother. She s-said it was b-boring."

Prince Alonzo scowled at him furiously.

"You f-fucked my m-mother, you m-murdered my f-father, you tried to p-poison me . . . W-which one of us d-do you think deserves to d-die?"

"You should never have been born."

"If you'd m-managed to p-poison me p-properly I wouldn't have b-been." Marco grinned. "You're t-too stupid for plots."

Someone among those watching laughed and that was enough. Incensed, the ex-Regent hurled himself forward and planted the spike of his axe so firmly in Marco's chest his breastplate bent. The crowd gasped. Soldiers hurried forward and Captain Weimer shouted to hold their position.

"It's not over yet," he yelled.

"Q-quite r-right," whispered Marco. He leant backwards over the waterfall's drop and everyone realised the only thing stopping him falling was the strap fixing Alonzo's wrist to the axe. As Alonzo fought to free his hand from the straining strap, Marco calmly swung his own axe, nailing Alonzo's hand in place, then kicked from the edge of the drop and smiled.

Tycho swallowed the scene in a glance.

Rosalyn all sharp cheeks and high amusement. Amelia, wide-eyed but clever enough to know Marco and Alonzo killing each other could only do Venice good. Captain Weimer and his men – the men Tycho had fought beside – unable to believe what they'd just seen. And Rosalyn's ragged children watching it all in silence.

This was where the world changed.

Tycho was moving in the instant. Time slowing as he crossed the trampled dirt, drew his dagger and launched himself from the edge into the dark pool below. He hated water, hated it with a fierceness, but knew he had almost no time to act. Ahead of him Alonzo was hitting water first, Marco tumbling after. The weight of their armour took both under.

Tycho followed.

46

The marriage of Lady Giulietta de Felice di Millioni to His Highness Prince Frederick zum Bas Friedland, natural son of Emperor Sigismund of Germany, took place in the middle of the afternoon in the Millioni's private chapel, otherwise known as the Basilica San Marco. A church widely agreed to be Europe's most beautiful.

San Marco was at its most magnificent. Mosaics had been mopped, the floors swept and the bodies in the crypt discreetly buried. One in a pauper's grave on an island to the north, another under the flagstones of the Millioni crypt, an act of respect from the new duchess to a woman who was probably her cousin for all neither of them had known this. The last body, that of Duchess Alexa, had been interred with great splendour beside that of her husband, Marco the Just, father of the late Marco the Great. The new duchess did this because she hoped her Aunt Alexa's ghost would approve. Almost everything Giulietta did and had done since that hideous morning on the ship at Sveti Stefan, when they brought her news of Marco's, Uncle Alonzo's and Tycho's death had been based on what she thought Aunt Alexa would do.

Aunt Alexa would demand Giulietta be crowned before being

325

married so no one could doubt she married Frederick as a reigning duchess. If the basilica was clean, aired, swept and lavishly decorated for the wedding it was because Giulietta had demanded her coronation that morning be magnificent. Aunt Alexa would have wanted it magnificent. She would have wanted Giulietta to marry Frederick, too. So that was going to happen.

He was Sigismund's bastard. Her city had thrown in its lot with the Holy Roman Empire, allied to it but not part of it. Byzantium was an enemy now. Sigismund's power was needed as a counterweight. The only problem with this was that Giulietta and Frederick had barely exchanged a word since she received the news on the quayside at Sveti Stefan of Marco's death.

Maybe it was guilt? Frederick had thrown guilt in her face.

Why else would she refuse to talk to him? Why else would she refuse to let him talk to her? He'd greeted the news that she'd agreed to go through with the marriage suggested by Emperor Sigismund with disbelief, fury and then contempt. Having disappeared for three days, he was found drunk in a brothel. Far from being publicly outraged, Lady Giulietta let it be known she was delighted to have proof his interests ran in the right direction, unlike his half-brother Leopold. That bit went unspoken – at least by her.

Aunt Alexa would have been proud.

Just as she would have been impressed by the icy dignity with which the Duchess Giulietta entered the basilica and made her way in stately procession through the nobles and richer *cittadini* gathered under the stern gaze of the messiah painted on the dome above. Prince Frederick stood before the altar, dressed in magnificent silks and velvets. His entourage occupied one side at the front of the congregation. They were as magnificently dressed and as unsmiling. It had taken a direct order from his father to make this marriage happen. His friends knew exactly how Frederick felt about that and their scowls showed they felt the same.

They believed he'd rescued Lady Giulietta from certain death, and his reward was to be cold-shouldered and treated with contempt. The two Venetian knights who rode with the *krieghund* to the coast agreed. Giulietta's reading of this . . .? If Frederick had stayed he could have stopped Marco's stupid duel. Everyone was talking about how magnificent his death was. Marco the Simpleton finding his common sense and courage and beating his fearsome uncle in hand-to-hand combat, just the two of them, under traditional rules.

How could anyone be stupid enough to let Marco fight a duel? Why had Tycho not stopped it? And why had he then been stupid enough to die trying to rescue Marco from the pool into which he'd thrown himself? They had fought in armour. How could Tycho possibly think he could save Marco?

Ahead of her, someone coughed discreetly.

Looking up, Lady Giulietta saw the Patriarch of Venice, magnificent in his embroidered robes. "Your highness . . .?"

Giulietta nodded. She was as ready as she'd ever be.

A dozen *Assassini* were hidden unobtrusively among the congregation, a noble from the mainland here, a *cittadino* no one quite recognised there. They were the only people in the basilica carrying hidden weapons. At least Lady Amelia hoped so.

She watched Duchess Giulietta from an upper balcony. Newly made mistress of the Assassini, she had her best people in the crowd. God knows, they were few enough and she'd be recruiting for months and possibly years to come. She'd summoned back every agent she had, using the month between Giulietta's landing and her coronation to send for *Assassini* from Paris, Constantinople and Vienna.

Her earliest shock, apart from Lady Giulietta accepting Tycho's recommendation of her without question, was how efficient his archives had been. For a libertine said to live in exotic squalor his notes on which agent was where, how many retirees could be drawn on and who had failed testing but could still be used in emergencies were frighteningly clear.

The squalor had been a disguise, Amelia decided.

Along with Tycho's house in San Aponal she'd inherited a Jewish servant called Rachel, who ran Tycho's house with quiet efficiency and knew more about the workings of the Assassini than Amelia expected or thought wise. Until she realised Rachel was the Assassini's unofficial archivist and the reason everything was so efficiently ordered. She'd also inherited oversight of Pietro, once a Venetian street child, then Tycho's servant and now Giulietta's page. Pietro stood just behind his mistress, his dark hair freshly cut and his scarlet doublet embroidered with gold and silver. Since the sumptuary laws banned servants from wearing silver thread and those below armiger from wearing gold, the duchess must have declared him noble. What *oversight* meant Amelia was waiting to be told.

She knew the boy was *Assassini* trained, and could see the advantage of having someone with that training close to the duchess. Lady Amelia's own title and noble status had been given for undefined services during the Montenegrin campaign. Since the official version of the campaign had yet to be written, she was also waiting to discover what these were. She doubted the slaughter of Duke Tiresias, briefly Byzantine patron to Prince Alonzo, would be numbered among them, at least officially. With the house and her title came a gold chain set off by her black skin. She still wore tarnished silver thimbles on her braids, though, simply because she enjoyed the disquiet they caused.

"What do you think?" asked the hooded figure next to her.

"What do you expect me to think?" Amelia glanced from Lady Giulietta standing stiffly before the patriarch to Frederick, stony-faced beside her. "This is a disaster. They can barely stand to be in each other's presence."

"I'd heard she loved him."

Lady Amelia turned to look at the monk also hidden in the

upper balcony's half-darkness, so invisible in the shadows he had to be *Assassini* trained. "Jealous?" she demanded.

"Of course I'm jealous . . ." Tycho stared at the couple at the altar and wondered why he'd risked daylight, no matter how well wrapped, to see this. Why didn't he simply stay in his room, stab a knife into his own heart and twist?

Amelia had seemed unsurprised to see him when he appeared at Sveti Stefan, demanding she smuggle him aboard Giulietta's ship. The real favour came a week later when she produced the formula for Dr Crow's ointment and the address of a discreet Moorish pharmacist who could make it up for him. Lord Atilo had the formula filed and Tycho had never thought to look. So now he had daylight freedom of a limited sort, although the sun's brightness still terrified him.

He had one more job to do, though, before he could leave the city, probably the most difficult of his life for all that no one would die. "You have good people in the kitchens?"

Amelia glared at him.

Of course she did. Poison and courts went together.

Pulling a leather pouch from his pocket, he untied its mouth and Amelia went very still as he rolled two pills into the palm of his gloved hand. The pills were tired-looking and grubby. One had once been silver but most of this had worn away. The other had fragments of gold leaf sticking to its surface.

"What are those?"

"The solution to that." He'd saved them the night Giulietta insisted they were unnecessary. Lying in his arms, she sworn she'd love him for ever.

"And what, *exactly*, do they do?"

The balance between Amelia and him had changed. She was mistress of the Assassini and took the responsibility seriously. She spoke from the assumption that she had a right to ask and he would answer.

"Well . . .?

"Dr Crow made them." A reply that did little to reassure her. "Remember the feast for Frederick?" Tycho asked.

"I was in Paris, remember?" She flicked her gaze to where the patriarch was asking Duchess Giulietta if she took Prince Frederick as her husband. Her answer was flat but it was still yes.

"She's in shock," Amelia said.

Tycho looked at her.

"The duchess is sleepwalking through this. She's been sleep-walking through everything since you and Marco died. *What would Aunt Alexa do?* I've heard her ask it aloud. Everyone close to her has heard it."

What would Aunt Alexa do?

"Aunt Alexa would want her to take these."

"Convince me," Amelia said.

The kitchens were steamy and filled with cooks screaming at undercooks about their failings. In one corner, a confectioner reduced his young assistant to tears with a fluency and vicious-ness that stunned Tycho. It seemed an egg white had not set properly.

An ox roasted on an iron spit over a fire pit. In the chimneys, whole hogs cooked on lesser spits turned by children over hissing charcoal that singed bristles as dripping fat sent flames jumping. The area smelt of crackling. Vast pies of salt pastry not meant to be eaten were being filled with a mix of hot mutton, black pepper and steaming winter vegetables. The last peacock in the zoo was honey-glazed and almost roasted. Barrels of red wine stood warming. More barrels of strong and weak beer were being trundled across stone floors towards a trestle table that held clay jugs for lower tables and glass ones for high tables.

The crowd in the banqueting hall beyond the doors were drunk and already half stuffed with fresh bread, their fingers slick with oil from a stew of chicken and root vegetables better suited to the table of a *cittadino*. Barely a scrap remained on the dishes being returned to the kitchens. Tonight might not be the richest feast Venice had seen but it was better than any given in recent months.

The great banqueting hall, first demanded by Marco the Just, and overseen by Duchess Alexa, had been finished on the orders of Marco the Great, the late and much lamented duke. Its panelling was waxed and the painted ceiling finally in place; even the windows had been fitted. Politeness demanded that no one mention the last time Prince Frederick attended a feast in that hall assassins had tried to kill him.

"Over there." Amelia nodded to the far side of the kitchens.

Two White Crucifers stood by a table watching the preparations carefully. Every so often, one would abandon his post to test food, sniff meat or examine dried peppercorns before allowing them to be ground. They were Giulietta's and Frederick's official food tasters. The Crucifers looked up suspiciously.

"Duchess Giulietta's orders," Amelia said.

For a second it looked as if the men would demand her right to use the duchess's name, then they took in the richness of her gown and the value of the gold chain around her neck and accepted she'd be stupid to use the name without authority. They had the closed faces of men who didn't like women at the best of times, certainly not ones who met their gaze. "And him?" the taller demanded.

Tycho was dressed simply, his robes long and priest-like.

"An alchemist," Amelia said. "Also here on her orders."

The priests scowled as Tycho guessed they would.

"You taste the food first," Amelia told them. "We taste it second. Only then does it go through to the duke and duchess." The Crucifers thought about that and scowled at each other as they tried to come up with a reason that having the food double-tasted was a bad idea beyond hurt pride.

"The first dish has already gone."

"True," Lady Amelia admitted. "But since Giulietta and Frederick have yet to seat themselves they will not have eaten it . . ." Maybe it was the familiarity with which the richly dressed young Nubian used the royal names, and used them with confidence . . . Perhaps it was simply that she knew the couple were not yet seated, which he didn't, but the elder Crucifer accepted defeat.

"We'll be watching."

"Especially him." The younger one nodded.

They were true to their word. They watched carefully as Tycho dug his borrowed spoon into a bowl of fish soup they'd already tasted, and barely bothered to watch Amelia take her turn afterwards. Over the next hour and a half they watched Tycho chew a slice of beef, pinch a succulent sliver from a piglet, and spoon mutton and winter vegetable pie into his mouth.

Food tasters kept their employers alive. They tasted the wine and the water, the bread and the meat and the wizened winter vegetables that had been plumped up by soaking in water and seasoned with black pepper and cinnamon to hide their bitterness. They tasted everything. "I think we're done," Tycho said.

Lady Amelia nodded.

"You don't intend to taste that?" The younger Crucifer pointed at a heart-shaped sweetmeat of diced fruit, honeycomb and spices carried by a young page. The heart was cut diagonally so Giulietta could take the top piece and her new husband the bottom. "You," the Crucifer said. "Here."

The boy glared at him.

He wore Millioni scarlet, decorated with gold and silver. At his hip hung an ornate dagger that he could only be wearing by dispensation of the duchess herself. "If you would," the priest added, more politely.

The boy brought his dish across.

His eyes widened as he glanced at Tycho's hooded face and his mouth opened. He was trembling when Lady Amelia stepped

332

forward and gripped the boy's cheeks with fingers that dug into his skin. "Has anyone else touched this?"

She tapped the dish – in a rapid sequence that announced *Assassini business*. When she released him, Pietro bowed. "No, my lady." He hesitated. "I mean, the confectioner obviously, but . . ."

She waved his fumbling away.

The priests tasted it first, taking tentative scoops from beneath both bits of the heart. Lady Amelia's interrogation of the page had given them a new respect for her. She had to be someone if she treated a royal page like one of her own. They watched Tycho, although less closely than before. There was little enough for them to see. He scooped out sweetmeat, tasted it and did his best to smooth the sides. His smile was bleak as he nodded to say he felt no ill effects.

It was Lady Amelia's turn. But the Crucifers were watching the page, wondering why he was standing so rigidly to attention and obviously fighting his emotions. The boy glanced at the hooded figure, who said, "I'm sorry for your loss."

The page stared at him.

"Your master, Tycho bel Angelo. I'm told he drowned in Montenegro trying to save Duke Marco after the duke slaughtered his traitorous uncle . . . It must be hard for someone so young to handle the loss."

Pietro's chin came up. *I'm not so young*, his gesture said. *Of course I understand.* A second later, he asked. "You think he's really dead?"

"So everyone says."

The boy nodded sadly and turned his attention to Lady Amelia, who was smoothing the exact points on the sweetmeat heart where the happy couple could be expected to scoop the first mouthfuls to offer each other. "Everything is as it should be," she said.

Pietro bowed to her, nodded to the Crucifers, considered

carefully . . . And bowed deeply to the hooded figure, touching his clenched fist to his heart. Then he picked up the sweetmeat and turned for the door.

Inside his hood, Tycho smiled sadly.

So much to give away in one day. His heart, his happiness, Giulietta's love for him, now Pietro "You want to see how this ends?" Amelia asked sympathetically, her voice pitched too low for the priests to hear.

Tycho didn't but he knew he should.

A balcony ran the length of the banqueting hall, fretted with gilded wood to let women watch from above without being seen by men at the tables below. It was years since feasts had been for men only, but the new hall had been designed by the late duke's father and Marco the Just had insisted on a balcony in the old style. Looking at the archers stationed behind the fretwork Tycho decided the old duke had known precisely what he was doing.

"The *krieghund* are targeted," Amelia said, nodding down to where Frederick's companions sat together. "But they can't prove it."

At the top table Giulietta and Frederick ate in silence. Every so often, Frederick would glance across and look away if she caught him watching. Occasionally, she'd look at him. There was something hard in her gaze. Yet puzzled, as if she wondered how she found herself sitting next to him.

"He's terrified of her," Amelia said.

"Why?" Tycho demanded.

"Because she's terrifying."

Is she? At times, she'd seemed to him spoilt, unhappy or miserable . . . At others, kind, gentle and thoughtful. One didn't make the other untrue. People were complicated.

"Are you leaving Venice because of Frederick?"

"No," Tycho said, "I"m leaving because of me." He looked

at Giulietta and his mouth twisted with sadness. "Well," he corrected, "I'm leaving because of us. Giulietta made me happy."

"And you?" Amelia asked.

"I made her scared."

Amelia looked surprised. "You knew that?"

Not until the words came out of my mouth just then, Tycho thought. Although he didn't say it. "Watch," he said.

Part of him was scared Dr Crow's pills were too old to be potent, and part of him hoped that was true, the dark part. Why should he want to help them fall in love with each other? Pietro was approaching the top table, carrying the gold salver containing the sweetmeat heart. He carried it steadily, staring straight ahead. Stopping in front of Giulietta and Frederick, he knelt and held out the plate.

Tradition said they should take the heart, lift it together and put it between them on the table. When Giulietta did nothing, Frederick reached for the salver and she hastily grabbed the other side. The plate tilted and the banqueting hall fell silent, fearing a bad omen. The dish made it to the table with only a slight clang.

Frederick's sigh of relief was so explosive Giulietta smiled, despite herself. She opened her mouth for the forkful he offered and her hand touched his as she steadied his fingers. Frederick looked as if he might cry in gratitude and Tycho had to remind himself that this was a *krieghund*.

At the high table, Giulietta lifted her own fork to Prince Frederick's mouth, nodding to say they could both now eat. He ate from the fork she offered, just as she ate from the fork he held, their arms twisted through each other's as tradition demanded. Both chewed as one, but Giulietta swallowed first.

Leaning forward, she asked something softly.

Prince Frederick looked at the crowd and nodded carefully. He swallowed his mouthful and asked something in his turn. It was like watching two children navigate their way through a field of thorns. Frederick's fingers touched the back of her hand and she smiled. It was sad but kind. He risked saying something else, something that mattered, because her lips trembled.

She wiped her eye crossly, then shrugged and nodded.

Frederick dried her tears as tenderly as if the great banqueting hall were empty and they were the only people there. No, as if they were the only two people in the world. "Remind me again how this works?" Amelia said.

Tycho ignored her.

The couple at the top table sat with their heads close together. He seemed to be apologising and she was apologising back. That was how their marriage would work out. She'd be protective, and he'd have fits of unexpected fierceness if he felt her threatened or slighted. They'd muddle through because that's what people did. Those on the lower tables returned to their own meals and conversation grew loud in a mixture of drunkenness and relief. The banquet would be remembered fondly and be coloured by myth. A feast to celebrate the end of winter as much as their marriage or Giulietta's coronation. A winter when ice covered the lagoon and the Grand Canal was so frozen carriages used it as a road. When hunger drove wolves down from their mountains, and Marco the Simple became Marco the Great in a single night by killing his uncle and clearing the way for Giulietta to take the throne.

"You're smiling," Amelia said.

"Look at them."

He had to be happy for Giulietta; how else could he survive without going down there and slaughtering the lot of them? She had her head bent even closer, and when Frederick dipped to kiss her forehead, she smiled. How much of it was Dr Crow's pills? How much forgiveness happened before the love potion had time to work its effect. Tycho didn't know and refused to let himself wonder.

"She'll forget you?"

"Not exactly. I'll simply stop mattering."

"And Leopold . . .?

"Only Frederick will matter." Tycho glanced down and corrected himself. "*Only he matters.* The rest of us? Fond memories at best."

Frederick would be faithful and Giulietta would be faithful, and they would become that most unlikely and dangerous of hybrids, co-rulers who liked and respected each other. She would deliver Sigismund a city. He'd give her imperial protection. The issue of an heir was already decided.

Tycho had no doubt she'd give Frederick children and he'd dote on them, the memory of his lost daughter ever in his mind. Smiling again, Tycho straightened his shoulders. Who knew what the future would bring? What he would see, what he would learn, what he would do. "I leave the city tonight . . ."

"You travel alone?" Amelia asked.

"Of course. Who would come with me?"

The night he dived off the edge of the waterfall Tycho acted on impulse. After the chaos of his early months in Venice, he'd wanted to believe life unfolded to a plan but that night he simply reacted. Marco was the one with a plan, he realised now.

He'd always intended to sacrifice himself to clear the throne for Giulietta, unless he'd simply wanted revenge. There would be time to ask him later. A whole lifetime of it, then another and another . . .

Bending his knees, Marco had pushed away from the edge of the drop and pulled Alonzo after him. And time had slowed as Tycho crossed the trampled circle, drew his dagger and launched himself over the edge. Marco hit the water just ahead of Alonzo, with Tycho tumbling after.

The weight of their armour took all three under.

Freezing water closed over Tycho as he fought the weight of his own breastplate, the drag of the sword he'd slung across his back. It was dark beneath the water. As dark and cold and unforgiving as for ever. Finding Marco, he'd followed him down into the slime, grit and rock of the waterfall's floor. Where he slashed the strap fixing the axe in Marco's chest to Alonzo's wrist and kicked for the surface.

Alonzo he left there.

Tycho almost made it, although he had to scale the last few feet by clinging to rock and dragging Marco behind him, the weight of the duke increasing as they left the water. Rolling Marco on to a ledge, he looked down and saw the duke's eyes flutter open. The spike axe still jutted from his chest.

"You have a choice," Tycho said.

Marco shook his head. "I'm dying," he whispered.

"I'm offering you life."

The duke looked up and smiled. "My mother said you were a broken angel. Perhaps the last of your kind. You don't look that angelic to me."

Biting into his own wrist, Tycho held it out.

Marco's eyes widened and he nodded, drinking with increasing urgency until Tycho judged him strong enough for what came next. He pulled the axe free, and drank from the wound, feeling cold steel against his lips. The night was dark and the pool deep in shadow. High above, Tycho could hear shouts and cries, orders and counter-orders. No one saw what happened in the darkness at the edge of the pool. At least no one who'd be telling.

Acknowledgements

As the third of the Tycho novels comes to an end, and his history ends on a high and a new beginning for him, and those involved in bringing the three acts of the Assassini to the page having been thanked already in previous books, it only remains to apologise to the ghosts of those historical figures whose lives I've stolen and dip my knee to the *Serensìma Respùblica de Venesia* herself.

I remain as convinced now as when I was a child that Venice is alive and deadly and beautiful and dangerous. She has outlived empires and kingdoms, republics and revolutions. I pray she outlives many more.

Jon Courtenay Grimwood was born in Malta and christened in the upturned bell of a ship. He grew up in the Far East, Britain and Scandinavia. For five years he wrote a monthly review column for the *Guardian*. He has also written for *The Times*, the *Telegraph* and the *Independent*.

Shortlisted for the Arthur C. Clarke Award twice and the BSFA seven times, he won the BSFA Award for best novel with *Felaheen*, featuring Asraf Bey, his half-Berber detective. He won it again with *End of the World Blues*, about a British ex-sniper running an Irish bar in Tokyo.

His work is published in French, German, Spanish, Polish, Czech, Hungarian, Russian, Turkish, Japanese, Danish, Finnish and American among others. He is married to the journalist and novelist Sam Baker, currently editor-in-chief of *Red* magazine. They divide their time between London and Winchester.